I0590200

Going Viral for Christmas

CEDAR JAMES

Copyright © 2025 by Cedar James

All rights reserved.

No part of this book may be reproduced in any form or by any electronic or
mechanical means, including information storage and retrieval systems, without
written permission from the author, except for the use of brief quotations in a
book review.

The characters and events portrayed in this book are fictitious or are used
fictitiously. Any similarity to a real person, living or dead, is purely coincidental
and not intended by the author.

All brand names and product names used in this book are trademarks, registered
trademarks, or trade names of their respective holders. Cedar James and North &
Anchor Co. are not associated with any product or vendor mentioned.

Published by North & Anchor Co., Houston, TX

Cover Art: Artscandare Book Cover Design

ASIN: B0FFN7H7JL

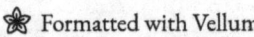 Formatted with Vellum

Oɴᴇ

AVA

You know what's trending right now? My downfall.

Sponsored by pacing issues, heatless handjobs, and one very dramatic ShelfSpacer with editing software.

Recent Goodreads reviews include:

Cringe writing.

Painfully boring.

Flat characters.

And a third-act sex scene so anatomically confusing that someone made a diagram. With arrows. Labels. A red circle that read, *"This is not where the clitoris lives."*

So yeah, I'm a little on edge.

My latest book, *The Boyfriend Deadline,* was supposed to be my swing at the big list. Instead, I overshot the heat and landed in humiliation instead. It's flopping in real time—memed, mocked, and massacred—by readers who think my heroine deserves jail time for her metaphor choices.

In the cruelest twist of irony, I'm expected to smile through a live panel today with fantasy's favorite weapon-wielding himbo, Soren "The Blade" Pembry.

Apparently, the internet isn't satisfied with mocking the

Queen of Steam's latest disaster. It wants a front-row seat to my public execution.

No pressure.

Renata—my publicist and resident sadist—calls being here a *"relatability rebrand."* She swears the solution isn't another aesthetic reel or annotated-edge giveaway, but me getting "authentic." Reader intimacy. Real-time charm.

So, here I am at *The Great Booksgiving Festival.* AKA a hotel ballroom with pumpkin towers leaning like Pisa, lo-fi remixes of "thank u, next" by Ariana Grande, and a rogue turkey mascot gyrating in slow motion. It's like someone gave a former sorority social chair a corporate Amex and a line of cocaine, then shouted, *"Make it festive."*

One more maple-spice latte and I'll combust.

A squeal detonates across the room. I flinch, sloshing foam on my wrist, then turn.

There *he* is.

Soren Pembry.

My viral rival.

Six feet of swagger in leather boots and a face that makes readers forgive war crimes. A long, gleaming sword hangs at his hip—because subtlety died with chivalry.

The crowd parts like he's biblical. He signs books, kneels for selfies, probably cures seasonal depression with a single wink, all while blessing the people with his cheekbones.

A cluster of women in *Dagger Daddy Fanclub* tees swarm him with their glitter pens and questionable boundaries. One of them hands over her chest as though she's offering up real estate. Soren signs his name across her skin with a smile that could power a small city. The turkey mascot nearly face-plants trying to watch.

Jesus! These people treat him like he's a collectible action figure with limited shelf availability with an NSFW accessories pack.

Can't say I blame them. On-screen, he's hot. In person, he's gravitational. Pure filth and fantasy. A morally gray villain who

smirks from the shadows—a little dangerous, a whole lot cocky, and swoony enough to make you forget he poisoned a village three chapters ago.

I must say, I wasn't prepared for this level of attractiveness. He's clearly winning.

The crowd.

The algorithm.

The vibe.

All of it.

That realization sucks an even bigger dick than my sales chart.

Parked in my booth, doom scrolling, I'm one vent-blast away from becoming a puffball with trust issues and a caffeine dependency.

I hate him.

I hate his stupid shoulders—so broad they're practically blocking out the sun, along with my common sense. His offensively symmetrical face. That mess of hair that somehow flops perfectly, like angels styled it.

Don't get me started on the cocky beard shadow. Probably scratchy as hell. Bet it feels like sandpaper between your legs, makes you all red and raw.

Terrible.

Sipping my latte, I remind myself I don't care. Not about his crowd. Or his rabid *Fanclub*. Definitely not about the way one girl purred when he handed her a signed bookmark, as if it were his hotel key.

Wait! Was it his hotel key?

Honestly, wouldn't put it past him.

Soren's gaze holds mine for a solid heartbeat. For a fraction of a second—barely longer than a breath—the look he gives me strips away space and sound until it's just the two of us, air charged. It feels as though I'm no longer across the ballroom, but standing right in front of him. Vulnerable. *Unsafe.*

He winks. My lungs forget what to do. His mouth curves. It's

in that moment that I know I'm screwed. Or...want to be? *What the hell?*

No, Ava. No ma'am. One wink from Soren "Whoren" Pembry and my underwear is filing a workplace hazard complaint. Unsafe conditions. Zero protection. Immediate evacuation required.

"Think *his* sword dangles as far down as the one on his hip?" An ever-so-posh British accent curls against my ear, and I jolt, nearly sending a passing woman's latte flying.

I whip around. *"Fisher."*

"If the comment threads are to be believed, that mammoth sword everyone's fawning over isn't the only thing worth unsheathing." Fisher's tone drips with a conspiratorial glee. "Legend has it, Soren Pembry's packing the kind of pants magic that derails plot lines and bankrupts pelvic floors."

I choke on foam. "Oh my God, stop talking."

"I would, but look at him." Fisher presses his lanyard to his chest, starry-eyed, as if he's witnessing the second coming of Henry Cavill. "He's signing that woman's tit with finesse. A signature flourish. I'm jealous."

Fisher Wallen, everyone. Personal assistant—also known as chief enabler, snarky therapist, the couture brooch holding my whole shit show of a life together. He grins like he's delivered a Shakespearean sonnet instead of an R-rated observation.

I look back over my shoulder. Sure enough, he's scrawling his name across some woman's boob. His ridiculously full lips curve as he caps the Sharpie.

"Unprofessional," I mutter.

"Said the woman making moon-eyes."

"I am *not* making moon-eyes."

"Please. Your pupils dilated. You blinked in slow motion. The next step is spontaneous ovulation."

"It's the lighting."

Fisher retrieves a sugar cookie, shaped like an open book, from his cross-body bag. He takes a bite, talks through the crumbs.

"Also, you're blushing. So you're either into him...or just plain horny. Do you need a moment? A privacy curtain?"

Classic Fisher. Sharp as a diamond stiletto. Baby-faced. Merciless. He's been my mainstay since my first indie signing a year and a half ago, where I sat behind a table no one noticed. Fisher, then a volunteer, declared it a "tragic waste of pink lipstick and raw talent," redecorated the booth, hollered at strangers, and sold a hundred books before lunch.

I hired him on the spot. Best impulsive decision I've ever made.

Now, I have an agent, a tiny but mighty backlist of USA Today bestsellers, and a brand that primarily runs on a mix of sweet romance, spice, and sheer delusion.

One of Soren's large hands is steady on the hilt of his sword while people practically swoon in line to touch it.

"I've never been into the brooding, cosplay types." Not typically, anyway.

"Sure," Fisher draws the word out. "And I hate gossip along with all things sugar." He takes another bite. "All I'm saying is, Soren Pembry is one fine specimen. No wonder the line wraps around the ballroom. He's literary lust in human form. I bet his special editions come scented with pine, musk, and male validation."

My eyes slide back to where Soren is standing tall, like a king ruling over his kingdom. Fisher's right. The line to see him coils across the ballroom, vibrant and alive.

Mine...not so much. It wilted the second he walked in, as though every reader suddenly remembered who they really came for. My shoulders slump.

"Flirting is a blood sport to him. He probably has a groupie rotation synced to his release schedule." Fisher perks up. "Do you think there's a sign-up sheet for that on his table? Or like... a QR code? Maybe a Google Form with checkboxes for preferred positions and safe word creativity?"

5

"Gross." I steal his cookie, snap it in half, and chew my frustration.

Fisher licks sugar off his thumb. "So, are you all set for the Genre Feud?"

"No."

"You'll be brilliant," he says, grinning like he knows exactly how not brilliant I'll be. "The two of you together—in the flesh—will kill the internet. Honestly, after a year of online sparring, this feels less like professional rivalry and more like the longest foreplay in history. The sexual tension in your comment threads alone could power a small country."

"What we have is *far* from foreplay. It's loathing."

"It's lust."

I roll my eyes so hard they nearly detach. "You're deranged."

"Mhm. Then explain why you're staring at that man like you want to suck his soul out through his dick. Because honestly, same babe. Same." Fisher bites his lip. *Oh God, he's visualizing it.*

I swat his shoulder. "Stop playing it out in your head."

"Can't stop, won't stop." Fisher crosses his arms. "It's not like you haven't thought about it."

My mouth drops open. "I haven't."

Fisher arches a brow. "Luv, you've been staring at him since he walked in here."

"I'm observing. Sizing up the competition."

Fisher barks a laugh. "Sizing up, huh? Judging by the way you keep sneaking glances at his...sword, I'd say you're not observing, you're measuring."

"I'm not!"

"Well, why not? The two of you together are enemies-to-lovers crack. Everyone in this room knows it. Act on it. Go over there and rub that magic sword, babe. Do it for the people. Do it for me."

As if he heard us, Soren looks up. Stormy grays rake over every inch of my body in a sweep so slow and thorough it should come

with a parental advisory. He stares as though he's got me pinned against the nearest wall, dress hiked up, whispering something indecent in that deep, gruff yet somehow smooth voice of his.

Heat soars straight to where it absolutely shouldn't. Lower belly. Inner thighs. And—

That particular traitorous place clenches. Typical. She's never met a bad idea she didn't want to sit on—Soren's cock included, which, if rumor threads are true, could probably be classified as a public safety hazard.

Nope. Delete. Backspace.

I shake the thought away so hard, I nearly sprain a neck muscle. *God, I need holy water. Or at least another latte.*

Fisher raises a brow. "You just disassociated into a sexual fantasy sequence, didn't you?"

I school my face into innocence.

He retrieves a water bottle from his bag and unscrews the top. "Did it involve brooding, biting, or begging?"

"...shut up."

"Oh my, Lord! It was all three. You hussy."

I sneer at him.

"I'll repeat myself. You should go for it."

"Go for what? His book? His fanbase?"

"His unbelievably well-defined forearms, which could double as murder weapons. All of the above, really. Preferably while riding him into oblivion."

"Gross, Fisher."

His lips twitch. "What? The heat in your eyes tells me you're one well-placed comma away from a sexual awakening."

"You're fired."

"You threaten, but I know too much."

"Ugh. Rescinded."

Fisher drapes an arm over my shoulder. "Sooo...Renata not-so-subtly suggested I try to snag a photo of you—or, God willing, a *video*—with Soren to 'play into the rivalry,' especially since every

time he so much as breathes in your general direction, your book sales mysteriously spike."

I shrug him off. "Not happening."

"Suit yourself–"

"Ms. Bell?" A young woman with a bright smile and barely contained excitement approaches, wearing a headset and carrying a clipboard. "Hi! I'm Jessica, one of the event coordinators. We're ready for you for the panel. Just follow me."

My stomach drops to my toes.

Right.

The *Genre Feud*.

Romance vs. Fantasy.

Me vs. Him.

Cinnamon rolls and soulmates vs. sword-swinging alpha types who wouldn't know healthy communication if it stabbed them.

This whole thing seems fun in theory—less so when you're the one about to walk into the arena.

"Great!" I force a smile.

"Off you trot." Fisher shoos me away. "March into that panel and give him hell and a half-chub."

With a groan, I follow Jessica, each step heavier than the last as I make my way toward the one and only Soren Pembry, who is drinking me in with a grin that could end nations.

This panel isn't just content. It's my chance to prove I belong here—that one bad release doesn't make me irrelevant. That I'm more than the algorithm's latest casualty.

That I'm somebody.

Problem is, I have to pull it off beside *him*. The author whose fantasy books top every list. Whose fandom treats his sword like it's Excalibur. Whose smirk is a direct threat to my sanity.

Lord help me. I'm about to endure a fan-fiction trope in front of a hundred people and a livestream audience.

Shoving every tremble, flicker of doubt, and the ache of insecurity deep, *deep* down, I step in front of *The Blade* himself, wearing my invisible mask of confidence.

Chin up. Smile nice. Shoulders back.

Show them fire.

Because no one—especially not Soren Pembry—gets to know what I'm actually feeling inside.

Two

SOREN

The crowd hums like a live wire.

Lighting: Tolerable.

Energy: Feral.

In the crush of perfume and paper, a woman in full *Beneath the Bloom* cosplay—from my latest bestseller—glides past, complete with a red corset, thigh holsters, and attitude.

Usually, that level of dedication would start a small riot in my pants. I'm a simple man: put a heroine in leather and I'm halfway to plotting a bonus scene. But somewhere between the third tear-streaked hug and the girl who asked me to press my sword against her thigh for a photo, someone yanked the plug on higher brain functions, short-circuiting my mind altogether.

That someone is Ava Bell.

Queen of Steam, Mistress of Meet-Cutes, the woman whose entire brand is chock-full of cinnamon-roll heroes and guaranteed happy endings. She's my rival, my foil, the bane of my ShelfSpace existence. And she's across the ballroom, blazing like fire and defiance.

This is a whole different battlefield than online. There, Ava's words on a screen, a sparring partner I can mute with a swipe or

outmaneuver with a post. In the flesh, she's devastating, not to mention so fucking beautiful.

My heart slams once, twice, then forgets how to recover. Fingers tighten on my sword hilt. Sweat sneaks beneath my collar despite the AC's arctic blast.

Battle scenes don't faze me. Crowds don't faze me.

Ava Bell in cable knit, absolutely does.

She's making it physically impossible for me to concentrate.

Okay, fine. It's the tight sweater dress.

My brain said, *Be cool*.

My dick said, *We are absolutely not being cool*.

Ava bent—just to fix a zipper. The hem of her dress lifted a fraction, flashing the underside of her ass. The air left my lungs. And downstairs? Captain Pembry—who, let's be honest, isn't exactly known for subtlety—sprang to attention. Full salute. No hesitation.

Standing with a Sharpie in one hand and a situation down below that would embarrass a lesser man, I nearly came in my leather. One more millimeter of curve and I would've been handing out signed paperbacks with post-nut clarity.

When she straightened, Ava's gaze hooked on mine—autumn bright, impossible to dodge—cleaving straight through the armor I didn't realize I was wearing.

Captain Pembry, ever loyal, reacted once again with enthusiasm.

What Ava doesn't know. Nor will ever know, is that I've spent a year losing sleep over her. Writing letters I'll never send. Wondering how her laugh sounds. Imagining the warmth behind her most cutting quips. Fisting myself to the point my body can't tell the difference between tension and need.

Now she's real. And right in front of me.

No amount of flirtation, attention, or bare skin from another woman means a damn thing when the one with the cinnamon-colored curls and glasses perched on her cute little nose undid me with words alone—words that sliced and sparked, sank under my

skin, and have stayed there, because I've let them. Because they're hers.

Another satisfied reader approaches. Flashing a practiced grin, I drag my pen across her book with a flourish that's become muscle memory. The ink bleeds dark against cream pages, my signature a bold slash of black that matches the leather wrapped around my wrist. I hand it back with a smile that once came naturally to me. Now, it's just me putting on a mask. Every. Single. Time.

The woman's fingers tremble as she clutches the book to her chest like a holy relic.

"Thanks for reading."

She lets out a squeak so shrill, I half-expect steam to shoot out of her ears. Full kettle meltdown. Then she floats away.

The next wide-eyed person in line steps up immediately, radiating with a mix of desire and hero worship that once fed my ego. Not anymore. Not for a long time.

Please don't mistake me. I love my readers. Christ, I do. They've changed my life in ways I'll never be able to repay. They've funded my ridiculously overpriced sword collection, my downtown loft in Seattle with floor-to-ceiling windows, and so much more.

But this version of me—the carefully crafted book boyfriend persona that ShelfSpace devours? Well, he's slowly suffocating the man underneath.

I'm caged by my own charisma, forced to perform the same seductive dance until my soul feels scraped bare.

The Blade.

Fuck, I hate that name. It tastes like copper and lies every time anyone says it.

I finish another signature, the pen sliding smoothly across the paper, and force out another laugh that grates against my throat.

As if drawn by some cosmic pull, my focus veers left—straight to where Ava Bell is standing. Little does she know, she's my lighthouse in this bookish storm, surging inside this ballroom.

Somewhere between the cheers, the selfies, and the hundredth book shoved under my nose, my mind drifts toward the woman who's labeled as the thorn in my side.

Ava's polite smiles never quite touch her eyes. The little waves she gives look genuine enough, but there's tension simmering beneath them. She plays her part, posing when readers ask, but it's her hands that betray her—nails chewed down to the quick. She's holding herself together, bite by bite.

Every so often, she glances at me. Quick. Curious. Checking to see if I'm still here. Each time she does, hope burrows under my ribs and yanks. I feel it everywhere. Gravity. Hunger. Want. Desire.

Dread.

Ava's fan line has dwindled to almost nothing. Not because she isn't magnetic—she is. That woman is whip-smart, sharp-tongued, and funny as hell. *She* deserves a line out the damn door.

The second I walked in, the energy changed. Heads turned. Lines shifted. Phones came up. My name trended. I didn't plan it, didn't want it—but, I stole the room just by existing in it.

That reality nags at me. Gnaws, if I'm being honest. The worst part is, every smile aimed at me feels like I'm robbing her blind. I hate that because I like her. A lot. Even though I don't even know her. Even though she hates me.

I'm not wired for empathy; it was never standard issue. Charm, sure. Graciousness on cue. Genuine concern, however? Rare.

Yet watching Ava fight to stay composed stirs something unfamiliar inside me. It reminds me that beneath the sharp edges and the sparring, a real magnetic pull has always been there, dragging us closer.

We started as a feud.

Ava showed up on my *Got You* page in a video that disemboweled my entire genre with pinpoint accuracy, triggering a fan war that crashed the app's servers for two days.

I retaliated with candlelight melodrama and a poetry-slam

wig. She countered with a stitch that said my heroes had the emotional depth of a puddle.

In the span of one week, that tiny, five-foot-nothing female managed to pick apart three years of carefully crafted brand identity.

I decided to go full scorched earth.

Reading the steamiest scenes from her book, *The Lumberjack's Love Letters*, I wore a flannel button-down, no shirt underneath, boots, and sawdust in my hair—because if I was going down, I was taking her libido with me.

At the time, it felt deserving.

Ava didn't even wait a full day. She posted a video captioned, *Two can play the forestry fantasy game.*

The clip opened with her in a cute, checkered dress, featuring delicate straps and a daring neckline that tested my self-control.

In the video, Ava's voice dropped into a mock-serious narrator cadence as she started reading one of my most tortured passages.

"I want to touch her," Ava read, tone perfectly flat, expression bored. "But I shouldn't." She glanced up at the camera. "Touch her, you jackass. She wants you to. We *all* do."

She flipped a page. With the same disinterested, almost teacherly delivery, Ava read one of the steamiest scenes I've ever written—every filthy, fevered word—like she was dictating a grocery list.

The effect was devastatingly funny. My passionate prose had never sounded more virginal. Ava wasn't just roasting me; she was dismantling my ego with a witty scalpel. I watched it on loop, hand in my hair, half mortified, half turned on.

By the time she shut the book, took a prim sip of wine, and said, "Five stars. Would recommend for anyone suffering from insomnia," the internet had blown up.

#BellAndTheBlade was trending by morning with two million views.

It was war. Beautiful, vicious, intoxicating war.

Until it wasn't.

After that, I actually read *The Lumberjack's Love Letters* in its entirety, rather than skimming the spicy parts for ammunition. I discovered Ava's not just good. She's fucking brilliant.

Between the catalyst and the climax, tectonic plates shifted beneath my feet. I ended up staying awake until 4 a.m., wrecked beyond reason.

That ending? A gut punch wrapped in flannel and burning sincerity, dipped in whatever literary witchcraft she uses to make fictional kisses feel like sacraments.

The prose? Gorgeous.

The pacing? Immaculate.

Her character arcs? Absolutely lethal.

I will never admit this to anyone, but I cried—big, messy, not-cute, ugly sobs. Then I preordered the special edition. Twice. Downloaded her entire backlist and tore through all ten in under a week.

Her words revealed a part of her that she never shares. The part that bleeds into the pages. The part only another writer would recognize for what it was.

After that, I saw my online nemesis in a whole different light. In those late-night moments, while reading her works, I developed a *very* real, *very* inconvenient, *major* thing for Ava Crowley Bell.

Yes, I know her middle name. I did some light internet stalking. Mind your business.

I tried to deny it at first. Then, I caught myself anticipating her posts, like a teenager waiting for a text. Watching her lives with the sound turned up, studying the way she laughed at her own jokes.

My sparring changed, too. It became something else entirely. My comebacks stopped being defensive. They turned smokier, more intimate, charged with an energy even I didn't recognize. Her razor-blade insults started landing differently, no longer feeling like attacks, but invitations to dance.

Ava Crowley Bell became the highlight of my week. As we traded barbs across the digital divide, I felt good. I was me. I

wasn't "The Blade," or the fantasy thirst trap—just Soren. Unfiltered, vulnerable, alive in a way I'd forgotten was possible.

She made me want to be wittier. Also, deeper, more honest. That stopped me from viewing her as my enemy. In return, I saw her as the woman who could, and did, cut through all my bullshit with a single, perfectly crafted comment like the one she wrote in my "Brooding Heroes Need Love Too" post:

Soren, your heroes don't need love. They need therapy, a personality transplant, and maybe a dictionary so they can learn words other than 'mine,' 'claim,' and 'destiny.' But sure, let's call it romance.

Yep, I was in trouble.

With all her fire and brains, Ava drags on my tropes as though it's her civic duty to educate the masses on everything wrong with a dark fantasy. She *loathes* my genre, my face, and the fact that I once called her "adorably demented" during a live.

I meant it as a compliment, by the way.

For months, I've kept up playing the fantasy author *slash* book boyfriend role, flashing the grin that's becoming more of a grimace each day, spinning the sword that's become more prop than passion, and feeding the fandom the version of me they crave while quietly wondering: *what if I dropped the mask for once, and let people see the man drowning beneath all this leather and manufactured mystique?*

Between you, me, and the smirking devil on my shoulder, Ava Bell is the only person I want to witness that drowning. Which is, of course, peak irony, considering she's also the one who keeps handing me the metaphorical bricks.

She hates me—publicly, enthusiastically, and with just enough lingering eye contact to make me think she's either plotting my murder or imagining hate-fucking me with the lights on.

Which I'm all for.

And know this, if she ever gave me the chance to, I'd destroy that pussy of hers with every ounce of pent-up hunger she's stuffed into me since the day we started exchanging verbal daggers.

Captain Pembry twitches. *Down, boy. Nope, not today.*

Ava's watching me, so I send her a wink to see what she'll do. Predictably, she pivots back to the guy beside her, suddenly riveted by whatever brilliance he's pretending to offer.

She laughs easily, the sound hitting me square in the chest. His hand grazes her arm, and a territorial burn courses through me. He's too close. Too familiar. I'm building a list of reasons to hate him—none of them rational, all of them mine.

Ava's rattled, though. She won't look back at me. That small tell makes my morning. Because it's all *mine*.

I continue watching her a moment longer. The soft amber in her eyes has gone watery at the edges, speaking louder than the smile she's forcing. Her shoulders stay tight even when she laughs, like she's bracing for impact. Her fingers worry at her sides, flexing in and out, again and again, as if stillness might make her unravel.

My focus returns to Ava's whiskey-colored eyes. Much like her stories, they hold multitudes—grief tucked beneath the beauty, ache threaded through every line, a quiet pain hiding even in her happily ever afters.

If that wasn't enough of a clue, the guarded flame in her gaze is. That wary, wounded kind of look comes from surviving, and never quite believing you're safe.

Someone shattered her faith in love, and she's been writing her way through it ever since.

It's evident that Ava Bell is a fortress—mentally, emotionally... maybe even physically. I respect that. I understand caution. How it wraps around your heart like barbed wire, and doesn't let go. She's rebuilt herself with walls *no one* gets past.

Bet she can spot a threat from miles away. Which, for her, is me. Except I'm not a threat. Not even close.

While whispering in her ear, the guy next to her demolishes a cookie with the dedication of a man on death row. A blush creeps across her skin, from her throat to her ears, almost like spilled wine.

I'd sell my soul to know what caused it. Hell, I'd kill to be the reason for it.

But alas, Ava Bell is immune to my swagger and smirks, too intelligent for surface charm, too scarred to trust a stranger.

"Mr. Pembry?" A clipboard-wielding volunteer suddenly materializes, headset askew, chest heaving, cheeks flushed. *Has she been running?*

I nod, point to her nametag. "Jade, right?"

"We're ready for the Genre Feud panel with you and Ms. Bell."

My heart kicks against my ribs at the sound of her name. I cap my Sharpie with a soft click, letting the persona slide back into place with one last practiced grin for the girl still waiting in line.

Drawn by that same magnetic pull that's been torturing me for over a year, I turn to see Ava striding toward me. That sweater dress hugs her tight little body like a love letter, clinging to curves I've tried very hard not to imagine touching, but failed miserably.

Her curls bounce with every determined step, glasses sliding down the bridge of her nose until she pushes them back up with the same fingers I wouldn't mind curled around something far less innocent.

My lips twist at that thought. Ava looks straight at me. A pull tightens deep in my chest, uninvited, undeniable.

She moves with purpose, light catching her hair, defiance in her stride. Ava's fierce, and she's not going to spar with my words up on that stage today. She's going to aim for my soul.

And the sickest part?

I very much want her to hit her mark.

Three

~∽∾~

AVA

"This is so exciting," Jessica chatters on, clearly oblivious to the silent showdown happening behind her—where Soren and I are locked in an intense, slow-blinking stare-down. "The whole team has been talking about this panel for weeks. The social media buzz is incredible. Everyone's calling it the literary event of the year."

The banter war begins the second our gazes collide.

Soren sweeps over me, taking inventory of every curve, curl, and guarded breath I'm pretending not to take. "I can't believe I'm actually face-to-face with the Queen of Emotional Catharsis."

His mouth curves, mine tightens. It's all instinct now—words as armor, wit as weapon.

"Yes, and here he is—the Sultan of Sword Porn, in the flesh."

A hit of his cologne flies up my nostrils when I step closer. It's woodsy, clean, hellaciously distracting.

I gesture to the sword on his hip. "Tell me, did you have to check that thing as luggage, or did you register it as a service animal?"

His laugh is genuine, unlike the masterful charm he uses on his fans. "Service animal. I like that. It does provide emotional support. Mostly to the lonely and the curious."

"Mm. Judging by the crowd, you're running a full-on support group."

His eyes darken with amusement. "You sound jealous."

"Hardly," I shoot back. "Though I am curious. Does it grant wishes and orgasms on contact, or is that just part of the folklore? It's been fondled more times today than I care to count."

Soren's grin goes pure mischief. "Only one way to find out."

I scoff. "Right. Let me guess—step into the enchanted realm, hike up my skirt, and moan your name?"

"Only if you want the deluxe package. Includes a sticker pack, a commemorative T-shirt, and the sudden inability to think about anyone else."

I'm smiling, despite myself. "Wow. Did that line come with a training manual or years of unchecked ego?"

Soren steps closer. The air tightens. "No manual. Only excellent instincts."

I lift my chin. "Funny. My instincts are telling me to run."

"Toward or away?"

The moment stretches between us like taffy, sweet and tension-filled, daring someone to make the next move.

Show them fire.

I offer a sugar-laced smile. "This has been fun, Pembry. Truly. But, enough games. I've got a panel to carry."

"Ouch." Soren presses a hand to his chest in mock pain. "Right in the ego. I see you're bringing your A-game today."

"Not even my best stuff. I'm saving *that* for when the cameras are rolling."

"Guess I'll have to step it up, then." Soren leans down toward my ear, the heat in his words licking across my skin. "Let's give 'em a show, shall we?"

The volunteer standing next to Soren—Jade, her nametag says —clears her throat pointedly. "If you two are done flirting, we *really* need to get you mic'd up."

Heat prickles at the base of my neck, crawling all the way to my scalp. "We weren't—" I begin, too fast.

Playlist

Click on the QR code to listen to the Going Viral for Christmas playlist. Music is inspired by Ava and Soren's story, and is available on Spotify. Enjoy!

right here waiting. Ava and Soren will keep their place on the page until you're ready.

Stories are meant to hold pieces of us, but they're never meant to hurt us. I hope this one makes you laugh, makes you swoon, and maybe, in the moments between, makes you feel a little Christmas magic.

With love and holiday hugs,
Cedar James

Note From the Author

Before you dive into this story, I want to take a moment to say: please take care of yourself while reading.

Going Viral for Christmas is, at its heart, a swoony, slow-burn rom-com full of banter, fake dating, and holiday mayhem. But beneath the sparkling lights and mistletoe, there are threads of grief, complicated family relationships, public scrutiny, and self-doubt that can sneak up on even the strongest among us.

This book also touches on themes of mental health struggles, as well as moments that reference narcissism. These topics are not the central focus of the story, but they are present in ways that may be triggering for some readers. They are handled with care and without graphic detail, but your well-being matters most.

If you've ever felt the sting of depression, the ache of being misunderstood, the weight of mental health battles, or the pressure of living up to other people's expectations, some moments in these pages may feel closer to home than expected. There's joy here—so much joy—but there are also hard conversations, quiet heartbreaks, and the reminder that love is never as simple as it looks from the outside.

Take breaks if you need to. Skip ahead, that's okay too. And if you need to set the book down and come back to it later, I'll be

write love. Also hope. You create longing as if it were a living, breathing thing.

You made me feel acknowledged in a way that's different from the public version of me. I felt like the boy I was before the world told me to be clever instead of soft. Sharp instead of sincere. A persona instead of a person.

I write about men with storms in their chests. Men who carry swords. Who don't speak unless it's life or death. But your lumberjack felt things. He said them. And it didn't make him weak. It made him unforgettable.

Thank you for showing me, through your words, that vulnerability can be power. Wanting isn't weakness. Love stories, the real ones, aren't just fantasy. That they could be reality, with the right one.

And this is going to sound like a horrible insta-love trope. I promise this isn't that. But I believe it might be the beginning of something truly beautiful between us.

Always,
S

Soren Pembry

New York Times Best-Selling Fantasy Author

Dear Ava Bell,

You've changed me.

I didn't expect it, and I wasn't looking for it. But here we are.

In the spirit of online roasting, I picked up The Lumberjack's Love Letters as a joke. I went into it thinking your book would have too much sap and not enough swordplay. I was ready to roll my eyes, skim a few pages, then get back to brooding warlords and doomed quests.

I stayed up all night reading. Not necessarily due to the spice (though, Jesus, chapter nineteen), but because your words split my heart wide open.

On top of fun, flirty, and filthy, I got a mirror I wasn't ready for. A man holding so much inside he split in half. I felt that in my bones. And it scared the shit out of me.

I didn't know romance could hurt like that. Or feel like coming home to a version of myself I hadn't met yet.

I'll never recover.

There's an ache and a grief in the way you

"That wasn't—" Soren says at the same time, far too calmly.

Jade arches a brow. "Mhm."

Smooth, *way* too satisfied with himself, Soren laughs. "That's a new one for us."

My head tilts.

Light, almost silver, storm-colored eyes slide to mine, lazy and amused. "Though if we *were* flirting, I'd probably open stronger. Less mutual denial, more meaningful pressure."

"We weren't flirting," I snap with force, hoping it'll erase the heat lingering in my cheeks along with the flutter in my stomach—the one I'm trying very hard to ignore.

Soren's grin deepens, full of slow-burning trouble and quiet ego. "Noted. But for the record, if we *were–*"

"We weren't," I cut him off.

Was I?

Was he?

No. No, absolutely not.

Except maybe—

I need to focus. Or get laid. Preferably by anyone *but* the six-foot-four fantasy menace staring at me like I'm halfway out of this dress.

I wish the floor would open up and eat me.

"Let's just get this over with." I square my shoulders like a soldier in formation, ignoring the tremor building inside my chest.

After Jade finishes with our mics, she walks off, shaking her head, muttering on about authors and their unresolved sexual tension.

"Right this way," Jessica forces us forward.

The buzz of the ballroom dulls behind us as we make our way through a back hallway. We pass several doors before Jessica opens one marked: *Event Center.*

Slipping into a utilitarian space smelling faintly of dust and stale coffee, the low thrum of backstage chatter, along with the occasional jump scare of a walkie-talkie, drifts through the air.

Exposed pipes line the ceiling. Folding chairs, extension cords, and cardboard boxes labeled *SWAG BAGS - PANEL 3* are stacked haphazardly along one wall. A half-eaten muffin sits forgotten on a metal table beside an open laptop looping the event schedule.

Another woman—this one with a headset, and the aura of someone keeping twelve flaming tasks in the air—spots us approaching. She waves enthusiastically.

"Ava Bell! Oh my goodness, I'm Shirley Whitemire—" her badge says *Chaos Coordinator* "—I'm such a huge fan! I've read *The Boyfriend Deadline* three times and teared up at the puppy yoga scene each re-read."

Despite my nerves, I instantly love this overly vibrant woman wearing a burnt-orange blazer with a pilgrim hat pin. Her excitement is infectious. And the fact that she read and liked my bomb book makes my anxiety dial down a notch.

"Thank you so much, Shirley." I beam back at her. "That means the world to me."

"And Soren Pembry!" She bounces on her toes. "The Blade!"

"A pleasure to meet you." Soren holds his hand out for her to shake, which she vigorously does.

"Oh, the pleasure is all mine." Shirley is still shaking his hand. "You know, I have to admit, I'm more of a contemporary romance girl. However, my book club devoured the Court of Thirst and Thorns. We spent two hours debating whether Kael was a green flag or a red flag in leather pants."

"What was the verdict?" he asks.

"Unanimous red flag," Shirley giggles. "But we'd all still climb him like a tree."

I snort-laugh before I can stop myself, a full-on, inelegant, traitorous laugh.

Soren's eyes immediately shift to me. "Don't knock it till you try it, Ava."

"Oh, I've tried red flags," I retort. "But I don't usually line up for the sequel."

"Usually, huh?" His growly tone slips under my skin as if it's received clearance. "Never know. A walking red flag could ruin all the green ones for you."

"Ruin? Cute. You write brooding weapon racks with abandonment issues. Let's not."

Soren's gaze is a caress on my skin. He's every bit the smoldering anti-hero he writes.

To my utter horror, he moves closer, his proximity sending a shiver skittering up my spine.

"I could rewrite how you burn, Ava."

My jaw falls to the floor at the same time my vagina throws confetti. What the fuck did he just say?

Before I can ask that question out loud, I snap my mouth shut and tilt my chin, refusing to let him see how my pulse is trying to breakdance.

I know what Soren's doing, turning the heat up on purpose, tossing out loaded lines and sinful smirks, hoping I'll lose my footing before we even reach the stage.

Let them see fire.

"Not today, Blade Boy. I've faced worse than some cocky fantasy author with a fandom that probably sells scented candles in your honor."

"They do, actually. Body mist too. *Storm-Kissed Leather* and *Brooding in the Sheets*—both sold out in under an hour when they launched." His tongue darts out to lick his bottom lip. "If you want a sample, I'm wearing both."

My eyes narrow at him.

"Oh, you two are going to kill it out there," Shirley gushes.

"That's the plan," Soren says, eyes still on me.

"This is the biggest crowd we've ever had for a panel." Shirley peels back the curtain.

My stomach drops.

The energy vibrates with anticipation. Every chair is filled, and the rest is standing room only, with people lined up against the walls three deep. Phones are already recording from the back rows.

"That's way more than a hundred people," I whisper.

"Two hundred fifty," Shirley says. "To be exact."

I close my eyes for half a second. Breathe in. Try to remember my own name. Breathe out.

Camera flashes, excited voices, overhead lights. They're all making my skin feel too tight. The world is loud and bright and pressing in from all sides. I can't find enough air to suck in.

Deep breaths. One. Two. Three.

It's not working. Anxiety and ambition are locked in a bare-knuckle brawl behind my ribcage. Both are losing.

Soren's voice pulls me back. "Ava, you okay?"

Breathe in.

I reopen my eyes to find him watching me with the tiniest crease between his brows.

Breathe out.

Refusing to let him see me crumble, I smooth my dress, flash a smile sharp enough to slice through my own panic, and reply with a light tone, "Of course."

"You sure?"

"Absolutely. This is me, mentally preparing for our classic death match."

"Classic death match," he parrots.

"Yeah. We're about to go up there and do some real *Clash of the Titans* stuff, you know, debating over men who *show* their emotions vs. sword-wielding angst machines."

With a chuckle, Soren's head drops for a half-second. "Some might argue that those sword-wielding angst machines *are* showing their emotions. Only, they do it with bloodshed and battle cries. In my books, war isn't just war—it's foreplay with a body count. Because let's be honest, most of those epic clashes start with a woman. Or end with one. Or a kingdom burned down in her name."

"So you're telling me your warlords are romantics with rage issues? That all this sword-swinging and kingdom-toppling is their way of writing love letters in blood?"

For My Parents

Growing up, the holiday season made itself at home within our walls, with the house always smelling of cookies and woodsmoke from the fire. You wrapped our world in warmth and joy so generous it spilled into every corner, turning even the hardest years into something beautiful, and making every Christmas feel like stepping into a snow globe. That magic stitched itself into the fabric of who I am. And it's why I still believe in the power of Christmas, and its wondrous miracles, even when the world feels heavy.

Thank you, Mom and Dad, for a magical childhood, for always loving and supporting me, and being there through every moment.

I love you!

(Dad, you can't read this one either)

"Exactly."

Pulse tripping over itself, I manage to roll my eyes. "Fantastic. Murder with emotional depth. Be still, my heart."

His gorgeous lips twitch. "See, you get it."

"Yep. Nothing says love like a little light decapitation."

"Ready?" Shirley asks.

We nod.

She slips through the curtain, strides up to a podium, and taps the mic. "Welcome, readers and guests, to our most anticipated event of the evening—*The Genre Feud: Romance vs Fantasy!* Featuring the reigning queen and king of controversy themselves: Ava Bell and Soren 'The Blade' Pembry!"

The crowd goes feral.

Soren and I exchange glances. Mine, a mix of dread and painfully rehearsed professionalism. His full of cocky charisma and a smolder dialed so high it might violate a fire code.

I pretend my heart isn't trying to do jump squats inside my chest and walk out onto the stage.

Soren, of course, is pure showmanship and ease, tossing out waves like he's stepping onto a red carpet instead of into a literary lion's den.

Once seated, I survey the contents on the table in front of me. Three bottles of water. A notepad. Pen with hotel logo. A metal tin of mints. *Thank you, Fisher.*

On an exhale, I paste on my best fake-it-'til-you-make-it grin and lift the pen with a shaky hand to give myself something to fidget with.

I look out at the crowd.

"Thank you for having us—" Soren says at the same time as I do. We both halt mid-sentence, then scramble our words.

"Sorry—" I start.

"Go ahead—"

"No, you—"

"We'll be here all day." Half-smiling, he gestures to me with a sweep of his hand. "After you, Ava."

My lady parts flutter at the sound of my name on his lips.

Ignoring it, I start again. "I'm so excited to be here with all of you today. And... with you, Soren."

There's a beat of silence. Then another, stretching long enough to make my armpits second-guess my deodorant.

Apparently, I'm supposed to keep talking.

So... I do.

"I love how you've captured everything about fall here at *The Great Booksgiving*. The warmth, the coziness, that feeling you get when you cocoon yourself in a soft blanket with a good book and a steaming mug filled to the brim with a cinnamon-spiced drink."

I should stop there. That's a perfectly fine continuation. Warm. Professional.

My mouth has other plans.

"And the lighting in here? Stunning. Yet eclectic. Comforting."

Shirley nods. Smiles. She's clearly thrilled.

The audience? Dead silent.

Soren delivers the save. "Honestly, I think it looks like Thanksgiving and Christmas got drunk, picked a fight, and they both redecorated with their last dying breaths."

"But, in a festive way," I add quickly, not wanting to offend Shirley or the staff. "Not a crime scene kind of way. More of a 'let's bake cinnamon rolls and work through our trust issues' vibe. Know what I mean?"

What am I saying?

More silence. One long, dangling moment where I seriously consider flinging myself off the stage and into the *Dagger Daddy Fan Club*.

Shirley clears her throat with the energy of a kindergarten teacher redirecting a class. "Let's jump in with our first question from the audience. Ready?"

Soren and I nod.

Shirley reads off a card. "What's your favorite trope to write, and why? Soren, you first."

"Enemies to lovers. It's timeless. The tension. The banter. The delicious descent into obsession." He side-eyes me. "Especially when one character pretends to hate the other, but secretly wants to strangle them *and* make out with them. You know the type—morally gray with a tragic backstory and hands you definitely shouldn't trust... but want all over you."

"Interesting," My mouth says before my brain can stop it. "You sure you're a writer, Pembry? Or just fanservice with a sword?"

Fucking hell. He's going to make me regret every ounce of confidence I just faked.

Soren's grin falters. He turns toward me in his seat, eyes white-hot. *Here we go.*

That easy smile of his snaps back into place, this time with a little more edge to it. It's when stormy grays spark like steel on flint that I know I hit somewhere I wasn't supposed to.

"Oh, we're doing *that* today?" His voice is velvet and venom. "So, tell us then, what's the Queen of Pumpkin Spice and Flannel-Wrapped Feelings favorite trope?"

I try to swallow. Forget how.

"Second chance romance," I manage.

"Why?"

"Sometimes the one who hurt you the most is the only one who can help you heal."

Soren's brow lifts, intrigued. "How so?"

"It's messy and rooted in forgiveness. When done right," I let my tone smooth out. "It shatters you... yet somehow makes you whole again."

A hush settles over the room. Soren suddenly appears flustered.

Point: Bell.

"I love that." Shirley plucks the next card from the stack, reads it to herself. "Oooh, this one's fun." She wiggles in place. "If your co-panelist were a romance trope, what would they be... and why?"

The crowd hums.

"Oh, that's easy." Soren's grin is that of a wolf locked inside a henhouse. "Ava's the grumpy sunshine with a gooey center trope."

"Excuse me?" I chuckle. "I don't have a gooey center."

"I'd be willing to fact-check that," he says, wicked and amused. "And if you ever need help locating it—"

"Don't finish that sentence."

Soren's voice goes syrupy-smooth. "Ava, I'd be willing to bet that you have a spreadsheet for your feelings, and a planner to schedule when you'll actually deal with them. Color-coded, of course. Deep down, though..." He looks straight into my soul. "You're just a knife-wielding cupcake... sugar and spice stuffed inside a very stabby exterior."

Point: Pembry.

My cheeks burn. I open my mouth to respond, but my brain is buffering. It lost signal somewhere around "knife-wielding cupcake."

"However," he adds, lifting a finger, "she's also the 'falling for the enemy' trope. Which is definitely one of my favs." Soren winks.

Shirley's attention bounces between the two of us. I glance at the exit, calculating my odds of escape. Then to Soren, who's very clearly enjoying himself. *Asshole.*

"Fine." My chin lifts defiantly. "If we're assigning romance tropes, then you're the cocky fantasy anti-hero who's secretly one soft touch away from crumbling."

The audience gives a collective *ooh.* Soren hides his smile behind a closed fist.

"And the heroine doesn't fall at his feet?" My voice is sugar-dipped steel. "She makes him *work* for it."

Gasps. Laughter. Applause.

"Is that an invitation?"

"Only if you beg."

Oh, shit. Of all the things I could've said, I basically handed him a loaded innuendo and dared him to pull the trigger.

My words linger between us, dripping with temptation, and I *know* Soren's preparing his response. Sure enough, his eyes light up, and that mischievous grin unfurls as though it's been waiting all day for this exact setup.

"Do *you* beg, Ava?"

The question coils around my throat, silk and smoke and heat, pulling tighter with every heartbeat until I can't breathe, let alone answer.

"Chances are, you'd fight it," Soren continues. "Pretend you're above it. But when you finally break beneath my touch..." His eyes drag over me like he's watching it happen.

I swipe a strand of hair from my eyes, then flatten my palms against the table.

"You'd be poetry," his voice darkens, "breathless, un-fucking-forgettable."

Someone in the crowd gasps. Might've been me.

"Imagine it, Ava... or better yet, let me show you."

Momentarily stunned, I stop breathing. *Who says shit like that?*

His smirk deepens. Case in point. Soren *Whoren* Pembry, that's who.

"If you *really* want to see what *fanservice with a sword* can do, I'd happily tie you to that four-poster bed you love to write about. Strip you slow. Kiss you slower. Then worship your moans as gospel. You won't be able to walk once I'm done."

The silence is deafening. People in the audience are live-streaming my internal meltdown. My uterus side-eyed me, then whispered, *You brought this on yourself.* And Soren leans back and sips his water like he didn't just verbally fuck everyone within a five-mile radius.

Set.

"I—Y—You can't say that on a live panel."

Unapologetic, he shrugs. "You started it with the name-calling. I just finished it. Besides, the conference asked for a panty-melting experience. I deliver."

"Not *my* panties, Pembry," I blurt, immediately regretting it.

Soren pauses, the pounces. "Are you admitting I've got your attention... where it counts?"

Match.

In that exact second, my brain decides to betray me with a mental highlight reel of Soren Pembry on his knees, murmuring filth against my clit while my thighs practically levitate. Tongue, fingers, that deep, growly voice of his, telling me to stay still while he ruins me in chapters.

Abort. Abort mission.

My core clenches so hard I nearly black out. *Nope. No. Bad brain. Naughty vagina. We are* not *envisioning oral fixation in front of hundreds of people. Pull it together, Ava.*

I'm overheating—no thanks to that visual.

Shifting in my seat, I press my knees together like that'll stop the traitorous flare building beneath my skin. My palms are useless—clammy, restless—so I drag them down my dress to give them something to do.

When I risk a glance up, Soren's looking right at me, the corners of his mouth tilted like he's enjoying the show.

In no rush to stop, he studies every fidget, breath, and flutter of my lashes. It's making me severely uncomfortable, but I *cannot* let him see that I'm falling apart inside.

"Soren, I'll say this..." My tone is slightly higher than usual. "...some of us prefer our fiction with a functioning moral compass and pants that aren't vacuum-sealed."

"Vacuum-sealed?" He twists the cap off a water bottle and takes a swig. "More like battle-ready. Every blade needs a sheath, after all."

Laughter erupts, along with a few scattered cheers.

I clear my throat. "Can we get back to the task at hand here?"

That smirk of his turns complete villain. "Sure. I've got very talented hands."

More laughter. Audible wheezing. Shirley appears seconds away from imploding.

I glower at Soren. His brows raise, pompous as hell, and it's a huge reminder of why we fight. *Because he's the worst!*

"I'd be happy to demonstrate," he adds. "Purely for research purposes, of course."

The room rustles from Soren's latest verbal crime against my sanity. I'm hanging on by the frayed thread of my dignity. Somewhere offstage, I'm positive my publicist is popping Tums like candy. Wonder if she has extra?

Trying to salvage what's left of this panel, I clear my throat *again*—because the first time didn't cut it—and shoot Soren a withering glare that only makes his villainous smirk spread further across his face.

"Alright." I reach for the mints, fingers trembling as though I'm defusing a bomb. "What if we tried something wild and talked about books?"

A few scattered chuckles ripple through the audience.

Soren makes a grand show of zipping his lips. "Scout's honor."

I huff a laugh. "You were never a scout."

"Wanna bet?"

"Moving on," I cut in, before that becomes a whole thing.

"Okay," Shirley takes back control. "This next question is a more serious one."

"We'll behave." I smile.

"No promises," Soren says.

Shirley waves him off. "What kind of world do you build in your stories?"

The change in the air is immediate. Still warm. Still very much alive. But calmer. More focused.

I skim the audience—the readers clutching annotated paperbacks, wearing homemade merch, holding pieces of our books in their hands as if they're treasures.

"The aesthetics at this event, the decorations, they're exactly the world I try to create in my books." My answer is all heart.

Soren watches me—quiet, curious—and for one suspended moment, the tension between us fades.

"Stories that hit like emotional comfort food," I continue, "all the feels, with a happy ending guaranteed."

There's a softness in the silence that follows.

Then—

Soren snorts.

My head whips in his direction. "What?"

"I'm wondering if we're talking about the same kind of happy ending." He tries and fails to suppress a smile.

My jaw drops. "Oh. My. God."

"Hey," he replies with mock innocence. "Reader satisfaction is important. I support all forms."

There's a collective sigh, the front rows are full of giggles, and one very dramatic, *"Marry me,"* from a reader hugging a special edition of one of his books.

Shirley grins awkwardly, fanning herself with her clipboard. "My, my, Soren. You certainly know how to get the crowd going."

"I aim to please."

Oh, I bet you do.

"Well, let's dive in with another question. Ava, this is for you."

I sit straighter.

"What's the appeal of a holiday romance to you?"

Pausing to consider what the best words for this would be, I think through all the scenarios Soren could use against me.

Finally, I answer with, "It's about hope. Kissing under mistletoe. People falling in love. Not in spite of the conflict around them, but because of it."

Soren fake yawns.

"Oh, I'm sorry," I snip at him. "Is a heartfelt connection boring you, Soren?"

"Not at all." He straightens in his chair. "I love when epic love stories come with gingerbread cookies and a snowball fight."

"I'll have you know a snowball fight is a time-honored metaphor for intimacy."

Soren nods solemnly. "Nothing screams passion like concussions and frostbite."

"Well, Soren," Shirley turns toward him, "that leads us into a question we have for you. What's the *fantasy* take on holiday stories?"

He folds his hands, just like I imagine a biggity little sorcerer might. "Give me a solstice curse. A kingdom at war with itself. Star-crossed lovers hiding in a frozen forest with only a dagger and a shared cloak. Doom and destiny...that's for me."

"You know," I say sweetly. "Swords and daggers, it's all starting to feel a bit Freudian."

"Funny, coming from the girl who uses 'throbbing tension' excessively."

"Sir, I will have you know, I use meticulously crafted, emotionally secure sensuality, thank you very much. Classy smut. Grown-up spice. I know those two words are hard for you to relate to."

"Smut and spice? Oh, Ava, I relate to those very well." That wicked fucking grin spreads across his face again.

"Funny." I sneer at him. "But I was referring to classy and grown-up."

"Right. Well, since you brought up the smut and spice. To clarify, you mean the kind you pretend you're reading for the plot while your tingly girl parts are composing thank-you notes to your bedside drawer's top shelf, correct?"

The crowd erupts in a fit of laughter. The conversation spirals from there. We debate elves versus werewolves, the legitimacy of magical coffee shops as a viable battle strategy, and whether baking cookies counts as a love language.

We argue over the superiority of hayride meet-cutes versus enchanted-sword soulmate bonds, and a woman from the back yells, "What about Santa smut?"

Neither of us knows how to respond to that. My voice is bright and biting, seasoned with a healthy dose of nervous laughter. His is shadows and seduction.

And then another woman in the audience calls out, "How about Romantasy?"

Soren groans theatrically. "Ah, yes. The genre where emotional longing appears, wielding a destiny map, and magical powers serve as metaphors for unspoken feelings. It's interesting, the villain always knows when to strike. And the sex is a little too good to be healthy, where you don't know if you're about to be claimed or cursed, and half the time someone's growling 'touch her and die' before burning off a corset with that metaphoric magic I mentioned earlier."

The room cackles.

"No offense, Ava."

Tossing my hair over my shoulder, I shrug. "None taken. I'm thrilled *some* fantasy authors are finally discovering what romance readers have known all along."

"Oh?" he challenges. "What might that be?"

"That emotional stakes matter. That sexual tension doesn't need to be buried under fifty chapters of Elvish prophecy."

"Ouch," he muses. "That hit harder than my MMC's betrayal in the *Court of Thirst and Thorns*."

"Time for a few rapid-fire questions," Shirley announces, shuffling through the pages on her clipboard. "First up—favorite writing snack?"

Soren: "Whiskey and Goldfish."

Me: "Trader Joe's peppermint bark and caramel blondie latte."

"Writing music?"

Me: "Phoebe Bridgers–haunting lyrics, soft emotional destruction.

Soren: "War drums. And occasionally Hozier."

"Your characters are trapped in a cabin during a snowstorm. Who confesses their love first?"

Me: "The woman, because she's emotionally mature."

Soren: "The man, because she threatened to stab him with a candy cane."

"Enemies to lovers or friends to lovers?"

Me: "Friends. With unresolved tension."

Soren: "Enemies. With knives and one bed."

"What's your most-used word during a sex scene?"

Me: "Clit."

Soren: "It's 'moan.' Followed closely by 'thrust.'"

"Last one!" Shirley says eagerly. "What do you think your co-panelist's most quirky habit is?"

Me: "Soren treats his swords like they're pets. Probably snuggles them."

Soren: "Of course I do. They have feelings, Ava.

"And Soren, what do you think Ava's might be?"

"I bet she uses oversized mugs for her coffee. Probably has animal shaped ones, possibly one that's a Highland cow."

The audience howls. Shirley wipes away tears of laughter.

My skin heats under the weight of Soren's attention on me. Then—*damn it*—there it is. A flash of charged eye contact. His smile loses its bite, and a gentler, more intimate expression blooms in its place.

Soren's tongue flicks across his bottom lip, and my entire body commits treason.

My core clenches, trying to send a flare signal. The bees in my stomach? Yeah, not anxiety. *Desire.*

How dare my libido clock in after sitting dormant for so long. And for *him* of all people? I blame the drought. I haven't... You know... done anything in a *while.*

Soren Pembry—with his carved-by-chaos cheekbones and perfectly trimmed facial hair—is the *last* person I should be reacting to in *this* way.

Yet, here I am, one smolder away from applying to his *Dagger Daddy Fanclub.*

Oh, God! Stop, Ava.

"Ava, you okay?" Shirley asks, yanking me from my spiral.

Thankfully, I recover quickly and nod. Years of moderating Q&As while crumbling internally have made me a professional.

Soren's watching me even closer now, like he's seeing beyond the veil. His expression softens. "You know, Ava. Showy banter aside..." His tone holds no heat, but something startlingly sincere. "When I read *The Lumberjack's Love Letters* after that vampire video I did, I actually stayed up half the night finishing it."

"Soren, it's not like you to roast the same book twice. My lumberjack must've made quite the impression on you."

"He did. The ending—phew." He gives a quiet, self-deprecating laugh, and for a few seconds, he's not Soren Pembry, sword-wielding sex symbol. He's a man talking about a book that hit him somewhere deep. "It made me realize that the world could use more heroes like yours."

"What are you getting at?"

"I mean, men who fight with their hearts instead of their fists, who believe in things like love and that it can conquer anything. Men who make good on their promises and show up—despite the odds. Despite everything."

"I'm sorry." I shake my head. "What realm did I just cross into?"

Soren chuckles. "I'm being completely genuine. I swear on the Dagger Daddy Fan Club."

A wave of high-pitched screams rings out.

My mouth forgets how to form words. Whatever that was, it wasn't for the crowd. It wasn't for content.

That was for me.

I'm utterly unprepared for it.

I will my pulse to calm down, and the flush in my cheeks not to give me away.

"Oh. My. God." Shirley clutches her mic like it's the bouquet at a wedding. "You two are the swooniest thing this convention has ever seen."

Soren's eyes lock on mine. "I certainly hope so."

Something in the air changes. I *feel* it in my spine. In my knees. In the places I shouldn't.

Someone yells, "Ava Bell is a Sword Whore."

Soren smirks at the crowd. "You have to buy the special edition for that scene."

I roll my eyes. Except, I'm smiling.

The panel ends in a standing ovation. Book bloggers rush the stage. People wave copies of our books. Soren autographs a leather-bound spell book someone shoved in front of him. I pose with a woman dressed as my main character, complete with tinsel in her hair.

It's insane. It's magical. And I'm completely overstimulated.

Slipping backstage to catch my breath, I hide behind the stack of swag boxes, trying to slow my pulse.

"You okay?"

Soren appears, one hand on that stupid sword, the other grazing over the thick stubble on his jaw. He leans against the wall, his silver eyes start trying to decode me.

Good luck with that.

I plant my hands on my hips and nod. "Yeah. Why?"

"You ran off." Soren continues watching me.

"I'm fine," I lie.

"You were a good sport out there," he offers.

"Thanks," I manage, voice an octave too high. "You were... *tolerable.*"

While my lungs fight to breathe, my brain crashes out like someone dumped my hot cider into its wiring.

Who uses tolerable anymore? Literally no one.

I want to crawl into a pile of signed paperbacks and disappear forever.

Soren's head tilts as if trying to decide whether I'm adorable or unwell.

I'll save him the trouble. I'm unwell. Very much unwell.

"You know, the crowd ate us up out there." He moves toward me. I retreat backward. "We make a good team."

"*We*...are not a team." My back hits the wall. "That...that was strategic opposition. Nothing else."

He's standing right in front of me now. "Funny how strategy looks a lot like chemistry."

His gaze dips to my mouth. Before I can reply, my publicist barrels backstage, waving her phone at us. She's either discovered a new planet or a disaster.

Renata's not alone. Another woman is with her—tall, severe, and wearing the shade of dark lipstick that means business, and holding a tablet. Both of them are grinning in a way that makes me deeply worried.

"You two?"Renata points at us both. "Viral gold."

"They're calling it enemies-to-lovers in real time," the other woman adds, flipping the screen to show us ShelfSpace flooding with clips. "*Bell and The Blade* is trending."

"I'm sorry," I say. "Who are you?"

"Camille," Soren answers, "My manager."

Camille taps a pen against the tablet. #BellandtheBlade is in bold. In italics. In stitched-on-a-throw-pillow font.

"It's not just a hashtag," she says. "It's a generational movement. A siren call to the masses. A viral juggernaut rolling through ShelfSpace with reckless abandon, taking no prisoners."

Confused, my brow furrows. Soren cranes his neck to look at the chaos on the screen.

"So," Renata takes over. "We have an idea."

Soren crosses his arms. "Should I be scared?"

Bracing for the worst, I swallow.

They glance around to ensure nobody's listening.

Then, in a hushed tone, they say it.

Together.

"Fake. Dating."

Four

SOREN

Today's panel fucked me. Rammed me right in the feels. It's the first time Ava and I have ever sat side by side. Semi-close. Same air. Real words instead of digital daggers.

I spent the entire time cataloging her, watching how her eyes lit up each time she was about to deliver a killing blow. I took every hit willingly. Except the fanservice one. *That* one lodged itself right in my ego.

She said it with such fake sweetness, turning my whole persona into a punchline and smiling while the audience laughed along.

Maybe I deserved it. To her, I am the brand, personally providing her with ammunition almost daily online.

Still, hearing it live and in person hit different. Felt personal. She saw straight through the performance and aimed for the man beneath it.

Then I went and told her I'd read her book—the whole damn thing. The words just slipped out as if a part of me needed her to know I see her beyond the banter.

She startled, a faint flush crept up her neck, and for a moment, the room tilted on its axis. The noise, the lights, the people, all of it blurred until there was only her.

Ava Bell.

For all the fire and fight inside her, she wears a mask for the crowd. A lot like someone else I know. I see it now. We're two people pretending a little too well.

Whatever anger I'd been clinging to burned off in an instant. What replaced it wasn't gentle—it was fierce, inevitable. A pull that starts in your chest and doesn't stop until it's carved your name into someone else's heartbeat.

And damn me, Ava has certainly carved hers into mine, because I am so fucking gone for this woman.

After the panel, I'd planned on asking her to grab a drink. Nothing serious, just a ceasefire over something stronger than caffeine.

And if she said no? Fine. I'd fall back on my original plan: sit on my hotel balcony with a fall-spiced bourbon, pretending the quiet didn't feel like punishment while prepping my breakout session for tomorrow. *Why battle-mages with trust issues deserve cuddles too.*

Catchy title. Tragic subtext.

What I didn't plan on was being herded into my manager's hotel room to hammer out the details of a fake dating scheme between *The Blade* and *The Queen of Steam.*

Her publicist paces the room while she and Camille deconstruct every angle of this PR stunt—equal parts absurd and genius. They talk numbers: follower metrics, engagement spikes, viral potential. On paper, it's flawless. Strategic. A guaranteed visibility boost for both of us.

I, for one, love the idea.

Ava, however, clearly doesn't. She's sitting stiffly on the edge of an armchair, ready to jump out the window if someone says "holiday boyfriend" again.

This plan gives me the perfect excuse to orbit Ava Bell without anyone questioning my motives.

This isn't a strategy.

It's not a crush.

It's bigger. Messier. Something more that doesn't fit into neat, professional boxes.

"This is the stupidest idea ever." Ava's fingers keep drifting to the hem of her dress, tugging, smoothing, more tugging.

I wish she'd stop doing that. Every nervous pull hikes the fabric a little higher, and my focus a little lower. It's torture in high definition.

Yeah, I should look away—be a gentleman, or at least pretend to be—but the truth is, I don't want to. Those legs are toned, restless, impossible not to notice, and have officially rerouted my moral compass.

I force my eyes upward, to her face. My heart squeezes. Ava's nervous. Guarded. Human in a way that doesn't fit the image I built of her online. She's not the clever nemesis I spar with for clicks—she's layered, real, entirely herself. That combination does something to me I can't disguise with arrogance or charm.

Because it's not *just* her body I want.

It's her *pages*.

Her chaos.

Her order.

Her unapologetic logic and that soft, stubborn heart she tries so hard to tuck away.

I want to burrow under every one of those layers, especially the ones wrapped in cable-knit and hiding in plain sight.

And this fake dating scheme is my chance.

Except, I have so many questions.

Like, are we supposed to hold hands at events?

Are we kissing? In public? On camera?

Do I tell her I've read every single one of her books, not just *The Lumberjack's Love Letters*, and loved them all?

Am I looking at her right now like she's the love of my life... all while she stares at me like I'm a fungal infection she can't legally sue?

Did I say that last one out loud? Or in my head?

Either way, her eyebrow twitched. So... not great.

Fuck. Me. *What* am I thinking?

Ava Bell *hates* me, so unless this plan includes a step-by-step guide on how to win over a woman who's made a brand out of slandering my literary kinks—this thing's going to go down in flames.

Renata stops pacing, turns, addresses Ava. "We're talking a few more appearances. A dozen posts per event minimum, and at least five shared videos for ShelfSpace. You two are already trending. Let's keep the momentum going."

Ava makes a noise that's somewhere between a scoff and a dying reindeer.

My publicist, Camille, nods approvingly. "We'll soft-launch the relationship with a teaser post tonight, then make it official with a pumpkin patch press conference. Full couple content. Cozy aesthetic. Bonus points for falling leaves. You'll be the hottest couple on the internet. Next to Asher Cross and Celeste Monroe, of course."

Ava turns to me, an expression full of pure heroine betrayal on her pretty face. "This is insane."

"Possibly," I say, because yeah it is. Or is it?

Shaking her head in disbelief, she grimaces. "What's in it for you?"

"It's good marketing," I add, trying to get her to look at me again.

She does. With narrow eyes. I'm pretty sure she's mentally hurling the decorative ceramic pumpkin at my face right now. I'll take it.

Camille clears her throat like she's been waiting for her cue. "And it'll be good for Soren's image. A relationship makes him more relatable. Less... untouchable bad boy, more fan favorite."

"You do know I'm sitting in the room, right?" I say. "You don't have to speak about me in third person."

"Are you actually considering this?" Ava folds her arms over her chest, which pushes her tits up in a way that does *very* unhelpful things to my concentration—and Captain Pembry. "You don't need the extra numbers, Soren."

No, but apparently I do need a moment to remember how words work. Or to stop imagining what my name might sound like with less judgment and more breathlessness.

And true. I'm not hurting for attention. My last book broke the preorder record for fantasy that month. Sure, the movie adaptation for my most popular series has been in "development" longer than most celebrity marriages. Needless to say, I'm fine. But Camille isn't wrong. And publicity never hurts. Especially when I'm about to launch a spin-off with an ambiguous demon prince and a possessive, foul-mouthed shadow wolf, with a flair for violence.

Ava, though? She could use the win. She's brilliant, legendary good. I don't understand why the numbers don't match the hype.

So, maybe this fake dating, staged proximity, and sudden spotlight will give her the boost she deserves. If I can help with that, I will.

Never mind the fact that I plan to use every second of this scheme to my advantage and get to know Ava beyond the screen.

Also, if we're being brutally honest... I'm extremely curious what it would feel like if Ava Bell had to touch me in public. Or at all. Pretend to flirt. Pretend to adore me. She's sassy-tongued and tightly wound, allergic to spontaneity and joyfully resistant to fun —which means she's *precisely* the kind of woman I want to peel apart. Layer by stubborn, sarcastic layer.

And yes. I mean clothes too. I want to know what she hides under her armor, her attitude, her hemline. All of it.

It'd also be... I don't know. Nice, I guess. To have someone to spend the holidays with.

I'm not getting into that right now, though. That's a different chapter.

Or maybe an epilogue.

One I haven't written yet.

"You're right, I don't need the numbers," I say, rubbing my thumb back and forth over chin. "But tell me, Bells—when else am I going to get the chance to fake-date the romance author who claims she hates me? That's fun waiting to happen."

Camille's attention shifts to Ava. "It's two months. Max. In January, we end it. A joint statement. Focus on writing. Blah blah, creative growth. Everyone moves on."

"Two months," Ava repeats, voice brittle. "Of pretending we're dating. In public."

"In matching outfits," Renata adds with zero remorse.

Ava groans. She gets up and walks over to the mini bar, snatches a tiny bottle of whiskey and takes a sip. Based on the face she just made, it's not strong enough to process what's happening.

"We should set some ground rules," I offer.

"Ground rules?" Ava asks, her brow furrowed in that adorable way she gets when she's still working everything out in that whip-smart, controlling head of hers.

"Sure. That way you don't accidentally stab me with a candy cane at the Snowflake Gala when I try to put my arm around you."

Camille, ever the opportunist, steps in. "Boundaries are good. Let's make a list."

"No sharing a room," Ava replies immediately.

"Actually..." I clear my throat, eyes flicking over at our managers for a brief second. "If we're trying to make this believable, wouldn't it be weird if we didn't share a room at least once? Or dare I say, thrice."

Ava whips her head toward me, her expression full of disgust. "Absolutely not."

"It's not like I suggested we film a sex tape and leak it on Shelf-Space." I drag two fingers slowly down my jaw, skimming the edge of my beard with mock thoughtfulness. "I mean, I wouldn't be opposed to the sex tape—strictly for realism, of course."

Before Ava can protest, I hold up a hand. "It would be for

optics. We're supposed to be a couple. If anyone finds out we're not staying together—at some point—it'll kill the illusion before it starts."

Silence follows, settling heavy in my chest.

Camille and Renata both glance at each other but say nothing, clearly crossing every PR-obsessed finger they have that Ava might actually agree to this.

I won't lie—I'm crossing mine too.

"No weird touching," she finally says.

"And your definition of weird would be..."

She shoots me a glare. "No touching unless it's for the camera. And even then, I pick the pose."

"Understood. No unsanctioned snuggling."

Renata scrolls through her tablet. "We'll need a few public moments that suggest intimacy—breakfasts, post-panel hangouts, maybe a cozy bookstore date. Let's make it swoony, and memorable."

Ava glares at her for a long while. "I don't understand."

Camille cuts in. "A date. Low-key. Paparazzi bait without being obvious that it's paparazzi bait. Coffee shop window seats and a shared pastry. It's about the illusion of closeness without forcing it."

Ava sneers. Shakes her head at me. "You're enjoying this entirely too much."

"Can you blame me? If pretending to be your boyfriend comes with flannel sheets and strategic cuddling, sign me up. I'm only trying to be thorough in my role."

Ava stares down at the glass in her hand, quiet. Her brow furrows again. This time, I don't see irritation or confusion. She's thinking, turning it over, weighing the options, treating this as if it's a negotiation for her soul. I hate that for her. But I also, very much, want to do this.

So I nudge a little.

"How have your sales been the last few days?" I ask casually.

Renata answers for her. "Steady. Good, even."

I look right at Ava. "And today?"

Renata lifts her tablet. Scrolls. Then beams. "She's up eighty percent."

Boom. Mic drop.

Ava's face changes. There goes the fight between pride and logic. Control and possibility.

It's settled.

"So, you in, Bells?"

Ava lifts her gaze. "Don't call me that."

"All couples have cute nicknames for each other." I cross one leg over the other. "What's mine?"

"Brood Lightyear," she replies instantly.

"To infinity and beyond, huh?" I tilt my head. "Is that... a request?"

Ava rolls her eyes then moves toward her publicist. "I want a detailed itinerary, a veto on all captions, and the right to block his number after New Year's."

"Deal." I raise my glass. Her attention snaps back to me. "Cheers to love."

Renata lights up. Camille starts on the paperwork.

My eyes slide over to Ava. She's ringing her hands, twisting them all up, probably rethinking every career decision that led her here.

Fake dating.

Me and Ava Bell.

This might be the best worst idea ever.

Or the best.

Five

AVA

After the meeting, I headed down to the hotel bar, regretting everything, and immediately texted my agent, Victoria, like a tattling younger sibling.

> Renata's gone rogue.

> She's fake dating me to Soren Pembry.

> Send help or legal fire.

> She told me my only option is to smile, nod, and basically do whatever she tells me to.

> Her words. Not mine.

Unfortunately, Renata sidled up next to me and saw my text messages. In her sweet, condescending tone, she assured me it's too late to pull the plug—everything's been signed, sealed, and delivered to Victoria for approval.

Then she ordered herself a victory drink.

I ordered a chai martini, hoping for something strong enough to taste like fall and mild self-destruction.

I love my publicist, truly—she's exceptional at her job and wants the best for me. But that doesn't mean she's always right.

47

As much as I trust her, I don't trust *this*. Not when my name is on the line.

Victoria will fix this. She's a bulldog in designer heels. A terrifying, whip-smart advocate who shreds contracts for sport.

She'll do the same to this one.

Except she hasn't replied yet. What if she agrees with the plan? No, think positive. She's just super busy sharpening her teeth to find an out for me.

God, please let that be the case.

After two drinks, Fisher joins.

When we move to grab a table, Renata excuses herself.

"Gotta go work on some of the logistics with Camille for tonight's soft launch," she says, slinging her purse over her thin, bony shoulder. "Ava, you must be present in the comments. It's your number one top priority. Understand?"

Nodding, I decide not to tell her that I'm two seconds from Googling "how to fake your own death and disappear before a fake dating contract goes viral."

As Fisher and I follow the hostess to our table I check my phone again. Still nothing. If Victoria doesn't answer, Googling might actually become Plan A.

The hotel restaurant is all rustic chic and forced tranquility, featuring cornucopia centerpieces, amber lighting, and instrumental jazz playing overhead; everything is built to convince you that peace can be manufactured.

It's not working. My chest is tight, my thoughts won't stop circling, and my stomach feels like it's hosting a corn maze made of dread. I am not calm. I am not okay.

Sitting here, about to have a perfectly normal meal with Fisher, pretending that I am, feels like I'm throwing thin fabric over something still thrashing underneath.

I've spent almost two years carefully cultivating a routine of control and predictability. And now I've willingly walked into a stunt designed to implode it all.

Once seated, the waiter takes our orders. Maple-glazed pork chop for me, and Fisher goes full drama with the truffle risotto.

"It pairs well with unrequited love and a chilled rosé." He drapes a napkin over his lap and takes a sip of said rosé.

I order another chai martini, swallow it down like it might quiet the noise, and gesture for the next. Fisher's gaze tracks me the way one might watch someone step willingly into quicksand.

Thankfully, the food comes out fast. I need something in my stomach before the chai martinis convince me to start trauma-dumping in public.

Fisher digs right into his. "Delicious."

Cutting a piece of pork chop, I shovel it into my mouth and grumble.

"What's wrong?" Fisher asks. "Is it not cooked right?"

"No, it's perfect," I whine through a mouthful. "But I can't enjoy a single bite. All I want to do is crawl under the table, curl up in a napkin cocoon, and cry into a breadbasket. I don't even need a reason. Just five solid minutes of ugly crying and an emotional support breadstick."

My assistant rolls his eyes. "Ava, it's fake dating, not a hostage situation. You'll survive the comments and a few photo ops. Now eat your feelings like a normal person."

"This online nemesis thing I have with Soren Pembry was never supposed to turn into something personal."

"Until it did," Fisher retorts.

I groan, thinking back to how this all started. I made a tiny throwaway post during a late-night doom scroll. It was a satirical "Dear Fantasy Authors" rant, centered on how *some* characters from the fantasy genre have the emotional range of a teaspoon.

I never mentioned Soren by name, but if the emotionally-stunted warlord boot fits...

His fans lost it. They mass-reported and ShelfSpace tagged me for "slanderous content."

Soren responded with a video of him reading a steamy scene from my book, *The Lumberjack's Love Letters,* using an overly dramatic gruff voice. And since humiliation is a layered art form, after that, he followed it up with a second take: suspenders hanging low, shirtless, a ridiculous wind machine blowing through his cheap romance-cover wig as though he was shooting a woodsy Fabio reboot. The man even had the audacity to rub sawdust across his abs for "authenticity."

It's hard for me to admit how my traitorous eyes immediately zeroed in on the trail of hair leading south from his navel, like it was a fucking treasure map.

At that moment, I was a sinner. A fraud. A woman two seconds from licking her screen and renouncing every opinion she'd ever had about fantasy authors and their egos. Or at least, this particular fantasy author.

That post was a declaration of war.

Then, he took it too far.

In order to make me homicidal, he capped it all off with a black-and-white "dramatic reading" reel—lit similar to a poetry slam, jazz music in the background, one eyebrow raised as though he was interpreting Tolstoy instead of a five-page ode to cabin fever and creative use of furniture.

"Some say love is a fire," Soren read, *"but in the woods... it's a slow burn."*

My book was trending within the hour, along with his six-pack. And that's when viral rivals *Bell and The Blade* were born. Dueling hashtags and all.

"You're chewing like someone just served you a side of roasted octopus dick," Fisher's voice slices clean through my spiral.

I realize I've been mauling my maple-glazed pork chop. "No, I'm chewing like someone who agreed to fake-date her rival. For *two* months."

Across the table, Fisher looks effortlessly elegant as he stirs his cocktail with the cinnamon stick garnish.

"What?" I snap.

"You're overthinking."

"So what?"

"So, regret isn't exactly your best shade, Luv," Fisher says with glittering judgment.

"You're right." I blow a stray curl out of my face, sit up straighter, summoning whatever scraps of composure I have left, and stab my pork chop with my fork. "I am in control. This is a strategic career move."

"Ah." Fisher tilts his head. "Is that going to be your new daily mantra, or are we still pretending the reason you're this worked up isn't because he gets under your skin?"

My fork freezes mid-air.

"You don't hate him, Ava. You're curious. And curiosity, my dear, is foreplay's favorite cousin."

"He doesn't get under my skin," I deny it. "I told you already. I *loathe* him."

"Loathing is simply another brand of lust?" Fisher seems pleased with himself. "Call it strategy all you want, but we both know this isn't about exposure or clicks. This is about curiosity."

"Curiosity over what, exactly?"

"Soren Pembry's flesh sword, of course."

My eyes narrow on him. "*This* scheme has nothing to do with *that*."

"Mhm." Fisher takes a bite of his food. "You're telling me you've never thought about it?"

"Not. Once."

Lie. That's a lie. I've imagined it. More than once. If a particular scene in *The Boyfriend Deadline* reads suspiciously close to a fantasy involving a hot tub and a man whose likeness resembles Soren Pembry... well, all I can say is creative minds pull from the strangest places.

Fisher arches one perfectly plucked brow. Busted.

"Even if I have, I can't act upon it. That would be a disaster waiting to happen. One with unfairly broad shoulders and the potential to tank my career."

Fisher shakes his head at me, his dark skin radiating under the golden light. Long, tightly woven dreads are pulled back into a half-up style that makes his cheekbones even more mysterious. "I have a feeling this is going to be exactly what you need."

"What? Public humiliation?"

"A personality exfoliant."

"Excuse me?"

"Ava, you are layers upon layers of self-control and perfectly paced romance. Fall scented candles, color-coded bookshelves, and repressed sexual tension. You need a sledgehammer. Well, congratulations, you have been granted a fantasy fuckboy whose bone structure, and I mean *bone structure*, was blessed by the gods. Soren's aura radiates with the promise that he could destroy your vagina, *with said sledgehammer,* and you'd beg for seconds, maybe even thirds, with his hands still cupping your ass and your morals left in the sheets."

My jaw falls open. "First of all, eww. Second of all, I thought you were on my side."

"Of course I am," he says, dabbing the corners of his mouth with his napkin. "But your dry spell is longer than the runtime of Titanic. And right now, you get to be your very own Enemies-to-Lovers trope *in public* with a man who probably smells like bergamot and leather."

"He smells like trees and sweat."

"Even better." Fisher takes another bite of his food.

"How is that better?"

Fisher swallows, sips his water to wash it down. "The man looks like he was hand-forged by those same gods in a thunderstorm—he's gritty, and built to last. If you get what I'm sayin."

I stare at him. "Okay, calm down."

Fisher shrugs. "Hey, if Thor's morally gray cousin wants to rail you into inner peace, who am I to stand in the way?"

"Fisher!"

"What? Maybe a little swordplay—*literal* or otherwise—will loosen you up."

I slap a napkin over my face and groan.

"You'd better conquer that man like he's the last enchanted keystone holding the gate to total satisfaction."

"Lower your voice," I hiss as a pair of authors walk past our table.

He ignores me. "I wonder if he moans while reading sexually charged scenes out loud when he's writing?"

"Fisher."

"Do you moan when you do it?"

"Not funny and none of your business."

"So, yes then?" Shameless, Fisher grins, arrogant charm dialed to the max. He enjoys poking the bear to see how loud it roars.

I glare at him. He winks.

Over this conversation, I stab a crouton, then shove it into my mouth.

"You're still chewing aggressively," Fisher states.

"Why are you judging my chewing so harshly tonight? And what does that even mean?"

"Repressed sexual tension always shows up somewhere. For some people, it's the gym. For you? It's how violently you murder carbs. Like people who eat ice. *Aggressively.*"

A flash snatches my attention. Across the room, someone snaps a selfie with a best-selling romantic suspense author.

The whole place whirs with the low-grade buzz of industry mingling over cocktails, influencers recording content, publicists schmoozing, ShelfSpacers scouting angles.

Then there's me, sitting at the corner table, pouting, while my very judgmental PA cleans his plate and sips his drink.

"You're crashing," Fisher says. "It's not a good look."

See? Judgy.

"I'm not crashing."

"You're doing the thing where your brain over-stirs and your inner monologue gets mean."

I scowl. "My inner monologue is always mean."

"Yeah, except now it's directing all the anger inward." Both hands gesture toward his chest.

"You're right. I'm angry. At Soren. At our publicists. At myself. I'm part of this whole manipulative charade, and we're supposed to act as though it's all okay. It's not okay."

Fisher's expression folds, the snark stripped back to bare concern. "Ava—"

"We're using fake affection for clicks and comments and virality, and painting it as a perfectly acceptable marketing strategy. It's crooked, Fisher. It's deceitful. I mean, how did I get here? Why is this stupid stunt necessary? Worse, why am I doing it with someone who clearly has no shame playing into it?"

Fisher lets the silence sit heavy for a beat, then says it plainly. "He brings the numbers. Whether you like it or not, Bell and the Blade is the type of story people eat alive."

He's right. And I hate that.

"Admit it, deep down, part of you wants the world to see him looking at you like you're a riddle he intends to solve."

"Fisher, that's not—" I start, but stop. The protest tastes bitter on my tongue. I shake my head, forcing steel into my voice. "So the only way my career survives is through him?"

Fisher plops backward against his chair. "No, Luv, of course not. But think about the what if's?"

What if?

Those two words throw an even bigger coup in my brain. Because...

What if it works? What if it doesn't?

What if I sell more books, gain more followers, boost my brand, but what if I lose the part of myself I actually like in the process?

What if all this pretend affection and flirty manipulation starts to affect me?

What if the Dagger Daddy Fan Club comes for me?

What if I become someone I don't recognize? Or someone *I* wouldn't respect—someone who sells intimacy as merch. Flirts for metrics. Trades integrity for trends, all in the name of the almighty algorithm.

Someone like Soren "Whoren" Pembry.

I've officially stooped to his level. I want to scream into a throw pillow and then immediately light it on fire. I can't be like him.

That ballroom was Soren's personal colosseum. He didn't casually stroll in—he *owned* the room. Worked the crowd. The women. They *loved* it.

How much of that was real? How much of it was a calculated performance? He can't be *that* fake. Right?

Those questions, unfortunately, bring me to a more unbalanced one.

"Uh oh," Fisher's voice cuts in. "What storm is swirling inside that beautiful, overthinking brain of yours?"

I hesitate before asking, "How much pussy do you think Soren Pembry actually pulls?"

Fisher looks genuinely surprised by the question.

"Because statistically, it's gotta be disturbing." I wave my hands fast, like I can physically swat it away. "No, I don't want to know."

Fisher grins sardonically. "And that's the worst part, isn't it, Ava?"

"What do you mean?"

"Not wanting to know feels a little too close to being jealous. Which is a whole new emotion you're not ready to unpack." He leans on the table with his elbows. "What are you actually afraid of?"

My reply is instant. "Failing. I'm cautious, Fisher. And honest. This whole lying thing is hard for me."

"Is this about a certain someone we shall not name?" His tone carries a dash of faux innocence and more than enough shade to make my stomach tighten. "Mr. I Hate Your Face?"

"No," I lie. "It's not about him."

He hums, skeptical. "Well, good. Keep that sore excuse for a man in the past where he belongs. With his pretty words and practiced hands."

"The ones that took everything from me," I mutter.

Fisher's face softens. "Luv–"

"Look, I can't do what Soren does. He's so good at being... well, *him*. He treats every woman like she's the answer to his prayers, laughs with them, signs books with personalized notes that are probably *very* intimate. And now I'm stuck in this fake dating stunt with a man who uses charm as a weapon."

"Which is very close to Mr. I Hate Your Face."

"True," I agree. "But I'm not worried about that. I'm worried associating myself with a walking man-whore, like Soren, will screw over my credibility?"

"So, you're worried about the Whoren Pembry persona?"

"Yeah, I've worked hard for my reputation. It's spotless. And he's out there passing out orgasms with every autograph."

"Let's unpack that jealousy now."

"I'm not jealous," I insist, although part of me hated how my body responded to him today, blushing and buzzing, thighs clenching.

Fisher gives me a look so dry it could sand furniture. "You sound as though you're trying to convince TSA you're not smuggling a vibrator in your carry-on."

"Cute, coming from the man who *did* smuggle, not one, but two, actually."

He shoves his empty plate aside with flair. "Ah, memories. Romanticom last year. Security pulled me aside, thinking I was harboring state secrets. All I could say was, 'It's rechargeable and body-safe, officer.'"

"You're the worst human I've ever loved."

"Correct." He grins briefly, then hits me with a pointed glare. "But seriously, Ava. You need to remember that Soren plays a *character*. Emotional connection is merely another arrow in his hot-boy quiver. It's an illusion. Theatrics. The man doesn't bare his soul when he bares his chest."

I open my mouth to object, but Fisher steamrolls ahead.

"What you're actually saying with this long, self-righteous

monologue of denial is your loins lit up like a goddamn Christmas tree when you saw him in person today. And that panel?" He fans himself with a cocktail napkin. "*Hot.* I went to my hotel room and jacked off to it."

I choke on my martini, then gag. "Why, Fisher? Why must I know what?"

"Because we tell each other everything. And hey, if *I* got that worked up, I can't imagine what was happening in *your* panties. *Miss Dry Spell.* I'd bet money that you've officially tumbled into Soren's horny abyss. And all it took was one wink from that deliciously handsome, arrogant son of a bitch. *A wink!*"

I'm staring at him like he pulled a secret out of my pants and waved it around like a party flag.

The alcohol is *finally* doing its job. I point a finger at him. "Let's make one thing clear. I don't 'tumble' anywhere. If I wanted Soren Pembry, I'd *stride* into his lair in full control, heels clicking as though they were a countdown to his inevitable destruction."

"With the way Blade Boy was staring at you today, if you're striding, he's kneeling." Fisher lazily circles the rim of his glass with a finger.

"Whatever," I say, blinking away the blur in my eyes. "He hates *me* as much as I hate *him.*"

"Nah, Luv. He wants to fuck you. And I think you want that too."

I shake my head. "Um, no."

"There's nothing wrong with it. In fact, I'd argue it's the most natural response your body's had in years."

My lips part—then snap shut again. Great! My mouth has become a faulty garage door.

Fisher clocks it instantly. "You're cautious. I heard you. Thou-Whom-We-Shall-Not-Name torched your heart, your trust, and your career. We won't mention the other failures since him. I get it. You're afraid of stepping back into the fire with anyone, let alone an industry peer."

I don't have to say anything. It's all true.

Fisher's voice dips to a teasing whisper. "But don't go pretending your clit didn't salute *The Blade* today... probably still is."

My shoulders tense. I cross my arms in a too-tight hug, willing the heat in my cheeks to cool down. "No."

Fisher nods. "Yes."

"That's the stupidest thing I've ever heard."

"You like him," he sings.

"I do not," my voice cracks.

"He likes you."

"He does not."

Fisher's eyes glint. "Your voice cracked. That was your shame talking. Your horny shame."

I go silent. Which, of course, is all the proof Fisher needs.

Fiddling with the button on my sleeve, I yank a stray thread. The button pops off. *Shit.*

"Let's consider for one moment the what-ifs." Fisher crosses his arms.

I exhale. "I already have been."

"Mhm, I'm sure you have. Except what if the *opposite* of what you're worried about happens?"

"What do you mean?"

"What if all this boosts your approval rating *and* cleans up his image in the process? Makes him less the fantasy fuckboy of Shelf-Space and more... a genuinely good guy who's with a genuinely good girl." His tone drops a few decibels to his deep, silky, dark romance narrator voice. "Come on, Ava Bell, be a *good girl* for Dagger Daddy."

Despite myself, I laugh at the same time a shadow falls across the table.

"Am I interrupting?" Soren drawls, setting a hand on the back of my chair. "Or did I just hear my government-assigned nickname?"

Well, speak of the smolder. Soren Pembry stands beside me in a forest green cardigan layered over a white V-neck that shows his golden, muscled skin.

Somehow, this is worse than the sword, the smirk, or the signature fan service swagger. He's normal. Casual. Achingly touchable. Almost resembling a character right out of *my* books– one who reads literary fiction on their porch and owns too many flannel shirts.

It's doing things. Inappropriate, unprofessional, wildly inconvenient things.

His hair is slightly damp, which means he took a shower.

Great, now I'm picturing him in the shower. Clothes off. Naked. Water beading down carved muscles.

Fisher eyes me skeptically. Soren tilts his head, waiting for an answer. I can't speak. My brain is a traitor. My hormones are holding my sanity hostage as Soren's gaze flicks to Fisher, then back to me.

"Please do join us." Fisher gestures to the open chair with a shit-eating grin.

"Thanks." Soren sits. "Didn't want to interrupt anything private."

"Not at all, we were just discussing Ava's dramatic flair for denial," Fisher replies cheerfully.

"Denial? Well, that doesn't sound like her at all."

My attention bounces between them. "Wow. A two-man improv set. How lucky am I?"

"Fisher Wallen." He offers his hand to Soren across the space.

"Soren Pembry." Their handshake is brief but weighted.

"She's been singing your praises, by the way," Fisher muses. "Can't stop talking about your... sword."

I choke on air. "Okay, nope. Absolutely not."

Soren's villain smirk is back. "I'm flattered. Not everyone appreciates true craftsmanship."

"I appreciate silence," I deadpan.

"Not my style," Fisher says. "You know that."

"Mine either," Soren agrees.

I fold my napkin with a little more aggression than necessary. "You two should take this show on the road. Maybe open for a band called *The Misogynotes.*"

Fisher chuckles. "Careful, Soren, she's spicy tonight."

Soren's dark yet amused gaze cuts to mine. "She writes spice, Fisher. It was only a matter of time before some of it rubbed off on her."

I sneer at him.

"When I started roasting your books, I thought you were all cardigans and clean kisses." Soren leans an inch closer. "But there's filth hiding under that sweater dress, isn't there?"

Fisher props his chin on his hand and sighs happily. "God, I love live theater."

I ignore him. My eyes are set on the enemy. "You want to say that again with fewer contract violations?"

Soren's grin deepens. "Not particularly."

Fisher continues to listen, unbothered as always. He waves to the waiter for another drink. "Don't get too close, lover boy. She bites."

Soren smirks. "Even better."

"Oh, I like him, Ava."

"Thank you, Fisher." Soren claps a hand on Fisher's shoulder and squeezes. "How about you, Bells? Do *you* like me too?"

"*Don't* call me that."

Soren leans on the table with his forearms, then twists his neck to survey the gathering of influencers. "We should cause a little trouble while we're here. You game?"

"No," I say immediately. "You're not staying."

"Admit it," he replies. "You'd be disappointed if I were anything other than trouble."

To avoid looking at him, I stare down at my plate. His trees and sweat scent from earlier now smells more like magical pine needles, sultry smoke, and some enchanted elixir that was probably brewed under a full moon, possibly by a sexy wizard from another realm with one hand on his hip and a prophecy on his tongue.

Jesus, I'm really leaning into the fantasy genre all of a sudden.

"What, no witty quip?" Soren teases. "Should I be worried?"

"Oh, I've got plenty." I stab my fork into a roasted carrot. "But I left my ego-dismantling kit back in the hotel room."

"Fisher was right, you are spicy," Soren laughs, clearly enjoying himself. "Now I'm definitely staying."

I exhale, shove a forkful of pork chop into my mouth, and chew.

A smile curls on Fisher's lips, but he doesn't comment.

"So, have you two been plotting my demise this whole time?" Soren asks, waving over our waiter.

"Not yet," I answer. "Still weighing the pros and cons."

Soren grins. "Let me know if I can help tip the scale."

One side of Fisher's mouth curves back because he can't resist a golden opportunity for a dirty joke. The second Soren said "tip," Fisher's expression changed immediately. Now he's halfway to drafting an entire erotica novella based on that one word.

I kick Fisher under the table, mentally screaming at him to focus, then I fix my face to resemble a fake sweet smile, turning my attention back to Soren. "We were discussing the plan."

"Ah, yes. The *romance* of it all." Soren savors the word as though he likes the taste of it.

Does it taste good in his mouth?

Fisher jumps in. "Well, I for one love what you two are doing. You know, I've always said Ava needs someone to shake her out of her tight little bubble. Someone tall. Charming. A little maddening."

Soren raises a hand. "I'm available."

They both laugh. I don't. My vagina might file for emancipation, possibly with Fisher as her lawyer.

Another round of cocktails shows up per Soren. This one is an autumnal concoction with a cinnamon rim and a festive garnish.

Fisher insists we toast to "inevitable choices." I drink mine faster than I should, which might explain why my edges start to blur a little.

Across the room, a few content creators pretend not to stare. One of them definitely snaps a pic. Another tilts her phone, acting like she's getting B-roll footage for a post captioned "Enemies to Lovers in the Wild."

Soren's presence changes the air. It's hotter now. Looser. With a sexy, fire-in-the-fireplace sort of vibe.

My pulse jumps when his knee brushes mine under the table, subtle, but it still shoots lightning straight up my spine.

Scenes start playing in my brain—one with a one-bed trope, then another with me getting completely railed on the oversized window seat in my hotel room while city lights glimmer in the background as if cheering him on, while that smirk of his presses against my skin.

What the fuck is wrong with me? Why does he affect me this way?

My phone buzzes, yanking me from the visual of my breasts pressed against the cool pane of glass, one of Soren's hands tangled in my hair while his other works my clit apart with devastating precision.

Group Chat with Fisher and Renata: **PLOT THICCENS** (named by Fisher, obviously)

Shifting in my seat, I swipe open the message from PR Queen Supreme:

> Fisher, you've stirred enough. Time for the heroine and the hot guy to suffer in forced proximity. Shoo.

Fisher checks his phone, then grins so wide it could break a camera lens. "Well–" He rises. "—the goddesses of Spin and Sparkle are summoning me. You two enjoy your drinks and your mounting sexual repression."

I want to die.

He winks. At me. At Soren. Maybe at the table itself. And then he's gone. Leaving me alone. With *him*.

Soren twists to turn his full attention toward me. His gaze simmers, as if he's trying to peel back layers I won't give him permission to see. He's making me deeply uncomfortable, but also a little feral.

No, the drinks are making me feral. *Soren* is making me tiptoe straight into an area I'm not ready for.

"So..." His smooth voice pitches so low and deep, my back arches slightly, "what were you thinking about just now in that pretty head of yours?"

The panic sets in. "Lighting," I lie. "The...warm tones. Great ambiance. Excellent food. Stellar drinks." I take a sip of mine. It's tart. Hints of cloves and spiced pear—comforting in theory, but strong enough to tear through the anxiety thickening in my gut. Not strong enough to take the edge off, though.

"Oh, too bad. I could've sworn the flush creeping up your neck meant you were visualizing me... and you... doing *very* naughty things."

My stomach flips. My ability to form proper words shuts off. "I-I wasn't," I stammer, too fast, too high-pitched.

Soren chuckles. "Well, I for one have thought about it. I thought about it five times today, actually. Once before the panel, twice *during* the panel. Again, in our little meeting with Camille and Renata. Then in the shower, right before I came down here."

My brain is buffering. All I manage is a wide-eyed stare as my entire nervous system goes offline, then comes roaring back online, sparking up like I've licked an electric fence. The clatter inside my brain persists as my thoughts circle themselves.

Is he joking? Is he serious? Who says that out loud? Who says that *to me*? And why is my face suddenly ten degrees warmer?

He said shower.

He said *shower.*

Which means he...

I say nothing. How the hell can I?

Soren smirks. He knows exactly what he's doing–throwing me *way* off base. He's proud of it.

Well, fuck him very much. Soren Pembry will not get the best of me.

Squaring my shoulders, my voice becomes the same sugar-dipped blade it was at the panel. "Let me put this into words you'll understand."

Soren crosses his arms, bracing, a smile tap dancing across those perfect lips.

"I wouldn't think about you if it meant ending a thousand-year curse and restoring my orgasms in the process."

His grin widens, infuriatingly cocky. "Good thing curses aren't real, huh? But orgasms? Those I can help with."

I nearly choke on my drink. "In your dreams, Pembry."

Soren laughs, the sound softer this time. "Relax, Bells. I'm messing with you." He tilts his head. "You're easy to ruffle. And might I add, you're gorgeous when all riled up."

A warm and traitorous feeling slithers through my chest. The compliment lands so unexpectedly, I don't even realize I haven't breathed in a few seconds.

I've got to get out of here.

Pushing my chair back, the loud scrape of the legs against the floor reverberates through the air. I grab my purse sitting on the table and toss my hair over my shoulder as though I'm a woman who storms off in stilettos and high-budget confidence, not one who's barely holding her composure together.

Inside, I'm a tornado of emotions—full-body static and a pulse that won't quit. I don't have a plan. I'm not thinking. I'm moving because right now, motion is the only thing keeping me from exploding in place.

Soren's utterly confused. His brows pinch, brain rewinding the last sixty seconds, like a play tape he can't untangle.

Little does he know, I'm caught in the same mental spiral, replaying every second of his compliment, my reaction, the heat in my chest, the way I bolted with every cell screaming, "Get the fuck out!"

I stand quickly. Before I can storm off, his hands grip my waist with a firm, careful touch, and he yanks me into him so his mouth is near my ear.

"There are dozens of influencers and press people in here right now," he whispers, breath dancing across my skin. "They're all about to pick up on your *sudden* departure. The angry scowl on your face. And the steam pouring from your ears. That's not the image we signed a contract to portray."

"Get your hands off me," I whisper, my voice cold enough to crack glass.

Soren immediately releases me and slides his hands into his pockets. Jaw tight, concern feathers across his face as a flash of softness appears beneath his usual smirk. He wasn't expecting me to sound so cold.

This charade feels very close to standing on a tightrope over a canyon with molten lava running through it.

My eyes sweep to the table and back again. "Charge everything to my room."

Soren pauses, seemingly weighing his words, then replies with, "No worries, I'll get the check. Your last book bombed, remember?"

A sound somewhere between a growl and a hiss escapes my chest—a primal noise reserved for when someone insults your work, your talent, and your dignity all in one casually devastating sentence.

My fists clench. If rage were flammable, the linen napkins would be ash. "How kind of you."

I walk away. Don't look back. I *will not* give that cocky asshole the satisfaction. Even though every fiber of my being is currently debating between flight, murder, or channeling this rage into a revenge plot so satisfying it could launch a bestselling thriller series. Maybe I should seriously explore switching genres.

Oh, and fantasizing about Soren? No longer on the table. Not after what he said just now. *That* visual has officially been redacted, deleted, and burned in effigy.

Feast & Fiction

Snowflake Gala

Bookmas Bash

Midnight Kisses & Paper Wishes

Six

SOREN

The groupies were relentless inside that restaurant tonight. It took twenty minutes, three fake phone calls, and one emergency escape through the kitchen to pry them off.

I'm finally alone. My phone's on silent. My boots are by the door. And I'm standing in front of the window in my suite, watching the wind chase dying leaves across the sidewalk below.

The city glows in a burnt sienna haze, with a moody, fall-evening atmosphere that should feel comforting. It doesn't. All it does is make the loneliness louder.

Resting my forehead against the glass, the chill seeps into my skin. I'm not used to this kind of silence. At home, I'd fill the space with music or keyboard clicks or the sound of Ava Bell's videos to break the quiet. But here, there's nothing except the echo of my own shitty words bouncing around in my skull.

No worries, I'll get the check. Your last book bombed, remember?

Fucking hell. I don't know why I said it. No, scratch that. I do. It was a defensive verbal middle finger to cover up how Ava was about to storm off, all gorgeous and furious and entirely out of my reach.

I've been a lot of things in my life—reckless when it served me, selfish when I thought it protected me, charming when I needed to be. I'm not cruel. Not intentionally.

When it comes to Ava, I seem to fumble—like on that damn panel stage, inside Camille's hotel room, tonight at dinner, and even in the way I watch her too long, thinking she won't notice.

I let out a breath, letting it fog up the glass.

Ava Bell. Fake relationship contract.

Being tied to her, having to touch her, talk to her, pretend she's mine? Man, I wish it were real. I want it to be. More than I should.

Except she doesn't know. I've been living with my secret for so long now. And I'm not sure if I can ever tell her how I feel, seeing how she hates me like it's her full-time job, benefits package and all.

Sinking into the nearest armchair, the leather sighs under my weight. I drag a hand down my face. My facial hair is getting a little too overgrown. I haven't had time to care. Between back-to-back events and being swarmed by fans who believe my characters are their next book boyfriends, I'm nothing more than a role. A glossy cover propped up at signings.

The whole persona's a shield, though. The real Soren—the one who hasn't spoken to his father in over five years, my only family left—isn't someone people want to read about. The fantasy version is easier. Shinier. More marketable.

Ava sees through the bullshit. That's one of the reasons why I'm so drawn to her.

My messenger bag is sitting next to the armchair. I pick it up, start rifling through it until I find my very worn copy of the *Lumberjack's Love Letters*.

A shirtless lumberjack stares back at me from the cover. He's holding an axe, and a well-folded love letter.

I flip through the pages, remembering back to when I first picked up this ridiculous book. At the time, I expected a shit ton of fluff. Some polished, trope-heavy romcom with axe jokes, maple syrup innuendos, and enough sexual tension to fog up a forest.

What I didn't expect was that gut punch of vulnerability. A wounded, funny, fiercely loyal male lead who wanted to fix everything but couldn't fix himself. A man who fell in love with someone despite every damn reason not to.

Somehow, Ava had reached into my chest, stolen the parts of me I don't talk about, and stitched them into her fucking manuscript. She had written me, without even knowing she did. Nobody has ever done that. And now I've gone and made her hate me. Even more than she did.

Rubbing the back of my neck with one hand, I reach for my phone with the other. It lights up with a flood of notifications—ShelfSpace clips from the panel, edits of Ava and me with heart filters, tagged posts with the captions: *Enemies to Lovers? We vote YES.*

I scroll past them, then open my camera roll. There's Ava's author photo. I may have taken a screenshot of it from her website after reading her book. The picture is of her, in a simple blouse, soft red waves of hair around her face, eyes direct. Honest.

Beneath the surface, there lies a bit of unease, of tightly leashed anxiety. She's smiling through static. There's a power in her stillness, but also a quiet fragility that makes me want to lean in, understand it, protect it.

My mind wanders to that panel earlier today. The curve of her smirk. The fire behind every word. Then later, when it looked like she'd rather set herself on fire than fake date me. Somehow, that only made me want to know her more.

My thumb hovers over the screen. I should delete it. I won't.

I set the phone down on the armrest and stare at it. At her. My pulse stirs, languid and thick from longing and need. I want to show her I'm not just the guy who signs cleavage and wears dragon-print sweaters for clout. Under the layered charm and the manufactured smile, there's a man who read her book and finally felt understood. Who watched her walk away tonight and wanted —*desperately*—to chase after her.

I didn't, though, did I?

Yeah, I'm a coward. I've been one for too long. But I'm done with that. I've been granted a Christmas wish—to turn pretend pages into a real story before it ends.

So, Santa, if you're listening, I'm cashing it in for Ava Bell's heart, wrapped and delivered.

Tucking the book between the chair and my thigh, I shift forward, elbows braced on my knees, breath shallow. After a beat, I dig through my messenger bag again and fish out a page of letterhead. It's blank. Quiet. Honest in the way a glowing screen never is.

I need to write to her. It's a habit I stole straight from *The Lumberjack's Love Letters* to become that hero who lays himself bare because words are all he has left.

I started out writing a letter a week, but it soon became whenever I felt the urge to talk to her. Not as *The Blade*. As me. Just me.

It's become my ritual. My confession. My way of whispering to her in a world too loud to hear it otherwise. I don't know if she'll ever see them. Maybe one day I'll be brave enough to share.

I put pen to paper and let my heart spill across the page. When I'm done, I stare at it. The ink blurs where I pressed too hard—like my hand knew how desperate I was to let this out long before my mind caught up.

I don't put it away. I let it sit there on the table–a declaration scribbled too fast to be pretty. Too honest to erase.

This letter isn't just for her. It's for me too. For the part that still doesn't know how to say what I feel out loud without screwing it all up. Writing it down instead of hiding behind a keyboard makes the silence a little less loud.

I set the pen down and lean back in the chair, dragging both hands through my hair. The page stares back at me. Unspoken. Unignorable.

Bells,

I'm sorry.

I was an asshole tonight. No excuses. You didn't deserve what I said.

You started walking away from me, and I had to get the last word in to feel like I wasn't the one being left behind.

The truth of it all is, you make me nervous.

There, I said it.

You're beautiful. That part's obvious. But your looks are not what frays me. It's your fire.

You wield silence better than any insult. Your eyes pin me like you're three moves ahead and ten seconds from being done with me. You see through me in a way I've never let anyone do, and it knocks the ground out from under me.

I panicked tonight. Built up my defenses and said something I can't take back because the thought of you being done with me, before we even begin, gutted me.

But here's the thing: I'm grateful for this arrangement we're in. It's insane and probably stupid, and stitched together with PR tape, but it's

also my chance to show you the man you deserve.
Outside of The Blade.

Just me.

The me who wants to be worthy of your time,
your trust, maybe even more.

You don't owe me forgiveness. You don't owe me
anything at all. But I owe you the truth. And the
truth is this: I want to do this right. For the
cameras, sure, but mostly for you...and for us.

If you keep hating me, I'll deserve it. But I
won't stop trying to prove I can be more than the
man who panicked when you almost walked away.

Love,

S

My phone buzzes. I pick it up, glimpse at the screen.

> Please tell me you didn't agree to fake date
> Ava Bell without running it by me first.

Matthew Chen. My agent, best friend since college, and the
only person who calls me on my shit while getting paid for it.

> Um...maybe...

> Soren. What the fuck?

> It happened so fast. Our managers ambushed
> us backstage.

> Very corporate.

> Very aggressive.

I may have been in shock.

What's Camille thinking by not including me?

You realize I'm going to have to renegotiate this contract now, right?

That's literally your job

My job is keeping you from making terrible life decisions.

This is a terrible life decision.

It's good PR. Trending keywords. Cross-genre appeal. You love that shit.

Mhm

And how long have you been in love with her?

I stare at my phone as though I'm trying to defuse a bomb and forgot which wire is red.

What the hell are you talking about?

Bro. I've watched your videos about her. I've also watched YOU watch HER videos. You get that stupid, dopey face. Last month, you spent twenty minutes telling me about her "narrative structure" like you're some kind of literature professor.

I appreciate good writing.

You screenshotted her author photo.

How do you know that?

Because you're an idiot and you left your phone unlocked when I borrowed it to call the car service in Chicago.

...and?

And I swiped. Don't act like I wouldn't.

That's a violation of privacy. Illegal, even.

Is it though?

What's criminal is that you've got some gothic-ass ruin as your lock screen, but your ACTUAL background? Ava.

It's a candid moment of her. I like the lighting.

Bullshit. You can swap lock screens all you want, but we both know which one you stare at fifty times a day.

Seek help, man.

Matthew has known me since we were nineteen and stupid. He's seen me through several bad decisions, messy breakups, and more than a few 3 AM drunken crises. Of course he figured it out.

It's... complicated.

Oh my god, you're so fucked.

Thanks for the support.

Ava Bell doesn't strike me as the type who tolerates bullshit.

And you, my friend, are approximately 73% bullshit on a good day.

Your confidence in me is overwhelming.

I'll make the fake dating thing work. The optics are actually brilliant. But if you're using this as a way to try to make her catch REAL feelings for you, you're deranged.

That's a special kind of emotional masochism even for you.

I can handle it.

Can you?

You've been gone for this woman for so long, and now you get to hold her hand and stare into her eyes and convince the entire internet that you're soulmates.

That's psychological torture, not a marketing stunt.

When did you become a therapist?

When I started representing idiotic fantasy authors who fall for their genre rivals.

You're the worst.

I'm the best. That's what you pay me for.

Speaking of which, I'm billing you extra for this conversation. Emotional labor surcharge.

Of course you are.

One more thing. If this shit goes sideways, I will personally make sure every book blogger on the internet knows you cry during Pixar movies.

> ONE TIME, and it was Up.

> That movie is everything.

My point stands. Don't fuck this up, Pembry.

> No pressure

Now go to sleep. You have a fake girlfriend to NOT screw things up with tomorrow.

Matthew is correct, as usual. This whole thing is going to be a disaster.

I toss my phone onto the coffee table and sink deeper into the chair. The Lumberjack's Love Letters bites into my side. Yanking the book from where it got wedged between the cushions, I stare at the Lumberjack for several seconds, thinking.

Disaster or not, I'm done being a coward. Ava Bell terrifies me, and electrifies me in ways I don't know how to contain, but I want her anyway. Her brilliant mind, stubborn fire, and silences that say more than a hundred interviews ever could.

So let this thing crash and burn. Let it be messy. I'll still walk through the ashes with her, because it's the only place I want to be.

Seven

AVA

The gym smells like overused disinfectant, synthetic citrus, and a type of sterile clean that never quite lets you forget where you are. Which is, and always will be, a germy gym, despite its five-star status.

It's barely six a.m., and my anxiety got me out of bed faster than any alarm could. I told myself movement would help clear my head. Burn off the leftover humiliation still stewing in my bloodstream after last night's encounter with Soren.

So far, the only thing I've managed to burn are the muscles in my inner thighs from the world's most vindictive treadmill.

I should've gone for a walk outside. Got some fresh air. But no. I opted for pain and torture instead, because I'm a rational adult with control issues.

I'm gripping the handles so tightly my knuckles ache, and tension coils from my shoulders down to my fingertips. Each step is a desperate attempt to outrun the anxiety gnawing at my brainstem.

My playlist says: *Power Mode.*

My head says: *Panic Spiral.*

And my legs say: *screw you, Ava Bell* in Morse code made of lactic acid.

My phone buzzes with a notification. Then another. Then seven more.

Fumbling to check it mid-stride on the treadmill, I nearly face-plant into the emergency stop bar. Graceful, I am not.

Emily Lawson. Best friend, extraordinaire.

> BELL.

> WHY AM I LEARNING ABOUT YOUR LOVE LIFE ON THE INTERNET??

> #BellAndTheBlade?

> What the actual hell is happening?

> I thought you hated that guy?!

> Pictures of you two are everywhere!

> Damn girl, I leave you alone for ONE minute and you go full fantasy porno?

> Wait, are you two fucking?

Groaning, I jab at the incline, slow down, then snatch my phone to text her back.

Emily has been my best friend since undergrad at Amherst—back when we were both broke, brilliant, and stubborn enough to believe we could change the world through fiction. She's the calm to my chaos, the steady voice that talked me off ledges I didn't even know I was standing on.

When things were bad with *I Hate Your Face*, she was the one who saw through the highlight reel. While I was crumbling, she stayed—quiet, patient, unflinching, anchoring me back to myself every single time I forgot who that was.

Emily took a professor gig at Seattle Pacific University, and plans to finally finish her manuscript there.

I haven't told her about this whole fake dating Soren Pembry debacle yet. Obviously. Which is why I almost crashed out on the treadmill the second my phone buzzes with her name.

> Can I plead temporary insanity?

> I was tricked. There were cocktails.

> And contractual obligations.

And an audible purring sound from our managers.

Soren Pembry??????

I'm scrolling through pics from the panel. Why does it seem like you and Mr. Sword Daddy are about to kiss and/or kill each other?

> It's called professional tension.

Ava. His eyes are doing "I'd burn down a kingdom for you" things.

> Pretty sure that's his default setting. All part of the fantasy brand.

Uh-huh.

You haven't answered the question! Did you fall on his "sword" or just look like you wanted to?

> We haven't. And we won't.

Are you trying to convince both of us?

> Nothing's happening.

CEDAR JAMES

Yet.

Please stop. I'm in a public place. And sweating. Profusely.

Girl, same. It's because I was writing until 3AM, and now I'm on my third cold brew, and the barista put way too much AXE body spray on today.

Still. EXPLAIN.

Can I call you later? I'll tell you everything.

You *fucking* better. I'm in Port Townsend for the weekend working on my novel, but my phone is by me.

Also, please know that if this ends in scandal, heartbreak, or a surprise wedding—I'm flying down, slapping you once with love, then officiating.

There will be no wedding. Can't promise the other two won't happen though.

Uh oh.

Yeah. Remind me why I let you leave me for the Pacific Northwest again?

Tenure and peace and less nonsense.

Right, I forgot.

For what it's worth, you two are cute together. You would have gorgeous babies.

Again...NEVER happening.

Don't think I won't board a ferry back to Seattle to drag your romance-avoidant ass back into emotional alignment.

80

Tell Fisher he still owes me a rematch in Mario
Kart. I want blood.

I'm wiping away the sweat from my forehead when the gym door swings open behind me.

Soren struts in as a mix of lust and temptation, wearing black joggers, a fitted white shirt that emphasizes his built chest and arms. A towel is slung over one shoulder. His hair is messy in that deliberate way, and the stubble lining his jaw could probably file steel.

Surprisingly, he doesn't smirk. Or wink. Doesn't say a damn thing. Only nods. Like we're two regular people in a regular gym doing regular things and not co-starring in the ShelfSpace rumor mill's hottest romance of the season.

Correction, fake romance.

I refocus on the treadmill, which is hard when my brain starts writing smut based on how his biceps flex when he stretches his arms behind his head.

Focus.

I glimpse the timer. Ten minutes left. I can survive ten more—

After a few more seconds, he says, "Morning," voice still rough with sleep, like sand mixed in honey. It's sexy. And I hate that. Kind of.

I try to reply, but my throat has decided to be dramatic. So, I nod instead and jab at the elliptical incline setting with slightly more force than necessary.

Soren moves to the weights and starts doing bicep curls. I try not to watch him in the mirror, which of course means I absolutely do. His shirt rides up a little, revealing a line of skin that shouldn't be legal before coffee.

After he finishes a set, he approaches. "You want to lift with me?" He towels off his forehead.

I nearly trip again. "No, I'm doing cardio."

"Right." He grins, crooked and cute. I hate that too. "Well, if

81

you're planning to brave the weight rack after you finish your *cardio*, let me know. Don't want you getting pinned under a barbell. I'd be obligated to save you, and then you'd owe me your life."

"I'd rather take my chances with the barbell."

His smile falters, then he exhales. He's clearly tiptoeing across eggshells with me. After what he said last night, he deserves to.

"Listen," Soren's voice drops so low I have to slow my pace to hear him, "about last night—I'm sorry. What I said was out of line, and it was shitty of me."

I'm caught off guard. Soren Pembry, offering an actual apology?

He scratches the back of his neck. "I didn't mean what I said."

There's a brief silence. One beat. Two.

Softer, he adds, "Anyway. I don't want to walk around, pretending it didn't happen. Or have you thinking that's how I am when it's not. I'm not that guy."

This is the official moment my brain abandons cardio mode and enters full emotional glitch.

"Okay," Soren drags the word out. "Um, good talk then." He taps the side of my treadmill twice before walking back toward the free weights.

His words bounce around my head, along with a few more smutty visuals, because when Soren rolls his shoulders, his shirt clings tighter across his chest and back, making my mouth go dry. Bone-dry. Dust-bowl dry. I have to gulp down half my water before my voice even works.

"Hey," I call out right as he's about to resume lifting.

He looks back over his shoulder.

"Thanks." My voice comes out quieter than I intend. "For the apology. Seriously."

The smile he gives me might be the worst thing that's ever happened to my heart. It isn't the practiced Pembry grin he unleashes on fans. It's gentle. Almost shy. And I know right then that if I'm not careful, it'll split cracks in the foundation of every wall I've built to keep men like him out.

We dance around each other for the next half hour—subtle glances when we think the other isn't paying attention. Except we are. I catch him watching me in the mirror more than once, his gaze sweeping over me every time.

When our eyes meet head-on, for a split second, his jaw tightens, and his brows twitch. It's like we're standing under a spotlight and I'm not sure whether to step away or lean in.

What if Emily is right? Would he burn a kingdom down for me?

Nah. Soren's too selfish. Best to remember that.

When I finally move to the mat area to do a few half-assed crunches, Soren follows. I stretch out, trying to ignore him. He picks up a medicine ball.

I'm mid-sit-up when he suddenly kneels beside me. "Don't engage your neck so much," he says. "You're going to strain it."

"I'm fine."

"You're going to hurt tomorrow."

"I write for a living. My entire body already hurts every day."

"Here. Try this. Lift from here." Before I can slap it away, Soren's hand slides behind my shoulders and adjusts my form.

His palm warms my back while his other rests lightly on my stomach, above the waistband of my leggings. The heat of his touch and the soft steadiness of his voice manage to flip a switch I didn't want turned on. Especially by him.

Soren doesn't say much else. He helps, then backs off. No lingering. And somehow that makes it worse because if he were only being cocky or flirty, I'd know how to deal with it. I've been defending myself against his charm since the ShelfSpace algorithm started feeding me his stupid, seductive videos.

I don't have defenses for this quiet, gentle, *helpful* Soren.

Sitting up, I grab my water bottle, trying not to let him see how flushed I am. My eyes betray me, darting back to the weight bench where he's racked a barbell stacked heavier than twice my weight.

Gripping the bar again, his arms tense, veins standing out along his forearms. With his brows furrowed in concentration, Soren lowers and lifts with impressive control, and my mind... wanders.

Suddenly, I'm not at the gym—I'm in a full-blown fitness musical where Soren's biceps are the leads, and I'm just the understudy for *Woman Who Melts in Public.* Backup dancers in neon leotards chant *press it, Pembry,* while a disco ball drops from the ceiling and fog machines kick in for dramatic effect. There's even a key change as he grunts through a rep, which feels personally targeted at my hormones.

That's about when I catch myself mid-daydream and nearly drop my water bottle. Nope. Absolutely not. My brain is officially on time-out.

Soren completes another few reps, and I imagine those arms braced on either side of me, holding me down while he drives his cock into me with punishing strokes. His muscles flex with every thrust. His jaw clenches, muttering filthy praise in that sexy, coarse voice of his.

Moaning his name, my back arches, thighs shake. Soren's hand slips between us to toy with my clit as his hot breath dances across my neck.

"Bells?"

Snapping back to reality so fast, I nearly choke on my sip of water. "What?"

"You okay?" He curiously asks, wiping his hands on his towel.

"Yeah, why wouldn't I be?"

Soren's gaze lingers, like he wants to say more. And then he does. "Because you moaned my name, soooo... thought I'd check in." There's a teasing lift to his brow. A mischievous gleam in his eye.

I want to die. Right here. On the mat. On this day.

"I did not," I deny it.

"Okay then. My mistake." Grabbing his towel, Soren heads for the door, and I don't exhale until it clicks shut behind him. Even then, his absence doesn't help because the flutter in my chest isn't frustration. It's desire.

Oh my God, I want to fuck Soren Pembry.

I don't want to feel that. I want to cut it out with a dull blade and kill it, then burn it to ash. But it's already taken root, and I'm the idiot watering it.

Soren strolls by the glass windows on his way back to his room, then disappears.

Falling back onto the mat, I stare up at the ceiling and exhale, but more visuals enter my brain, and before I can fight against them today, they launch a full-blown attack.

Questions take over next.

What exactly would Soren do to me if he turned around and stormed back into this gym?

Would he drag me back to the corner, pin me to the mat, and fuck the tension right out of me until I forgot every insult I'd ever thrown at him?

Or would he fuck my sassy mouth with that *rumored-to-be-huge* flesh sword of his—one hand fisted in my hair, the other gripping my throat with enough pressure to make me behave... until I begged for him to spill his pleasure down my throat?

Would I moan for more with the taste of him on my tongue?

Shit, I'd probably beg for it.

I bolt. No cool down. Or stretches. Only a desperate grab for my water bottle and a beeline to the women's locker room, my pulse hammering, and my pussy pulsing.

The second I'm inside, I throw the lock on the nearest private bathroom stall and press my back to the door, chest heaving.

I'm soaked. From the workout, yes, also from the way Soren watched me out there. From the sound of his voice, his touch, the scent of his skin, the idea of that mouth between my thighs, and that cock inside me, filling me up.

The image slams into me so hard I almost crumble to the floor

—Soren pinning me down, sweat slicking our bodies, his growl vibrating against my throat as he drives me open, over and over, until the only sound left in me is his name.

My hand's already shoving itself down the waistband of my leggings before a conscious thought kicks in, the damp fabric peeling away from my overheated skin. This isn't a slow tease. This is primal. It's survival. Release. Sanity.

Biting down on my bottom lip to keep from making a sound, I squeeze my eyes shut while my fingers find what they're looking for. I'm slick, aching, and the first touch shoots electricity up my spine.

Circling my clit, I picture his mouth—that sinful, smirking mouth—between my thighs, those strong hands gripping my hips as he takes me apart with his tongue. The arrogant spark in his dark eyes when he calls me that stupid nickname. His voice would sound rough and growly when he tells me exactly what he wants to do to me.

"Drench me, Bells. I want you screaming while I lick you raw."

I pump my fingers in and out, circling my clit with ruthless precision, punishing the traitorous little bundle of nerves for daring to think of him. For twitching at the sound of his voice, for throbbing at the memory of his smirk. Every stroke is a reprimand, each press a reminder that Soren Pembry has no business living rent-free between my thighs...and yet here I am, grinding into my own palm like he's already claimed me.

And when the orgasm hits, it's not gentle. It's not sweet. It's a flash flood—violent, necessary, scorching, and so intense I have to press my free hand against my mouth to muffle the sound that tears from my throat.

"Soren."

My legs give out completely, sending me sliding down the stall door until I'm trembling on the cold tile floor. Yes, of the locker room. The same floor where people track in dirt, sweat, and whatever unspeakable horrors live on the bottom of a tennis shoe.

And here I am, author of *The Boyfriend Deadline*, masturbating in a bathroom stall, reduced to a sad tale titled *Girl Meets Germs: The Romance Nobody Asked For.*

Slumping to the side, I breathe hard against the cool metal wall, my entire body pulsing with aftershocks. The harsh fluorescent light is bright and unkind, and the silence is loud. Reality crashes back as a slap to my face.

Holy shit. I regret this. I do. But for a moment—one brief, wicked moment—I don't feel like I've lost control.

I feel like I've claimed something back.

By late afternoon, Soren and I are seated side-by-side at a small round table outside the hotel atrium café, a modest attempt at a "private" strategy session that's anything but.

Guests wander past, craning their necks. A few pretend to check their phones while clearly filming.

Soren slides a coffee in front of me without a word. It's a caramel blondie latte, non-dairy foam, extra sprinkles of cinnamon.

I stare at it for a beat.

"I pay attention." The sentence lands in my chest. Soren shrugs a shoulder, acting as though it's nothing.

It's so much more than nothing. It's not *just* a coffee. It's a gesture.

Don't read into it, Ava. Not too much, anyway.

Renata clears her throat, drawing our attention to her. "Let's move this to somewhere a little more private. Camille is waiting for us in the business center."

Right. Business.

That's all this is—fake dating between two people who roast each other on the internet.

A coffee doesn't mean anything.

A glance doesn't mean anything.

A moment of sexual weakness doesn't mean anything.

This isn't personal.

It's branding.

We follow Renata out of the lounge, down the hall to an aggressively beige room with too much lighting and too little personality. Perfect for selling your soul one bullet point at a time.

Camille greets us and gestures to a tablet sitting on the table. We sit as she flips to a digital press packet, stylus moving in quick, decisive strokes.

"Alright," Camille begins, eyes bright. "*The Bell and The Blade* buzz is white-hot. Your numbers are climbing by the hour. Ava, your book is trending under three different tropes. Soren, your Goodreads page is practically melting. Tonight is the hard launch of you two being a 'couple.' Although the internet pretty much made you official after yesterday. Still, the press conference is scheduled for six. We've prepped the host, planted a few smart questions, and booked a cozy corner of the courtyard for the post-panel photo ops. After that, I'll send some assets over to the social media teams. Renata, do you want to go over the interview?"

"Gladly." Renata taps her pen against her notepad. "You'll sit down, share how things unexpectedly shifted in your DM's over the last few months, and then drop that magic word we all agreed on: *connection.* Don't say relationship. And for the love of God, stay away from anything that says, 'exclusive.' You're not committed. Just 'connected.' Leaves room for intrigue *and* interpretation."

Not loving this at all, I grip the coffee cup a little tighter.

"Afterward," Camille continues smoothly, "you'll take a walk through the pumpkin patch outside. There will be fairy lights. Fire pits. A super cute, aesthetically pleasing food truck with mugs of cider. Families, other couples, someone walking their dog, probably. We've staged the entire mood."

"And then," Renata adds with a wink, "The two of you will walk hand in hand into the hotel and retire in Soren's suite.

Preferably with swoon eyes, Ava. Can you please work on those today?"

"Wait—his suite?" My head swivels between them and Soren. "As in... the room where he sleeps?"

Camille nods, entirely unfazed. "It's more believable than you heading back to yours.

"That makes no sense," I counter.

"You're a couple now, remember?"

"Right. Sure. Totally. Super couple-y," I mutter through gritted teeth, heart rate spiking. "Because nothing says believable romance more than swanning into a man's hotel suite after *one* panel and a dinner that was less date night, more emotional hostage situation."

Renata steps in. "Ava, the internet already thinks you're halfway to a shared toothbrush. Don't ruin the magic with logic."

I gape at her. "You want me to casually wander into his room like I'm auditioning for a holiday soft porn called *Cider & Sex*?"

Camille lights up. "That's actually a great title."

Soren chuckles. "We could go full hard-core porn, if you prefer."

My breakfast threatens to resurface. "Not funny."

Renata points a perfectly manicured finger at me. "That energy, right there, and all that sass and sarcasm is what we need. Channel it. Use it. Just with less panic and more bedroom eyes."

"Do bedroom eyes come with a user manual? Or do I blink slower and hope for the best?" I ask, snarky as fuck.

Soren peers at me over the rim of his own coffee.

This isn't happening.

While I'm trying to wrap my brain around this entire nightmare, another woman steps into the room—tall, angular, and terrifying in the most sophisticated way possible, her blonde hair scraped into a bun so tight it could slice diamonds, and her expression could cut someone down at the knees from a hundred yards away.

Dressed in a tailored black blazer that I know cost more than my entire college tuition, she carries a leather portfolio that probably doubles as a blunt-force weapon. I'd know this woman anywhere. A massive sigh of relief exits my lungs.

"Victoria Hartwell," she announces, extending a perfectly manicured hand to Soren. "Ava's agent."

Taking it, he only half-masks the wince. Her handshake has the energy of a corporate chokehold.

At only thirty years old, Victoria Hartwell is a legend. An agent who closes seven-figure deals between spin classes, dismantles predatory contracts over kale salads, and has been known to reduce senior editors to tears using only a Post-it and a glare. Having her on your side is adjacent to hiring a legal assassin in Louboutins.

"Victoria," I beam. "Are you here to save me?"

Her return smile possesses the warmth of an ice sculpture. "When Renata called about this... *arrangement,* I deemed it best to oversee the legal framework myself. I don't trust her–" Victoria's eyes slide from Renata over to Camille. "–or anyone else to make it solid. No offense," she says to both of them.

They exchange a nervous glance.

Victoria unzips her briefcase, pulls out her tablet, and produces a neatly tabbed contract the length of a medical textbook. "I've taken the liberty of contacting your agent, Mr. Pembry—Matthew, yes? We've completed the preliminary negotiations."

Soren raises a brow. "Negotiations?"

"Yes," she replies crisply. "The standard terms: image rights, social media deliverables, joint content creation, and public appearance obligations through New Year's Eve. You'll find a detailed engagement calendar on page eight, along with travel accommodations and the exclusivity and termination clauses."

His eyes narrow. "Termination clause?"

Victoria's sneer sharpens. "In the unlikely event either party chooses to dissolve the arrangement prematurely, there are contingencies for PR mitigation, NDA reinforcement, and reputational damage control."

"Reputational damage control," Soren echoes. He seems a tad confused, or maybe disappointed by that. Interesting.

"We don't want any ShelfSpace drama unless we're the ones monetizing it." Victoria swipes the page on her tablet with a soft *sweep*, then her eyes bounce between the two of us. "Any questions?"

"Is there an out?"

"Not unless one of you dies or develops a scandal juicier than this deal." She checks her perfect manicure. "The internet loves this. So, congratulations, you're officially half of the holiday campaign. Play nice, smile pretty, and for the love of engagement metrics, make it believable."

Soren's visibly trying to decide whether he should laugh or bolt. "I'll have my lawyer review it."

"He already has," Victoria replies to him. "You'll find his notes in red, which is the color I assigned to him. I find it keeps things honest."

Standing, she turns away to answer a call without a backward glance. "Victoria Hartwell speaking." Pause. "No, I said exclusive rights, not excuses. Try listening for once—it's a dying art, believe me, I know."

I exhale, disappointed.

Soren nudges me with his shoulder and whispers, "Your agent scares the shit out of me."

"She once made a VP at Random House cry with a single sentence."

His eyes widen, then he lets out a low whistle. "Hot."

"Smoking," I agree.

Even though Victoria might legally own my soul, I'm feeling a little more grounded knowing she's got my back, on paper anyway. She's terrifying, sure. She's also the reason I sleep at night. After the first—very large, and almost career-ending—mistake I made in this industry years ago, I promised myself I'd never trust anyone to fight for me who couldn't take a punch, or throw one.

Cue Victoria.

Sharp teeth. Iron spine. No mercy.

But better.

Feast & Fiction

Snowflake Gala

Bookmas Bash

Midnight Kisses & Paper Wishes

Eight

SOREN

The second I step back into my suite, I press my back against the door and breathe.

What a fucking day!

Tossing my leather jacket across the back of the couch, I then grab a bottle of water from the kitchenette, down half of it walking into my room, and collapse onto the edge of the bed.

Battle-mages with trust issues got their due, and I somehow survived the onslaught of selfies, swooning, and a very enthusiastic grad student who tried to hand me her annotated thesis, complete with contact info and lipstick kisses. It was a standing-room-only crowd, three people in tears, one guy who fist-pumped at every mention of "shadow-forged vulnerability." All in all, my lecture was a smashing success.

So, why do I feel like a fucking mess?

Oh, I know why? Because I just finished a three-act play called *Keeping My Shit Together in Front of Ava Bell.* And I deserve a fucking Tony for it too. Maybe even an Oscar.

For the last few hours, I've been in performance mode—smirking for every reader, nodding at every question a panelist asks me to make it appear as though I'm actively listening, and delivering charm to hundreds of people in pre-approved doses while internally

93

trying not to replay every second of this morning's gym confronta-
tion, which has been damn near impossible. To my surprise, I was
given the director's cut. It's been on repeat in my head all damn day.

Ava Bell. Ava *Fucking* Bell.

Snark and guarded glimpses, along with way too much
vulnerability hidden under sarcasm—they're all a challenge I can't
stop rising to meet.

I saw her three times today. Backstage, I tripped over a cable
and nearly face-planted into her heels. Another time, at her
signing table, a reader approached me. I grabbed a pink glitter gel
pen instead of a Sharpie and started signing, staring awkwardly at
Ava the whole time. And in the hotel café, I swerved to avoid her,
nailed the sharp corner of the pastry table, and got decked right in
the balls.

Every encounter with her was a battlefield.

We played our parts—smiles sharp, voices pitched—but
underneath? Total carnage. Rigid shoulders, molars grinding,
avoiding eye contact as if it were radioactive. The crowd probably
bought it. We didn't.

I've got maybe two hours to breathe before the Camille and
Renata Variety Hour, aka hell in couture.

I run a hand through my hair and collapse backward onto the
bed as though gravity's finally had enough of my shit.

My phone dings. I remove it from my pants pocket. Lena.
Fuck my life.

> So... no reply?

> That's how you're playing this?

Rolling my eyes, I flip it face down. Not right now. Or ever.

After toeing off my boots, I scrub a hand across my scruffy
jaw, where Ava's eyes lingered earlier. I think she likes it. It was
barely a second. But I saw it. Felt it. I'm not imagining that.

Am I?

I drive her crazy. I'm pretty sure she wants to throw her phone at my head, but maybe also ride my cock. I'm not opposed to either.

This tension I generate with women isn't new. The sultry smiles. The heated silences. The stares that say, *just once.*

I've always known how to leverage lust. How to bend it. Manipulate it. Let it get me what I want, whether it's the deal, the gig, the attention, or the cleanest exit possible.

Ava's different.

I want her heart.

That's corny. And yet, true.

I'm one thousand percent sure Ava is attracted to me. Based on what I witnessed in the locker room this morning, I could argue that point in a court of law and win. With exhibits. Possibly a PowerPoint.

But it's more than that. It's in the way she looks at me when she doesn't realize she is. There's a hint of curiosity in her eyes. The real trick won't be seducing her.

It'll be *earning* her.

If I play this right—if I stop being the version of me that leans on the swagger and charm, and start being the man who listens, who shows up, who's there for her...

I can turn that heat into something deeper than surface level. I'll be the man she can't walk away from just because the lights went off and the keywords died.

Because I don't want to be Ava Bell's fantasy.

I want to be her reality.

One arm flops across my face. The sheets smell clean, clinical, unlike everything else I've felt today. Ever since sunrise, my body's been wound tight. The only release I've had was lifting weights. I was raging during those reps.

No. That's a lie.

There was another release inside that gym. Just not mine.

I still can't believe I caught Ava masturbating in a hotel locker room. The images of what she must've looked like inside that stall flood back in.

Ava's flushed skin. Pursed lips. Her voice when she cried out *my name* when I was lifting. I heard it again inside that bathroom. And now it's *all* I can hear, or see.

My hand slides down my stomach, fingers skimming the waistband of my pants.

I retract. I shouldn't.

Then again, my cock's rock-fucking-hard, and when I close my eyes, the visual is immediate.

Ava—breathless, head thrown back as her hand between her thighs, working her clit.

I know it's real. Per the visual I received.

Before you judge me, know this: I wasn't trying to be a creep. I'd doubled back to the gym two minutes after leaving to ask if she wanted to grab coffee. Or breakfast. Something normal. Something that isn't staged, scripted, or buried in sarcasm. Something human.

When I walked in, the gym was empty. The women's locker room door was cracked. I thought I heard a sound—soft, choked.

At first, I panicked, thought Ava might be hurt. Or sick. I called her name. No response.

So naturally, I pushed open the women's locker room door.

There she was. Inside the stall, legs braced wide. The sounds she made were unmistakable. One hand was most likely clamped over her mouth, while the other punished her clit.

I backed out immediately. Fast. Silent. Adrenaline coursing through me as though I'd committed a crime witnessing it.

It certainly felt like one.

No matter how hard I try, the image won't leave my brain. The heat. The desperation.

Now I'm stuck.

Hard as hell.

Mind unraveling.

Palm twitching, caught between guilt and obsession.

I want her.

But I shouldn't have seen that.

Except I did.

Fuck me—*I loved it.*

My hand moves lower. Unthinking. Needing more.

Unzipping my pants, I push them down. My cock springs free, hot, heavy, leaking from the mental reel on repeat.

Ava.

Hand buried. *Soren* on her lips.

I pump once. Twice. A breath escapes me. She's behind my eyes, hips shifting, breath catching, thighs trembling.

I'm circling the edge of control, tugging harder now, chasing the same high she found when she thought no one was watching.

Ding.

The sound cuts through the room.

Another *ding.*

I groan. My phone starts ringing. I grab it, turn it over. Matthew.

He can go to voicemail.

I wrap my hand tight around myself, chest heaving when yet another *fucking* text message comes through. Matthew.

> We have a problem. Call me. Now.

Of course we do. And of course it happens when I'm several strokes deep into a fantasy about the woman I'm *faking* a relationship with.

Nothing like real-world drama knocking at the door and a very real, very hard problem in my hand.

I exhale, then grab my phone. "Fuck."

I swipe the notification and hit call. Matthew picks up on the first ring.

He doesn't bother with hello. "That Lena chick posted something. She's not naming names, but it's *damn close.*"

My gut knots. "What do you mean, *close.*"

"She tagged a 'certain sword-wielding author' and said, quote, 'It's not okay when someone uses power, popularity, and charm to seduce during a professional collaboration—then tosses you aside like it never happened. Being magnetic doesn't excuse treating people like they're disposable.'"

The floor tilts beneath me.

"Jesus Christ," I mutter. "I told you—we hooked up *once*, last year at the Christmas in July series. She came on to me *again* at the Summerween Festival a few months ago, but I shut it down. She's sent a few texts since, but I haven't answered."

"Good. Don't. This is Lena we're talking about. She doesn't throw shade. She constructs narratives. And right now, she's laying the foundation for a damn exposé. Comments are stacking up—people are connecting dots that were never even in the same damn coloring book."

I start pacing the hotel suite like a lion in a trap. "She's pissed because I told her no."

"No," Matthew corrects flatly. "She's pissed because she showed up to your signing in a corset dress and six-inch stilettos, tried to kiss you, and you turned her down as though she was a drink you didn't order. You bruised her ego, man."

I rub the back of my neck. "I didn't want to make a scene. So yeah, I pulled her aside. Told her we were nothing. I gave no mixed signals. There was no flirty bullshit. Only the truth."

"And now she's framing it how she wants it."

"She's trying to twist this into something it isn't because I didn't want her."

"And according to the internet, you've got someone new, beautiful, and not her. Hate to break it to you, man, but hell hath no fury like a scorned ShelfSpacer."

"Not funny."

"Didn't say it was." Matthew sighs through the phone. "Just pointing out the obvious."

I drop onto the chair by the window. My elbows hit my knees, and I press my palms into my temples. "What the hell do I do?"

"I'll get with legal. Start drafting a statement in case this hits critical mass. You've gotta stay clean. Stay visible, but not reactive. And for the love of God, don't try to explain yourself online."

"I wasn't planning to."

"You stick to the script with Ava. Let the world see you as genuine and *taken*. That story has traction. People are rooting for it. They'll see Lena as a jealous ex."

"She's not my ex."

"You know what I mean."

"And if it blows up in my face?"

"We pivot. We don't let Lena own the plot. Okay?"

I sigh. "Okay."

We hang up. I stare at my reflection in the mirror. There's a flush along my neck, and a flash of darkness behind my eyes. Shame. Frustration. Fury.

I look like the villain.

I feel like the villain.

I'm not the villain.

And I'll be damned if I let Lena write me as one, no matter how many irrelevant hashtags she hides her lies behind. She can't twist the past and ruin my future. I'm finally holding something in the palm of my hand that could be true.

What I have with Ava might be fake on paper. But *she's* not. Neither are the feelings clawing their way up every time she laughs, snaps, or looks at me. I may be the last person she wants, but I'm the only one she needs. Even through all the denial she's fighting against.

I won't let Lena destroy that.

There's possibility with Ava and me. A spark. A chance. I'll prove I'm worth more than the worst version of someone else's story. Even if it kills me.

Nine

~

AVA

After the panels and signings finally wrap, the ballroom transforms into a press gauntlet—rows of folding chairs, camera rigs, and a podium bathed in blinding bright lights.

The press conference is about to start. Reporters are buzzing like bees in a hive. Renata and I are standing off to the side, tucked just far enough into the wings that no one could overhear. She's filling my ear with a final round of reminders.

"Mention the panel chemistry. Remember, things developed naturally. Laugh when he touches you."

My arms cross. "That's not in my contract."

"It is now." Renanta turns and skitters away, toward Camille. The two of them have grown quite close during this charade.

Soren approaches, annoyingly calm in a perfectly fitted dark jacket over a charcoal t-shirt that matches my blouse a little too well to be an accident. The scent of pine needles and expensive cologne wafts off his freshly showered skin. I'll never admit out loud what it does to me.

Bending down toward my ear, his voice scrapes over my skin. "You nervous?"

"Yes, I hate lying," I reply, honestly.

His gaze dips to my lips for the briefest second. "Then let's give them something to believe in."

A spark zips straight through me, lighting up nerve endings I haven't felt in years. And when my breath hitches, his eyes zero in on my lips, which part on instinct. *It's not an invitation, Pembry.*

This is stupid. But I drift toward him anyway and whisper, "We're supposed to keep it professional. Wait until the interview starts. Read the statement. Smile. Nod. That's it. Okay? No off-script stuff."

"Understood." He winks.

What does that wink mean? That he *won't* behave? Or that he *will*?

Soren sidles up close, his cologne slithering up my nose, and my body reacts. My ovaries stage a walkout. My brain drafts a cease-and-desist. My spine tries to hold the line, but my resolve? She's grabbing her purse and hailing a cab.

I'm fucked. Not literally. Tragically, figuratively.

The host for tonight's interview is a perky ShelfSpace influencer who goes by the name *RaeReadsRomance.* She's in seasonal plaid, looking cute and festive.

Painting on the same careful mask I've used for book signings, launch parties, and awkward family dinners, I breathe in and then out.

The ring lights are hot, the cameras relentless, and every laugh from the audience feels like it's been sharpened to a point.

Rae flashes her cue cards, eyes gleaming with mischief. "Let's talk holiday love stories and unexpected sparks. You two have become the internet's favorite slow burn. The clips. The banter. The public bickering that somehow feels like foreplay." She giggles, then pauses. "So tell me—on a scale from staged to soulmates, what spice level are you two?"

I open my mouth, ready to give a rehearsed line about connection with mutual respect and shared passions, when Soren steps in, shadowing my voice.

"What an excellent question, Rae." A hand slides to my waist, and before I can process what's happening, Soren dips me back and crushes his mouth to mine, bold, claiming, all tongue and heat and zero warning. My gasp is swallowed whole. So is my sanity.

This isn't a simple PR smooch. This is a hands-in-my-hair, world-tilting kiss that knocks the breath out of me without ever lifting my feet off the ground. Or maybe my feet are off the ground. I don't know. All I know is that his mouth is hot and firm against mine.

A slow rush blooms through me until everything else fades. For a heartbeat, it feels like I've found something I didn't even realize I'd been missing.

The kiss goes from insistent to patient, unhurried. It asks instead of takes. When his tongue grazes mine, I melt into it, curious and hungry in a way that feels like remembering. I taste him, learn him, breathe him in, every second sinking deeper until I feel it all the way down to my toes.

That magical forest scent envelopes my senses. For a second— one dizzying, blinding second—it doesn't feel like a stunt. It feels...real.

Oh, shit.

Soren lifts me back up, and when we break apart, we're silent. I look at him. He looks at me.

His attention shifts back to Rae. "Does that answer your question?"

The crowd roars with excitement. Someone near the front drops something. Camera flashes explode. Rae literally squeals.

"Holy *fuck*, that was hot," a man from a publishing blog whispers too loudly.

Soren drapes an arm over my shoulder. "No truer words have ever been said."

Fireworks rip down my spine then detonate in my core. I'm frozen, stunned, unable to breathe, because—

What the hell was that?

A joke?

A confession?

I want to believe him. Wait, why do I want to believe him?

Rae recovers first. "Wow. *Okay*. So that was... a capital M *Moment*. I think I speak for the entire internet when I say, Replay button, please?"

Laughter ripples through the air. She peeks down at her notes, then her eyes are on me, glittering. "Ava, would you care to comment on that display of swoon-worthy chemistry for the ages, or are you still kiss concussed?"

My cheeks burn. "We're... enjoying the season."

That's what I say. That's what my brain—still drunk off Soren Pembry's lips—decides is appropriate to offer the public.

I could've said "help," "thank you," or even "excuse me" while I went to crash out in private.

Nope. Just: *We're enjoying the season.*

What does that even mean? Am I a Christmas card now? Did my vocabulary flee the scene of that kiss like a coward?

"Clearly." Rae laughs. "Soren, you definitely know how to put on a show."

Oh my God, I need a do-over, a teleprompter. How I managed to get *any* words out after Soren's tongue did illegal, yet delicious, things inside my mouth, I honestly cannot say.

Speaking of the man with the incredible tongue, he's grinning as though he slayed a dragon, signed another seven-figure book deal, and dropped a scented candle line called *Victory & Vanilla.*

"I *could* say I believe in committing to a story arc." Soren lounges back on his heels like the arrogant bastard he is. "But that makes it sound like I'm following a script." Eyes glinting, he glances sideways at me.

What is he doing? Is he about to reveal to the world that Ava Bell asked him to fake date her in exchange for better reviews and algorithmic sympathy? Right here, right now, in front of Rae and the ShelfSpace community?

It would be the ultimate roast video for him.

My stomach drops straight into my boots. I frantically scan the crowd for Renata.

"Trust me," Soren continues, "nothing about us is scripted. We are as real as it gets."

I gape at him, forgetting basic human functions—swallowing, blinking. Words are hard.

Soren seems totally unfazed by the puddle I'm rapidly becoming. "So, am I putting on a show? Maybe a little." He winks because that's what he does. "Can you blame me? I've got Ava Bell on my arm. She's not exactly background noise. And okay, full truth, I'm marking my territory a bit."

His smirk deepens as my mouth parts uselessly. No words come out.

Watching me intently, Soren brushes a stray hair from my face and whispers, "You're doing great."

A hand shoots up from the press pool. "How long have you two been...romantic?"

Renata gives me a thumbs-up from the back of the crowd. *Go with it.*

"We've been talking for a while now. Things escalated in the DM's around late summer." Soren pauses.

I'm searching for words, but I've completely lost them. Along with all the ones Renata stuffed into my brain. Just gone. Then I blurt, "There was a connection."

Everyone stares.

"Yes," Soren cuts in, recognizing my mental breakdown. "One of those lightning-strike moments you don't plan for."

"Any plans to collaborate on a book?" Rae asks.

"Not unless it's about a woman murdering her co-author," I mutter under my breath, finally able to speak somewhat coherently.

Soren replies, easy and cocky enough to charm the front row. Let's be honest, every row. "It's still very early. We're asking for a little space to enjoy the sparks. No pressure, or labels. We want to see where this goes."

Says the guy who just kissed me like he was trying to win a trophy, ruin my panties, and claim my soul all in one go.

Mission fucking accomplished.

See where this goes? God, he's so good at faking it. He sounds like he actually means it.

A traitorous, warm flutter kicks me down below. My body gets the memo before my brain can object, and I cross my legs tighter, trying to appear composed while my pulse sprints a victory lap.

While the crowd eats it up, a burning sensation settles in the pit of my stomach, accompanied by guilt and frustration. This is a game to him. I'm not good at games. Especially when I can't tell what's pretend and what isn't. This story feels like it's taken control and is now writing itself.

Rae begins talking with the audience.

Soren whispers in my ear again. "You rattled, Bells? Still thinking about our kiss? Or is your mind stuck on what happened at the gym earlier today?"

My jaw drops open. I turn toward him. "What are you talking about?"

His grin is the devil himself. "Pretty sure you were imagining me pinning you down, making you beg for more reps. With my mouth."

My elbow finds his rib. He doesn't even flinch, only laughs low in his throat. I laugh, too, but it's shaky. Forced. Fake as fuck.

"Such a vivid imagination you have, Pembry," I try to play it off.

Soren gives a knowing smile. My stomach dips as my mind rewinds that moment. Wait. *Wait.* Oh God. Did he *hear* me? Did he *see* me?

The flush crawling up my neck has nothing to do with flirtation. It's pure panic. I can't meet his eyes. If he *knows*—if he has even an inkling of what I did in that locker room—I'm going to have to dig a hole and throw myself in it.

"Mhm." To my utter shock and horror, he presses a kiss to the side of my cheek, like *I'm cute for trying*, and walks off as though he didn't detonate a bomb in my pants or my brain.

An hour and several photos later, Soren and I are walking in the pumpkin patch under a canopy of fairy lights as dusk settles over the courtyard, crisp fall air thick with the scent of cinnamon and cider.

I've calmed down a little. Thankfully, the adrenaline from the kiss has faded to a low simmer, and my heartbeat has returned to a normal pace. I've stopped mentally replaying that moment in the locker room like I'm studying film footage from a car crash and a sex dream at the same time.

Mostly.

Now, as I walk beside him through the faux-rustic fantasy Camille designed, something feels...different. Less performative. More tangible.

It could be the quiet between us, or the fact that his fingers keep brushing mine, testing what I've dubbed *the Contact Theory* —that little experiment where a man pretends he isn't trying to hold your hand. Still, every accidental touch is actually a question. It would be sweet any other time. Harmless, even. But with Soren, it feels like a fuse waiting to catch fire.

His attention is on the families nearby, the kids in matching scarves, the older couple sharing a caramel apple, the man walking his golden retriever.

What would this scene feel like if it weren't staged? If the camera wasn't watching? If the lights weren't for show, and this were a *real* date?

"You okay?" Soren asks softly, eyes still forward.

I shake those previous thoughts loose. "Yeah, just taking it all in."

He hums a low note, not fully buying that answer, but isn't going to push. I'm glad. If he did, I'm not sure what would come out of my mouth.

The two of us fall into step again. Oddly comfortable. And that might be the craziest part of all.

Camille, Renata, and Fisher trail behind, giving the illusion of privacy while still managing the optics.

And Soren and I? We're on.

Walking beside me, he tucks his hands into the pockets of his coat. We pass rows of pumpkins stacked high on hay bales and kids running around, hiding behind corn husks and scarecrows.

I'm tense once again. My smile stiffens at every click of a camera lens. It's like a countdown to implosion.

Soren nudges a tiny pumpkin with the toe of his boot. "That one kind of reminds me of you. Compact. Seasonal. Outrageously cute."

I snort despite myself. "You calling me small?"

"I'm saying you pack more impact than most of the oversized ones put together."

He's teasing. There's a gentleness in the way he says it—a softness I hadn't expected.

Pausing at a cider stand set up beside a decorative fire pit, Soren orders two and hands me mine before I can speak. The tension in my shoulders doesn't entirely disappear.

Settling on a bench near a fire pit, warm mugs in hand, I glance around, making sure no one's directly pointing a lens at us.

"So," he starts after a beat, "is this the weirdest fake date you've ever had?"

"It's the only fake date I've ever had."

"Mine too."

Silence lingers.

My mind jumps back to the Genre Feud when Soren told me he read *The Lumberjack's Love Letters*. That moment's been gnawing at me ever since, chewing through every wall I swore was indestructible. I've tried to write it off, to file it under "irrelevant nonsense," but it keeps coming back.

"Why did you read my book?" I finally ask, even though I already know this question has claws.

Swirling his cider, his gaze fixes on the firelight. "The guy in it... I saw a lot of myself in him, except, you know, with more restraint and less flannel."

A nervous laugh escapes me.

"What inspired his character?" Soren inquires.

I hesitate, my response snagging like fabric on barbed wire. "He was based on someone I used to lo—" I choke the word back, because even after all this time, it still tastes like rust and regret. The memory of it hovers anyway, daring me to set it free, but I bite down hard, refusing. "He's just a made-up book boyfriend."

My chest twists. On so many levels, that answer is true. The man in my book isn't real. Neither is his inspiration. He's a wish —a dream stitched together in the dark—of someone I needed to exist.

But wishes don't come true. They blur lines and make monsters look like miracles.

I don't look at Soren. I can't. If I meet his eyes, he'll see the jagged, unfinished edges of me—the parts I've spent years patching over. I don't want to share that part of my story with him.

"I know you're lying," he calls me out. "So, what happened?"

He wasn't who I thought he was. And he didn't love me back. "He wanted other things." Women, to be more specific.

Soren's gaze snaps to mine as though I've said something blasphemous. "Well, he's a fucking idiot."

The air stalls between us. It's been almost two *years*, and still, there's a part of me that flinches when I talk about it out loud. That relationship carved its name into my bones. Don't mistake that for poetic. It was more like scar tissue.

I've told myself countless times I'm over it. That *he* no longer controls me. I'm stronger now. But somehow, hearing Soren call him a fucking idiot makes my insides ache. I guess there's a soft place there I didn't realize was still bruised.

"And now?" he asks, quieter this time, like the answer matters to him.

"Now, I write about the guy I *wish* existed instead. It's safer that way."

Soren studies me for a second, brows lifting slightly. "That's kind of devastating, Bells."

Shrugging, I stare into my cup. "Yeah, well. So is dating in real life."

Another pause. The hiss and pop of wood from the fire and the occasional bell of laughter from across the patch fill the silence.

Soren leans forward, cradling his cup in both hands, fingers tapping a slow, distracted rhythm against the paper sleeve. He draws in a breath. The crease between his brows tells me he's weighing the thoughts in his head, rolling them around on his tongue before deciding whether or not to let it go.

That tongue. The one that did wicked, swirly things with mine during our kiss. My lips recall how it moved, with confidence and hunger. An uninvited thought slinks in: *If that's what his tongue can do in my mouth... what kind of magic could it work lower?*

Heat floods my cheeks. I clear my throat. "What about you? How come the hottest ShelfSpacer ever to live is single?"

Soren huffs a laugh. "I'm single by choice."

"So much magical pussy, so little time?" I quip, lifting my cup in mock salute. "The burden of the chosen one."

His jaw tenses, and that casual lean he had a moment ago is gone. Soren shifts in his seat. He sets his mug down on the bench with more force than necessary. Long fingers flex once. He's tamping something down. It's subtle, yet unmistakable.

"Am I wrong?"

"Yeah, you are. I'm not some horny asshole who collects conquests for power points." His voice is suddenly less amused. "That's not why I'm here. And for the record? If I wanted a harem, I wouldn't be wasting my time sitting here with someone who views me as just another trope."

The words sting. I deserve them.

I try to laugh, brush it off, but the sound catches in my throat. Soren managed to open up a sealed door inside me with a tiny crack, but I slammed it shut with a cheap line. Because that's what I do, make jokes when things start to get heavy.

"I'm sorry–" I start.

"It's exhausting sometimes. Not gonna lie." There's no exaggerated delivery. Only soft and stripped-down honesty. He's not putting on a show right now.

And I feel like a total shit.

Turning toward him, I open my mouth to apologize again, but he silences me by adding, "I'm not trying to earn sympathy points from you right now."

I pause before replying, "I didn't think you were."

His eyes set on a couple holding hands. "If I... if *we're* going to do this, we should be honest with each other."

I don't speak. I listen.

"I'm not into lying either, Bells. Even though I do it every goddamn day for people who want the version of me they make up in their head." He's quieter now, thumb and forefinger rubbing together, slow and absent. I'm surprised by this new fissure in his usual cocky veneer.

Exhaling through his nose, he continues, "They demand that persona. The flirt. The fantasy they follow on ShelfSpace. I created a glossy, thirst-trap book boyfriend to build a brand. It worked." He shrugs. There's no pride in it. "I'm a New York Times Bestselling author. So, I play for the cameras, give the people their wink and bite, keep the mystery alive. I do what I have to do."

Soren's gaze finally meets mine again, and my stomach sinks at the vulnerability I see tucked behind his eyes.

"The point is...I'm not always what you see." A soft, sad smile touches his lips. "There's more to me, despite what you think."

That phrase cuts right through me. What is wrong with me? Soren's not a character. He's a person. A living, breathing human being with feelings and fatigue and walls I just helped reinforce. One who's been performing for so long, I'm not sure he even knows who he'd be if he stopped. And I reminded him why he doesn't. Shit, why did I say that to him?

Fingers tightening around the cup, my heart shifts a fraction. I don't want to like him. But he's making me want to see past the layers. Past the swagger and the smirk, down to the man who hides inside the spotlight. That's risky.

"I need you to know." Soren turns entirely toward me, his expression steady and unbearably sincere, "that during all of this..." His eyes roam over my face, trying to see the parts I've hidden behind my own brand of armor. "You don't have to smile if it hurts. I'll do it for you."

The words slam into me with quiet precision, right into the softest part of me. Soren sees my mask for what it is. And he's telling me that with him, I can take it off.

My throat tightens. The air feels suddenly too thin, like I've been caught naked in a room full of strangers. If I drop the smile, if I let him see the ache underneath, there's no taking it back. No pretending I'm untouchable. The terrifying part is that a small, traitorous piece of me wants that.

It's too dangerous.

"I don't even know you."

"Yet," he says. "When you're ready, I can be a safe space for you. You can breathe with me."

That undoes me more than anything else he could've said. It's not a line. Nor is it a flirtation. It's an offering–one that doesn't ask anything of me.

You can breathe with me.

I try swallowing around the lump rising in my throat, and remind myself it's not about my past anymore. It's about what that ending did to me. I internalized it. After what happened, I started shrinking, sanding off edges, making myself harder to love, and easier to leave.

Now, I'm sitting next to someone who's offering safety in

moments where I least expect it. I want to lean into it. If only for a second. Long enough to experience what it feels like to be *wanted* and not used. To be *understood*.

But I don't. I can't. Never again.

A shaky breath leaves my lungs, and I pray to whatever deity is in charge of emotional boundaries that Soren Pembry never figures out how close he is to breaking me open.

"I appreciate the offer. It's not the smiling that hurts, though," I whisper, even as the truth pulls loose, stitch by stitch. "It's the recklessness of this whole thing."

His brows merge. He breathes a laugh. "I've been reckless since before this fake dating thing even started."

"You must be tired." The words come out shaky.

Soren nods, thoughtful. "I am."

A beat of silence.

"What about you?" He runs a hand through his hair before laying it across the back of the bench. "You wear any masks, Bells?"

My shoulders tense. I've worn them all. The good girl. The dutiful daughter. The rising author who smiles for the fans, signs every book with a perfectly rehearsed flourish, and laughs off the questions that hit too close to home.

I've painted on cheer when I've felt like splintering. Pressed on concealer over sleepless nights. Bottled up heartbreak, fear, doubt–then pretended I'd never tasted any of it. Because if I cracked, even a little, everything underneath would come spilling out. And once it did, I wasn't sure there'd be anything left worth saving.

"A few."

More silence.

Soren laces his fingers together, his gaze drifting across the courtyard at the twinkling lights strung overhead, voices in the distance, and the hum of forced festivity pressing in from every direction.

I don't say anything.

Neither does he.

Camille is off to the side, scrolling through her phone, while Renata chats with a journalist who attended the press conference earlier. She's using her 'I'm totally relaxed' fake laugh.

Fisher's nowhere to be found—probably retreated the second he sensed real feelings were on the horizon.

It's just me and Soren. Close, but not touching. Quiet, but not disconnected.

You don't have to smile if it hurts.

Could Soren be a safe space? He offered it so freely. What if we actually became friends?

No. No, that would never happen. There's too much bad blood between us.

"Where's that assistant of yours—Fisher? He seems loyal."

I let out a breath that's more of an exhale, thankful for the topic shift. "He is. Adopted me at my first signing when nobody came to my table. Talked a bunch of people into buying books because he believed in me. We've been stuck together ever since."

Soren's gaze lingers with an intensity that makes me readjust. I'm not uncomfortable, exactly. More like... exposed. Which is new. And terrifying. Somehow, he's yanking out a version of me I'm not used to showing.

Wrapping my fingers around the edge of my scarf, I twist the ends into knots I don't intend to untangle. "What about you? Is Camille your ride or die, or something more?"

Soren huffs out a sound that's not quite a laugh. "Camille definitely has my best interests at heart... at least the financial ones." He rubs the back of his neck, eyes sliding over to our managers before returning to me. "I pay her to manage me, Bells. Not fuck me."

"Right," I blurt, instantly wishing I'd just nodded and moved on after I told him mine and Fisher's story. "I didn't mean—just, you know, like... who's really in your corner? Friends, family— someone else?"

The second the question is out, I hear the careful curiosity in it. I sound like a woman fishing for information she has no busi-ness wanting. Like the kind of girl who refreshes social media to see who he's been tagged with.

My fingers pick at an invisible crumb on my jeans, because apparently I can't handle eye contact or basic conversation.

Soren's jaw works. His fingers curl tighter around his knees, the rhythm of his thumb halting mid-tap. His back goes straighter. I know this reaction. I've touched on something he's spent a long time trying to bury. But what?

"Matthew," he finally says. "My agent. Well, he's more than that. He's been with me from the start. One of the few people who saw through the noise and told me to write what scared me. Not what sold." There's such reverence in his answer—a truth he doesn't hand out often. "M's the reason I didn't quit after my first book deal. Or the second. Or when everything went sideways after a disastrous film option. One of those Hollywood fever dreams that promised a big-screen blockbuster and ended up as a half-written script, a lawsuit, and six months of my inbox filled with nothing but tabloid gossip and refund requests. He's part mentor, part therapist, and part whiskey-fueled life coach."

That last part earns a small smile from me, and from him, too. This tug of recognition hits me. There's a thread tying me and Soren together. Different lives, different people, but the same kind of loyalty holding us both up.

"Matthew sounds amazing. I have a similar friend. Her name is Emily."

"Maybe I can meet her someday."

"Slow it down, Pembry." I smile. "We've only had one fake date."

Soren smiles back. "Well, any friend of yours is someone worth knowing."

He reaches over to pluck a loose thread from the sleeve of my coat. I'm surprised by the casualness of it. Soren doesn't even seem to register the gesture.

After, he picks up his drink, drains the cider, and shoots the cup into the nearest trash can. "You know, you're not what I expected, Bells."

"What did you expect?"

"I don't know. More... glitter? You've got this whole sunshine-and-sweaters aesthetic, but underneath, you're kinda terrifying."

My face scrunches. "Um, thanks? I think."

Soren grins. "It's a compliment."

The warmth of his words settles deep inside my chest. "I'm mad about that kiss," I firmly say. "You didn't give me a fair warning."

"Sorry, not sorry." Heat simmers beneath the humor. "If it's any consolation, I've been thinking about it ever since."

I blush. "I... It was unexpected."

His smile curves, satisfied. "Not always a bad thing."

"Still should've warned me."

"Next time, I'll give you a ten-second countdown."

I'm smiling—dammit—and he sees it. His mouth opens as if he wants to say more, but he must decide against it, and he closes it instead.

What was he about to say? Was it weighted with banter? Something that could crack open whatever fragile truce we've built? Hopefully, it wasn't anything that would tip us both too far into territory we can't walk back from. Or at least from somewhere *I* can't.

"You two look good together," a couple walking by says to us.

"I think so too," Soren replies, sitting back against the bench where our shoulders brush.

I look away.

"You got cagey all of a sudden," he mentions.

My body tenses. Soren rises and extends his hand. Against my better judgment, I place mine in his, and the moment our palms meet, he pulls me gently into his orbit.

Suddenly, we're not Ava Bell and Soren Pembry, enemies turned marketing experiment. We're two people standing together in the dark, both a little broken, both trying not to let anyone see it.

And I can't help but hate him a little less now.

Ten

SOREN

It's not the first time I've shared a suite with a woman. But it's the first time the woman is Ava Bell—romance's golden girl, my fake girlfriend, and the human embodiment of a soft sweater hiding a stick of dynamite.

The moment we step inside, she wants out, acting like we've just entered a cage, with her eyes darting to the corners, calculating exits, arms tucked tight across her chest as if they might physically hold her together. The space isn't small. It's one of those obnoxiously nice penthouse-style setups with a gas fireplace, modern edges, muted gold accents, and two bedrooms connected by a shared living space.

Her suitcase sits next to the leather bench by the door, a scarf draped over the side—one of those thick, romantic ones she wears on book promos.

I nod toward the bag. "Fisher?"

"Renata thought it'd be more seamless if my stuff were already here." Ava's eyes continue surveying the area as she heads straight to the left bedroom. "I'm gonna rest," she says without looking back.

"No problem," I reply gently. "Need anything?"

Shaking her head, quick and quiet, she keeps moving toward

the bedroom without another word, then disappears inside. The door clicks shut.

Good talk.

With an exhale, I let go of everything this day threw at us, and the air finally stops vibrating with tension. I set my phone on the bar counter, peel off my jacket, and make a beeline for the liquor tray.

Vodka. Tonic. Ice. Lime. Mechanical muscle memory.

The air outside on the balcony bites with a fall wind that threads through your clothes and hooks its claws in your chest.

In the distance, our little pumpkin patch glows inside the hotel courtyard with strings of lights blinking like sleepy stars. Voices drift from below, laughter caught in the edges of conversation. It's all so alive. But up here, it's as though I'm watching a party through glass.

I take a slow sip. Bitterness blooms first, cold like frost edging a windowpane. Then the lime drifts in, bright but fleeting, a dash of sweetness gone too soon. It settles in my chest, the taste numbing, reminding me that the woman of my dreams is less than a hundred feet away. And she's nervous.

Ava's not wrong for being so. I don't come with the cleanest of reputations, and I've been putting on a show for so long that I forget what it's like to be *in* it.

And now, the line between performance and reality blurred so fast for me, I can't pinpoint the moment it disappeared—only that I wasn't fully prepared when it did.

Unselfishly, I meant for the kiss to be marketing gold.

Selfishly, it was everything I've been craving for over a year.

All I felt was her.

All I tasted was her.

It wasn't a kiss. More like an undoing. Of her. Of me. Of everything I thought I could control. It was the best damn thing I've ever felt. And the second her mouth met mine, she showed her hand. It was a risk that could've ended with a slap across my face or a knee to the balls. But Ava Bell kissed me back. Fingers threaded in my hair, her palm gripping my cheek, staking a claim.

When I stumbled upon her in that locker room—her voice breaking on my name, her body shattering under her own touch —I knew this wasn't smoke and mirrors. This is fire. And it's ours.

I'll be damned if I let fear or reputation snuff it out. Come hell, high water, or every headline in the book world stacked against us—I'm not letting her go. Not now. Not ever.

The only problem is, she doesn't like me. Not how I want her to. Which makes this whole fake dating, make-believe closeness thing, so damn frustrating.

I drain half my glass in one swallow. The burn is a welcome distraction. I should've apologized earlier when she told me she was mad. But like I told her, *sorry, not sorry.*

What started as a small crush for me—stubborn, and maddening—has only deepened over time. I fed it with banter, long-distance sparring, obsessively watching her videos, and categorizing her expressions.

The moment our eyes met for the first time in person, I knew...this isn't a crush.

It's destiny.

It's inevitable.

It's her.

Tonight, in that pumpkin patch, the air turned silent, and the world slowed down. She *almost* let me in. There was a spark of vulnerability. She nearly accepted my offer, let herself believe I could be a safe space for her. Then she slammed the door to her emotions shut before I could wedge my foot in.

Ava Bell is a woman who'll fight herself harder than she'll ever fight me. She'll armor up with sarcasm and call it healing. I've already waited a year. Watching from afar and wanting her in silence. What's a little longer? She'll come around. I have to keep showing up until she realizes I'm not the enemy.

I'm the ending she didn't see coming.

CEDAR JAMES

I stand out on the balcony a minute longer, letting the cool air sting my cheeks, then head back inside, leaving the glass on the patio table. The warmth of the suite hits immediately. Soft lighting and stillness make the whole place appear as though it's holding its breath.

I stand in front of Ava's door, press my ear to the cold surface. Everything is still inside her room. No music, no TV, no sound of water running. Just quiet. I don't knock on her door. I leave her be and retreat to my own.

Inside, I open my bag, pull out the portfolio holding Ava's letters. My fingers grip the pen for a second before I start writing.

Soren Pembry
New York Times Best-Selling Fantasy Author

Bells,

I told you tonight that you don't have to smile if it hurts.

I meant that.

You don't owe anyone your composure. Not to the cameras. Definitely not to the crowd. And certainly not to me.

I saw your hands shaking when you picked up the cider. I saw you twist your scarf as if it were the only thing keeping you strapped to this earth. And when someone said we looked good together, I saw you look away.

We did look good, by the way. You were

120

autumn sunlight caught in motion. Someone I
shouldn't want this badly, but do anyway.

I wish I could make this simple.

I kissed you and I meant it. And you felt it
—the undeniable magnetic pull between us.

The fear in your eyes confirmed that. But
there's no denying you kissed me back.

I understand your trepidation with this whole
thing. Fake dating. Public charades. All of it.

I've messed with your quiet life, but I will
not be careless with it. I know how hard you've
worked to protect it.

So here's what I can offer:

The bigger bedroom's yours, nonnegotiable.

Vodka in the freezer, comfort on standby.

If you want silence, I'll shut up.

If you want noise, I'll make it.

If you need space, I'll give it.

But if you ever decide to let me get close, even
an inch, I'll be there.

I won't take that lightly.

Love,

S

It's barely past midnight when I wander into the kitchenette, shirtless, feet bare, hair mussed. I can't sleep. My brain won't shut off, and my stomach's grumbling.

After filling a glass with water, I grab a handful of trail mix from the bowl Camille stocked and lean against the counter, chewing and staring blankly toward the balcony.

Soft footsteps sound behind me. I crane my neck to see over my shoulder. Ava's shuffling toward me, wearing an oversized hoodie that I wish were mine, and fuzzy socks that barely make a sound on the tile.

"Couldn't sleep?" I ask, keeping my voice low.

She shakes her head. "You?"

"Not a chance."

Ava hovers a second, then crosses to the island stool. "I feel antsy."

"Yeah." I slide the trail mix bowl toward her, followed by a bottle of water. "Being fake-coupled-up is shockingly stressful. Who knew?"

She cracks a smile. A small one, but it still lights me up inside.

After a beat of awkward silence, she randomly asks, "How'd you get into writing?"

I shrug, sipping from my glass. "Grew up reading fantasy, old school stuff, Narnia, Earthsea. Got obsessed with mythology. Needed a way to channel it. Also, I was an odd kid with insomnia and too many notebooks."

Ava hums. "I was the girl in the back of the class writing breakup scenes during math. My teachers thought I was depressed."

"Were you?"

She lifts a shoulder. "Maybe a little. I never felt accepted by the other kids in school. Writing gave it shape."

A moment passes. I lean on the counter, facing her. "So, why romance?"

She taps her nails on the counter once, twice. "I love the guarantee of a happily ever after and that they're going to choose each other. Even if it's complicated at first, and messy along the way."

"And the spice?" I tease gently.

She glares at me over the length of her water bottle. "It's called realism. Most adults have sex. Some even enjoy it."

"Do *you*?" I ask, shamelessly.

She chokes on the sip she just took. "Kind of personal, isn't it?"

"You opened the door with all the 'realism' talk. This is me, trying to run through it."

She sets the bottle down with a little too much force. "Well, realism also includes boundaries. Maybe try knocking first."

"So that's a yes, then? You enjoy it." I prop my fist under my chin. "Man, Bells, you *do not* want me thinking about you enjoying sex."

We stare at each other for a long beat.

Tilting her head like she's assessing a wild animal that sat down and asked politely for tea, she asks, "Is this flirting or some sort of elaborate literary chicken game?"

I grin. "Why not both?"

Bemused, Ava shakes her head and lets out a half-laugh, half-sigh. "If you try to turn this into some tortured enemies-to-lovers subplot—"

"Too late. I already outlined it while you were finishing that sentence."

She groans dramatically and snatches her water. "I need a stronger drink."

"So that's a yes?" I ask again. "You enjoy sex?"

Still no answer.

"Who inspires those scenes?" I press.

"Excuse you and your prying questions."

"I'm sorry. It's just...the way you write—you've either got a lot of experience or one *hell* of a vivid imagination."

Her lips purse. "Wouldn't you like to know?"

"I would actually. It's fascinating."

Ava scoffs. "You wouldn't last two minutes inside my imagination. It's broken glass and plot deadlines in there."

"I'm not afraid of a little structure that might bite in the process."

"Okay," she shifts on the barstool, "to answer one of your *intrusive* questions, maybe a few people inspired them."

Jealousy flares in my chest. I try to conceal it, but don't do a very good job. "Lucky few."

"To be completely honest," she continues. "I watch a lot of porn and Passionflix to help me write those scenes."

My cock stirs instantly, hit with a bolt of heat straight to my core. I attempt to ground myself by gripping the edge of the counter with one hand, but it does nothing to stop a mental narrative from crashing in.

I'm picturing us curled up on the couch, Ava tucked into my side, watching porn with that wicked gleam in her eye, tossing out dry commentary as though it's another Thursday—

Until it's not.

Until the scene on screen shifts, and she goes quiet.

Until her breathing changes.

Until she squirms.

Until my lips brush the shell of her ear and I ask: *Want to try it?*

Then her hand slides over my stomach, lazy at first, turning purposeful, diving into the waistband of my pants to find my hard cock, leaking, and ready.

Dipping my own hand into her leggings, palm between her legs, I circle her clit with coaxing strokes as her grip on my cock tightens. And those sounds—filthy, high-pitched moans I've only ever heard through a screen, now coming from *her*. Louder. Needier. My name is rooted in the middle of it.

Jesus.

Subtly, I adjust myself behind the counter, praying she doesn't notice. This girl has no idea what she's doing to me. Or

124

maybe she does. Either way, if I don't walk away soon, this conversation is going to take a very, very hard turn. Pun intended.

"Yeah?" I manage, voice lower than before. "That explains the accuracy."

"What about you?" she asks. "You write spice in your stories, don't you?"

I pick up a walnut and roll it between my fingers, much like I would her clit if I ever had the pleasure of meeting it. "I do when the story calls for it. Most of mine have been fade-to-black—until recently. Only because my publisher wants more." My eyes meet hers. "It's been an adjustment. I've always been better at doing it in real life than describing it in prose."

Ava's glare intensifies.

"Want me to show you?"

Her eyes go wide.

I waggle my brows.

"You're the worst."

"Am I?"

"Yes, you absolutely are."

Rounding the island, my hand drags lightly along the counter. "You're stalling."

"How so?" She's not looking at me as she says it. So much defiance in this one.

"First, you dodge my question. Then you try to swap the spotlight. Why are you so uncomfortable?"

Still not looking at me. "I'm not."

My expression becomes more arrogant before I ask, "Do I make you nervous, Bells?"

Ava's throat works around a swallow, and when she finally answers, her voice is lighter than she means it to be. "Nervous? Please. I'm not nervous. I know better than to play with fire when it's standing six feet tall and grinning at me." Her gaze finds mine, quick and betraying, before darting back to her glass.

My grin deepens. "So you admit I'm fire."

"Don't flatter yourself." She takes another sip of water, but her hand trembles just slightly.

"Too late. Definitely flattered."

Ava sets the glass down with a bit of *clink* and lifts her chin.

I move another inch. "I'll ask again—do you enjoy it?"

Her lips part slightly. "Sex?"

"No," I reply. "Christmas tree assembly."

A flush rises in her cheeks.

"Yes, sex."

"I'm not answering that."

"Which tells me everything." I'm so close to her now. One more inch and I could touch her. "Guess I hit a nerve."

Ava's body stiffens. Even her breath locks up. Her gaze can't help but roll down my naked chest before she catches herself, and those pretty autumn eyes snap back up. I can tell she's mad at herself for looking. Love that.

"Good night, Soren." Ava moves to stand. I block her. She peers up at me, a little angry, a little confused, but a whole lot breathless.

"The thing about fire, Bells." I lean down, so my voice sweeps over her skin. "You can run from it, hide from it, try to smother it, but once it's in you? You don't get a choice. You burn."

Ava angles away, fists balled up at her sides. It's not anger. It's need, shuddering through her muscles, aching in the spaces between us. If she lets go, she'll touch me. And if she touches me, we'll both ignite.

And then—

Fire.

Burn.

"Please move." Her hand drifts toward her throat, like she could hide the furious pulse hammering there.

Turning slightly to let her pass, she quickly disappears down the hall, into her room, and locks herself inside.

I pop the walnut in my mouth and smile.

Eleven

AVA

After the glitter-storm circus that was the *Great Booksgiving*, Renata and Camille whisked Soren and me away like romance novel fairy godmothers on a caffeine bender.

Apparently, "organic relationship building" is done through a carefully organized weekend getaway with the enemy.

Our destination? Washington, D.C.

Reason? Content.

Camille and Renata have decided that before the *Feast & Fiction* event next week in Boston, we *must* detour through the nation's capital for what they dubbed "a picturesque lovers' weekend."

Their words, not mine.

The itinerary reads like a Buzzfeed listicle titled *Top Ten Cliché Couple Dates You've Already Seen in Every Rom-Com Ever*.

• A carriage ride. Nothing screams timeless love like horse manure on Constitution Avenue.

• Candlelit dinner cruise on the Potomac.

• Matching scarves for a Lincoln Memorial selfie. (Yes, they actually packed us scarves.)

• A bookstore stroll with only one copy of a hot new release, which we're supposed to "playfully" fight over.

It's all designed for ShelfSpace clips and stories—slow pans of the monuments, moody filters, close-ups of us gazing at each other like we're the stars in a holiday rom-com movie.

Please note: I do not gaze.

At least not willingly.

Soren, to his credit—or maybe to his vexing charm—plays along better than I expected. He's not the insufferable Sword Daddy he is online. Or how he was at the *Genre Feud*. He holds doors. He tips generously. He even made a joke about winter scarves that made me snort red wine out my nose during our pre-fake-date cocktail hour. Which is...unfortunate, because I do not want to find him tolerable.

The carriage pulls up—with actual white horses—and I'm one fake laugh away from bolting.

Soren leans in, so only I can hear, "Tell me you don't feel like we're in a low-budget Regency reboot."

I bite back a smile. "Oh, we absolutely are. And you're underpaid background talent."

A grin flits across his face, and my chest does a stupid rolling cartwheel in response.

The horses clop forward, hooves striking sparks off the pavement, and the carriage rocks us into a rhythm that feels far too intimate. The velvet bench offers no mercy, forcing me tight against Soren, his thigh a steady press into mine every time the wheels find a crack.

When the carriage lurches hard, his arm shoots out across me —an automatic, protective *Mom Arm*. His hand hovers so close to brushing my breasts that my pulse kicks like I've been caught doing something illicit.

Soren jerks his arm back like the velvet burned him, but not before color floods his neck, crawling up his cheeks in a slow, betraying bloom, all the way to the tips of his ears. And here's the problem: the flush doesn't make him look guilty. It makes him look adorable. Soft in a way he shouldn't be. Cute, even. It's infuriating because there's nothing cute about the way my body wonders what it would feel like if he didn't stop short.

Did he mean to? Did he want to? The thought lodges itself into my brain, needling at me. If he didn't—why do I want him to?

I fold my hands in my lap, eyes fixed firmly on the lampposts skating by. "This is ridiculous."

"Agreed," he says easily, settling back. "If Camille and Renata wanted authenticity, they should've stuck us in a rideshare with a driver who plays the same EDM song on repeat."

I almost laugh. Almost. "At least then I wouldn't smell horse poop."

"Correction—you'd smell Axe body spray and despair."

That earns him a smirk I don't mean to give. Soren notices, and his grin deepens, wicked and sweet at the same time. His stormy eyes are calmer tonight, like moonlight dancing on water, and he's gazing at me as if he's trying to chip away at my carefully constructed armor to see the fragile girl underneath.

It's unnerving.

I hate it.

"Why do you look at me like that?" I shift my attention to the Washington Monument glowing in the distance.

"Like what?"

"Like you like what you see."

Soren's arm lifts, stretches across the back of the carriage behind me, casual in posture but not in intent. His heat is everywhere, surrounding me, closing in.

"I do like what I see." His tone is certain, like it's the simplest truth in the world. "I've liked it all night."

My pulse jackhammers against my ribs. I should laugh it off, toss back a witty remark, shove him teasingly. But my throat locks, because Soren isn't smirking. He isn't joking. He means it.

And that—more than his cocky grin or his ridiculous fans or his rumored flesh sword—terrifies me most of all.

Silence.

Soren removes his arm, clasps his hands between his legs, and chuckles. "You're adorable when you're suffering."

"I hate you."

"No, I don't think you do, Bells." The words thread under my skin like the chilled air curling through the open side window.

The carriage jolts again. I grab the edge of the seat. His hand twitches like he wants to reach for me, but he doesn't. Instead, he leans a little closer, his shoulder brushing mine deliberately.

"So," I say quickly, desperate for distance. "Do you plan on any more impromptu kisses tonight? Or was that strictly a one-time-for-the-cameras thing?"

Soren's head tilts, and those stormy grays hold the reflection of the passing lights. "Depends."

"On what?" My voice comes out thinner than I'd like.

"On whether you'd hate me for it."

For the briefest, most intense second, I'm not sure what my answer would be. His gaze stays on me, intent, until I have to look away, pretending to be fascinated by a group of teenagers snapping selfies.

Fake, I remind myself. This is supposed to be fake. Just content. Survival until *Feast and Fiction*.

My mind wanders back to what he said:

"The thing about fire, Bells. You can run from it, hide from it, try to smother it, but once it's in you? You don't get a choice. You burn."

Heat lashes down my spine at the memory of that statement, and it makes me wonder, *What would it feel like to step straight into that fire? Just once. To surrender to it? Would it burn me clean, forge me into something stronger, or leave me as nothing but ash?*

Soren's too much. Bold words. Shameless questions. The same confidence that makes the entire internet swoon. But beneath it, in these private moments with him, he's a different man—one that doesn't fit the Sword Daddy persona he's perfected for the world.

That's a problem, though. I don't want to see it. Don't want to like it. Don't want to wonder who Soren Pembry is when the cameras aren't rolling, and the banter isn't staged.

But here I am, doing exactly that.

The carriage slows, wheels crunching against the curb as the driver calls out something about the "romantic dismount." Kill me.

Soren swings out of the carriage first, shoes hitting pavement with unfair grace. He turns, arm extended, palm open, like this is an episode of *Bridgerton* instead of a rom-com death trap with horses.

I hesitate, but eventually slide my hand into his. The second I start down the teensy, metal ladder, my heel snags on the step, my ankle twists, my balance falters, and the world tilts.

Soren's grip tightens, his other hand latches onto my waist, and he pulls me against him before I can eat asphalt in front of a row of gawking tourists.

My body slams into his broad, solid chest, smelling faintly of magical pine trees and *him*.

"You okay?" he asks, his tone worried, and laced with an emotion that doesn't feel fake at all.

I make the mistake of looking up. His gaze crashes into mine. Suddenly, there's no Capitol dome, no clopping horses, no cameras waiting to catch a candid. Just his hands on me, my pulse sprinting, and a silence that feels like it's keeping a secret we haven't confessed yet.

Soren's mouth curves into a sexy half-smile. "Should I start the ten-second countdown?"

The weight of his hands, the heat in his eyes, the memory of that first kiss—all of it makes the air knot in my throat.

I manage a slight shake of my head. "No."

Soren lets me go, slowly, as though reluctant to hand me back to gravity, then tips the driver and gestures for me to start walking.

Next up on the evening ticket—the dinner cruise, which is precisely what you'd expect: white tablecloths, violinists playing a slightly off-key version of *All of Me*, and a photographer, who

Renata definitely hired, is pretending to be a "staff member" for better shots.

I sit across from Soren at a table that's a little too small, with a view of the Potomac gliding by in moody darkness. Candlelight reflects off the window, turning this whole setup into the opening credits of a CW drama.

He lifts his wine glass. "Cheers, Bells. To our love story."

"Fake love story," I correct.

"Right." His brows knit, then he sets his glass down without taking a sip from it.

"Cheers." I clink my glass against his anyway. "May our story die a noble death in the new year."

A hand covers his heart. "You wound me. At least pretend all this sweeps you away." His words are meant to be playful, but his eyes hold a hint of hurt behind them. Why though?

"Oh, I'm swept." I tear a piece of bread off the loaf. "Mostly toward the lifeboats."

Soren chuckles genuinely, and the sound burrows into my heart in a way I don't appreciate. It's nothing like the overproduced laugh he uses for fans during livestreams. This one he keeps hidden away from the general pubic. But not from me.

Again, why?

Our entrées arrive—expensive salmon, capers, and a vibrant garnish that looks like a small weed plucked from a sidewalk crack. I spear it with my fork. "I bet Camille Googled 'romantic meals that photograph well' before picking this."

"She totally did," Soren agrees, cutting into his salmon with infuriating calm. "We're one rose petal away from a Nicholas Sparks novel."

I snort laugh. "More like the parody version."

He smiles at that, then wipes his mouth with his napkin. "So, are you planning to push me overboard before dessert?"

"I considered it. But you probably float. Too much hot air."

Soren laughs, and that treacherous little flip my chest did earlier has traveled to my stomach. Not fair. Definitely not okay.

As the dinner wears on, the boat glides past the Lincoln Memorial, glowing in the night. Our reflection is in the glass, but it dissolves once the photographer's camera snaps like a vulture in the distance.

I plaster on the fakest grin I can muster. Soren does the same. Our eyes meet, and for one split second, my smile isn't fake at all.

Quickly looking away, I stab another piece of salmon. *Fake. This is fake. He's fake. I'm fake. We're fake. Everything is fake.*

Except my pulse doesn't seem to believe any of that.

We finish dinner, drink the rest of our wine, and decide to head out onto the deck. The air is cold and biting when we step onto it, our breath fogging in little puffs that drift off over the black water.

Renata and Camille are nowhere in sight—probably inside strategizing how to caption our next "candid." In the meantime, it's just the two of us, leaning against the railing, the city sparkling in the distance.

"Romantic enough for you?" Soren asks, tugging his coat tighter around him. His grin is a little crooked and a whole lot boyish. "All we're missing is a boombox and John Cusack."

I chuckle, hugging my own coat closer. "You'd probably pick the wrong song."

"Not a chance. I have impeccable taste."

"Please. You'd go full drama—*Highway to Hell* or something equally ridiculous."

"Wrong. *Careless Whisper.* Every time." He hums the tune until I roll my eyes.

Banter fills the space between us for a few minutes. We keep things safe and light. I ignore the wind as it catches strands of my hair, as well as how Soren subtly steps closer to block it. He's being a gentleman, and that's messing with me. Everything about him is.

I grip the railing tighter and decide to be bold with my own questions, like he is. "So, there's still one thing about all this I don't get."

"What's that?"

"The day we signed the contract, you said you were doing this for entertainment value. But you've got the whole internet drooling over you. You could fake date anyone. Or...real date them. You can get your kicks with anyone you want. Why me? I live a stale existence. And our ideas of fun are painfully different."

His eyes lock on mine, unflinching. "That's exactly why you're perfect for me."

My response is a short, disbelieving laugh. "Perfect?"

"Yes." His voice sounds calm, but with a slightly rough edge. "My life stopped being mine the second one of my books hit big. Crowds, panels, livestreams. People don't want *me*, they want the Dagger Daddy. *The Blade.* The walking thirst trap that banters through everything." He shakes his head once, presses his lips together. "But you? You don't buy the act. You bulldoze right through it. You call me on my bullshit and don't care if it makes me uncomfortable. You remind me I'm still a man, not just a persona. That's not stale, Bells. That's the only thing that feels real to me."

Soren's words settle in places I don't want them to. And in this one fragile, terrifying second, I believe him. I think maybe he understands me, beyond our internet feud and our curated captions. He sees past the girl who's been stumbling through bad reviews and worse memories, and is looking at me, Ava Bell. The broken and fragile. The steadfast and strong.

That scares the fucking hell out of me.

I can't let myself buy into that notion, not even for a moment. If I do, then this stops being harmless make-believe. It sprouts claws. It becomes a weapon that could slice me clean open.

I wet my lips, level my voice. "But it isn't real. It's fake."

Soren's smile fades, twisting into one I haven't yet seen from him. He shakes his head, gaze fixed on the rippling dark water. "Everything in my life is noise. Fun, sure. Addictive, sometimes. But it's not—" He pauses, mouth pressing shut, as if the words he was about to say were too heavy to. "You see," he starts again, pauses. "You don't want anything from me. Personally, that is. I find that...refreshing. And you intrigue me, if I'm being honest."

I look at him, and the cocky Dagger Daddy from ShelfSpace isn't standing here next to me. This Soren is gentler, fervent, and —for reasons I refuse to admit to—he makes my heart beat extremely fast.

So I do what I do best. I deflect. "Deep thoughts for a dinner cruise."

His lips twitch. "What can I say? The water makes me poetic."

"Dangerous combination." I turn back toward the glow of the Lincoln Memorial, my pulse still drumming, traitorous and loud.

The lit monument spills over the water, fractured light shimmering between us. I swipe a stray strand of hair from my face, pretending it's the wind that makes me shiver.

Behind me, I hear the rustle of fabric. Then a scarf, smelling faintly of pine and sexy Viking warrior, slides around my neck. Soren tugs the ends together gently, doubling me up in it. His fingers brush my collarbone before retreating.

I freeze, because this is not in the itinerary.

"You don't give yourself enough credit," Soren says, voice stout like it's been waiting to be spoken. "For what it's worth, I wouldn't fake date anyone else. Or re—" His words cut off. It's becoming a pattern with him. One I don't understand. He finishes with, "You're fun to rile up."

I should cut down these warm emotions taking root inside me before they overtake me.

But then Soren adds, "And for some reason, I want to help my enemy succeed. I told you, Bells—I'm more than what you see online. Maybe one day, you'll believe that."

I stare straight ahead. Looking at him right now would be a mistake. A fatal one. My pulse hammers against the scarf he just tied around me, as if it knows whose hands were there seconds ago.

Fake. This is fake, Ava.

What if it could be real?

No. *Fuck no.* I crush that little whisper in my brain before it grows teeth and turns into a beast I can't cage. That's not the deal. Definitely not the plan. And if I let myself believe otherwise, it won't be Soren Pembry who breaks me. It'll be me, all over again.

Twelve

~∞~

SOREN

The suite is too damn quiet.

Ava's holed up in her room, typing away like the world depends on it, the faint clack of her keyboard drifting under the door.

I'm sprawled across the couch, long legs hanging off the end, thumbing through the spoils of our staged "bookstore stroll."

The book in question? *The Dragon Slayer's Secret.* Yeah. That's what Renata and Camille staged us "playfully" fighting over in the Romantasy aisle while a dozen onlookers live-streamed it for ShelfSpace. A single copy left, two fake enemies turned lovers reaching for it simultaneously. A setup so on-the-nose, it should've come with a laugh track.

I "won" the book. Technically, Ava let go first, which is hilarious, because she's the one who could kill a man with her death glare and a witty line.

Now here I am, flipping through the pages for a distraction. Not gonna lie—some of these spicy scenes are hotter than they have any right to be. And reading them is safer than replaying the words she stabbed me with earlier. *It isn't real. It's fake.*

She's not wrong. That's what we agreed to. Fake. For content. For optics. For *The Bell and the Blade* ship.

But fuck, I want the opposite.

She looked so beautiful tonight. That little silk dress clinging —no, *sculpting*—to every curve. Her hair caught the light like flames. When I wrapped my scarf around her neck, her pulse jumped beneath my fingers.

I wanted to lean down and kiss her right there. See if the heat in my chest matched the heat in hers.

Instead, I settled for hoping the scent of my cologne in the fabric would loosen her up. It didn't. Ava Bell is one tough egg to crack. But that's what I like about her.

I toss the book onto the coffee table, drag a hand down my face, and grab my phone to text the one person who won't feed me a line of fluff in their advice.

> You awake?

It takes thirty seconds before my screen lights up.

> Unfortunately.

> I know you said fake dating Ava is basically the same as psychological torture....but...

> I want to make it not-so-fake.

> How do I do that?

> Simple. You don't.

> Encouraging as always.

> I'm serious, man. That girl hates you.

> Yeah. Except she doesn't. Not completely.

> As your agent, I can't support this.

> I'm not asking my agent right now. I'm asking my best friend.

138

There's a pause so long, I think he bailed on me, until the dots appear again.

Best friend says... it's risky. It's not a good idea.

Yeah. I know.

And yet here you are, texting me at one in the morning.

...you complete me.

What's the plan? Hope she trips and falls into your arms, instantly falling in love with you?

Also, caught the carriage video on ShelfSpace. Didn't know you moonlighted as Prince Charming.

Only on the weekends.

The plan is... I don't know. Figure out how to show her I'm more than the asshole she thinks I am.

Be careful.

I won't get many chances with a woman like her.

Which is why I can't waste a single one.

Then my advice changes. Best friend says: stop bullshitting her. Show her you're more than "The Blade."

That's the only chance you've got.

How?

Easy. Start by not trying so damn hard.

That's your big advice? Don't try?

No. DON'T PERFORM. According to her scary as fuck agent, Ava's got a bullshit detector so sensitive, it probably goes off when you tie your boots. You want her to see you? Then actually let her.

You make it sound simple.

It is simple. It's just not easy. Stop hiding behind your quips and sword jokes. Show her the guy who reads her books and still has eighth-grade poems memorized. Show her the guy who'd rather carry her bags than carry his ego.

...Jesus. Who writes your stuff? That was almost romantic.

Shut up. I'm not your ghostwriter. I'm your best friend telling you the obvious: if you want Ava Bell, then give her the one thing nobody else has—*you*.

And if she still hates me?

Then you'll hurt. But at least you can walk away knowing you didn't fake it.

AND YOU TRIED.

I leave my phone on the coffee table and head to Ava's room, hovering outside her door for too long, fist half-raised like an idiot.

Finally, I knock.

There's a faint shuffle of movement. When the door cracks open, Ava blinks at me through her glasses, hair piled on her head in the world's most chaotic bun.

"Do you need something?" she asks, confused.

"No," I say swiftly, then realize how weird and somewhat creepy I sound. "I mean...do *you* need anything?"

Her brows lift. "No."

140

Silence swells between us for too long. I clear my throat. "Uh...how's the manuscript coming along?"

She leans her shoulder against the doorframe, like she's guarding the entrance. "Fine."

Fine. Nothing more. Nothing less. The verbal equivalent of a locked gate.

Pursing my lips, I nod several times. "Cool, cool. That's great. Okay, I don't want to interrupt your flow." I step back, hands shoving into the pockets of my gray sweatpants. "But I wanted to say thanks. For tonight. I had fun with you."

Sparks flash in her eyes, quick and unreadable.

I push a little further. "I've been enjoying getting to know you, from behind the screen."

That earns me a furrowed brow. But she doesn't speak. So I retreat.

"Sleep well, Bells."

I start down the hall before she can respond, leaving the words —and the weird, awkward weight of them—hanging in the air between us.

Real smooth, Pembry.

That's all I can think as I stalk down the hall, hands jammed into my pockets as though that'll keep them from trembling. Who knocks on a woman's door at almost two a.m. to ask if she needs anything? A butler? A psychopath? Definitely not the guy trying to prove he's more than a Dagger Daddy meme in leather pants.

She looked...soft, glasses slipping down her nose, hair a mess, sweater swallowing her frame. I caught her off guard, and instead of saying something worth remembering, I babbled on like I was asking about the weather. And, *Sleep well, Bells?* Really? That's my closer? Weak. Limp. Verbal lukewarm tea.

By the time I get back to my room, I'm chewing on every word I didn't say. All the lines I wanted to, but couldn't push past my own tongue. My chest feels tight, restless. If I don't get this out, it'll rip me apart from the inside.

So, I do the only thing that has ever worked for me. I grab my leather messenger bag, yank out a piece of letterhead, and uncap a pen. Blank paper stares back at me, daring me to screw it up.

I don't.

Not when it's her.

The words pour out the way they never do when she's standing in front of me. On paper, I'm brave. On paper, I don't choke. On paper, I can tell her that today didn't feel fake—not for me. I liked watching her roll her eyes at the carriage, hearing her laugh, and seeing her reflection in the glass of the boat when she forgot to guard her smile.

On paper, I can tell her the truth.

That I'm falling for Ava Bell, and I don't know how to stop.

Goren Pembry

New York Times Best-Selling Fantasy Author

Bells,

I need to get these words out of my head before I lose my mind.

Tonight was supposed to be a performance. That's what Renata and Camille wanted, right? Slow pans, fake laughs for the camera.

The thing is: you make it impossible to separate the act from the truth. We laughed together. We gazed at each other. I liked it. All of it.

Too much, maybe.

That's the part I can't say out loud. If I did, you'd run. Which is the last thing I want.

You're different from what the internet thinks of me. You don't buy "The Blade." You don't bow to the persona. You call me out. You see me. And that terrifies the hell out of me, because I want you to keep looking.

Today wasn't fake for me, Bells. Not a single second of it.

So...

Sleep well. Dream better. And if I'm lucky, maybe one day you'll believe me when I say this isn't a game.

In the meantime, here are some words, inspired by you. Enjoy.

Love,

S

A Poem For You, Ava Bell:

At the carriage,

you were laughter spilling through the cold night air,

a sound that made me want to believe in things I'd given up on.

At the table,

you glared at your plate like it deserved the blame

for every scar the world ever handed you,

and I loved you for fighting even then.

On the water,

the lights crowned you in silver,
the marble envied your stillness,
your strength, your flame.
And when the wind stole your breath,
I wrapped you in warmth,
but you—
you gave me something I've never known before.
Hope.
A glimpse of a home I've been aching for my
entire life.

Thirteen

AVA

Feast and Fiction, my ass.

They should've called it *Chaos and Crippling Foot Pain*. Or *Herding Bookish Cats: Live!*

Either way, my voice is gone, my Sharpie smells like betrayal, and I've officially hit my social limit for the week. Maybe the decade.

The Massachusetts leg of our book tour was supposed to be the calm before the family storm. One more round of panels, photo ops, and pretend-you-love-each-other banter before I escape to Salem for Thanksgiving and let my mom feed me into a coma.

Nothing about this day was calm.

By noon, the fire marshal was threatening to shut us down due to the line snaking through the hotel lobby and out the front entrance.

By two, someone threw a pair of lace-trimmed panties onstage during mine and Soren's fantasy-romance panel.

By three, I'd lost a contact, and Fisher had to sprint up eight flights of stairs–because the elevators had been overtaken by enthusiastic readers–to my hotel room for a replacement. When he finally returned, he was muttering about "diva-level ocular emergencies."

And by the signing hour, security had to escort a woman, who was visibly upset, out after she demanded Soren write his phone number inside her book.

He gave her *mine*.

"I panicked," he said, later in the green room. "And it felt... thematically appropriate."

I should've murdered him. Instead, I laughed. Because as much as I pretend to roll my eyes at all this—at him—there's a part of me that doesn't hate it. The routine, the rhythm of being with him in these tight spaces, the banter we slip into so easily.

He watches me like he's trying to burn every square inch of me into his brain. And, okay, so it's fake. For the fans. For the tour. For the algorithm. But it doesn't *always* feel fake. It didn't in D.C. It especially doesn't now, hours after the day has ended, when we're back in the suite and the world is finally quiet.

The buzz of the crowd is still ringing in my ears, and my feet ache in that deep, satisfying way that means I did something productive.

The air smells faintly of lemon polish and the warm, plasticky scent of overworked electronics. The floor lamp beside the couch throws a soft amber glow across the room, catching the dust motes drifting lazily in the air.

My hoodie sleeves are pushed halfway up my arms. I'm absently rubbing circles against the bare skin of my forearm, chasing a kind of comfort that never quite settles.

Curled up in the corner of the suite's overstuffed sectional, one leg tucked under me, the other bouncing in a slow rhythm, I turn on the TV.

I *tried* to write earlier. Opened the doc, stared at the blinking cursor, and rearranged the same three sentences twelve different ways. Deleted them all.

My deadline's breathing down my neck. It's a fire-breathing

ghost, and my brain's decided to check out at the worst possible time.

So, Netflix it is. A temporary distraction-slash-bribe for my creativity. Maybe if I feed it enough angst and banter, it'll finally come out of hiding.

Some old cooking show plays on the flatscreen, quiet background noise against Fisher's monologue as he flits around the kitchenette. He's methodically organizing the minibar, muttering about electrolytes and avoiding sugar crashes–which is comical coming from him. He's acting like we're prepping for a summit in the Andes.

My fingers toy with the tassels on one of the couch pillows, twisting them until they coil tight, and I let them unwind again. It's either that or check my phone, and I'm not ready to scroll through any more tagged posts of *Bell and The Blade*.

"You know," Fisher says, voice casually laced with intent, "you *could* invite him to Thanksgiving."

One brow raises. "What? Who?"

"Pembry. He mentioned he didn't have plans." He shrugs, no big deal. "Could be good for PR."

A dry laugh escapes me. "It's enough that I have to maintain this charade in my daily life—I'm not dragging it into my family's home."

The thought hovers in the air.

Soren. Alone.

Nobody should be alone.

I recall the lull between panels, when I asked what he was doing for the holiday. He gave a half-shrug and said, "I don't do Thanksgiving," then promptly redirected his attention to the sad little bowl of unwrapped caramels on the refreshments table.

That was the safer conversation. It wasn't nothing. And I felt it.

Fisher disappears down the hall, now mumbling about immunity boosters and burnout, and I find myself rising from the couch.

I tug down my leggings from where they've ridden up on my calves, rub a hand over my face, and suddenly I'm standing outside *his* door, with fuzzy socks heating my feet.

One hand raises, then hesitates.

This is dumb. I should go to bed.

I knock anyway.

The door creaks open a few seconds later.

Soren stands there shirtless. Again. Apparently, half-naked is his normal state of being while in the confines of a private space.

I take him in. The muscles of his chest are carved, lightly flushed from the warmth of the room, a faint sheen glistening along his collarbone—as if he's been pacing. Or maybe just existing too hard.

Ink sprawls across him, a mix of calculated and cluttered—snatches of script, bold strokes, and fragments of poetry etched into skin. But it's the runes that catch me, hidden messages along his ribs, curling down the slope of muscle. Old shapes, honed edges, ancient and private, as though the man himself is written in a language nobody else gets to read.

I caught glimpses of them that first night at the *Great Books-giving*, when neither of us could sleep. Shadows of ink beneath dim light, not enough to see their weight or meaning. But here, in full view, they're impossible to ignore—impossible not to wonder about.

Every mark tells a story. Why do I suddenly want all of them?

A pair of reading glasses sits low on his nose, and he's holding a pen in one hand, a stack of pages clutched in the other.

Soren glares at me from behind the lenses. "Hey."

"I—uh..." I clear my throat. "Sorry to bother you."

He opens the door wider. "You're not. Come in."

I stumble at the threshold and try to play off the embarrassment by blaming my fuzzy socks for slipping on the floor.

Soren chuckles.

His now familiar scent of pine trees and magic fills the room, mixed with a new one—old paper and lukewarm coffee. I inhale as if I'll never get another chance to breathe it all in while surveying his room.

His bed is unmade. The desk is tidy, covered in color-coded sticky tabs, a coffee mug full of pens, and a printed manuscript thick with handwritten notes.

Soren sets his pages down carefully. "Working through my latest draft." He rubs the back of his neck. "I know, wild Saturday night."

Curiosity tugs at me. I move closer to where the manuscript sits, highlighted in blue and green ink, with some lines circled with arrows and others marked with blunt comments: *cut this* or *not relatable.*

I trail a finger along the edge. "Let me guess...you are your own worst enemy." Catching a line, I read it out loud. "When Daxion kissed Elira, the moan that escaped her was etched into his memory by moonlight—sacred, trembling—and now he's retracing it with reverent hands, the rhythm of her body a sacred text written in heat and breath, and worshiped in silence."

"Bit much?" he asks, nervous.

"No," I say, surprised. "It's good. Excellent, actually. You used sacred twice though."

Soren's head tilts. He checks it. "Hm, so I did." His eyes peer up at me, mischief swimming in them. "Wanna trade notes?"

I hesitate—then nod, grinning. "Sure. I'm warning you though, I'm ruthless with adverbs."

Soren's eyes crinkle in the corners when he smiles. "That's okay. I overuse em-dashes like I get paid for it."

We settle side-by-side on the edge of his bed, knees brushing, a nervous quiet filling the space between us.

This is where he sleeps. Right here, in this space. Probably sprawled out with one arm behind his head, the other thrown across the pillow, owning the universe.

The thought shouldn't feel so intimate, but it does. And now I can't stop wondering what he dreams about—if he tosses and turns, if he wakes up swaddled in the sheets.

Has he ever thought about me while lying right here?

I shift slightly, and my knee bumps against his. Neither of us moves to break the contact.

He hands me a page, and I pass one back.

Our notes start playful, him teasing me for a sarcastic margin comment, me calling him out on an overly brooding line of internal monologue. Somewhere along the way, the tone morphs into thoughtful.

"You could go deeper here," I say, tapping a paragraph. "You keep pulling away right when it starts to hurt. Let it sting."

After reading over the spot I marked, he glances up at me. "You always this thorough in revisions?"

"Yeah, I am."

He's quiet for a second too long before he says, "I appreciate thorough."

A heavy invisible weight settles between us. Surprisingly, it's not uncomfortable. Just... honest. Unexpectedly easy. A little scary. Okay, a lot.

Eventually, I circle back to the real reason I knocked on his door.

"So, listen." I fold one knee under me. "About Thanksgiving."

His expression shutters slightly.

"Why don't you come home with me. Fisher is coming too."

One of his brows quirks.

I rush ahead. "PR, of course. Fisher thought it might solidify how serious we are. Show the fans a softer side. Make you more 'relatable.'" I hold up a piece of his manuscript with the word scribbled next to a highlighted paragraph and smile.

Nodding once, his shoulders fall, and the space between us suddenly feels a lot wider than it did a second ago.

Pressing my lips together, I swallow my pride. "Nobody should be alone on the holidays. Least of all you."

His head turns. Our eyes meet.

"I'd like it if you came with me," I add. "Us, I mean."

Stormy eyes search mine, trying to decode the real reason

tucked between the words. He wants to believe me. He just doesn't know how.

"You sure?" he asks, voice stripped of its usual swagger.

Nodding, my fingers brush against a corner of the pillow resting on his bed. "Yeah. I mean... my mom's going to freak out. I haven't even told her about us. My dad will want to know what your true intentions are with his daughter, which will prompt the 'what about grandchildren' questions from my aunts. My uncle will absolutely tell you his theories about time travel while mixing you a mind-altering cocktail. And there's a ninety percent chance you'll be force-fed pie by someone you've never met, but will absolutely fall in love with, which is my grandmother."

His lips twitch. "Sounds terrifying."

"It is," I say. "It's also loud and warm and weirdly comforting. And... you'll love it."

There's a beat of silence. Then another. And another. Is the room getting smaller?

Soren releases a measured exhale. "Alright. Only if I get to fashion a battle helmet out of tinfoil and whipped cream."

"What?" I ask, confused. "Why?"

Straight faced, he says, "If I'm going to wade into the war zone of awkward family Thanksgiving's with my genre nemesis, I need armor. And snacks. Hence, battle helmet."

Laughing at that, relief bubbles up. "Okay. Deal. Just so you know...you're very strange."

The corners of his mouth curve, soft and genuine. And for a second, we sit there as two writers, two disasters, in a hotel room filled with stories and subtext, quiet and connected.

And–*right now*–it's not pretending. Tomorrow...it will be though.

Soren leans back on his elbows, legs stretched out, expression thoughtful. "Since we're making deals..." His voice trails off, debating whether to speak the next part aloud.

I narrow my eyes. "What?"

"There's a scene I've been stuck on. For my current WIP."

"Oh god. You're not going to ask me to fact-check your sword names, are you? The last one I read sounded close to a venereal disease."

He lifts a finger. "First of all, *The Blade of Eternal Reckoning* is iconic and you'll regret mocking it when it wins a Goodreads award."

"No one is giving your herpes sword an award, Pembry."

Soren chuckles, then drags a hand over his face, suddenly a little more serious. "It's not about the sword. It's a scene. A...spicy one. I told you, my publisher wants more sex. It isn't my strength. Not in print anyway. But now that I have the Queen of Steam here, maybe you could take a look?"

"Okaaaay?" I drag the word out.

"It's...I—" His jaw flexes. "I'm not doing it justice. I can't figure out how to make it read real. Right now, it sounds like a man trying to write a woman's orgasm while overthinking what nipples do."

I snort-laugh. "Do I want to know what you think they do?"

"Obviously, they're dial knobs to an alternate universe." He smirks. "Or at least that's what my writing describes them as, currently."

"You're not wrong."

"Will you guide me?" he asks innocently, which only makes it worse. "Sensory language. What feels true. Realistic. Maybe read over what I've got so far and—"

"*Read* it?"

He shrugs, oh-so-casual. "Unless you'd rather act it out."

My brain breaks in seven places at once.

Soren grins, but there's tension under it. He wasn't *entirely* joking.

"You are—without question—the most infuriating man on this planet."

"I'm trying to be accurate." Soren stretches, not fully aware that his muscles ripple when he does. Or maybe he's very much aware. He flexes.

Okay, yeah, he's aware.

I'm suddenly wondering how *accurate* his spice really is.

Soren grabs his laptop off the desk, opens a document with an adorable tilt to his mouth.

"We're doing this?"

"Hey, this is only fair," he says. "I'm meeting my fake-future-in-laws."

"Right, because being paraded around by my family is *equal* to helping you construct your Romantasy sex scene."

"Dark fantasy," he corrects, handing it over. "Chapter nineteen. The part in the cave."

"Oh for the love of—of *course* there's a cave." I settle back on the bed and adjust the screen, ignoring the way my palms suddenly turn clammy.

"Read it."

"Okay, fine," I huff. "Elira's breath hitched as Daxion knelt between her thighs, the heat of his mouth dragging lower. He knew every inch of her better than she did. The silky glide of his tongue—"

Pause.

Soren coughs. "Too much?"

"No, so far...it's fine," I say, even though it's very *not fine* that this man is sitting three feet from me while I read the phrase *'the silky glide of his tongue'* without exploding into a million fragmented pieces.

Soren focuses on my mouth before meeting my eyes.

I keep going. "Daxion murmured spiritual words, as if her body were scripture and he was willing to worship it until the gods themselves begged him to stop."

My mouth drops open slightly. I peek up.

Soren's not smiling anymore. He's *watching* me. Carefully. Anxiously. My reaction matters to him. I soften.

"Not good?"

"That was... poetic, Soren."

"Too poetic?"

"Maybe a little. It's still good. Almost as if a sonnet and a thirst trap had a baby." I clear my throat. "But, uh, maybe we dial down the divine imagery? Unless Daxion's literally summoning orgasms with sacred incantations."

"I mean... he *is* a high priest of the Shadow Order—"

I hold up a hand. "Nope. Not unpacking that."

A beat of silence.

"What if instead of scripture, he *listens* to her body. Responds to the way she squirms. The little catches in her breath. Stuff like that."

Nodding appreciatively, Soren jots it all down on a notepad, acting like we're in some unholy writer's room from hell.

"And the kissing?"

"What about it?"

"Am I overdoing it? Would you..." He scratches his eyebrow. "Would you mind reading the next paragraph out loud? To hear how it flows."

The next paragraph. Right.

I take a breath. "Daxion kissed Elira's lips, desperate and seeking, then pressed his forehead to hers as his fingers sank inside her. She was sanctuary itself, the one place he no longer had to be strong."

A pulse flares in my stomach. Heat rushes through me so fast it feels akin to a betrayal—my body's officially joined the Dagger Daddy's without looping me in.

I struggle to finish the line and shut the laptop so hard, Soren jumps. "I'm not reading any more of that unless you want me to explode into dust and shame," I announce, standing up and fanning my face.

"I take it that's a no on the act-it-out option?"

"Soren!"

He's breathing a little faster. It appears I'm not the only one imagining how those kisses might taste.

Planting both hands on my hips, I pace, trying to shake the

mental image of the *Shadow Order High Priest Oral Sex Magic* out of my brain.

Soren watches me the way someone might watch a cat approach a priceless vase—hoping for the best, fully expecting destruction.

"Ava," he says, "I'm desperate."

"Clearly."

He scoots to the edge of the bed. "You're the best spice writer I know when it comes to female POV."

"I'm probably the only spice writer you know."

"That too," he replies. "I need this scene to work. I've rewritten it eight times. Camille said the early version sounded like a campfire tutorial, and the last one made her yell the word *'clammy'* out loud in a meeting."

I wince. "Yikes."

"I'll buy you all the caramel blondie coffees you want. Just..." He clasps his hands in mock prayer. "Help me."

When I hesitate, he ups the stakes. "I'll take you to your favorite indie bookstore—it probably has creaky floors and a small dog who'll hate me—and I'll do the ShelfSpace challenge. Three minutes. As many books as you can carry. I'll be your pack mule. I'll finance the entire thing."

"That sounds expensive."

"I'm prepared to drop thousands," he says solemnly. "Possibly tens of thousands. My credit score will never recover. But your advice? Worth it."

With a groan, I flop back onto the bed beside him. "You're lucky I'm a sucker for suffering artists."

Soren grins. "Is that a yes?"

"Give me the laptop before I come to my senses."

Beaming, he passes it over.

I reopen the document. Find the spot. And start reading again.

"Elira arched beneath him, thighs trembling as Daxion

dragged his mouth over her breast and up, so slowly it might've been cruel if it didn't make her whimper for more."

My throat tightens, but I power through.

"Daxion's hand settled low on her mound, thumb teasing her clit, holding her steady as his tongue found her heat once more and tasted her as though she was holy. As though he'd been starving for her."

My face *flames*. Soren's eyes are fixed on me, brows raised in anticipation.

"Well?" he asks, voice far too casual.

I press my lips into a tight line.

"Based on the color of your face, I'm guessing I got it right."

I swallow.

He chuckles, pleased with himself. "So the 'starving for it' line works?"

"It's... evocative. But I'm getting déjà vu. It's been used a million times."

"Evocative like *holy shit, take me*, or more like *eh, we'll cut it in edits*?"

"Both," I reply. "Mostly the first. Aggressively the first."

I stare at him.

He stares right back.

The air turns thick with heat. And the fact that I'm still picturing that scene—with *his* voice. *His* hands. *His* mouth.

God, please make it stop.

"Do you want me to keep going?" I ask, barely above a whisper.

His answer is immediate. "Yes."

So I do. Slowly. Carefully. Reading each word aloud with as much detachment as I can fake. That façade cracks the second I hit the next page:

"Elira rolled her hips, greedy now, chasing the friction. And when Daxion's fingers curled just right—she broke, shattering with a cry she tried to muffle. But he didn't care who heard it. Let it ring out for all the realms."

My voice falters. Soren shifts closer. The warmth of him sweeps over me. His thigh brushes mine, and my breath hitches. The laptop between us is a loaded weapon. I'm afraid that if I look up, his eyes might match the desire in mine.

That invisible tether pulls taut between us–the ache of proximity daring us to make it more. I'm desperately trying not to fall into something that's already happening.

His voice is raspy when he asks, "That last line? Was it too much?"

"No," I say quietly. "It wasn't enough."

The space between us narrows by a breath.

Clearing my throat, I shift on the bed and tuck my hair behind my ear as though the movement might sweep the tension away. "So, where did you get the inspiration for Elira?" I aim for light, but the question holds more weight than I want it to. I find myself jealous of the woman behind the character.

Soren leans in, as if he's about to share a secret or touch me. Maybe kiss me. I don't know which would be worse. Or better.

His throat bobs, then he whispers, "You."

My mouth falls open. A shiver rolls across my skin. Those three little letters dance *everywhere*. My knees gravitate toward him on instinct. My hand flutters to my neck, a nervous tic or invitation, I don't even know anymore.

A storm brews inside Soren's raging silver eyes. Lifting his hand, fingers ghost along the curve of my jaw, marking the moment. If he moves forward one more inch, we'll shatter the fragile line we've drawn.

His gaze drops to my mouth. Mine stays locked on his.

And then—

"*Knock knock knock,*" Fisher sings, striding in without warning.

Lurching away from Soren so fast, I fall off the bed and hit the floor with a *thud*. Soren immediately reaches for me, but I scramble back up.

Fisher halts and sniffs the air. "Why does this room smell

faintly of sexual tension and burnt popcorn?" His eyes bounce between Soren and me. "Oh my God, were you two about to bang?"

"Nothing was happening," I stammer.

Fisher crosses his arms. "Ava, blink twice if *The Blade* is seducing you." He doesn't mean Soren's nickname.

"There was no seducing."

"Uh-huh." Fisher flops into the armchair and pops a piece of gum into his mouth. "Well, *something* was happening, and I just saved you from turning this into Chapter Thirteen of *Things That Complicate Book Tours.* You're welcome."

Soren coughs and casually grabs a throw pillow to cover his lap. "Thanks, man."

Fisher squints at Soren's crotch. "Oh no. Were you pitching tent? Don't get mad at me because I'm the plot twist you needed."

"Get out," I mutter, cheeks still flaming.

Fisher grins wider. "Fine. I'll leave you to your slow burn. But if you're going to combust spontaneously, can you at least wait until I've had dinner?"

Sauntering out, he leaves the door wide open behind him.

Soren and I sit there in stunned silence.

I bury my face in my hands. "I'm sorry about him."

Soren's voice is laced with reluctant laughter. "No worries."

A beat passes.

Then another.

Neither of us moves. Neither of us dares to look at the other.

My cheeks are still hot. The pillow is still covering his lap. The computer is still open on the bed, glowing with all the things we're both thinking and don't say, and all the things I want him to do to me.

I clear my throat. "Um, well, I'm gonna head to bed."

Soren huffs out a quiet laugh. "Dream sweet, Bells."

Even though the moment's passed, even though Fisher blew

in as the world's most bonkers chaperone, the tension growing between Soren and me is a song waiting to restart.

We could pretend we didn't gaze at each other the way we did. But that would be a lie.

I leave the room and hurry straight to mine, grabbing my phone off the nightstand, and shooting a text to my mother.

> Hey, quick heads-up.

> I'm bringing someone home for Thanksgiving.

> Please don't panic. Or do that thing where you text the entire family.

OH MY GOD. Is it the hot fantasy author with the smirk??? THE ONE I SAW KISS YOU ON THE INTERNET???

> Um-yeah.

Ava Bell, how DARE you casually drop this at 10:46 PM like it's a weather update. Also, we're going to discuss why you haven't told us that you're dating him.

> I've had so much going on.

I'm your mother. We're your family. Nothing should ever get in the way of that.

> I'm sorry.

OMG you're bringing Soren Pembry into my home?! To eat MY stuffing?!

> Please don't make it weird. It's new.

Are you sleeping together? Are you in love??

I need to buy matching pajamas.

> Don't do that!

I'm doing it.

Mom. I literally just said it's *new*.

He didn't have plans for the holiday and... I didn't want him to be alone. So I asked.

😭😭😭

That's so kind of you, baby.

You've always had such a big heart, even when you pretend to be a snarky little hedgehog.

Did you call me a hedgehog?

An adorable, prickly one.

Oh, I need to deep clean the guest room.

Aunt Hilda stayed in there last when she visited for the 4th of July. There's been a weird smell ever since.

Oh God.

What does he eat? Does he eat pie?

Too many visuals enter my mind with that question.

Is he allergic to anything?

I'm sure he can handle all of the above.

Fisher is coming too. FYI.

She gives a thumbs up on the Fisher info.

Oh honey, Soren has no idea what he's walking into. The aunts are going to attack him. Your father will suddenly take up whittling just to "talk man to man." And G-Ma's going to fall in love with him and feed him until he can't move.

Sounds about right.

I'm proud of you.

For opening up to someone again.

And also for snagging a fantasy villain with abs and a fanbase.

Wow. Thanks, Mom.

Nice to know none of my other achievements in life count unless they come with pecs and a ShelfSpace following.

Oh hush. I'm also proud of your books, your independence, your brains, and your perfectly arched eyebrow of judgment.

Let me have this. He's *SO HOT*.

I'm not showing him this thread.

Too late. I already drafted a welcome banner.

"WELCOME TO OUR HOME, SOREN PEMBRY. PLEASE REMOVE YOUR SHIRT."

I take it back. He's not coming.

No refunds. See you both Thursday 🩶

Fourteen

SOREN

The ride into Salem is a kaleidoscope of color and nerves, and, in my case, a mental battlefield of horniness and restraint.

I've spent the past three hours with ear buds in, flipping between different porn sites and Passionflix adaptations—thanks to Ava—and I'm taking notes for the spice scenes in my current WIP like a diligent scholar of smut.

The research has been solid—cinematic thrusts, poetic moans, a truly inspirational use of whipped cream—but every time I manage to get Captain Pembry to stand down, I glance up and see Ava in the front seat, then he perks right back up.

Looking beautiful, she's riding shotgun, haloed in sunlight. She's the freakin' goddess of romantic tension. Neck exposed. Lip caught between her teeth. Fingers tapping on her thigh. I've caught myself staring at her several times. She's seen me doing it, too. Her eyes don't know the power they hold. I'm a weak man when it comes to Ava Bell.

The rental SUV buzzes beneath us as Fisher drums along to *Mr. Brightside* blaring from the speakers. It might be his personal anthem. He's at the wheel, sunglasses on, belting out every word with the confidence of a man born for the stage, or a karaoke bar.

Once we enter Salem, I take my earbuds out, close out the

porn, and watch the town unfurl like a storybook—white picket fences, amber-leafed trees, and porches dressed for fall with garlands and gourds.

Ava leans forward, arms resting against the dash, posture relaxed in a way that tells me this place lives in her bones.

I gaze out the window. I don't have to roll it down to know the air is different here. Cleaner. Even in the confines of the car, I taste it—coastal sea salt, rustling leaves, life unburdened. Obviously, it's never been forced to carry the weight of pretending.

We pull into a gravel drive flanked by towering oaks and a front porch that's been lovingly decorated for a Thanksgiving special. Wind chimes jingle, and two pumpkins perch beside a welcome mat that probably says: *HOME IS WHERE THE HEART IS.*

The phrase feels less like a cute farmhouse quip and more like a multigenerational warning label, dipped in nostalgia and marinated in family history.

It might as well say, *YOU DON'T BELONG HERE, PEMBRY.* The thought flits through my mind before I can smother it to death, unwelcome and jagged—but true. I can't help it. My past has a way of hitching a ride, even when I'm sure I've left it behind in a different zip code.

"Here we go," Ava says with a tight smile.

The three of us pile out of the car, and the second my boots hit the gravel, the chill hits me too—crisp, edged with spice. It smells like November should.

I'm grabbing the last suitcase from the back when the front door swings open.

Before Ava even makes it up the porch steps, a woman who could easily be her older sister rushes out, arms wide. "My babies!"

Ava groans. "Mom, please."

Too late. The woman has already engulfed her daughter in a hug, then whirls to face Fisher, who lifts her off the ground and spins her in a circle.

Then it's my turn.

"Ava, introduce me to this strapping piece of literary meat," her mom commands.

Ava pinches the bridge of her nose. "Mom, stop."

Her mother waves her off.

"Mom, Soren Pembry." Ava gestures to me. "Soren, my mother, Mandy."

Momma Mandy yanks me in for a hug. A mix of apple pie and Chanel No. 5 swirls up my nose.

"I've read all your books," she supplies. "The pirate one drained my battery supply."

"Mom!" Ava barks in horror. "What the hell?"

Her mother releases me. "I'm sorry. I'm just so excited to meet you."

I flash her an appreciative grin even though I should probably feel a little awkward here. I'm used to women saying outrageous things about my books. And me.

Still, hearing it from the mother of the woman I've got a very real thing for? That's a little different.

Accepting my praise with a gracious nod, I say, "Thank you, ma'am. I'm honored."

"Oh, no, call me Mandy." She smiles, swaying side-to-side.

The screen door creaks open again, and a tall man with a head of silver-streaked hair and warm, watchful eyes emerges. His jeans are total Dad jeans, and he's wearing a quarter-zip that reads *Salem Innkeepers Association.*

"I figured I'd better come meet the man causing all the commotion."

Ava brightens. "Dad, hi!" She launches into his arms, and the way she tucks against his shoulder shows years of safety.

He hugs her back just as tightly, his hand patting her hair in a rhythm that says *mine, always mine.*

"This is Soren Pembry." Ava pulls back but keeps a hand on his arm. "Soren, my father."

The introduction barely lands because I'm still watching them—how their smiles mirror each other. Her whole face softens in his presence. Their connection doesn't need words. It's an unshakable tether that's held her together through every storm. And it makes my chest ache with respect. And maybe a bit of jealousy. I want to be that tether for her.

I wipe my palms on my jeans before reaching out. "Mr. Bell. It's a pleasure."

His grip is firm, eyes locked on mine the entire time. "Call me Tom. And welcome to our home. You got tossed into the deep end with this crew, huh?"

I chuckle. "It's been a ride. Honestly, one of the best."

Tom strikes me as a man who means what he says and listens twice as hard. I take to him immediately, probably because he reminds me of the father I never had... or the kind I always wished for. The one who didn't vanish without looking back. The one who didn't trade blood for distance. The one who didn't leave a son wondering why he was never enough.

He claps my shoulder, then lifts the gravy boat slightly. "Hope you're hungry. You'll need your strength around here."

"Come inside before your good looks freeze off," Mandy says.

We roll our suitcases into the house. Fisher and her father shove them into a hallway to the left while Ava takes a right, and we're met with a full-blown sensory ambush.

The living room wraps around me in plaid throws and soft armchairs, twinkling lights woven through garland that climbs the banister like ivy.

Every wall bursts with framed memories—smiling faces, graduation caps, baby feet, decades of haircuts—and the entire place is enveloped with holiday essentials, gravy, cinnamon, and something fried and life-affirming simmering in the air. My stomach lets out an actual growl.

Fisher comes up behind us and mutters, "Martha Stewart and Betty Crocker had a baby and let her redecorate with Ina Garten's credit card."

We're barely two steps inside before the chaos swallows me whole, cousins coming in hot with loud hugs and perfume clouds, aunts who reek of spicy cloves, one named Hilda who is doused in eye-watering perfume. They throw out unsolicited opinions, along with a rapid-fire of names that I immediately forget. After only two minutes inside, my brain hurts. And I absolutely love it.

A rogue neighbor named June–who swears she's a psychic and calls me "a brooding Capricorn with a restless third eye"– introduces herself.

And then there's Brinley.

Ava points to a woman with a toddler fused to her hip. Two blur-speed boys circle her like caffeinated satellites.

The woman turns her head and yells across the room, "Do you need to go potty? You're holding your penis!"

"That's my cousin, Brinley."

I choke on absolutely nothing.

Ava smiles sheepishly beside me. "Welcome to my family."

Off in the distance, another small boy screams about poop and sprints down the hallway with a glowstick.

Bouncing the toddler, Brinley approaches, offering me a one-handed wave. "Hi! Sorry, we're...a lot."

I raise my hands in surrender. "I'm adaptable."

Ava starts popping her knuckles. That's the first time she's done that, that I've noticed.

To help ease the commotion, I whisper something funny in her ear. "Might want to fashion those tinfoil hats, Bells. This is the kind of battlefield training no one's prepared for."

She smiles, then suddenly straightens. "Oh God."

"What?" I brace myself for her answer.

"Uncle Marty's mixing a fall cocktail."

"I call it the Gallows Gulp," Uncle Marty calls out, hearing her. He waves us over to the side bar that resembles more of an apothecary than a drink station.

"What's in them?" Ava asks, skeptical.

"It's pumpkin-spiced tequila with a splash of ghost pepper vodka and a floating eyeball candy," he says proudly.

Ava narrows her eyes at the swirling orange concoction. "Halloween is over."

"It's *never* over in Salem." Eyes twinkling, Uncle Marty grins. He adds a cinnamon stick with theatrical flair, then holds it out for me to take. "Witches don't hang up their hats because the calendar flips. We marinate in spooky around here."

I accept the glass, admiring how smoke billows out of the top. Ava snatches it out of my hand before I can take a sip.

"Absolutely not," she says, shaking her head and placing the drink back on the countertop of the bar. "Learned my lesson last year when Marty's drink made Fisher believe he could summon ravens."

In that same moment, Fisher gets whisked away by the neighbor, June, for a tarot reading. He goes willingly, appearing mildly concerned yet intrigued.

And then the real showstopper arrives.

Who I can only assume is Ava's grandmother struts into the room, wearing leopard-print leggings, has two rings on every finger, and wears a confidence that suggests she's outlived at least three scandals and enjoyed every second of them, probably even started them. She's holding a wine glass in one hand and her sweatshirt proudly proclaims in sparkly letters: *GRANDMA KNOWS BEST, DON'T TEST.*

"Ava!" The woman sets her wine glass down on the nearest perch and then cups her granddaughter's face in both hands, squishing her cheeks like she's still five. "You brought me a man who clearly doesn't eat kale on purpose. That's progress, sweetheart. Maybe I'll live to see my great-grandbabies after all."

"G-Ma, don't start."

I step forward. "Ma'am, I'm Soren."

She eyes me like I'm a horse at auction. "Hmph. Good voice. Nice jaw. Decent hips. Strong thighs."

"G-MA," Ava grits out.

G-Ma ignores her. "The last man Ava brought home had

wrists smaller than mine and thought mulch came from a can. You though? I bet you could split a stump by winkin' at it."

I bite the inside of my cheek, fighting the snort of laughter clawing its way up my throat. "I haven't tried. Maybe I should."

G-Ma nudges Ava's arm. "Big hands. That's important. Gotta know if the stock is hardy before you plant the seed." She waggles her gray brows. "This man could plow a field and still have enough stamina to churn the butter. If you catch my drift."

Ava might die where she stands. I can't stop laughing.

"You did good, Ava Bean." G-Ma pats Ava's cheek, then swivels her attention to me with laser focus. Before I can brace, she clamps my hand—shockingly strong—and yanks me forward.

I expect a sweet, grandmotherly hug. What I get is a rib-crushing tackle that knocks the air straight out of my lungs. My spine pops. My eyes water.

Her mouth is right by my ear when she growls, "You hurt her, I'll break your legs."

She squeezes once more for emphasis, and I'm ninety percent sure one of my ribs waves goodbye.

"Yes, ma'am," I say. "I won't. I promise."

"You're a man who knows the value of a good woman." She bops my nose. "Eat my heart out, why don't you?"

I smile because I don't know what else to do.

G-Ma pauses and inspects my face again. "I'm jealous. If I were thirty years younger and didn't already have four ex-husbands in the grave, I'd keep you for myself." She snatches her wine glass up and drains the rest of it. "I'm off for a refill."

Ava glares at her grandmother's disappearing back. "I'm *so* sorry."

"Don't be," I grin. "She's a queen, Ava Bean."

Ava rolls her eyes. "Better than Bells."

"Is it?" I dip my head close to her ear. The air between us vibrates. "Because it makes me think of something dirty."

Ava's eyes widen, her mouth dropping open like she's caught

between outrage and intrigue, and for one glorious second, I think she might fire back, until her mom rounds the corner, smiling.

"Go on upstairs and get settled." Mandy's tone is sweet but commanding. "You and Soren are in your old room."

Ava's reply stumbles out. "My...what now? No, Fisher and Soren are rooming together."

Her mom's grin only grows. "Fisher's in the guest room."

Heat streaks across Ava's face, and I bite the inside of my cheek to keep from grinning like an idiot. She'd clearly been banking on Fisher as my bunkmate. But her mother—God bless her scheming heart—had other plans.

Ava whirls toward her mom, voice dropping into a hiss. "Mom. *No.* Absolutely not. You cannot put us in the same room."

Mandy blinks innocently. "Why not?"

"Because—" Ava flails one hand at me, like I'm Exhibit A in a trial, but says nothing. She can't. She's contractually obligated to me now.

"Handsome, polite, smells faintly of cedar and magic?" Mandy offers, completely unhelpful.

"Mom!"

Coughing into my fist, I fight down a laugh. "I don't mind bunking with Fisher."

Ava presses her palms to her temples. "This family is deranged."

"Correct," Mandy chirps. "And also correct is that you and Soren will be in your old room. Enjoy."

Ava's glare could melt steel. "Come on. The good news is, there are two full beds in there."

I nod, somewhat disappointed, and follow her to the hallway where our bags are. When she tries to take hers, I swoop in and lift it from her grip.

"Soren," she warns. I smile.

"Let me do one gentlemanly thing before your family roasts me alive."

She crosses her arms but lets me take it. We head upstairs. Ava opens the door to our room, which is filled with sunlight and an overwhelming number of throw pillows.

"There's only one bed," Ava mutters, noting the queen-sized mattress in horror. "Mom!" She whips back around and shouts down the stairwell. "What happened to the beds?"

"Gone!" Her mother calls back, "It's modern times! We know you're not virgins."

"Mom, we aren't *that* together."

Yet... I want to say.

"Well, honey, you'd better start being *that* together," Mandy yells at us. "Open those legs, Ava. The man has options!"

I'm literally dead.

Ava stalks back inside and slams the door. "I hate this family."

I drop the bags and suitcases in the corner of the room. "I doubt that very much."

With a groan, she falls onto the bed, draping an arm over her eyes.

"I can sleep on the floor," I offer.

"The extremely *hard* hardwood floor?" she replies, rubbing her temples. "We're adults. We'll figure it out. Just... wear a shirt. No funny business."

I nod solemnly. "What's your definition of funny?"

Ava throws a pillow at my head, her aim sharper than it has any right to be. I catch the pillow mid-air, plop down on the bed next to her, shaking my head, grinning as a fool who wouldn't trade this moment for anything else.

She scoots over, but I lean down so our faces are inches apart. "I promise to stay on my side. Unless, of course, you ask otherwise."

She huffs a laugh. "Please. That'll never happen."

"Stranger things have," I counter. "Like us, in this house, in this bed. Your mom was practically shoving me up the stairs with a neon sign that flashed, 'Breed Here.'"

Ava's groan could register on the Richter scale. "Do not say 'breed' in my childhood bedroom."

"Fine. Multiply?"

She yanks another pillow and hurls it at me. This one actually connects. Square to the chest. I let it drop dramatically to the floor as if she's slain me.

"Dead," I gasp. "Killed by Ava Bell and her throw pillows."

Her lips twitch, the faintest betrayal of a smile slipping through, and the tension in the air between us lifts. Just a hair. Just enough to tempt me.

I roll onto my back, hands folded behind my head, pretending not to notice how close she is, how her scent hovers, how the ceiling fan hums, holding its breath for us.

"Your family's amazing, by the way."

"They're insane." Ava runs her hand over the quilt. "But yeah... I know. Even though I complain."

I hesitate, fingers tugging at the hem of my shirt. "You're lucky."

Her eyes flick to mine. She sits up. "What about your family? Are they as crazy as mine?"

I swallow, shift in place. "They're—uh...not in the picture."

Ava goes quiet, then says gently, "You don't have to talk about it."

"No, it's fine. But being here? It's a lot. In a good way."

Her hand covers mine, and the touch sends a jolt of warmth straight up my arm. "You're doing awesome. I'm impressed by your fake boyfriend acting skills. You make it seem real. They're totally buying it. Which means they'll be crushed when I tell them it's over between us in January."

She says it lightly, teasingly, but every syllable scrapes against me like a jagged blade.

I want to tell her it's not acting. That none of this—her hand on mine, the warmth of her skin, how her smile turns this family circus into a dream I never want to wake up from—feels fake. I want to tell her I'm not performing. I'm not *The Blade*, Dagger Daddy, or her viral rival. Definitely not her fake boyfriend. I'm a man who's finally found someone worth wanting with his whole damn soul.

But I don't.

I squeeze her hand once, let go, and smile like I'm still in character. It's not the right time to tell her any of that. If she knew the truth—that every second with her is the most real I've ever been—she'd run.

A yell from downstairs, "Somebody get the turkey hats!"

Ava sighs. "Get ready. You ain't seen nothing yet, Pembry." She stands. "And for what it's worth...I'm glad you came."

"Yeah. Me too."

She smiles at me, and sugarplum fairies start dancing in my stomach at that. I'm about to throw my previous thoughts out the damn window, man up and confess my true agenda—maybe not all of it, but enough—when she flashes a small, wistful smile and adds, "I'm glad that through all of this fake dating debacle, we managed to find a way to be friends."

Friends.

The word is a dull thud in my chest.

Ava heads for the door. "See you downstairs."

I watch her go, the echo of that word still ringing in my ears. *Friends.*

I should be grateful. It's better than enemies. Better than rivals. Better than being blocked and reported.

Damn, I was hoping after our little mutual stare down over my spicy scene the other night—and the way she glared at me as if I'd read her mind—that this trip to see her family might thaw the glacier of ice between us.

But nope, I'm friend-zoned.

Still, that's a step up from nemesis.

Progress, right?

Yeah. Tell that to the part of me that's picturing her wrapped in one of those ugly holiday sweaters, curled up next to me on a couch, stealing sips of cider and letting me kiss her without an audience.

Exhaling, I scrub a hand over my stubble and mutter to the empty room, "Baby steps, Pembry."

Following the scent of roasted Turkey, buttery potatoes, and denial downstairs, I find my way to the kitchen, where Ava flits about as though she's the eye of the storm, the calm surrounded by the chaos.

Leaning against the doorway, I watch her. Curls wild, cheeks flushed.

Her mother barks orders about marshmallow ratios while Ava steals forkfuls of pie like it's a sport. After rolling out cookies for the kids to decorate, Mandy palms her daughter's cheek, leaving a white handprint. Ava doesn't even notice the small spot of cranberry sauce on her sleeve.

When one of the uncles offers to help them, Mandy waves them off with a "Don't you dare touch that pecan pie." She's running a ship and a sitcom at the same time.

Ava's engulfed by a mix of craziness and comfort, and she's completely in her element. One of her little cousins barrels from out of the living room and launches himself at her full speed. She catches him midair on instinct and wraps him in her arms, kisses the top of his head, and keeps right on talking while he clings to her like a koala.

Everything inside me twists.

Ava's beautiful. She's *rooted*. She's effortless, capable, full of fire and softness. She's something I've never let myself want.

Until now.

The next hour is a blur of being passed around as though I'm the last deviled egg at a church potluck.

I'm answering questions about my books, my skincare

routine, and whether I'm "the one who wore the poet blouse on ShelfSpace."

Before I can even finish my sentence, Mandy starts corralling everyone for family pictures. I politely offer to take them, phone already in hand, but she waves me off.

"Nope. You're in them too, sweetheart," she says, already dragging me into the frame with a grin that promises she'll be telling this story at our wedding someday.

I hope that comes true.

There's the full family shot. One with the cousins. The siblings. And then—because Mandy is on a mission—she insists on a few of just Ava and me.

"Smile," she chirps, snapping away before Ava can object. She shows us the pictures afterward, and a fist of feelings punches me right in the gut.

I grin. And it's not forced.

I'm standing next to Ava, her shoulder brushing mine, her family buzzing around us, and I belong here. I don't have to fake much of anything. There's something disarming about it all. The warmth. The noise. The way her little cousin just slipped his hand into mine as though it's the most natural thing in the world.

And then there's her.

Smiling through clenched teeth. Barely holding it together. Still the most magnetic person in the room.

Fisher comes up behind Mandy. "Could you send those to me?"

"Of course," Mandy replies.

Guilt worms its way through my veins. This photo isn't for ShelfSpace, followers, or press tours. It's a picture of us that no one's staging. There's zero branding. Zero spin. It's Ava and me... Pretending to be something we aren't.

Reality hits. *Shit.*

My shoulders fall. I want it to be real. God help me, I want this fiction to become fact.

"Can you send them to me, too?" I ask Mandy.

Ava's head snaps in my direction. "Why?"

She's squinting up at me like I asked for a lock of her hair to add to my voodoo shrine.

Shrugging, I keep it casual. "We look good together. It's a nice picture."

Her eyes narrow. "You planning to doodle devil horns on me and post it with a snarky caption?"

"Tempting. But no."

Ava crosses her arms, clearly unconvinced. "Seriously. Why?"

There's a pause. My gaze meets hers. "Because this—" I gesture around us, at her family laughing in the kitchen, pumpkin pie wafting in the air, the photo that captures us, together. "Feels nice. And I want to remember it."

A mixture of confusion and uncertainty flies across her face. Ava opens her mouth, but doesn't speak. Her arms drop slightly. She moves into my frame so nobody can hear her say, "You being sincere when you're not on camera is messing with my head."

"Get used to it."

Her cheeks flush the faintest shade of pink. "I might draw horns on *you*."

"I hope you do."

I love this version of her. She lets me in—grudgingly, sarcastically. I'll take it.

Afterward, someone hands me a staple gun, and suddenly I'm on a ladder helping string lights while Ava's aunt tells me I have "good shoulder posture."

I carry folding chairs, open a stubborn jar, fix a rogue cabinet hinge, and sneak not one—but *eight*—sips of The Gallows Gulp from Uncle Marty's thermos, which tastes like cinnamon, jet fuel, and is sure to turn into a horrible decision later. Or possibly a good one. We'll see.

Dinner is an explosion of colorful conversations. Not one soul can escape the turkey hats. Even Tom is wearing one—though he keeps muttering about losing a war for this.

Mandy passes the rolls. Tom drops a turkey leg in a toddler's lap. G-Ma leads a toast that turns into a eulogy for her third husband—who's very much still alive but 'dead to her.'

"Didn't she say she had four dead exes?" I ask Ava quietly.

"Honestly, we stopped counting years ago."

Confused, I nod anyway and set my attention back on the craziness before me. Ava's little cousin insists I'm a wizard. I might be. The Gallows Gulp is doing things.

"So," Uncle Marty pipes up, eyes glassy from his own drink, "how long have you two lovebirds been together? This is all so sudden to me."

Ava stiffens beside me. "Oh, um—"

"Did you meet on one of those apps?" Aunt Lo asks, shoving a casserole at me.

Before Ava can answer, her mother chimes in with a knowing smile, "No, he's the online nemesis, remember? He made fun of her books on all those videos. Went viral."

"Actually," I start, trying to help, "we—"

"Is he the one you called 'that cocky writer boy with a face for sinful things and a womb broom to boot'?" Another aunt—I forget her name—adds from down the table.

Ava chokes on her wine. "I never said that."

"Sure you didn't." G-Ma clicks her tongue. "We've got the group texts, Sugar."

As the table erupts with laughter, I reach under the table and gently place my hand on Ava's bouncing thigh, hoping to reassure her, or ground her, but she jumps like she's been shocked. I retract my hand, the heat of her thigh still lingering on my palm.

Ava blurts, "Excuse me," before pushing back from the table.

Around me, the noise continues. I want to follow Ava, explain why I touched her, ask her—*no beg her*—to let me in, only a little, or at the very least, talk to me about what's bothering her. "Friend" to "friend."

But I don't. It's not the right time. Ava needs space.

Eventually, the crazy winds down. Bellies full and plates scraped clean, the group separates into little pods—some toward the back porch for cigars, others toward the living room to claim space in front of the football game.

Lingering at the edge of the kitchen, I offer to help clean. Mandy shakes her head no, then reconsiders when I insist a few more times.

"Alright, handsome, you're on drying duty."

"My favorite." I grin, clapping my hands and rubbing them together.

We fall into an easy rhythm, her washing and me drying. It's quieter now, the family buzz melting into a post-feast lethargy.

My gaze lands on a photo above the sink—a much younger Ava, gap-toothed and muddy-kneed, proudly holding up a pumpkin twice her size.

I nod toward the picture. "She looks fierce."

"She was," Mandy replies with a soft smile. "Still is. That was her in second grade. Refused to let anyone help her carry that thing to the truck. Said if she picked it, she'd handle it."

"Sounds about right."

"Ava's been that way since birth. Headstrong. Big-hearted. She's had it broken into a million tiny pieces, so be careful with her, Soren. If Ava gives you the chance to be the one she lets in, don't waste it."

I nod, throat tight. "I won't. Any other advice?"

"Guard your heart, though." Mandy's voice dips, a little heavier now. "My girl retreats when things get to be too over-whelming. It's her defense mechanism. There might come a time when you'll need her and she won't be there, not because she doesn't care, but because she's terrified. You'll think she's selfish, but she's not. She's just scared. Ava doesn't understand love the way she writes it... not yet. She can pen happily-ever-afters for everyone else, but when it comes to her own?" Mandy shakes her head slowly. "She's still learning what that looks like."

"I'll wait as long as it takes for her to learn."

Mandy stops washing, looks over at me. "I believe you. I can't wait for Ava to experience that. She's got these walls. Gorgeous things, built from pain and brilliance and stubbornness. If anyone's gonna tear them down, it'll be someone who sees the masterpiece underneath." She grips the edge of the sink, exhales. "She needs a man who's serious and won't walk away when it gets messy, Soren. I'm not asking you to promise that. I'm just asking for you to understand it."

My voice is hoarse when I answer, "I promise, Mandy."

She offers a gentle, approving smile and slides another dish into the drying rack. The scent of rosemary and lavender soap blends with the wood smoke drifting through the open window.

How badly I want this hits worse than ever before. Not just Ava. But this messy, complicated, nosy, wonderful family. I've been folded into something bigger than myself, and I want it permanently.

But the guilt creeps in like rot. We're lying to them. Every laugh, every toast, every photo snapped tonight with me beside Ava is built on a stunt. A PR move. An illusion.

These people deserve more than what we're giving them. Ava deserves more, too.

I close my eyes for a breath. Re-centering. I need to remember that I didn't come here to keep up appearances.

She's what I want.

She's what I'm staying for.

I'll prove that to her.

After Mandy and I finish drying the last dish, I go searching for Ava.

I pass through the den, where a handful of her relatives are engaged in a loud debate about the Red Sox bullpen. I avoid that one.

In the front room, Fisher is standing on a chair wearing a fishnet shirt, dramatically reading everyone's fortunes from a tea-stained napkin. There are feathers in his hair. Why? I don't ask.

"Fisher," I call out, trying to snag his attention. "You seen Ava?"

He gives me a knowing look, climbs down off the chair, and

adjusts his shirt. "Tree house, friend. Goes there when she needs some peace." Fisher grabs two glasses from a nearby table and hands them to me. "Wine is on the rack on your way out. Good luck."

Snatching a bottle of red, along with a corkscrew from a basket holding several of them, I step outside and let the screen door close behind me.

The crisp air nips at my skin, scented with pine needles and the faint sweetness of fallen leaves. It's quieter out here. The laughter and music from inside are now muffled, becoming a memory I'm already starting to miss.

My eyes scan the backyard. Tucked beneath the arms of two old oaks, half-shrouded by shadows and strung with soft fairy lights, is Ava's treehouse. Elevated above eye level, it's more than a childhood hideout. It's her sacred spot.

And she's up there. And I'm suddenly very nervous.

I hesitate for a moment, debating on giving Ava the distance she so obviously needs, but my selfish nature takes over, driving me straight toward her.

Shoving the corkscrew in my pocket, I climb the ladder, strategically carrying the wine and glasses with me. Each step creaks under my weight, an echoing heartbeat in the quiet.

Ava's silhouette is my guiding light under the golden glow inside. Once I'm at the top, I see her. Knees tucked to her chest, a blanket wrapped around her, eyes on the stars beyond the little open window. She's surrounded by this space that's so precious to her. The secrets it must keep.

I want to be someone who belongs here, in this perfect, quiet corner of the world. With her.

She doesn't say anything as I ease onto the floor beside her, setting the wine down first. It's cramped in here, and my knees bump hers. The air is warm and fragrant with cedar and the fading scent of chimney smoke. It's intimate. As though the whole world forgot to press record on this moment—and I'm grateful for it.

I pour two glasses. Ava's fingers brush mine when she accepts hers. We sip in silence for a beat.

"This place is..." I pause, searching for a word that's worthy.

"Magic." Ava finishes for me. She smiles, leaning her head back against the wood-paneled wall. "My dad built it when I was six. Told me every girl needed a castle. I said I wanted a hideout instead. So he gave me both."

"You spent a lot of time up here, then?"

"Every weekend. After school. I used to bring my notebook and write for hours. Or read. Sometimes I'd lie here and listen to the wind."

"I didn't have anything this cool growing up." My eyes scan the space. "Not even close."

Her voice softens. "Where did you grow up?"

"L.A. But not the shiny parts." I take a drink, letting the tannins roll over my tongue. "Tiny apartment. Paper-thin walls. My dad was a mechanic, always working. Mom left when I was eight. Never came back. I have no idea if she's living or dead."

Ava winces. "Oh, Soren, I'm sorry."

"It's fine." It isn't.

"How did you cope?"

I think back. "My middle school English teacher saw potential in me. Taught me how to read for escape—and write for it too."

Ava is cradling her wine glass between her palms, listening. "Is that when your writing career began?" She smiles.

"Yeah. Stories were my way of running away. I'd stay up late making up lives for other people. Better ones."

There's a pause, and then she gently asks, "You ever write about them? Your parents?"

My throat nearly closes up. I stare down at the wine in my glass. "I used to. But sometimes it got too real, and I needed distance."

She nods. Questions are swimming in her eyes—waiting to be asked.

With a sigh, I shift to lean against the opposite wall, stretching out my legs. "Truth is... my dad and I haven't spoken in years."

Ava stills. "What happened?"

I run a hand through my hair, every word a weight.

"Shit," she says. "I'm sorry. It's none of my business. I can't believe I asked that."

"Please, I don't mind. My father didn't understand why I didn't want to work at the shop. Or why I quit that job at the ripe age of eighteen to write full-time. Said it was irresponsible. Said I was throwing everything away. We fought. I told him he never supported me anyway, so what did it matter?"

Her face crumples with sympathy.

"I published my first book a year later. I sent him a copy. He mailed it back—shredded."

"*Oh my God*, Soren—"

"It's okay, Bells. I haven't heard from him since. I certainly haven't reached out. I don't intend to. I think in the end, it was an easy out for him. He wasn't the most loving parent." My lids bat against the sting in my eyes. "Sometimes I tell myself I don't care. That he doesn't matter. But I do care. And he does matter. It all mattered."

"You matter," she says immediately, yanking my attention straight to her. The silence between us grows with each breath. Ava scoots closer. Her voice is barely audible when she adds, "That's not fair. You deserved better."

I don't respond. I don't trust my voice.

Ava reaches out and touches my arm briefly, causing a spike in my heart rate.

Staring down at where she's touching me, I let out a quiet breath. She smiles, sad and beautiful. Her fingers curl tighter around my arm, and then my eyes skim over the tiny wooden room, the bottle between us, the girl beside me, and everything in me aches with how much I want her. *Us*. But I do nothing to ease that ache. I sit in quiet with her, sipping and watching the stars twinkle into existence.

Ava speaks first. "I'm glad you came."

"You told me." I shift slightly so our shoulders touch. "And, me too." I'm not glad in a casual, polite sort of way. I'm glad in the bone-deep, don't-ever-fucking-let-go kind of way. But her calling me a friend earlier today was a punch to the chest wrapped in a bright, shiny, Christmas bow. "Thanks for inviting me."

Another small smile is her response.

I need to tell her I want more. That I *need* more. As always, I chicken out, and instead I say, "I'm sorry for grabbing your leg at dinner. I was only trying to be a safe space."

The words hang there, pathetic and limp. *Safe space?* Jesus Christ. I'm trying too hard. For being a New York Times Bestselling Author, I sure as fuck am having issues finding the right words to say to this girl.

Glancing over, her eyes are shadowed with warmth. "Don't apologize. I shouldn't have left you there. I don't know what came over me."

I study her face—defensive Ava is gone. What's left is more vulnerable. Still lit from within by the flame of whatever that moment between us was, when my palm met her thigh.

"My touch...it did something to you."

She doesn't deny it.

"Was it bad?"

"No." She exhales slowly. "I... I just wasn't prepared for it."

My heart squeezes in my chest. "Has it been a while since someone has touched you, Bells?"

After a long few seconds, she finally answers, "Yeah," her voice a whisper.

I swallow, fighting the instinct to apologize for something I didn't do. I don't care about who she's dated previously—or how many there were. Lord knows, I don't want to discuss my numbers. What gets me is the thought that no one before me made her feel like she mattered. So I reach for the only thing that might make her smile.

"Well," I say, aiming for lightness, "your grandma keeps telling me I hung the damn moon, so I'd say I'm officially in your family's top five."

A laugh. "To her, you're an upgrade. The last guy—whom I dated for a whole five minutes before deciding it would be a good idea to bring him home and meet the family—serenaded the turkey with Wonderwall."

"You're lying."

"I wish I were. He made aggressive eye contact with my dad during the chorus."

Laughter bursts out of me. "Jesus. Wonderwall?"

"He was a huge mistake."

"Clearly." My head tilts. "No wonder I'm in the top five?"

She bites her bottom lip, eyes dancing. "I brought home a male cat once. He's number one."

"And why's that?"

"He hissed at everyone and puked in my cousin's shoe. It went over about as well as *Wonderwall*, but I thought it was hilarious."

I shake my head, laughing. "Well, he was probably cute and cuddly, so that's hardly fair."

"He was definitely cute and cuddly." Her smile falters slightly. "And also... cats don't lie to you or—" She stops. The tension returns.

My smile fades. "Or, what?" The question comes out defensive.

"Not important." She lifts her glass in a toast, deflecting. "To emotional fortresses and extremely low expectations."

I clink mine against hers gently. "I don't believe that for a second."

Ava's eyes meet mine, defiant yet wounded. "Believe what? That it isn't important? Or that I don't let people in?"

"That you don't *want* to."

Her lips press together, she looks away, jaw tight. "Wanting's the easy part."

Her voice is soft. Almost like she's admitting it to herself more than to me. I don't push. I sit with it. And her. The silence between us isn't awkward; heavy rather, in the way truth always is.

Ava's fingers trace the rim of her glass, giving her something to focus on in this tense and now uncomfortable moment for her. I'm sure she's about to shut this conversation down and run. But then she surprises me.

"I used to think love was this beautiful thing. That it was supposed to fix things, overcome hardship, or conquer all," she says, opening up a little, but laughing it off at the same time. "I thought if someone loved me enough, it'd glue all the broken pieces back together."

"Do you not think that now?"

She wraps her arms around her legs, glass still in hand. "Now, I think love is a hammer. You let someone in, and they'll swing that hammer, making all your cracks worse."

My heart sinks. "Not everyone swings to hurt."

"I wouldn't know," she confesses.

My heart breaks when she says that. I actually feel it shatter inside my chest.

Offering something quieter than words, I reach over and gently brush my knuckles against hers, giving Ava something more peaceful than a promise. Presence. Patience. "I'm not one of them, Ava. If I ever swing, it's to clear the rubble, not to hit the person standing in it. Old walls come down, and then you build something more beautiful with that person."

Her uncertain gaze finds mine, searching.

I let the silence hold, so that it means something before I try to ease the weight between us. "But for the record," I add, smirking a little, "I'm terrible with tools. Probably best if you don't hand me a hammer."

Ava gives me the smallest laugh—a spark of light breaking through the heaviness—and I feel it in my chest.

"Better with swords?" she teases, the corner of her mouth lifting, eyes glinting in the low light.

"Infinitely," I reply with a smirk. "Though fair warning—

when it comes to you, I'd never fight fair." I'm resting my elbows on my knees, a grin tugging at my lips before I can stop it. "I feel like this has deeply bonded us." There's a tinge of mischief in my tone. "And now, I know the bar I have to clear is post-poultry Oasis covers."

Ava laughs again, pulling her hand to her chest, and for the first time all night, it doesn't feel like she's running. If anything, she's leaning in, and maybe, finally, I'm the one catching up.

Angling toward her, my knee brushes hers—just a fleeting touch, but enough to spark through me like flint on steel. She still won't meet my eyes, yet her hand drifts down from where it guarded her chest, a quiet surrender, as if the gates of her fortress have opened wide enough to let me step inside.

My fingers graze hers—light, uncertain—more question than touch. *Can I reach you? Can I stay here, like this, a little longer?*

"You don't have to keep bracing for impact," I say quietly.

Her gaze lifts, cautious but curious. "What?"

"For people to hurt you," I clarify. "Some of us show up to hold what's broken."

Her eyes search mine, wary and bright, and for a heartbeat, I swear she lets me in. The wall's still there—thinner now, splintering some. If I breathe too hard, it might finally give.

"If you ever gave me a chance with you, I mean."

We sit, suspended in the delicate and the dangerous until she moves, leaning into the moment without realizing it. I take it as permission.

One more inch.

My hand slides to Ava's cheek, tentative at first, then sure. Her skin is warm under my palm. Lowering my voice, because anything louder would break this spell, I say, "I'm going to kiss you now, Bells."

Her breath falters. I feel it. We're so close, I count the flecks of amber in her eyes.

"Unless you tell me not to."

Not a word comes out of those perfect lips.

One more inch.

Slow at first, testing the limits of a wish I never thought I'd get to make, I kiss Ava's lips. They're soft, warm, hesitant for a heartbeat... and then she exhales into it, and everything changes. She starts kissing me like she's been holding back for years and has finally stopped caring about the consequences.

And then–

Ava pounces.

The clink of wine glasses hitting the floor is faint, forgotten as she pushes me flat against the creaky floorboards of the treehouse.

I grunt in surprise, hands finding the curve of her hips as she straddles me, hair falling around us in a red curtain.

Her mouth is everywhere—my lips, my jaw, my throat. Slender fingers twist into my shirt, tugging, claiming.

I'm hard beneath her in seconds. No hope of hiding it. Especially when Ava starts to grind against me, chasing a need that's clearly been burning inside her, the same as it has in me.

A groan slips out. *"Fuuuck."* My hands tighten around her waist, guiding her rhythm, drinking in every gasp and shiver as if they could be my last.

She stops. Freezes, really. And sits up. One hand braces my chest, the other is curled at her side as though she's not sure what it's doing there. Her breathing is ragged. Her lips are swollen and parted. Her eyes were wide and glassy, darting away from mine.

"You okay?" I ask softly, not moving.

Her throat bobs like she's pushing razor blades down when she swallows. "I—" She scrambles backward like the floor's on fire. "I'm sorry. I didn't mean to—I don't—"

"Ava." I reach for her. My voice is firm, not demanding.

She tugs her sleeve down, needing armor. I can tell she regrets every second that just passed. "I shouldn't have—God, that was so stupid."

"No." I wait until her eyes meet mine. "That was *you* wanting something. And there's nothing stupid about that."

Ava's expression shows me she doesn't know how to process kindness from a man when it's handed to her without conditions.

"I don't know what came over me." The cracks in her voice gut me.

"Neither do I," I admit. "But I'm damn glad it happened."

I scoot closer. She scoots back.

I take a breath. "I like you, Bells. I'm not here for the version of you that always has it together. I want the chaos, the contradictions, the impulse-control failures, and the *oh shit* moments." I pause, let it land.

Her eyes well slightly. She wipes the tears away fast.

"And that kiss?" A soft smile tugs at my lips. "Best moment of my life that I wasn't prepared for."

Ava's chest rises and falls heavy with breath. "I—I can't," she whispers, eyes suddenly wide, voice raw.

The moment floats away into the cold night air as she slips out of the treehouse before I can say a word, leaving the ghost of her mouth on mine, her body on top of me, and the now familiar scent of cinnamon and cloves in the air.

Soren Pembry

New York Times Best-Selling Fantasy Author

Bells,

You're right beside me. I could reach out and touch you. But I can't do that. We're "friends." Nothing more.

You drew that line in the sand. And I'm trying to respect it, even though every breath I take feels like I'm choking on it.

Ever since this contract between us started, there have been nights I can't sleep. It's not the noise outside, or work, or stress, or headlines, or dead-lines keeping me awake.

Nope.

I can't sleep because my heart's too full of you. Your voice, your laugh. The way you say things like they're throwaways when they're anything but.

And right now, I can't sleep because the space beside me is cold, even though your stubborn warmth is right there. Despite anything that's happened between us, you're insisting this is fake while I'm falling harder every day.

For instance, take today. You showed me your world. You didn't treat me like an outsider looking in, but someone who might belong there also.

That's scarier than anything I've ever written.

Thanks to you, I can't stop replaying what happened in the treehouse. Your lips met mine of their own volition. You gave in, for one delicious, glorious second before pulling away.

My heart's recovering. Other parts... not so much.

After you went to bed, I stayed downstairs, couldn't bring myself to climb into this bed and pretend like none of it happened. I waited until I knew you were asleep. Then I crept in like a coward, heart in my throat, hoping you'd shift toward me in your sleep. You haven't.

Alas.

I'm not sure when I'll have the courage to tell you all this, so for now, I'll let the dark and this paper keep my secrets.

Love,

S

Fifteen

AVA

It's stupid early. Pale, blue-gray light is creeping in through the gaps in the curtains. Everything's quiet and still. The house, usually groaning with the morning bustle of my parents and coffee machines, is silent. I can't sleep. Not with Soren curled around me as though he was made to fit there, all heat and hard lines.

At some point in the night, we must've gravitated toward each other. His leg is notched between mine, and one arm is locked around my middle like I'll float off if he lets go. His breath brushes against my neck in warm puffs. And there's one more issue.

A very... *present* issue.

Soren's morning wood nudges my backside with its own agenda. From how thick and obscenely hard his "flesh sword" is, it could apply for its own zip code.

Jesus.

Then, as I lie there, caged between his arms, the unthinkable happens.

My brain cues up a smutty slideshow of every angle, all the positions, me panting as I imagine Soren burying himself deep inside me with his thick, obscenely hard cock.

Raging.

Punishing.

Fucking me in ways no one ever has.

A needy ache blooms low, and I squeeze my thighs together. As if that's going to help. It doesn't, obviously.

Fuck, what has gotten into me? I'm not supposed to want him. He's my fake boyfriend. My online nemesis. My one-man PR disaster.

And yet. Here I am. One sleepy thrust away from throwing all my emotional boundaries in a blender and asking him to rearrange my insides.

For research, of course. Something other than porn and Passionflix. Real-life, hands-on experience.

My eyes fly open.

Nope. Nope, nope, nope.

This behavior has to stop. From me launching myself on top of him last night, to now, enough is enough.

Inching forward, I manage to create a little space between us, but Soren's arm tightens. A soft, possessive murmur escapes him. Even asleep, he's got a sixth sense for retreat.

I stay still.

Mistake.

My body—traitorous, stupid, and apparently starved for touch—shifts back the tiniest bit.

That's all it takes.

Suddenly, Soren's moving, grinding against me with a seductive roll of his hips. He's solid and ready, and the shape of him is pressed firmly against the curve of my ass.

Another laggard grind, and that razor-sharp pulse ignites, heat blooming between my legs with humiliating urgency.

Closing my eyes, I bite back a curse, mortified that a half-conscious thrust got me wet.

Thankfully, Soren turns onto his back. Right when I think I might escape this unholy situation without dying of mortification

—his body turns again, his arm jerks, yanks me back, and I'm flush against a wall of warm, sleepy muscle.

My stomach nosedives. My breath is caught in my throat. I. Can't. Move. *Fucking hell.*

"Soren," I hiss. No response. Maybe he's dreaming. Maybe this is some involuntary—

He chuckles.

"Oh my God." I twist to break free. No dice, his grip is relentless. "You did that on purpose?"

"When you wiggle against it, what do you expect?" His voice is rough with sleep. He doesn't even pretend to be sorry. "Men can't help it. Especially when you rub up against us with your ass."

"How long have you been awake?" I demand he confess, spinning in his arms.

"Since the moment you sighed and did that little... arch thing."

"I didn't do an arch thing."

"You did."

I gape at him. "You're unbelievable."

One shoulder of his shrugs, cocky and clearly unfazed. "Hey, don't blame me. Your ass clearly has a crush on my dick. And full disclosure—he's into it. He thinks your ass is pretty damn cute too."

My mouth tumbles open at his crass words.

Soren grin widens. "They've got chemistry, Bells. Could be special. Beautiful, even."

I scramble away from him. Staying a second longer might shatter whatever's left of my resolve. And I'm too goddamn horny to fight against my walls.

As I near the edge of the bed, I nearly fall off in my haste.

He props himself up on one elbow, eyes dragging over me with zero shame. "I'm just saying... if you ever want to let them explore that connection, I've got a rock-hard invitation ready to go."

Snatching the throw blanket from the footboard, I wrap it around me. "I'm going downstairs."

"You always run." His voice is no longer teasing.

I pause at the door. "*Excuse* me?"

Soren sits up, the sheets pooling at his waist. His eyes lock on me. "Why?"

"Because this is fake." The words don't come out as cold as I meant them to. They sound... tired. Broken.

"You kissed me back last night," his tone is certain. "That's twice now." His legs swing off the bed. He walks to me. Barefoot. Bare-chested.

"I told you to wear a shirt."

Soren doesn't even acknowledge that statement, only continues to trudge toward me. "You pounced on me, *touched* me, ground on my dick because you wanted so much more from me than fake."

I'm retreating backward as he's stalking forward. Our eyes are latched onto each other's, and we do this little dance until my back hits the door.

"One kiss, you can fake. Twice? Nope. You can't fake twice. You also can't fake pouncing on me in your treehouse last night, *or* clenching your thighs together like your pussy's trying to cast a protection spell to keep me out. Which is what's happening right now." Strong arms cage me in. His body presses closer to mine. "Guess what, Bells. I already got past the wards."

I don't have an answer to that. Or I do, but it doesn't matter what I say, he's right.

Soren's hand reaches for mine. I yank it away. He sighs, head dropping for the briefest second before lifting back up.

His eyes connect with mine. "Stop denying what you feel."

"It's not *real*." The words are thin. I'm trying to convince a ghost of a truth I no longer believe. "Or professional."

Pine, musk, a hint of worn cotton, and an elemental scent– wild sage beneath morning dew wafts off him.

"That's what you're telling yourself."

CEDAR JAMES

The softness in his tone weaves through all the hollow parts of me before lodging in my chest, heavy and terrifying. If I let myself believe him—if I let myself believe *this*—there's no turning back. And I can't have that. I refuse to stand on the edge of a cliff that's too steep to climb if I fall.

So, I look away. It's safer than gazing into the eyes of a man who sounds as though he might actually mean what he's saying.

I know better.

"That burning inside," my voice trembles. "It's heat. Lust. It's not good, Soren."

"The fact that you can describe it to me tells me you feel it too."

Shaking my head, I duck under his arm to escape and retreat to the bed. "I'm not about to act on it."

"Except, you did."

My entire body goes rigid, nerves locking tight beneath my skin. I could tell him the truth—that I'm scared. That I'm in too deep. That he makes me feel things I can't control.

"That was a mistake," I say. "It won't happen again."

Soren strides up to me, closing the space and erasing every inch of distance I've tried to build. His hand comes up, fingers firm but gentle beneath my chin, tilting my face toward his.

"Yes, it will," he says. "And when it does, I'll make damn sure it doesn't feel like a mistake."

This is too much for me. So, I go for the jugular.

"You're confused," I say, both words clipped and cold. "Whatever fantasy you've built in your head over the last couple of days needs to end. Maybe you're just overwhelmed with the idea of family, since you don't have one."

The words hang between us like shrapnel. For a heartbeat, Soren doesn't move. Or blink. He stares at me, the color draining from his face as the hit lands exactly where I aimed. Then he nods once—pointed, contained—and looks away, swallowing hard.

I hate myself for it instantly. But hate feels safer than hope.

I plant my hands on my hips and turn away. I put the hurt in his face there, and I can't stand to look at it.

"That was a low blow, Bells."

I let out a long breath before turning back to face him. "Look, I don't do casual. And you don't do relationships. You're not the long-haul type. You're fireworks and flings that burn fast and bright. We wouldn't be right for each other anyway."

The air between us turns to ice. I'm really twisting the knife today, and I hate myself for it. But it's easier to strike first than wait to bleed.

When he speaks again, there's no anger, only quiet resolve. "It doesn't mean I can't want something different." His arms drop to his sides. "And that something different is you, Ava."

Ava? No Bells. Just... Ava.

"You don't want *me*," I say, angling my head to look back at him. "You just want to *fuck* me."

The silence that follows isn't soft or comfortable. Soren's stormy eyes flame with fire. His smile—ever-present, ever-disarming—is gone. What replaces it is ice and fury.

"Wow," he says, voice lethal. "You really think that little of me?" He steps into me, close enough to steal my air. "You think this is about sex? That I've spent *months* circling you, sparring with you, craving every damn second of you... because I'm what? Horny?"

I search for the right words, but come up empty. What does he mean he's spent months circling me? And craving every damn second of me?

"If all I wanted was sex, I could've had that with a dozen other people by now. People who didn't insult my integrity every time I gave them a piece of myself."

"Soren, I *don't* understand. We're rivals. It's a gimmick. A show. And now, that show has become a clichéd fake dating trope. For numbers. Nothing more."

Soren presses a hand to his chest as though he's physically holding himself together. Like if he doesn't keep the pressure

there, the wound I've just inflicted will split wide and spill everything he's trying so hard to keep inside. "That's where you're very
wrong." A shadowed sadness I'm not prepared for passes over his
features.

My chest tightens, a coil of confusion winding tighter with
every word. He sounds so certain, and I don't know what to do
with it. Or with him. I don't know if I should believe him or run
away before I start to.

"You, Bells," he says, softer now—dangerously so. "You're the
one I *want*. And not just in my bed." Big hands grasp my waist.
He leans down, his voice a whisper pressed between clenched
teeth. "So if you're going to accuse me of something, make it
something that actually reflects what I've *shown* you. Not this
bullshit version you've made up to protect yourself."

Soren releases me and steps away, breath ragged. I'm instantly
confused as to why I want him to come back.

"And for the record? Wanting to fuck you and *wanting you*
are not mutually exclusive." He waits, watching me as though I'm
the final page of a book he's not ready to finish. Then, that shadowed sadness reappears. This time, as his smile spreads across his
handsome face. "Maybe I'm not *known* as the long-haul type, but
I don't survive tarot readings, turkey hats, the whiplash you're
dishing out, and *family* for just anyone."

My heart is filling with emotions I've been pushing away since
the very beginning. I don't know how to trust them. Or him, for
that matter.

Wrapping my arms around myself as if I can hold in the pain
building behind my ribs, I keep my attention set on the floor. I
cannot look at him. "You don't get it."

"I do get it.' Soren approaches again. The heat of him immediately seeps into me. This man is impossible to escape.

"Those fireworks you mentioned. I want them with you. And
I'm not going anywhere until you believe it. I'll show you that
this," he motions between us, "can be real."

There's no teasing in his tone. There's not even a flirty smirk.

Only steady eyes that are locked on mine and an expression so earnest it robs me of air.

This is where my defiance kicks in. And I almost laugh. Soren *Whoren* Pembry thinks he's going to show *me* something real?

Please.

He licks his lips, tasting the promise—no, challenge–in the air. Strong, muscular arms box me in, one palm against the door behind me, the other brushing my waist. I don't move. Can't. Silver eyes dive into mine, lit with an intensely deep determination.

And then he says the line that could destroy a woman. Destroy me–

"Tell me to stop wanting you, Bells, and I swear I will. But mean it. Don't stand there and lie to me. Or yourself. Because you see...your pulse is racing. And I can tell your heart wants to leap out of your chest and into my mine."

My eyes narrow. Fuck this guy. He knows nothing about me.

"You say those same things to hundreds—maybe thousands—of women." The dig rushes out as a sharp little rustle of defense. "You make it seem easy because it is. You're practiced. Slick. *Fake.*"

Every word carves another piece out of him. His jaw ticks. He's hurt. It makes sense. I slapped him with something more painful than the truth—my doubt.

I'd be lying if I said I didn't mean it to be *so* harsh. I mean... I did, but not to that level. I wanted distance. I wanted armor. I didn't expect him to actually bleed.

That line though? About my heart wanting to leap into his? That's ridiculous. Over-the-top. Too much for most romance novels, including mine.

Yet it still made my lungs stop.

So, I stomped all over that line with spiked boots and sarcasm because I'm terrified of him.

And yes, the guilt tastes bitter in my mouth. Maybe I should've kissed him again. Or at the very least... not tried to burn down the one person who might finally understand me.

No. Don't be another one of his conquests, Ava, I plead with myself. *Don't give in. Don't yield. Don't make this mistake...*
Again.

There's a long silence between us. Soren's gaze never wavers. Neither does mine.

"Challenge accepted, Bells," he says, almost to himself, but loud enough for my rattled heart to hear.

At breakfast, the sun is higher and the smell of bacon, coffee, and toasted bread has replaced the early hush. I sit stiffly at the breakfast table next to Soren, who's maddeningly at ease.

Fisher is at the end of the table. Between bites of pancake, his eyes bounce between us as though he's watching a tennis match no one else sees.

My dad focuses on his food with monk-level devotion, and my mother... oh, she's in full Q&A mode.

"So in your book—*Fields of Fire*—what inspired that final scene in the rain?" she asks Soren, leaning in, treating him as her guest of honor on the *Morning Mandy Talk Show.*

Soren smiles, polite and impossibly charming. "Honestly? I always wanted to end a story with the rain doing the confessing when the characters couldn't."

"That's *so* poetic. God, I love that. Ava never talks about your work—why don't you talk about his books, sweetie? Then again, you didn't mention your *relationship* either, so I suppose I shouldn't be surprised."

Sipping my orange juice, I try not to glare. "We're not here to dissect my—" The word stalls in my mouth, unfamiliar but not unwelcome. "*Boyfriend's* career, Mom."

My gaze drifts to Soren. He's mid-chew, and there's the faintest smile tugging at the corner of his mouth.

The word surges through me—warm, electric. Dangerous.

I turn back to my mother. "I don't talk about his books because I haven't read them."

She appears genuinely offended. "Why not? They're literary masterpieces."

Literary masterpieces? My mother is comparing Soren's work to books like the Great Gatsby? Sure, if Gatsby railed Daisy in a cave and wore leather pants.

My head tilts. "What about mine?"

She waves a hand. "Oh, honey. Yours are cute. They're like Hallmark with cussing...and fucking."

I spit out my juice. Soren covers his mouth to hide his grin.

Oh, this is hilarious to him? Well, fuck him very much.

"It's not fair," my mother adds, "or good for relationships when one partner does stuff and the other doesn't. You need to read at least one of his books."

"He read mine to poke fun at it."

Soren clears his throat. "Actually," his voice is calm and certain, "I've read all your books."

Everything screeches full stop. My fork hovers in midair. Even Fisher quits chewing.

My mom's eyes widen. "You have?"

Soren nods, eyes on me. "Every single one."

I'm stunned into silence. Everyone, including my man-of-few-words father, is swooning.

What the fuck?

I bolt up. "I need to... get something." Grabbing my phone off the counter as an excuse, I rush up the stairs, cheeks burning so hot I'm surprised no one comments.

I don't stop until I'm inside the bathroom, the door locked behind me. Only then do I let out a shaky breath, hands braced on the sink.

The silence in here lets the weight of what happened at the table settle in.

He read them all?

Every single one?

The man I've labeled as my fake boyfriend, my online neme-sis, the one person I was so sure couldn't possibly understand me —read every single one of my books.

That's the most intimate thing anyone's ever done for me. My heart attempts to melt inside my chest, but I quickly ice it back over.

Get a grip, Ava. He read them so he could roast me with *detailed accuracy.* No other reason other than that.

Soren definitely didn't read them because he cares. Not because he might actually have feelings for me.

Maybe I'm not known *as the long-haul type, but I don't survive tarot readings, turkey hats, the whiplash you're dishing out, and family for just anyone.*

Guess we can add reading every single one of my books to that list.

Pulse pounding, throat tight, I stare at myself in the mirror. I need air. I need space. I need to not develop feelings for someone who's nothing more than a stunt. And a fuckboy.

But all I *feel* is him. His voice in my ear. The weight of his gaze. How my stomach flips when he looks at me like I'm the story he's been trying to write his whole damn life.

What the hell am I doing? I've locked myself in a bathroom, hiding like a teenager, because Soren Pembry turned around and shattered the line *I* drew between truth and fiction.

What do I do with that?

My reflection offers no answers. Only flushed cheeks, glossy eyes, and the faint outline of a girl on the edge of a cliff she swore she'd never approach.

I press a hand to my chest. Beneath my skin, my pulse races way too fast.

I can tell your heart wants to leap out of your chest and into my mine.

He can't be real.

He's not supposed to be.

He's not.

But he is. Flesh and bone, heat and heartbeat, steady where I spiral.

It takes me a few more minutes to get my shit together, and when I finally do, I head back downstairs, cheeks still warm, pride dangling by a thread.

The second my foot hits the bottom step, Mom peers up from the table with way too much interest. "Tummy issues, sweetheart?"

The room goes silent.

"What?"

Lowering her voice, she attempts to be discreet, but fails epically. "You were up there a while. I thought maybe your digestive system was acting up? You've always been sensitive to high-fat foods. Did you flush twice?"

I want to crawl into the breakfast casserole and disappear.

From that point on, every question my mother asks is one she's never asked me. Not once. And even though she means well, even though Soren is fascinating and brilliant and charming—it still stings. This charade continues for what feels like forever, even though it's probably only been a few minutes.

This isn't breakfast anymore. It's turned into a damn stage play starring Soren Pembry and featuring me as some poorly lit supporting cast.

I stab my eggs. My thigh bounces under the table, and Soren's hand captures it—either a comfort or a flirt, I can't tell anymore. That bothers me.

I allow it for the sake of the show. No dramatic flinching this time. I don't want another wide-eyed retreat. I've done that twice now.

His hand shifts. Higher. Fingers tracing at the edge of too intimate, too aware, too much.

Startled, I nearly knock over my juice, and his.

Fisher's eyes zero in on me. "You good?"

"Yeah." I side-eye Soren, who's wearing a cocky fucking smirk.

And God, he's beautiful. It's wrong to look that arrogant and that delicious before nine a.m.

My mom whispers to Fisher, "Remember that video where he said her protagonist gave him 'the slow burn of his life.' I nearly died."

Fisher swallows a bite of bacon, coughs once.

"Mom, we can still hear you."

She waves a hand, totally unbothered.

Pinching the bridge of my nose, I silently pray for a sinkhole. Or divine intervention.

Then Mom's spine goes ramrod straight, which is a sign that a *really* bad idea has sparked in her brain. "Ava, why don't you take Soren into town this afternoon? Show him the shops, the waterfront, that little bookstore you love. He's flown all this way—he should see more than our dining room and your bedroom."

I drop my fork.

"I love that." Soren beams.

This breakfast was never a meal. It was a setup.

"Great idea," I say, voice sugary enough to rot teeth. "Fisher can come too."

Soren raises a brow. Fisher freezes mid-bite. I flash a victorious smile.

Soren Pembry thought he was getting alone time with me today?

Yeah. No dice, buddy.

Feast & Fiction

Snowflake Gala

Bookmas Bash

Midnight Kisses &
Paper Wishes

Sixteen

SOREN

I've been accused of a lot of things in my life—broody, aloof, built for flings and random hookups, quick, dirty, and emotionally unavailable, but *never* of running from a challenge. *Especially* not one in the form of Ava Bell, with her stubborn heart and eyes that shoot lightning bolts.

Which is why I'm still here. Even after last night. Even after this morning. Even after breakfast. And especially after she fled the table like she was on fire and I was the gasoline.

Even now, standing in front of the house with my boots on the driveway, about to get into a car with her, for a day trip into the most ironic setting imaginable.

Salem, Massachusetts.

The town of witch trials. Of burning questions, ghost tours, and all the pent-up tension a pair of enemies-turned-fake-lovers—yes, *lovers*. I'm manifesting it.

"Where's Fisher?" Ava asks, standing on the porch, arms crossed, lips pursed, wearing a fitted black V-neck sweater that dips down, teasing at her cleavage and hugging her petite frame. Her hair is in a ponytail, giving all sorts of visuals of me gripping it tight while her lips wrap around my dick. And then again, when

I'm buried inside her from behind, tugging it back to make her moan my name.

My cock swells inside my jeans. *Down, Captain Pembry!*

"He said he was coming," she says, peering behind me.

I shrug innocently, knowing exactly how this is going to play out. I overheard Fisher and Mandy whispering in the kitchen this morning about a Christmas crafting sesh in her "She Shed," which Fisher replied with, "You mean your Smut Hut?"

Mandy pretty much gift-wrapped this solo tourist run with Ava for me. God bless her.

Just as Ava turns to head back inside, the front door swings open and there Fisher is, coffee mug in hand and fake innocence painted across his face.

"Why aren't you ready to go?" Ava asks him, confused.

"Oh," he says, British voice casual. "Forgot. Uh, I promised Mandy I'd help her with the hay bale staging for her Christmas nativity setup. Can't *bail* on the family."

Ava narrows her eyes. "You hate hay."

"Luv, I'm doing it for Jesus." He winks before backing into the house.

"Tell Jesus, I'm going to murder you," she hisses.

Trying to hide the smile spreading across my face, my chin drops to my chest. Fisher blows her a kiss, then slams the door.

Ava's cutting scowl could slice steel. I'm so thrilled for this development. No buffer. A whole day with a woman who drives me insane in every possible way.

I flash her a cocky grin. "Guess it's just you and me, Bells."

She doesn't answer.

I can't help myself. "It's also a great opportunity to prove we're the real deal to the world, don't you think? We can take a million pics and post a few vids."

The glare she levels me with nearly guts me. There's a storm brewing behind her expression that tells me her mind is grinding over a thousand unspoken questions while her heart pulls in opposite directions. She's rattled, caught between craving and caution, between the enemy she swore I was and the man she's already reached for. Twice.

I'm blurring the hell out of that line for Ava, and I can see her trying desperately to stitch the boundaries back together, to decide where the performance ends and the truth begins.

What's left is her fear—feral, stubborn. But armor *can* be broken. When it does, she'll finally see what I've known all along: none of this has ever been pretend.

I'll show her. And I now know, after everything—me laying my cards out on the table like I did this morning— that I need to be strategic with Ava. Cautious as fuck. I have to do it through the role she's *letting* me play.

Game on, Bells.

A beat of silence ticks between us, then she's stomping toward the SUV.

I follow.

The rental smells of stale coffee and cheap car spray when I open the passenger side door for her. She hesitates. I catch the unease in her eyes as she climbs in without a word.

After rounding the front, I open the door on the driver's side, and slide into the seat.

Now, it's just me, her, and enough awkward tension to power a Tesla.

Let's do this.

Ava fiddles with the hem of her sweater while I check the GPS. It's suddenly the most interesting thing on the planet.

My pulse thuds as though I'm about to face a firing squad instead of a girl with a brazen tongue and a wounded heart. But damn if I don't want to be in this small space.

Alone.

With her.

Even if she stabbed me multiple times the whole way there, I'd welcome the pain. We might be playing two different games here, but I know, without a doubt, I'm going to win mine.

"And we're off." I grin. She doesn't.

Salem in late autumn is a postcard come to life. Damp cobblestones shine beneath the sun, and amber leaves swirl in tight little tornadoes at every corner.

Colonial houses wear their history, proudly weathered shutters, creaky porches, garlands of dried corn husks and burnt-orange ribbon.

Storefront windows glow with soft light, fogged up from inside where baristas pull espresso shots and locals huddle over mugs. A brisk breeze cuts through it all, sharp and clean, carrying the scent of cold earth and a savory sweetness from the bakery two doors down.

I park near the town square, and I'm barely out of the SUV before I'm gawking like a tourist.

"You've got this dreamy gleam in your eyes. It's almost cute enough to make me forget how insufferable you are." She exits the car once I open her door.

"Insufferable's one way to put it," I say, brushing my thumb over the doorframe before she passes. "But if you think I'm letting go of the *dreamy* part, you're out of luck."

"Delusion does look mildly good on you." She pulls the length of her ponytail over to one shoulder.

"Bells, is that a compliment?"

"Don't get used to it." She's trying to hide that smile, but I see it. "So, this is your first time in Salem then?"

"Yeah, but I've always wanted to come here," I admit, my gaze zipping around.

The buildings look as though they might hypnotize me if I stare long enough. "Seeing it with you, though, might be the best part."

She rolls her eyes, but her blush betrays her. *I'm going to wear you down, Ava Bell. And then you'll blush for a completely different reason.*

We walk down Essex Street, her voice slipping into tour-guide mode. She tells me about the original Puritan settlements, the trials, the accusations. About Bridget Bishop—the first person to be executed in Salem for the crime of witchcraft. About the way fear twisted justice into spectacle.

She points to historic plaques, tugs me into the graveyard where moss-covered headstones lean with time, and pauses to buy us cider donuts she insists are the best in the state.

"I'm serious," she says with her mouth full. "This is a religious experience."

I take a bite. She's not wrong. They're warm, the edges crisp with sugar, the inside impossibly soft and apple-spiced. It tastes like fall got deep-fried and handed over in a paper bag.

Hours have passed by the time we reach the Witch House. I'm more than halfway convinced I need to set my next novel here.

"You know." I stare up at the black-gabled architecture, "I've never written about witches."

Her brow arches. "You're telling me the King of Dark Fantasy hasn't sunk his teeth into spellcasters yet?"

"Not yet." I grin. "But I may have found the perfect setting for a new witchy series."

And the perfect muse, I don't say.

Ava's texting someone when I glance over, her fingers tapping rapidly across the screen. When she finally puts her phone away, I'm about to ask who it was when the answer appears in the form of a man with a windswept ponytail and a giant skeleton key hanging from his belt loop.

"Uncle Marty," she calls out, waving him over.

He flashes us both a toothy smile and makes his way toward us.

Ava turns to me. "Well, Pembry, you're getting the exclusive after-hours tour of The Witch House. It's closed for the season, but I thought you might enjoy it."

My heart fumbles out of my chest and onto the floor. This... well, this is probably the sweetest thing *anyone's* ever done for me.

Uncle Marty leads us through the creaky old house, talking like he's the official mayor of all things spooky, his voice booming through the low-ceilinged rooms as he rattles off history, jokes, and the occasional "Don't touch that, it's haunted."

He shows us a replica of a 1600s kitchen, complete with cast-iron cauldrons and a fireplace large enough to roast a whole pig.

"They used to make beer in these," he says, slapping the side of a barrel. "Witch's brew. Probably still better than Bud Light."

Ava rolls her eyes. I laugh. Marty keeps going.

"This bed frame here? Hand-carved. Rumored to have belonged to one of the judges who sentenced the accused. Some people claim it creaks at night...empty."

I lean down toward Ava, my voice brushing over her ear. "Maybe the ghosts are fucking on it."

She chokes on nothing, eyes wide with half-laughter, half-mortification. Worth it.

I give her a wink. Before I can enjoy her full reaction, my phone buzzes in my pocket. Matthew.

> After you're done playing Hocus Pocus Boyfriend in Salem, maybe we take a breather from the fake? I'm serious, Soren. Publicity stunts at shared events is one thing. Meeting her family? That's rom-com quicksand, my guy.

> Deep in the quicksand. Bring rope.

After a pause, I add:

> Any updates on the Lena situation?

> No news is good news. For now.

I respond with another thumbs up, then tuck the phone away and set my attention back to Ava. "So... where were we? Oh right. Ghost sex."

With a waggle of his bushy brows, Uncle Marty steps aside, muttering about "special witch business," leaving us alone.

Silence creeps in like candle smoke, settling around us. Not going to lie, it's definitely on the spooky side.

Turning in a slow circle, Ava's eyes scan the low beams and warped windows. "You know, the walls remember everything."

"Maybe they do." I step closer, the pull to her a force I can't break. "So, let's revisit the fact that you set this up for me?"

She shrugs. "Don't make it a thing."

"It's a thing." I close the gap. "You didn't have to. But you did."

I'm so close now, the fruity vanilla scent in her shampoo drifts into my senses. The tension is electric.

Her eyes flick to mine, then away. "It was something to do, that's it. Nothing. More."

I fucking hate those two words.

"You know what that tells me, Bells?" Her throat bobs as I continue inching closer. "It tells me you care. Somewhere under all that sarcasm and self-preservation, you feel something, just like I do."

Ava stiffens. I watch her fold into herself, trying to disappear.

"Don't do that," I say, softer now. "Please don't hide from this. Or from me."

"I'm not hiding," she lies. I know this because her voice cracks halfway through.

Our chests nearly touch. "You could've let this be simple, kept it small. Instead, you made it personal. You reached out. You did a kind and thoughtful and terrifying thing, and you didn't even realize it."

"It doesn't mean anything," she whispers.

The war inside her rages, fueled by a desperate need to believe, so she doesn't fall apart.

"It means *everything* to me."

Ava's chin trembles. She swallows. "We've been over this. You're confused. You think your feelings are real and—"

"They're real. So. Fucking. Real." There it goes, whatever

thread of restraint I had left, snapped clean in half. So much for caution. It's too late to pull back now. I'm already in freefall.

Fuck it.

"The truth is, the second I saw you for the first time, standing with your chin lifted like you had something to prove and your mouth was ready to fight me on every panel point...I *knew*."

Ava's face scrunches in confusion.

"It wasn't in a convenient, romanticized, predestined sort of way," I clarify. "I knew in my chest. In my gut. In the part of me that never shuts up when it matters. My heart whispered: *Her. She's your journey.* And I've been chasing that whisper ever since."

Ava's eyes fly to mine. The world narrows to just us–just this. Her walls are up, but they're cracking. I can feel it.

She says, so quietly I almost miss it, "You only think you mean it, Soren. It's lust. It's the story. You're the plot twist. Not the ending."

The words hit so fucking hard.

My voice becomes a plea she can't run from. "Then rewrite me."

She flinches. I struck a buried nerve.

"Soren..."

"I want a story with you, Ava. No edits. No drafts. Only us."

The tears shimmering in her eyes catch the light like fragile glass. She swipes them away fast, as if blotting out a weakness she refuses to show. It isn't a weakness, though. It's proof. Proof that my words slipped past her walls, sank deep into places she doesn't let anyone touch. And for one staggering moment, I see her—unguarded, human in a way that makes my heart hurt and my resolve sharpen.

"No," she breathes. "When it ends, and it will. The internet will eat me alive. I won't know how to survive it."

That one, tiny word lands as a battering ram straight to the gut. I stagger under the weight of her fear. She's so sure, already written our ending in ink.

"What happened to you?"

"I told you last night." Her eyes stay locked on mine, broken and angry.

"Who did this?"

"Nobody of importance."

I exhale, slow and tight.

She treats it as though it's nothing. Like it didn't shape the way she pushes people out, the way she builds walls with jokes and barbed wire.

It mattered. Enough to break her.

The only thing that comes close to the truth is clawing up my throat. I let it out. "They were important enough to make you shut down. Important enough to make you wall up every time someone else tries to care. Important enough to make you doubt everyone." I pause. Let it sink in. Let her *hear* me. My hand twitches at my side, aching to reach for her, but not daring to push too hard. "So don't tell me they weren't important, Bells. Because I'm fighting their ghost every time I get close to you."

"You're right," she says immediately.

That surprises me. "What?"

"Someone made me feel safe." She turns slightly, angling away from me. "Right before they taught me that I wasn't. Not with them. Or anyone for that matter."

That isn't an explanation. It's a wound. I want to hold every delicate, shattered piece of it. Even if she never lets me, I still want to try.

Someone made me feel safe. Right before they taught me that I wasn't. There was no anger in her voice when she said it. Only this quiet pain, showing she's not bleeding anymore, but she carries the scar around, denying anyone else the chance to trace the outline.

And she and I, we stay there, locked in a stare with the air between us tightening, heavy with the sins of others.

My skin prickles. My pulse kicks. Ava views me as though I'm a cliff's edge—one dangerous step toward disaster. But what she doesn't see is that sometimes a cliff isn't a fall. Sometimes it's a view. A leap. The only way to learn you were built to fly.

There's a question in her eyes that gives me hope: *Would falling hurt more than standing still?*

I want to close the space. I want to fix it. I want to take the rough edges that cut into her and replace them with something soft.

So, I try...again.

"You say you won't survive it," I repeat her words. "Then let me show you how to live in it instead."

The tiny space between her brows creases.

One more inch.

Lifting my hand, I don't touch her, I hover—waiting for *her* to close the distance. "Be scared *with* me."

Ava doesn't move. Or speak. But she doesn't run either. That's enough for now. Even if she still won't let her guard down, the tremble in her breath is unmistakable. She's trapping a storm. But I'm going to help her tame it.

Ava's slender fingers twitch, her fists clench and loosen at her sides, as if she's one second from grabbing me by the collar—or bolting. It honestly could go either way.

The air between us buzzes, charged with a volatile electricity neither of us can run from.

"I'm not the enemy, Ava," I say, my voice a little gruff. "I promise."

"I know," she whispers, almost too soft to hear. Then, after a pause, Ava twists my heart with, "I am."

The words hollow me out. And all I can think, standing there in the wreckage of her self-blame, is that I'd give anything to show her she's wrong. That she's worthy. And I want her to be mine to protect.

"No." I brush her cheek with the backs of my fingers. "Look, I crossed the line. And you've seen the way I am with fans and heard the rumors. Read the headlines. We started this under false pretenses, sure—but I would love it if you could try to get to know the *real* Soren Pembry. Because I sure as hell want to know you, Ava Bell."

She still doesn't move. I lower my hand between us. Ava stares down at it.

"Hi," I say, with a small smile that's far too sincere. "I'm Soren Pembry. Yes, that's my real name. I'm a huge fan of your work. I've made some shitty choices in the past, as you've seen broadcast across the internet, but I'd *really* love to show you someone different."

Her gaze snaps up to meet mine. Still, she doesn't move. In this charged moment of almosts, it's definitely something I consider a win, even though it isn't a game for me. I need to show her she has me twisted up in ways I've never known.

Right now, I'll let the moment breathe. Let her have her space. If there's one thing I've learned about Ava in the last twenty-four hours, she's a wildfire dressed as frostbite, and you don't rush her thaw.

Standing here in this haunted house, witnessing her wrestle with her iron-clad walls and *nearly* letting me in, I make myself a promise. Patience, Pembry. Ava Bell is worth the wait.

I'm not walking away. Even when shit gets hard. And with her, it's bound to get hard.

But not in the way she writes about.

Unfortunately.

Feast & Fiction

Snowflake Gala

Bookmas Bash

Midnight Kisses &
Paper Wishes

Seventeen

~∽~

AVA

There's a spot past the old wharf, down a narrow, gravel path that tourists never find. It hugs the edge of the salt marsh where the tide breathes in and out as though it's the world's longest-held sigh. A single weathered bench tilts slightly beneath the bare-limbed willow tree, right where the coastline curves.

I've been coming here since I was a kid. It's my quiet refuge through everything—schoolyard disasters, heartbreaks that hollowed me out, rejection emails that felt personal, deadlines that tried to eat me alive.

It always smells of salt and damp wood, kelp clinging to rocks, and something older beneath it all. It's calming. So naturally, I brought Soren Pembry here.

Idiot.

In my defense, I didn't mean to. It wasn't meant in a *this is my sacred place, come share it with me, oh-so-handsome-boy* sort of way. I just needed air. Space. A moment that wasn't filled with haunted floorboards and Soren's devastating voice saying things I don't know how to process.

I nearly had a panic attack inside the Witch House. Right after, Soren stood there, six feet of messy sincerity, and told me that the second he saw me in the flesh, chin lifted with something to prove, he just... knew.

Knew what?

We've known each other face-to-face for what? Three weeks? Ish. Twenty-plus days of fake dating, public spectacles, and private moments that were never supposed to amount to anything except positive numbers.

What does he truly know about me? He doesn't know what I look like when I fall apart in a hotel room over a bad review. He doesn't know that sometimes I reread the first rejection email an agent ever sent me to remember how far I've come. He doesn't know how hard I have to work to feel like *enough* in this industry.

So what if he's read all my books? He's obviously created this bold, clever version of me in his head—one where the heroine possesses edgy dialogue and a soft heart that she keeps hidden until chapter twenty-two.

I'm not her.

Soren's swept up in the rush. The buzz. The fake romance, the unresolved tension pulsing with more lust than logic.

And for a minute—no, longer than a minute—I almost got pulled under with him.

I dove on top of him last night inside my innocent childhood treehouse, the same place I used to read library books and eat peanut butter sandwiches, and proceeded to grind over his very real, very hard cock. There was nothing *innocent* about it.

The wine and the emotions made me forget what boundaries were. And I *wanted* to forget. I *wanted* to let go and drown in that moment, in him, with him.

Thankfully, a tiny, screaming voice of reason yanked me back before I made a grave mistake and did something I couldn't explain or undo.

Lust is easy. Lust feels good. Whatever this is with Soren—it could burn through more than our clothes. It could level me.

The stakes are too high, the numbers between us too big. And he's the fuckboy of ShelfSpace. I'm already fighting an uphill battle to be taken seriously—I don't need to hand the internet a scandal with a bow on top.

I do want to believe him. When he looks at me, it's not for a stage. It's mind-bending. And *way* too risky for me to consider. Feelings are reckless and don't come with a safety net.

That's not romantic.

That's terrifying.

So, when Soren and I walked out of the Witch House and he asked me, "Where to next?" I just... pointed.

Now he's here, standing with his hands in his coat pockets, staring out at the water with an adorable expression that guts me even more.

"This place is magic," he says, turning to look back at me.

"It's a swamp," I reply, my voice coming out lighter than intended.

Soren doesn't flash the full grin—the one that has broken hearts from coast to coast—but the one he's seemingly reserved just for me.

I'm on the bench, arms crossed, legs bouncing. My pulse is a mess, and my mind won't stop replaying his outstretched hand and that: "Hi, I'm Soren Pembry."

Those words reached under my ribs and tugged.

"You should know I don't bring anyone here."

"I'm honored," he says, genuinely.

That makes it worse. Because here's the thing: Soren Pembry is the enemy. Or was. Then he became the fake boyfriend. And now he's the man whose tongue was in my mouth, whose body heat is still branded on my skin, whose cock—*dear god, that cock* —has no business rubbing up against me in the early morning. But did.

I shouldn't trust him. I certainly don't trust his dick. Worse, I don't trust *me*. Around him. Or around his... Well, you get it.

But I haven't let anyone in for a long time. The last time I kissed someone and felt it all the way to my toes was years ago. I haven't laughed like this, or shared quiet spaces, or...

Let myself *want*...anything.

"You're looking at me with such reservation, Bells." He lowers himself to sit beside me. "Is it because of the dick thing?"

My throat clogs. "What?"

"You said you don't trust my—and I quote—*massive dick,*" he teases. "So I'm wondering if I should be offended."

My face flames. "I did *not* say that out loud." *Did I?*

Soren smiles, wide and wicked. "You did."

Burying my face in my hands, I groan. My inner dialogue seriously needs a time-out. How is my brain not connecting to the part where we filter these things before they hit the air?

"Relax." His shoulder nudges mine. "It's cute, the way you talk out loud—like I've got backstage passes to your brain. And I'm only giving you shit. But let's be real, Bells—you've been staring at me for ten straight minutes as though you're running a private poll in your head: strangle me or straddle me. Figured I'd cut the tension before it combusted and took the wharf with it."

"This was a mistake."

As I move to stand, Soren palms my knee, stopping me.

"You keep calling me a mistake." His tone is now exasperated. "And yet... here we are. Sitting on a bench at your sacred spot. Just a boy, asking a girl—"

"Don't you dare."

A grin tugs at his mouth, but his eyes are serious. "You see the irony, right?"

I do. I *live* it. I write it.

The silence between us is loaded with the weight of all the things we've said. And the mountain of things we haven't hovers above–a volcano ready to explode open.

Soren angles his body toward mine. "Bells, I need to know?"

I eye him with caution. "Need to know what?"

"Well, actually, it's more of an explanation."

"What do you mean?"

His voice is stripped of charm and games. "What *exactly* happened to make you build walls tall enough to keep even someone as determined as me out? And I'm pretty relentless when I want something, but Bells, you have a full-blown fortress. Moat included."

I inhale a breath, not wanting to go there. *Again*. But also... I'm done with swallowing it down and tired of holding it in.

My pulse hammers, and my mouth moves before my brain can stop it. "Okay, you want the truth?" I ask, hoping I won't regret this.

"God, *yes*."

I stare down at my hands. "I believed someone when they said I was everything. Their person. Their *one*. And when that changed, I didn't get a warning. I got replaced. With several other women, actually."

Soren exhales a breath that's meant to be felt. "I'm so sorry."

"This someone was *good* at pretending." My voice cracks at the edge. "And I was stupid enough to believe it was real." I look away, swallowing down the painful memory. "So you'll have to forgive me if I don't jump all at once, because *you're* pretending too, Soren. And everything is so muddled, I don't know what's safe. What's wrong or what's right—"

"So now you don't trust what's in front of you?" I cut in. "Because of someone else who lied behind your back?"

"I trust myself..." Silence and tension swell between us. "...except when I'm with you."

"I know," he agrees, like he's Luke Freaking Skywalker after Princess Leia tells him she loves him. He grins, trying to lighten things between us.

I roll my eyes, look away.

Soren grasps my chin and turns me back to face him. "I want to be clear. I'm not going to knock down your walls, Bells. Not until you're ready. I'm hoping you might hand me a layout of the underground dungeon to your intensely built fortress. Or at the very least, let me keep showing up until the front gate creaks open a little."

My laugh is watery. "That's ridiculous."

"Maybe," he shrugs. "So is *pretending* the chemistry between us doesn't exist."

His smile heats my core. And I don't hate it. That's the problem, isn't it?

Soren dips his head to meet my eyes. "Do you ever wonder what would happen if you *didn't* run?"

I hesitate before answering, "Yeah. I do."

"And?"

My head turns to avoid his gaze.

"Bells, it kills me to say this, but... as your *friend*..." That word suddenly sounds poisonous. "Thank you. For telling me. For opening up a little."

My laugh cracks, surprised and shaky. "Do you hate the word, friend?"

"Abso-fucking-lutely. You used it to keep me at a distance."

"You're not wrong."

Before I can pull away, before I can deflect, he adds, "You're not a game. *If* you were... please know this...I'd still want to lose myself in every level of you."

Air is trapped inside my lungs. My knee bounces in overdrive speed.

"I mean it," he says, voice rough. "And yeah, it sounds cheesy or cliché, but some clichés are rooted in truth. You have burrowed under my skin. Fast. And I don't want you out."

I want to tell him to stop. He's making it worse. He's making it *so hard* to push him away.

All I manage is, "You're exhausting."

"That I am," he replies, smiling. "That I am."

I don't know what scares me more—that I might be starting to believe him. Or that I already do and I'm denying it.

The thought gives me pause. My lips press together. And my "What If Demons" fly.

What if I chilled the fuck out?

What if I did give in?

What if, just once, I stopped thinking about everything that could go wrong, and let myself want him—not in locker room stalls or treehouses, but fully, recklessly, here and now?

The thought is terrifying. Yet intoxicating.

Bare minimum? I could get a few orgasms. Maybe even a dinner. Or two. And a side of dessert.

At what cost?

When Soren's eyes drop to my mouth, electricity skitters across my nerves like someone just plugged me in. Every muscle locks, breath stumbles, and panic mixes with want. He's about to kiss me, and my body is all in while my brain is screaming abort mission.

He drifts forward.

"There's something that I don't understand," I say, making him halt.

"What's that?" Soren leans back, away from the heat sparking between us, and my lungs forget their job—because apparently, they were counting on him to finish what he started.

"You don't even know me."

"I'd like to."

Something slithers into my chest. Hope? Oh no. I know better than to let that beast get comfortable, so I look away.

"We'll see," I say, more to myself than him.

Soren hears it, though. "That we will, Bells. That we will."

He's relentless in his pursuit to prove that this isn't lust, or a publicity stunt, or some passing whim, but something that could actually matter.

I'm equally committed to shutting it down before it splinters through the seams I've spent years stitching shut. The stakes are too personal. This thing between us is a war of poached glances and loaded silences. Of confessions wrapped in charm and kisses.

All of which I haven't stopped dreaming about over the years. To have...with someone.

And now, with Soren, I've stepped onto the battlefield, heart half-armored, pulse fully engaged, and no idea which one of us will be left standing when it's over. As history has taught me, it won't be me.

By the time we pull into the gravel drive of my family's home, dusk has settled over the trees. The porch is lit, and the scent of roasted garlic and sage punches through the crisp air, enveloping us in a homecoming hug when I open the front door.

Inside, G-Ma is back. And hell hath no fury like a matriarch on a mission to celebrate her sweet Ava Bean and her handsome boyfriend before they jet off again.

Her *exact* words.

The moment we step over the threshold, she appears–lipstick fresh, arms flung wide. I know for a fact she's been stationed between the curtains, waiting.

"There they are!" she bellows, bustling forward in a blaze of holiday sweater sequins and scented hairspray. "My favorite couple! I've got cider warming, apple pie cooling, and June performing a little ritual in your bedroom to assist with all your future lovemaking needs!"

Soren chokes beside me.

"Oh my *God*, G-Ma!" I hiss, face combusting.

"I'm trying to help'," she huffs. "Memory foam absorbs everything."

Before I can die a thousand deaths, the front door bursts open behind us with a slam.

Spinning, I immediately collide with an armful of wild hair, tote bags, and the scent of familiar citrus and sandalwood.

"EMILYYYYY!" I shriek.

We launch ourselves at each other with a high-pitched, best-friend squealing that could crack stained glass. Bags drop. Hair tangles. Soren flinches like he's stumbled into an exorcism.

"You didn't tell me you were coming home for Thanksgiving!" I hug her so tight she squeaks.

"I wanted it to be a surprise!" She hugs back. "You know what else is a surprise?" She breaks free. "This tall drink of sex appeal standing in your foyer."

My face goes up in flames.

"You didn't mention anything about taking him home to meet your parents!"

"It's not—he's not—it's complicated."

Eyes wild with glee, Emily leans in. "It's horny. That's what it is. I get it."

Soren gives a little wave, a half-grin tugging at his mouth as he tries to follow the conversation.

Emily turns to him. "Hi! I'm Emily. Just flew across the country, got frisked by TSA—which, not gonna lie, was oddly affirming—and sprinted through three terminals to make it here. So, hello. Big fan of your face."

A hand runs through his hair. "I... uh–thank you?"

She points two fingers at his chest. "I've got questions. So many questions. And follow-ups."

"Too late now!" G-Ma trills into the kitchen. "Corn pudding's in the oven, and I whipped up extra cream for Ava's boyfriend. He's a man who's no stranger to dessert... or whipped cream. Are ya, honey?" She winks.

Soren's mouth twitches. "I love this level of hospitality."

"You're about to get all of it, in 4-D surround sound."

He grins at me, soft eyes and stupid charm, like walking into the crazy that is my family, is exactly where he wants to be.

We're barely through the door to the dining room before G-Ma's thrusting a plate of pecan pralines at Soren and pulling out a deck of cards. The Great Dalmuti. Our family's preferred battleground.

"Where's Dad?" I ask mom.

"It's his weekly poker game." She uncorks a bottle of wine. "So, Soren has all of us girls to himself. And Fisher."

Soren turns to me. "So, basically, I'm outnumbered?"

Nodding, I pat his shoulder and walk away.

A few hours later, we're gathered around the dining table: my mom, G-Ma, Fisher, Emily, me, and Soren—who, thanks to beginner's luck or actual dark magic, has become the reigning Dalmuti three rounds in a row.

"Of course he's good at this," I mutter under my breath as I collect the Peon hat for the fourth time.

G-Ma leans in with a sharp elbow to my ribs. "Well, maybe if you'd focus less on huffing and more on strategy, Ava Bean, you wouldn't be losing to your *future husband*."

I fake a laugh and shoot Soren a look that should've engulfed him in a fit of flames.

Raising a brow, his grin turns lazy, gorgeous. "Honestly, I'm grateful that you all let me join. This is the most fun I've had in a long time."

My mom beams. "You're a delight, Soren. So well-spoken. And tall. Strong. So intelligent."

"I'm literally right here," I deadpan.

She waves me off. "Yes, yes, we know. We've seen you lose four times in a row. Let the man have a moment."

Fisher snorts into his beer. "Can we make him our permanent Dalmuti? Forever?"

"Fisher!" I scold. "Wrong side."

"What?" he shrugs. "He's fun. You're all stiff and twitchy."

G-Ma throws her cards down. "Stop talking and let this man *play*. I haven't seen hands that good since 1972, and let me tell you, the man who owned them back then could shuffle more than a deck."

I groan. Soren laughs. My mom giggles. She's three glasses in and feeling it.

Emily crosses her arms, one brow arched. "Okay, real talk, Soren. What exactly *are* your intentions with our Ava Bell? And know... if you lie, G-Ma's probably got a meat tenderizer with your name on it."

Soren's mouth quirks. His eyes stay serious, staring straight at her. "Honestly? I know I want to make her laugh when she forgets how. I want to be the one she calls when everything goes sideways. And if I ever get lucky enough—*really* lucky enough—I want to be the reason she loves again."

The room goes quiet.

Traitorous heat pricks the corners of my eyes. Absolutely not. No tears. Not for him. I force a laugh, too high-pitched to sound real. "You should bottle that line, Pembry. Sell it on ShelfSpace. The fangirls would eat it up."

His jaw tics, the humor draining from his expression. "That's the part you don't get, Bells. I don't care about them. Not when it comes to this, or to you."

Emily stares, then nods approvingly. "Okay. Damn. No meat tenderizer for you."

G-Ma sighs, "Too bad. I had good aim in my prime."

I stuff a praline in my mouth to keep from screaming. Because here's the truth: they're all eating him up as though he's a sugar-dusted pie. And Soren's playing his part perfectly—as a damn walking, talking book boyfriend dream sequence.

And me? I'm faking it harder than ever because every time he meets my eyes, I feel *soooo* many things.

I'm not ready for this. I refuse to be.

"Okay," my mom says, clasping her hands. "Let's keep this grill going. Soren, what's your favorite thing about Ava?"

The table falls silent. G-Ma puts down her fork. Even Fisher stops chewing.

"Mom—"

"No interrupting," she sing-songs. "Let the man speak."

Soren's gaze slides to mine. His smirk fades into a softer version of his smile. "Her fire."

The air is too thick. I can't breathe.

"She comes in swinging," he says, voice deliberate. "She doesn't let people coast on charm or bullshit. She makes you earn every laugh. All her looks. Each inch of trust. You think you're ready for her, and then she proves you aren't—unless you're *all* in. That kind of fire doesn't burn you. It brands you. You know? Makes you understand what matters in life."

Another beat of silence. My heart is a bass drum against my ribs.

My mom breathes. "I knew it. He's the one."

G-Ma sniffs, dabbing her eyes with a napkin. "Lord have mercy, I'm gonna need a shot of bourbon and a handheld fan. Stat, Fisher."

Fisher jumps from the table. All eyes turn to me. Crap.

"What about you, Ava?" my mom asks. "What's your favorite thing about Soren?"

My palms are slick. I rub them on my jeans. "Uh..."

Don't say *the dick*, and definitely don't say he has a smile that could collapse a solar system.

"He's... unexpected," I manage. "He surprises me."

Soren clutches his chest. "Bells, is that *another* compliment?"

"Don't push it," I shoot back. There's no heat in it.

"I wouldn't dare."

"He's also... smart," I continue. "Thoughtful. Kind, in a way that sneaks up on you. And he makes me laugh, a lot, even when I don't want to."

The weight of his attention is the same as the sun burning through glass.

G-Ma chimes in, "Soren, baby, tell us about your family."

Soren's hand, resting lightly on the table, goes still, and the boyish charm dims behind his eyes. With one single question, G-Ma flipped off a switch.

"There's not much to tell," he says after a few seconds of hesitation.

My mom frowns. G-Ma opens her mouth, ready to dive in with something probably involving casseroles and trauma.

I cut her off. "Hey." I stand and grab the deck. "Who wants a rematch? I refuse to end this trip as the Peon."

Everyone shifts their focus. Laughter returns, and the questions stop.

Soren meets my eyes, gratitude swimming inside his stormy grays. He doesn't say thank you. He doesn't have to.

I sit back down, nerves buzzing, because I know what I just did. I didn't do it for the charade. Or for any cameras. Definitely not for some invisible contract.

I did it for him.

And that scares the hell out of me.

Fisher whoops, returning with a bottle of bourbon and a handheld fan for G-Ma. "Let's go. Dalmuti rules. No mercy."

Before anyone can deal, Emily lifts a finger. "No rematch for us. You three—out." She points at me, Soren, and Fisher. "We've got drinks to consume, places to be, and a week of shit to unpack." She grimaces. "Okay, that's not a good visual. Sorry about that. We have things to discuss."

G-Ma gasps. "But the casserole—"

Emily waves her off. "No can do, G-Ma. We'll be back for leftovers and feelings later."

Fisher grabs his coat and flashes a grin. "If we're not back by midnight, assume we've all eloped or joined a cult."

G-Ma huffs. "Same difference."

Feast & Fiction

Snowflake Gala

Bookmas Bash

Midnight Kisses &
Paper Wishes

Eighteen

SOREN

They've all stopped throwing.

Emily, Fisher, Ava—each of them holding drinks, jaws slack, not even pretending to hide the fact they're watching me.

I'm the evening entertainment. And I'd be lying if I said I wasn't performing a little.

Okay—a lot.

The second Ava's eyes went wide on my first throw, a primal feeling kicked in. I adjusted my stance. Tightened my grip. Threw harder. Showed off the forearms so she'd squirm in her seat.

She's sitting with her legs crossed now, trying to appear unaffected. Her gaze keeps dropping to my hands. My arms. My chest.

They can't possibly know I used to do axe-throwing events at cons, right? Or that I choreographed fight scenes for a LARP team that took it way too seriously?

Whatever. Tonight, I'm not Soren Pembry, fantasy author. I'm the guy making Ava Bell rethink every wall she's ever built— with every single satisfying *thunk* of blade against wood. While she tries to patch the cracks with fresh cement, I keep chipping away at her defenses like they were never meant to hold. And from the way her tongue darts out to wet her bottom lip?

Yeah. It's working.

227

The axe lands with a satisfying *thwack*, dead center in the target.

I roll my shoulders, pretending I haven't been watching every damn reaction from behind me since I walked into this place.

Sure enough, Emily's cocktail straw drops from her mouth.

Fisher mutters a statement that sounds suspiciously like, "Jesus, take the loincloth."

And Ava's sipping her drink, as though it's the only thing tethering her to God's green Earth, but the heat in her gaze is giving her away.

Good.

I take another axe from the pile and toss it in my palm. "You guys done throwing or...?"

Emily waves a dismissive hand. "Why mess with greatness?"

"Honestly," Fisher says, leaning back against the bar, "I'm reconsidering everything I thought I knew about fantasy nerds. Do any of your book signings come with a personal lumberjack demo?"

I smirk. "Only the premium packages."

Ava snorts into her drink, which makes me grin wider. Every laugh I can wring out of her is a win. She's loosened up. Thank you, dirty martini.

The air between us is starting to crackle again. And I fucking love it.

"Speaking of packages," Emily says, swiveling in her seat. "This is the part where we all share deeply personal and slightly inappropriate facts about ourselves."

I approach. "You first."

"Gladly." Emily readjusts in her seat. "I'm currently a professor of human sexuality at Seattle Pacific University."

"Wait?" Fisher's head whips around. "I thought you were...a philosophy person."

"I was. But then I realized people don't actually want to read about Descartes. They want to read about desire. Power. Pleasure." She shrugs. "So I followed the libido of academia and here I am."

Fisher raises his glass to her. "Respect. Sexuality is philosophy, but with better toys."

Emily laughs. "Exactly."

Ava leans over with mock whisper-shock. "Tell them the rest."

Emily eyes her, cheeks tinting a touch. "For real?"

"There's a rest?" I inquire.

"There's a manuscript," Ava sings.

Emily rolls her eyes but grins. "Fine. I'm writing a novel."

"A romance novel?" Fisher guesses.

Emily hesitates.

"A rom-com?" I offer.

"Definitely not." Her eyes flick toward the wall. "An erotic novel, with darker romance."

There's silence, then Fisher lets out a delighted gasp. "Shut. Up."

"Swear on my PhD."

Ava's nodding. "I've read the draft. It's *hot*."

"You're telling me your best friend—" Fisher points between them, scandalized. "—writes academic sex essays by day and scorching fuck fiction by night?"

"Multitudes." Emily stands, takes a bow.

"Where do you get your inspiration?" Fisher leans in with the same curiosity he reserves for gossip and glitter.

Emily sips her drink, eyes glinting. "Wouldn't you like to know."

"I would. *Desperately.* Are you pulling from real life? Academic journals? Late-night Reddit threads? Volunteers? I'm available." Fisher winks.

"My research focuses on digital intimacy—more specifically, online hookups and how technology mediates sexual exploration."

I sit next to Ava. "So...Tinder."

"Bumble, Grindr, secret alt Tumblr accounts, but Romance

Roulette is my main focus right now," she says. "There's a whole world of anonymous desire out there. And it's all data."

Fisher downs his drink, signals the waiter for another. Ava's laughing now, her hand lightly brushes my knee when she scratches her leg. My cock jumps at the contact. She doesn't seem to notice she touched me, or she's pretending not to. Either way, I'm not about to move.

"Don't let her fool you," Ava says. "Emily once created a fake dating profile as part of her research at Amherst. She went on five dates and ended up in a swingers bar crawl in Detroit posing as a couple with some guy named Vlad."

Emily snickers. "That guy's back tattoo said 'Penis Precision'—in Old English font. Like a medieval dick sniper."

Fisher wheezes. "I would marry him on the spot."

"He was very flexible. Definitely knew where to aim." Emily chuckles.

"You're the most fascinating person I've ever met," I tell her.

"I know," she says, without a trace of shame.

We all laugh again, but the energy has changed. The alcohol has warmed our limbs—and loins. The neon of the axe-throwing lanes casts a strange intimacy, and there's a magnetic pull in the air that keeps bringing my attention back to Ava.

Her hand is still near mine, resting on the seat of her chair. Her thigh brushes against mine every so often. And every time, my body reacts, the touch continues to shoot straight to my cock.

Ava catches my eye with a crooked smile. "You're good at this."

"At what?"

"Throwing sharp objects. Winning over my family. Making Emily blush."

"I haven't even started with Emily," I say. "Give me time."

Emily points at me. "You're on thin ice, Pembry."

"Good thing I brought *The Blade*."

Ava groans, but she's grinning. That's when I lean into her and drop my voice an octave. "I meant it, you know."

Her smile slips. "Meant what?"

"What I said earlier. To your family."

Her skeptical expression flits between longing and fear, both of them cycling in an instant. "Soren..."

"I'm not trying to trap you." My words are gentle. "Just asking you to stop running...for *one* second. Maybe catch your breath."

Those caramel eyes dive straight into mine.

Fisher, blissfully unaware—or pretending to be—says, "Okay, I need to know. In this erotic novel of yours, Emily, is there a male lead?"

Emily taps her chin. "There could be."

Fisher's eyes drag over the professor. "Any chance this mysterious male lead has excellent taste in sequined shirts and is tragically single?"

"Where is he going with this?" I ask Ava.

Ava gives me a double take. "He's obviously fishing to see if she'd be open...to *swapping notes*."

"I thought he was gay?"

She smiles. "Fisher is a lover of *all* people. Literally, figuratively, and physically."

I nod, getting it now.

Emily takes a sip of her drink. "Nice try, Casanova. This research is strictly academic... unless you're volunteering for a case study."

"Where do I sign?" Fisher asks.

Emily smirks. "We'll talk, Fisher."

"Fabulous." Fisher raises his glass. "To erotic fiction, found family, and men who can wield an axe."

We all clink glasses.

And while the drinks flow, the teasing continues, and Emily begins describing the very detailed arc of her bisexual main character with boundary issues, I keep watching Ava.

She's glowing. Laughing. Relaxed. I haven't seen this before.

But I'd throw a hundred more axes if it meant keeping her this close, this soft, this unguarded.

If it meant getting her to let me in.

Fisher offers his arm. "Shall we dance, Professor?"

She slides her arm through his with a grin. "Only if you promise to spin me."

As they make their way toward the open dance floor, Ava drapes herself over the table in the seat beside me, her smile turning a little lazy. The drinks have dulled her edges, and the night is closing around us.

My fingers skim along the hem of her sleeve. "You want to dance?"

"No." Her head turns, gaze skimming across my chest, up my throat, like her eyes are trying to decide where to land. The drinks have her loose, soaking me in as though I'm the next round. "I want you to show me how to throw."

Yeah, sure she does.

Except the way those autumn eyes are trailing over me, lips parted, pupils blown wide, tells me this isn't about throwing axes. There's heat simmering inside her. And that has nothing to do with aim or technique and everything to do with the space between us.

"Deal." I hold out my hand.

She takes it. We step toward the lane, music thumping behind us. I grab an axe and offer it to Ava, fingers purposely grazing hers.

Uncertain, she shifts her weight, trying to appear nonchalant as I move close behind her, so that my breath skates down her neck. Also, on purpose.

"Feet shoulder-width apart," I instruct. "Hands firm on the grip. Let your shoulders stay loose."

"Like this?" she asks, adjusting her stance.

"Almost." I reach around her, guiding her arms into place.

Ava's back presses lightly against my chest, and for one suspended moment, we're just... breathing. One inhale from her. One heartbeat from me. Everything tightens.

"This isn't about the axe, is it?" she whispers.

"Nope," I admit.

I step back to give her space. "Go ahead. Let it fly."

Exhaling, Ava adjusts her grip as I showed her, and with one swift, focused movement, launches the axe.

Thwack.

Dead center.

Stunned silence.

Then—

"Oh my god!" she squeals, spinning toward me. "Did you see that? I did it!"

She jumps into my arms before I can react, pure joy bursting from her. I catch her easily as her legs wrap around my waist, spinning her once, twice, breathless from the shock of how good this feels. She's laughing against my neck. I'm grinning like an idiot.

And then it stops.

The spinning. The laughter.

What's left is Ava in my arms, my hands locked under her thighs—well, her ass, actually—and her, staring at me with wide, gleaming eyes.

The world keeps turning, but the curve of her hips anchors me, and the sound of her laughter from a second ago echoes in my chest.

I want this moment to last forever.

I want to bottle her joy, the softness of her smile, and how her breath stops when she looks at me. I've waited my whole damn life to find the woman.

I promise Bells, I'm not a mistake.

The air sizzles when she presses against me, a slow collision of breath and want, her heartbeat brushing mine, our lips are so close, they're almost touching. The world is still dancing behind us, but nothing exists outside this moment.

One more inch.

My tongue darts out over my bottom lip. "What's next, Ava?"

Her wide eyes search mine—unsure, but burning.

"Do you want—"

She kisses me.

Every cell in my body explodes.

It starts out soft, tender, a door creaking open to reveal a bigger room. Her lips are warm, parted, and I forget how to think. All I can do is feel. And holy hell, do I *feel* everything.

Ava's fingers knot into the front of my shirt. Mine slides down her waist, over her hips, fastening her to me as the kiss deepens. Her body rocks into mine, and that's all it takes. My control snaps like a dry twig.

A guttural sound rips from me as I twist, pinning her to the wall. The thud vibrates through both of us. She gasps, and I take it, my mouth hungry, claiming. Pressing my hips forward, I grind against her, chasing that sharp edge of friction. The kiss turns rougher—tongue, teeth, breath—heat rolling off us in waves until there's no space left to fill, no air left to steal.

Ava grasps at my shoulders, arching into me, hips rolling forward in a rhythm that sends blood surging south with alarming precision.

And then—

WHAM.

A loud *clang* reverberates as the frame of a poorly mounted dartboard rattles off the wall and lands squarely on our heads.

Jerking back with a grunt, I manage to set her down gently. "Mother—ow!"

Giggling, Ava's hands fly to her mouth. "Oh my God, did the wall just attack us?"

"Apparently, the bar is anti-PDA."

Ava starts laughing harder, even as she tries to apologize. "I'm sorry! I didn't see it! I was too busy—"

"Kissing me senseless?"

She stops to take a breath. "Yeah."

I sigh dramatically, rubbing the sore spot. "Worth it."

She brushes invisible dust from my shirt—an excuse to touch me, which lights me up.

"You sure?"

I eye her. "Depends. Are we done?"

Fisher's voice cuts in, "And post."

We both freeze.

"ShelfSpace is gonna eat that one up," he adds, followed by the unmistakable sound of a wink in his tone.

Ava stiffens. Within seconds, the moment transforms into one that's no longer ours.

She steps back a fraction. Her smile dims, not all the way, but the sparkle behind it definitely dulls. Like a beautiful flower that got plucked too soon.

I don't say anything because I get it now. She wanted that moment for herself. Now it belongs to everyone.

After the kiss at the bar—the one *she* initiated, the one *I* wish never stopped—Ava got weird.

In the car, she insisted the boys sit up front while the girls rode in the back. She didn't say a word on the drive home. Emily and Fisher did all of the talking.

When we got back to her family's, the four of us all sat around the fire pit for hours, trading stories. Emily slipped in details about college Ava—wild streaks and hidden rebellion I wanted to pocket and keep for myself.

Eventually, Emily declared she was heading home. Then, Fisher, being Fisher, eventually proclaimed he was going to "take care of his blue balls" and disappeared inside, leaving me and Ava in the glow of dying embers.

That's when she did this fake yawn and said she was heading to bed. I let her go. Put out the fire. Gave it some time.

I finally made my way upstairs, crawled in beside her, careful to get as close as I could without crossing into creepy. She slept on her side, her breathing even, lashes fanned across her cheeks. I wanted to wrap myself around her, pull her close, but I settled for brushing a kiss against her temple.

"Thank you," I whispered so quietly it dissolved into the dark.

"For tonight. For letting me in a little. For kissing me. For not running."

The words kept spilling, tiny confessions meant for her walls. "You undo me, Bells, more than you know. You feel like home. And I don't even care if you never hear this, because at least I finally said it."

Her chest rose and fell steadily, untouched by my restless truths. And still, I stayed there, staring at the ceiling, one arm tucked behind my head, wondering how I could spend an eternity next to her.

When I wake, darkness seals the room—a velvet curtain pulled tight across the world. Silence hangs between walls creaking with the heaviness of night and old bones settling in the house.

My hand reaches across the bed on instinct, searching the far side.

Empty. Cold.

Fingers skim over the sheets that are still holding the shape of her. She's always curled tight to the edge, as though claiming space costs her something. But even that narrow corner of comfort has been abandoned tonight.

Sitting up, I rub sleep from my eyes. My phone on the nightstand reads 4:12 a.m. Wind brushes dry branches against the roof, a scratchy rhythm that slithers beneath my skin.

The weight of the hour presses in on me as I creep out of the room. The stairs groan beneath my weight, and every creak slices through the quiet as I pad down them.

A faint silver glow spills from the living room, drawing me forward. Ava is curled on the couch in the shape of a question mark.

Lurking in the shadows, I take her in. Ava's knees are tucked beneath her in a way that makes her look younger than she is, like a kid who wandered out of bed chasing nightmares.

She's wearing a threadbare hoodie that swallows her frame, the sleeves bunched around her fists, the collar pulled up to her jaw. Armor. Her hair's a messy knot, strands falling loose around her temples, wild and sleep-tousled. Her eyes are locked on her phone, lit by the glow of ShelfSpace, where my face fills the screen.

I know the video. It's me, mocking the ending to a Halloween rom-com she wrote, complete with fake tears and a dramatic reading in a bad Dracula accent. She watches without anger, but there's no smile on her lips.

In the glow of the screen, the edges of her face are different, fragile in a way she never lets the world see. The pressure to be adored. To entertain. To build a version of herself that always delivers, even when it costs more than she's willing to show.

The sight of her unguarded and alone in the middle of the night is heartbreakingly human. She isn't the stage version tonight. Not the silver-tongued rival or the viral name. She's not just watching a video of me mocking her book. She's holding her breath through it, bracing herself.

It makes my chest ache in ways I can't explain.

Whatever she's carrying with her runs deeper than I understood initially, with unspoken expectations she's placed on herself. Outside of the ones the industry throws at her. I can see now how they've piled up in her silence, and how she smiles through the exhaustion.

This is Ava. Unfiltered. Unmasked.

She knocks the wind out of me in this quiet, unraveling moment. It's a blow I never saw coming until now, standing here, watching. I'm breathless.

I take a step forward, but a soft voice stops me.

"Ava?" Her mother shuffles into the living room, wrapped in a robe the color of warm sand.

Ava jumps a little, locking her phone and shoving it under a pillow.

Mandy's slippers barely make a sound as she crosses the room. A silk scarf wraps her curls into a careful tower on top of her head. Tired eyes pass over me, but I'm too far hidden in the shadows for her to notice. They catch on Ava immediately.

"Honey," she murmurs, voice still thick with sleep. "What are you doing up?"

"Couldn't sleep."

"Everything okay?"

Ava presses her lips together and nods. By the way she closes her eyes, I can tell she's fighting back tears, and that fucking guts me.

Her mother nods, then moves toward the kitchen. "Come on, honey."

Mandy flicks on the kettle, leans against the counter, and watches her daughter with practiced ease.

Sinking deeper into the shadows, I plan to head back upstairs when Mandy says, "You know, snuggling a warm man is therapeutic."

Ava exhales hard, more a breath than a response. But her mother keeps going on about it. I almost laugh.

"What?" her mom says, completely unbothered. "It's true. Your father has the body heat of a radiator. You should take advantage while you've got one."

Ava groans, pulls the hoodie higher over her face. "Mother."

The kettle whines to life, a mechanical sigh filling the room. Steam starts to rise. Her mom goes quiet.

She turns, eyes sharpening as only a mother's can. "What happened. Did you two fight?"

"No." Ava shakes her head. "He's been...perfect. But I don't think he and I are meant to be."

Heat crawls up the back of my neck, and an edge of nervous energy coils tight in my stomach. I've stumbled into a moment too unguarded and too vulnerable for my ears. And suddenly, my chest is packed with everything I haven't dared to show. Yet.

Her mom stills. "Ah. And there it is."

"What?"

"The problem." She moves closer. "You're waiting for the other shoe to drop."

Ava doesn't respond.

"Honey," her mom says, softening. "You always do this. Focus so much on what could go wrong that you don't give yourself time to see what's going right."

"It's not that simple."

"Sure it is. You're afraid. You're strong, smart, independent— God, I'm so proud of you. But you've got walls around your heart so thick, I'm not sure anyone can scale them unless they've got a battering ram, some dynamite, maybe a nuclear warhead, and a security clearance. Baby, you're the emotional equivalent of Fort Knox."

"For good reason."

"Of course, for good reason," Mandy says, her voice delicate but her eyes never wavering. "Love has been unfair to you. It's knocked you down in a way no one should experience. But baby, hiding inside Fort Knox doesn't stop the bombs from dropping— it just means no one can get in to help you clean up the rubble. At some point, you've got to let someone through the gates. Not because you need saving—God knows you can save yourself—but you deserve someone who stands shoulder-to-shoulder with you, carries the weight when you're tired, and *adores* you. And that man definitely adores you."

"What if I let someone in, and they leave? What if I hand them the keys and all they do is... prove me right?" Her voice dips, thin and uneven. "I don't want to go through that again."

"You're scared because he's showing up right now," her mom says gently. "And deep down, you want to believe he actually means it."

Ava's voice cracks. "What if he doesn't actually mean it?"

Mandy steps closer, her expression firm, motherly. "He isn't Jon."

Jon? Who the fuck is Jon?

"You've got to let go of the past," she adds.

"I know he's not Jon," Ava responds, picking at loose threads on her sleeve. "But I've learned that what looks good on the outside typically comes with splinters underneath."

Mandy's face softens. "Soren probably will hurt you. At some point. That's love, baby. You hurt each other sometimes. Not on purpose. But we're human. And loving someone means handing them the sharpest parts of yourself and trusting they won't use them to cut you open."

Ava leans over onto the counter, her head falling forward and resting across her arms.

Her mom walks over, brushing a strand of hair from her cheek. "Love isn't a feeling. It's not butterflies or chemistry or what your brain says when watching videos at four in the morning. It's a choice. Every day. To trust. To forgive. To keep showing up, even when it's hard."

"I don't know if I can do that."

"Then you'll lose him. And you'll probably live a very lonely life."

Those words sound cruel, but they aren't. They're honest and slice straight through flesh, through ribs, into my beating heart.

"You like him, Ava." Her mother strokes Ava's hair. "I know my daughter better than she knows herself, and you are gone for that man. You just haven't accepted it yet."

"Guess I should get in line behind the thousands of others."

That sentence hurts.

It doesn't just sting—it burrows into my chest and splinters. She still refuses to see me as nothing more than the caricature I've been selling to everyone else.

I press a hand over my heart, holding it in place like it'll fall out if I don't.

"You know what I see?" Mandy says, glancing toward the hallway I'm hiding in. "Yeah, that man upstairs has women throwing themselves at him online, in person. And he could've spent the holidays with any of them. But he didn't. He chose to be here. He chose *you*."

Ava lets out a short, incredulous breath. "So, what? I'm supposed to be grateful? I'm supposed to gush over the fact that he didn't spend Thanksgiving holed up, sticking his dick into a pack of thirsty groupies?" Her voice wobbles at the edges, heat blooming in her cheeks.

"Watch that mouth, Ava," Mandy scolds.

Ava's expression isn't embarrassment, more shame, frustration, maybe even fear—a reaction that only happens when someone hits too close to the truth with her.

Mandy steps closer. "No," tone matter-of-fact, "but you do need to *see* it. His choice means something. He's not chasing attention. He's chasing you. And denying the version of himself the world expects. Maybe it's because he's found someone worth changing it for."

A pause. Then, the kicker.

"Maybe *you* are that change."

Ava's eyes water before she can stop them, and for a moment, the room holds its breath.

"We barely know each other," Ava counters.

Shaking her head, Mandy chuckles. "Still trying to hide behind those walls, baby? You get to decide. Stay safe and alone. Or risk it for someone who could be everything to you."

Mandy turns to pour the tea, humming a tune under her breath.

I stay put. Breath shallow, feet frozen to the floor. What I just witnessed wasn't meant for me, but it sure as hell was *about* me.

Per her usual, Ava's scared. Walled up. But she's thinking. *Considering.*

I'll fucking take it. And when she's ready—*actually* ready–I'll be there. This one's worth it. Every biting edge of her.

In the meantime, I've got a new mission: Find out who the fuck Jon is. Then figure out whether to send him a thank-you card or break his nose.

Maybe both. Depends on the story.

Nineteen

AVA

It's been a week since our Thanksgiving visit. A week since a one-bed trope, mashed potatoes, treehouse kisses, and a viral video—the one where Soren had me lifted off the ground, legs wrapped around his waist, my back pressed to a wall, one thrust away from total indecency.

The internet went sexually ballistic. Comment sections melted. Reaction videos flooded ShelfSpace. And, because the universe enjoys my pain, couples everywhere started recreating it.

Bell and The Blade is a full-blown trend, complete with slow-motion thirst edits, bad lighting, and a few ER visits from overzealous reenactments.

Our farewell from the Bell household included my mom tearing up, Emily emailing Soren a copy of her manuscript with a wink emoji, and G-Ma whispering, "Don't come back unless you're engaged or she's glowing—and I don't mean from bronzer. Create a scandal, Soren!"

Little does she know we already are.

Fisher filmed the whole goodbye scene and posted it with the caption: ***The In-Lawlessness***.

The internet didn't just eat it up—they licked the plate clean and asked for seconds.

But the real breakout star?

G-Ma.

Within twenty-four hours, she launched her own ShelfSpace account–@GlitterAndGumption—and gained over two hundred thousand followers.

Her tagline: *"Hot takes, hotter grandmothers, and arthritis-friendly spice recs."*

She's already reviewing both our books, giving unsolicited sex advice in the comments, and threatening Soren (affectionately) in DMs. She's somehow better at social media than all of us.

After that, Soren flew home to Seattle, a city wrapped in mist and contradiction. Rain-slicked streets, neon signs buzzing in the dark, indie bookstores tucked between glass towers, and coffee shops named after sea monsters or obscure literary references.

I ferried back to my little neck of the woods outside Boston, to the cottage I bought when my first advance cleared. I call it solitude. Emily calls it avoidance. Tomato, to-mah-to.

Point is, I'm home. That should bring comfort. Familiarity. Safety. But, truthfully, all it's bringing is a quiet that curls around my ribs like fog, making me restless, and lonely.

Outside my floor-to-ceiling windows, the world is soft and still. Pale blue sky painted with lavender streaks. The tree-covered hillside below is dusted in the last whispers of frost, the lake at the bottom shimmering like it's been brushed with silver leaf.

There's a mug in my hand, steam furling into the air. Almond milk latte. Homemade. Overpriced beans and a dash of cinnamon. Exactly how I like it. The tiny indulgence feels similar to control, even if it's one that can't patch a hole in your chest.

My phone buzzes from where it's sitting on the kitchen countertop. I set my mug down and pick it up, moving over to the window seat at my breakfast nook. Victoria.

How are the pages coming?

Translation: *I know they're not coming but give me something to work with.*

> I told Hope to give you a month. That was two
> weeks ago.
>
> Clock's ticking, kid.

I stare at the phone screen, thinking it might magically auto-fill with a brilliant response. No such luck.

> So good. So many pages.
>
> Overflowing, honestly.

> How many of those pages contain actual
> words?

> Semantics.

> If those semantics aren't swoony and sex-
> positive and ready to print, I can't help you.
> Are you okay?

I don't reply to that one right away. I don't know if I am or not. I'm not sure what okay looks like when my entire brain feels wrung out and hung over a wood-burning fireplace.

So I type what I know won't set off alarm bells and, with my free hand, start rearranging the throw pillows lined up along my nook.

> Working through it. I'll send them soon.

> That better not be code for "I'm rearranging
> my throw pillows again."

I snatch my hand back before I touch the next pillow, and type back.

> Rude.

And no. That's not what I was doing.

(Anymore.)

Ava...

I got this. Promise.

I need to write. For the deadline. For the people waiting on me.

For me.

And for the ache that's camped out inside my heart, humming his name.

Soren.

Once I slip my phone into the pocket of my cardigan, I head toward my office. Every surface of my house twinkles. There are not one, but four themed trees—each with its own aesthetic.

The main tree in the living room is what I call "Nostalgia Chic" with mismatched ornaments, family photos, and glittered macaroni frames from elementary school.

The second is a romance book tree, naturally, covered in mini paperbacks, tiny fake candles, and a sign that reads: *All I want for Christmas is fictional men with emotional availability.*

The third is all gold and white, strictly for ShelfSpace. And the fourth? That one's for spite. Red, black, moody ornaments, and a garland that spells out: *Jingle Hell*.

Every door frame is wrapped in garland. Every candle smells of pine, or gingerbread cookies, or one named "Snowman's Balls" that Fisher sent as a joke.

There are seven throw pillows on my "way too big for one person, but I love it" sectional couch, all holiday themed. I bought them in a fugue state at three a.m. while watching *The Holiday*, drinking two bottles of wine, and eating mini candy canes like they were painkillers.

I sit at my desk, open my laptop, and stare at the screen. Taking a sip of my coffee, I think maybe that will help.

Nope.

I survey my Christmas crime scene that is my house, breathe in the cookie scented air, glance back at the screen.

Nothing.

No matter how much tinsel I string or how many sugar cookies I stress-bake, the words won't come. My document remains blank. My brain is static.

I've never had writer's block *this* bad. It's not only the story I've lost, but also the thread that ties me to my work. Who I am. Who I was in those quiet, solitary moments with him.

Free.

Unmoored from the past that's kept me caged, the hands that once pressed me small. With Soren, I wasn't measuring, second-guessing, shrinking myself to fit someone else's needs. I was flame and flood. I was hunger, unashamed.

My body wasn't something to guard, to silence, to barter away —it was mine. And in his hands, in his arms, it became *more* than mine. It became infinite.

In theory, the distance sounded like a relief. I could finally breathe without his gaze heating me.

Except now, my thoughts surround only him, remembering back to how he watched me across the dinner table, sizing up my every reaction. He never flinched when my family grilled him and swooned over him. He kissed me. I wanted–no, let's be honest, *want*–more.

I take another sip of my coffee and exhale. I'm not built for this. For high heat and emotional vulnerability. For slow-burning sparks that are starting to develop into a raging inferno. I'm built for edits and deadlines, and I fall for fictional men who can't disappoint me in the end.

I wasn't always like this. Once upon a time, I believed in love.

Until Jon Perry happened.

Literary agent. Smooth talker. Promiser of the world. Destroyer of innocence.

I was a senior in high school when he found me on InkWell, a digital playground where authors uploaded half-finished chapters at midnight, and by sunrise had entire fandoms arguing about ships, tropes, and cliffhangers in the comments.

Jon Perry slid into my DMs and told me I was a genius. He was a twenty-five-year-old, fresh-faced literary agent—or at least, that was his story—who was scouting hidden talent, building a roster of voices the world hadn't heard yet. Mine, apparently, was the one he'd been "waiting for."

He said he'd help me shape my career, protect my art, guide me through the noise. He played the long game with patience and praise.

I mistook manipulation for mentorship. I was young. Hungry. Desperate to be seen and make a name for myself. I didn't know what red flags looked like yet. I thought attention meant progress. I thought charm meant respect. I thought being chosen meant I was something special.

That's what I was led to believe, anyway.

Everything between us was strictly professional. He was the teacher and I was the eager student, sending him pages and waiting for his praise like oxygen. He spent time challenging me to hone my craft. He'd mark my stories up with red ink and notes that made me better—tighter pacing, sharper rhythm, cleaner tension, taught me how to trust my voice, and for that time in my life, I did. Not so much anymore. But other than that, he showed me that my stories were worth finishing.

Once I graduated from high school and became a freshman in college with a laptop, a dream, and no clue how cruel life was about to become, Jon signed me, called me his star, his prodigy, the next big one.

After that, things between us mutated. The compliments started to drift. They weren't about the writing so much anymore. They were about me. My smile. My voice. My body language in social media photos. Lines dissolved quietly, *so* quietly I almost didn't notice until it was too late. What once felt like mentorship morphed into ownership. And by the time I realized what he'd taken from me, he'd already convinced me I'd offered it willingly.

Which leads me to the night I lost my virginity to him. I met him at a hotel outside of Chicago, still believing the promises he whispered into my skin. Still believing I was the exception. Still believing he'd make me a household name, build an empire around me.

Still believing he loved me.

That hope held my dream for the remainder of my college career. Three whole years of missed opportunities. Of silence instead of submissions. Of being told to wait, to trust, to stay small and grateful while he spun elaborate stories to cover his tracks.

In that time, I didn't just fall for him—I built my world around him. I gave him my work, my body, my trust, my first everything. In return, he conditioned me to believe that my worth was tied to his approval, that I was lucky he picked me. That I'd be nothing without him. It wasn't long before I became chained to the version of myself *he* created. It wasn't just a bad relationship. It was an education in how easily love can become a leash and ambition a cage.

Then... My whole life collapsed.

The girl in Miami messaged me first. The one in LA. was next. More girls. Different cities. Different names. Same script. Same lies. Same heartbreak.

Come to find out, he wasn't even a licensed agent. Never submitted my manuscript anywhere. Had three phones and a sob story for each.

When it all came out, I not only lost a fake agent—I lost the voice inside me that once believed I deserved more. Or anything at all.

My budding career, my fragile confidence, and my bleeding heart all flatlined at the same time. Everything was a fiction better than anything I could've written myself—one where he was the hero and I was another gullible girl who got in too deep.

It's been nearly two years, and since then, I've played it safe and guarded my heart. No more letting someone get too far in, or allowing anyone to see the soft places in me.

There have been others, a rebound, a few flings, nothing more, all of them huge mistakes.

A lawyer who quoted romantic poetry until I realized it was all generated by A.I. He was a man who knew the lines of Shakespeare but not the meaning of follow-through, and loved the performance of affection, not the intimacy of it. By the time I realized all this, he had already used those pretty words to fuck me, then dropped me. Completely ghosted.

A barista named Jules. This is the one I took home. He thought "emotionally available" meant crying after sex, but never once asked how my day was. He wore vulnerability as a party trick—loud, temporary. And yes, Wonderwalled the turkey.

Last Valentine's Day, there was a fellow author. He had some promise. He was talented, charming. Except, he didn't want *me*. Or a partnership. He wanted a co-writer with coattails he could ride. Even tried to steal my current WIP by sharing the Google doc from my computer.

None of them lasted. I should've never let them get as far as they did. Each one confirmed what I already suspected—real connection is rare, and I'm better off keeping most of myself tucked away.

I write about love. I just don't believe in it. Not like what my parents have–the messy, stay-through-the-hard-stuff version of love. Definitely not the *I choose you over and over again* kind.

I do miss being touched, though. *And desired.* Quite honestly, I'm not sure I've ever been properly fucked. Not how I write it anyway. Or imagine it.

These days, my sex life is strictly academic—just me, my laptop or phone, one hand scrolling through "research," and the other collecting empirical data...down there.

My bookmarks folder could make a priest faint. And yeah, I

take notes. Angles. Pacing. Language. Emotion. I build sex scenes the way engineers build bridges: one tension wire at a time.

But living that kind of ruin-me-down-to-my-soul fucking? Still theoretical. And when my brain goes there—which it has, at a rate that would make my vibrator blush—I picture Soren.

His hands.

His voice.

His mouth.

The treehouse.

Oh God, the treehouse.

I straddled him without thinking, ground down on his hard cock like some horny YA heroine who mistook nostalgia for permission. He tensed beneath me, one breath away from snapping. And fuck, did I want him to snap. I wanted to feel all that restraint break open and take me right there on the weathered wood.

And when that same hard length was pressed against my backside the next morning, I couldn't help but wiggle against him, testing the weight of it, the possibility. He wasn't wrong when he accused me of doing it.

My body hasn't stopped remembering since. I constantly think about him over me, under me, *in* me—hips angled, my hands fisting the sheets, that thick, soft steel of him pressing so deep inside me I see stars behind my eyes. I picture the drive of his body against mine, the flex of his muscles, the heat of his skin. How I would gasp into the pillow when he bottomed out, and groaned against my neck and whispered, *fuuuck,* into my ear.

I shouldn't be picturing any of that. Except I am. And it's getting harder to pretend I'm not. Soren said he wanted to show me we could be real. That he wasn't going anywhere, and whatever this thing is between us—it matters. At least, to him it does.

Except, here's the thing no one seems to get. I'm broken in places people can't see. I've patched over too many cracks with caution tape and sarcasm. I can't be what he deserves because I will always be waiting for the catch. For the change in tone. For the warmth to turn cold. For the hand that cups my face one moment to turn into the one that pushes me away the next. It's a pattern I know too well—the whiplash of being pedestal-high one second and unworthy the next. It's what always came after.

So I brace. I push. I test. I pretend I don't care to see if he'll walk away. I don't know how to let someone love me without checking for the fine print. Without wondering what it'll cost me later. And the scariest part is that sometimes, when he looks at me, like I'm *worth it*, I very much want to believe him, which makes me panic even more.

Why? Because we're not soulmates. We're a brand. A viral phenomenon. *Bell and the Blade.* And if I don't screw it up, this could mean everything for my career. Renata and Fisher can't keep up with the fan content. Camille's videos are now in the millions. There's even a rumor that ShelfSpace wants to do a holiday spotlight segment with us.

Which brings me to...

The Snowflake Gala.

Our next event. Hosted by my publisher: *Kiss & Tell Books.*

It's formal. Black tie is not optional. Readers, the Press, and the entire internet are watching. Soren and I will be paraded around as the power couple of the literary world. Hand holding. Smiling. Dancing.

Touching.

Kissing.

My stomach flips. I'm nervous. More than nervous. I'm terrified. Someone is going to get hurt because this thing doesn't feel fake anymore. I don't know how much longer I can pretend. Especially when he says things that crack open places I've cemented shut, and truly believes I'm worth figuring out.

And Soren's *nice.*

Before we left Salem, Emily and I took him and Fisher to our favorite little bistro, and Soren ordered me an extra dessert because I mentioned once—*once*—how much I loved marzipan.

Also, he was supposed to leave that day for an event in Houston, but he rerouted his entire schedule to see the joy on my face when I ate it.

He's attentive. Kind. Infuriatingly swoony. And somewhere between our snark battles and staged photos, I stopped hating him.

That's a major problem.

My phone buzzes. ⚔ **Brood Lightyear** ⚔.

> Been thinking about you.

I stare at the screen. My thumbs hover over the keyboard.

Do I answer?

I want to.

But should I?

> I'm starting to worry you're developing a real obsession.

> Already had one. It's named Ava Bell and she's taking up all the space in my brain.

> Gag.

> What are you wearing to the Gala so I can match you, like prom?

> You mean you'll actually be in a tux and not cosplaying as a morally gray elf lord?

> Don't tempt me. But yes, bow tie, cufflinks, the whole tortured gentleman fantasy. Unless you'd prefer me in nothing at all?

> 😊

> That's a blush, Bells. You forget I've seen your tell.

> It's the lighting. I'm near a fireplace.

Sure. Let's talk logistics. Touching okay?

In public?

Were you thinking elsewhere? Like in our suite, later.

Or before.

I'm down for either.

Or both.

Light touching.

Deflecting. Okay. Kissing?

Strategic kissing. For the fans.

Tongue or no tongue?

Please say tongue.

You're impossible.

Only for you.

We'll make a plan. We'll be PREPARED. Not like that stunt you pulled at Feast and Fiction.

Or we could improvise. Like I did at Feast and Fiction.

Dangerous game, improvising.

I love dangerous games.

My heart does a traitorous flip.

You're full of lines tonight, Pembry. Are you workshopping new material?

Only one muse these days. She's snarky, suspicious, secretly sweet. Killer mouth on her.

That mouth is used for espresso and eviscerating fan theories. Not fluffing your ego.

Fluffing, huh? Is that on the table?

Kidding. Kind of. Unless...

There will be no fluffing.

I get hard when you turn bossy. It's hot.

I'm ignoring that. Quick question though...

Uh-oh. That tone.

How experienced *IS* the tortured fantasy villain, exactly?

What do you mean by "experienced."

I don't know. How many... chapters have you written with other women?

Chapters?

Pages? Scenes? Acts? I'm being delicate here.

You mean my body count?

Yeah.

That WAS subtle. As you're aware, I'm not a saint, Ava. But I'm also not who the internet says I am.

You've got, what, a thousand women calling you their book boyfriend?

Mmmm, more like millions, but they don't know me. Or my heart.

And I do?

You're the only one I want to hand it to, bruises and all.

...You're flirting again.

Yeah, I am. But ONLY with you.

This whole thing is getting confusing.

Let me help un-confuse you. Dinner. A REAL date. Not like that staged, cringy monstrosity in D.C.

Tomorrow night. I'll fly back to you. Your turf. Just us. Real talk. No fans. No cameras. No pretending. Only you and me.

Why?

Because if we're going to pretend to love each other in public... we should know what it *MIGHT FEEL* like in private.

Dangerous game, remember?

Still my favorite kind. That will never change.

I set the phone down with trembling fingers.

His words bounce around in my head. *Dinner. Just us. No fans. No cameras.*

No pretending.

Only you and me.

There's nothing fake about the way my stomach dropped when I saw he texted me. Nothing staged about the heat

256

spreading under my skin at the thought of him, here, with me. There's probably flames flickering in those storm cloud eyes of his, smiling. He knows what I'll say.

My fingers move to type out my response, then halt, hovering. God, what am I *doing*?

Soren Pembry is everything I've trained myself to avoid. Beautiful, risky in the way a cobra dances—hypnotic to watch, deadly to touch. He's made for seduction. Built for it. A man who collects hearts just to hear them shatter.

And yet...

There's a transformation I can't explain. He's hiding a quieter Soren underneath the smirks and swagger. I *felt* it in Salem—between the banter and that moment in the Witch House where he looked at me like I wasn't Ava Bell the Author™, but *just Ava*. I haven't been *just Ava* in a very long time.

It's easier being the brand. The ShelfSpace Queen of Steam. The girl with the romance empire and the tragic backstory. He saw through that. Or around it. Or maybe he didn't care about the façade I've worked so hard to create.

He called me a muse. His current book has a female character inspired by me.

No one's ever called me that before. Or done that before. Not without wanting pieces of me in return.

What if he's doing all of this to get close for research? For his façade? Or his character?

What if I'm a sucker and it's all lies?

Like Jon's were.

That asshole called me talented, beautiful, special. Right before he destroyed every part of me I'd felt brave enough to share. And right before he turned my body into a stepping stone and my dreams into a joke. The others were no different.

So yeah—I've got baggage.

But I also have eyes. Ears. And a very vivid memory of Soren's hand curling possessively around my hip, his breath catching when I tilted my head and gave him a little more skin, his voice dropping half an octave when he said my name.

Ava.

I *relished* the heat, the ache, the idea of someone touching me without pretense. Someone sees me—not the viral moment, not the author persona, but the flawed, guarded woman underneath.

And that's where it gets complicated, because what if I say yes?

Deep down, I know Soren's not playing. He means it.

What if I do too?

I know I'm suppressing emotions. But I can't take a wrecking ball to my walls. Gamble everything on a man who lives three thousand miles away and has been trained to flirt for a living.

No.

...But maybe it *could* be.

Just once.

One night of leaning in instead of pulling away. *One* night where I don't play the cynic or the puppet master or the girl who's always watching her own back. One night, to *let go.*

My thumb taps against the screen, indecisive. *Your loneliness is talking, Ava.*

It's the sunrise and the coffee and the way the light spills across the floor. Hope I didn't ask for.

Or maybe... It's the idea of his voice in my ear again, murmuring my name like it's the only word he ever wants to say.

Whatever it is, I'm tumbling down a black hole.

> Fine. Dinner. But let's be very clear, Pembry. One night. ONE. A moment. No contracts, no promises, no keywords.

I don't type: *No holds barred.*

But I very much think it.

I stare at the message for a full thirty seconds before hitting send. My heart is beating fast. I just agreed to sign a treaty with the devil. Only this devil wears reader glasses and smells like a magical forest.

The dots appear instantly.

> Noted. But if we only get ONE night, Bells...
> I'm going to make damn sure you remember
> it.

The blush hits so fast, I nearly drop the phone.

> Wear a dress.

Feast & Fiction

Snowflake Gala

Bookmas Bash

Midnight Kisses &
Paper Wishes

Twenty

SOREN

I'm not nervous.

Okay, I'm a little nervous.

Which is a wild thing to admit, considering I've stood in front of packed convention centers, fielded flirtation from cosplayers dressed as succubi, and once gave a talk titled *"Pleasure and Power: Crafting the Fantasy Villain Readers Want to Bone."*

None of that compares to tonight.

Tonight isn't about readers or fans or keeping the Bell and the Blade ship trending on ShelfSpace.

Tonight is about Ava.

About us.

If I do this right, it won't be *one* night. And one night only. It'll be the beginning of so much more.

I pull my journal out of my bag. What started as a weekly routine has now morphed into nightly letters. Obsessive? Maybe. But it's become a mission I *have* to complete.

Some are funny. Some are rambling. Some read close to love poems and others similar to apologies I haven't earned the right to give. But every single one ends with the same tone:

Choose me, Bells.

I open my journal to a random page and trace the words with

my thumb. They're worn soft from revisiting them too often. Maybe tonight I'll let Ava see the proof–the ink on paper–that she's been my reality long before this fake-dating circus. That she's the only story I've ever wanted to tell.

I shrug into my coat, slip the journal into my inside pocket and smooth my palms down the front of my black sweater. Presentable, layered for cold weather, and exactly what I know she likes: low-effort hot. I even shaved. Well, trimmed, really. Which I never do unless there's a stylist hovering with a lint roller.

But Ava's different. Has been from the start. The world falls away when she talks. And I want nothing more than to keep her talking.

Hopefully, she doesn't think tonight is some prelude to casual sex.

A *one* night... stand.

Lord knows the girl is horny. And hell, I wouldn't complain. But I want her trust before I want her body. Because I know her well enough now to recognize the heat in her eyes, how her body leans toward fire, even when she swears she wants distance. Desire makes her reckless for a heartbeat, maybe two—but the traitorous hunger that I know she feels with me isn't what I want from her. I want the part she's afraid to give.

Hopefully, when she says yes to this—whatever *this* is—it isn't to silence the ache between her thighs, but to answer the deeper ache in her heart. The one I'm waiting for her to trust me with.

Tonight, I need to let her keep control while I rewrite the story she tells herself—the one where all men are lying, disappointing assholes.

I'm here because of *her*, not the cameras. Or our brand. Not even her... Well, you know.

I won't lie, though. *That* visual has forced me to cold shower every day since Thanksgiving.

She said *one* night. That's her boundary. So I'll give her the best one she's ever had.

I pull up the itinerary on my phone and double-check the

plan. She thinks we're going to dinner. And we are. But I've also arranged for a private viewing at an immersive book-themed art exhibit in downtown Boston—one I know she's been dying to visit but couldn't score a ticket to. Thanks to Emily, who's helped me set up a few things for tonight.

After that, we're hitting an indie bookstore. Not just to browse.

We made a deal when she helped me with my spicy scene. She gets three minutes to grab as many books as she can carry. No limits. Although there will probably be lots of judgment. Still, I'll buy every single one, no matter the cost.

I make good on my promises. And if I'm lucky, this night will be one she doesn't file away as fantasy.

And *after that*, something quieter. More personal. A stop that will remind her of childhood, of comfort, of the way books feel close to home. She said that when we were side-by-side at *The Great Booksgiving* panel. Probably didn't realize I was listening.

I was.

I am.

Ava Bell deserves a man who *listens*. Who shows up, doesn't walk away or lie or make her feel like collateral damage in someone else's story. She deserves a man who sees the fire *and* the fear and stays anyway.

That's exactly what I plan to do.

The car I rented for tonight is a Bentley Bentayga—ridiculously impractical, absurdly expensive, and worth every damn penny.

Let's be honest, Ava could care less about the car. She'd roll her eyes at the price tag and ask why it doesn't come with its own library.

I didn't get it for her. I got it for me. It handles icy curves like a dream, the cabin smells of leather and ambition, and every detail whispers: *You're worth it.*

The moment she slides into it, wrapped in winter and

wonder, cheeks pink from the cold, I want her to feel like the queen she'll never admit she is.

About thirty minutes and a couple of stops later, I park at the base of Ava's rocky drive, step out, and lean against the driver's side door with a thermos in hand—caramel blondie latte extra hot. Her favorite. She notices the little things, even when she pretends not to. So do I.

Ava appears on the porch, resembling a wary cat—poised, curious, and utterly unimpressed.

"You're late." She folds her arms. She's in a long camel-colored coat, scarf wrapped once around her neck, hair down and slightly curled. Adorable. Gorgeous. Completely unaware of how kissable she looks.

"I was busy seducing your favorite barista," I reply, holding up the thermos as a peace offering.

That gets a smile. Small, reluctant, but there.

She rounds the car to the passenger side. I follow her and quickly open her door before she gets a chance to.

Ava eyes me warily as she slides into the passenger seat. I hand her the thermos. She sniffs the drink before taking a sip. "If this is poisoned, it's a very Ava-specific way to go."

"Oh, ye of little faith." I shut the door and rush to get inside, to be closer to her, but there's a wide console separating us. Who picked this car?

"No—ye of sketchy track record," she says once I click my seatbelt.

I laugh, yank the car into drive, then pull onto the road, tires crunching over frostbitten gravel. "You wound me. I'm a changed man."

"Sure. And I'm the Queen of England."

"I'd believe it." I sneak a peek at her. "You've got the stare. Regal and slightly terrifying."

She chuckles into the thermos. The faint tug of her lips tells me she's trying not to love this. Or to like *me*. So, I must be doing something right.

The ride is quiet after that, but not uncomfortable. Her fingers tap against the thermos. Mine rest loose on the steering wheel.

Once we're in the city, she watches it glide by, lights reflecting across the windshield like falling stars.

"Where are we going?" Ava asks.

"You'll see." I pull up to the small brick building tucked between a florist and an indie cinema, she frowns, curious.

"This isn't dinner," she says.

"Correct." I hop out and jog around to open her door before she can argue. "It's better than dinner."

Inside, the smell of sawdust and aged paper hits us. The gallery is dimly lit, intimate. A woman with black marble glasses and a clipboard gives us a nod and slips away—she knows not to hover.

Ava stops short in the main hall.

Book *art* inspired by, well, books. The exhibit displays massive canvases splashed with quotes and character sketches, sculpture installations of iconic romantic moments carved in stone and light. There's one piece made entirely of burned paperbacks, forming the silhouette of two lovers kissing through ash. Another has typewritten love letters suspended in glass.

Ava moves cautiously, seemingly afraid that if she breathes too loudly, it'll all vanish. "How did you..." Her voice trails off.

"I called in a favor," I say behind her. "Private showing. Thought maybe you'd like—"

"Love it," she whispers at the same time, turning to me with wide, doughy eyes. "Soren... this is unreal."

She drifts from piece to piece, murmuring titles under her breath, fingers hovering, just shy of touching. *Jane Eyre, Normal People, The Secret History, Persuasion, The Great Gatsby*—I know her reading tastes better than my own heartbeat by now.

I get a little giddy myself when I see *The Princess Bride* and *A Court of Thorns and Roses*.

When she reaches the wall covered in framed first pages—

typewriter-font manuscripts mounted as museum pieces—her eyes shine. She turns to look at me then, and I hope to God she sees past all the jokes and banter and the stupid viral videos—to something solid. Something honest. Me.

This is who I've been trying to show her all along.

Ava's slender fingers trail the frame of *Persuasion*, hovering over the opening line.

"I used to underline this one in every copy I found," she says softly, almost to herself.

I step beside her. "Why?"

"At first glance, it's not exactly romantic." Ava tilts her head, her hair falling, creating a curtain between us and the rest of the world. "But it sets up the deeper themes. It's about second chances. About someone being worth the wait. It made me believe that even if I messed everything up—if I wasn't brave the first time—I might get another shot someday." She laughs once, dry and hollow. "Except real life doesn't work like that."

"No... it doesn't." The words are rough in my throat. I drag a hand over my face, wishing I could scrub away the truth of it. My chest caves in at her quiet pain, my heart pounding like it wants to argue otherwise, then her body turns toward mine.

"But you keep showing up like it might," she says.

A heavy silence surrounds us. What Ava just said means she's finally seeing me. And for the first time, she doesn't push me away because she's terrified of what happens if she doesn't.

"Because you're worth it, Bells." I slide a stray hair away from her face.

Her breath shudders, as if she doesn't believe that about herself. That tears me up inside.

"I used to get lost in these books," she says, waving toward the walls, moving the spotlight away from her. "Not for the happily ever after, but the yearning. The tension. That ache when someone's afraid to want too much, but wants it anyway. I know that ache."

"And now?" I ask because I *need* to know and understand her hurt if I ever want to be the one she doesn't run from.

"You know."

"Do I?"

"Yes, I write about it," she says. "About love that I'm too scared to ask for. I write about women who get it right, even if I don't."

I don't hesitate. "You deserve a beautiful love story, Bells. Not just the ones you give everyone else."

Her eyes narrow.

"Did the idea never occur to you?"

She shakes her head. "Not in a long time—or maybe ever. I wouldn't even know where to begin."

"Start here," I whisper, reaching gently for her hand. "With this chapter. With me."

Ava stares at our joined hands—mine large and callused from axe handles and book signings, hers delicate but sure. They've spent a lifetime bracing for impact.

Her thumb brushes the inside of my wrist. It's the gentlest touch. But surges through every vein in my body.

"If I let someone write their way into my story again, I'm scared of the ending," she admits, her voice trembling at the edges.

My heart thuds, deep and painful, against my ribs. "Then don't let them write it for you. Write it yourself. Write the terrifying and messy. I'll be whatever you need me to be—your plot twist, your cliffhanger, hell, even your tragic hero if that's what it takes—but I'll never take the pen out of your hand."

She laughs a breath. Then—God—she leans her forehead into my chest.

"I'm not good at this," she whispers.

"Good," I say, brushing a knuckle along her cheek. "Neither am I."

We stay like that for a breath... two... five. The world still spins beyond the gallery's tall, frost-touched windows. The city glitters in soft focus. But in here, in this small moment carved from pages and heartbeats, it's ours.

I lean down, but not to kiss her. Not yet. To feel her nose brush mine. To feel her exhale when she lets the walls drop an inch lower. And, gently, her lips press to my cheek—so light it's as though she's testing how it feels to let herself hope.

Ava pulls back, eyes swimming with unshed tears. "Ready for the next room?" she asks, voice thick.

I nod, hand still warm around hers. "Lead the way."

We linger a while longer, moving from canvas to canvas, exhibit to exhibit, letting the hush between us say what our mouths won't.

Ava stops to study a shadowed portrait titled *The One That Got Away*, I watch her instead—how her brow furrows in thought, how she bites her lip, as though she's holding something fragile behind her teeth.

Eventually, I slide my hand into hers again. This time, she squeezes back.

Neither of us says it, but we're both feeling the weight of what's clicking into place between us.

Outside, the December air nips at our cheeks, but Ava doesn't let go of my hand as she veers toward the car, cheeks flushed, eyes still sparkling from the exhibit.

I tug her back gently. "Not so fast. We've got a Blind Date with some books."

"What?"

I nod toward the indie bookstore glowing down the block, windows fogged and shelves lined like a siren call to every reader with a TBR taller than their fridge. "You've got three minutes. Grab whatever you want. As many as you can carry. I'm paying."

Her jaw drops. "I—Are you serious?"

"I'm rarely not, but..." I say, leading her across the street. "Clock starts once we walk through that door."

"Are you insane?"

"Yes."

The bell chimes when we step inside. She does a little spin in the entryway, trying to absorb every shelf at once. Then something clicks behind her eyes, and Ava Bell *activates*.

"I'm going full gremlin," she warns.

"Do your worst."

And she does.

In the first thirty seconds, she clears the new release table. She dual-wields tote bags the store owner hands her with sheer fear in her eyes.

At one point, she's muttering to herself in a frenzy: "Need the special edition. Ooh, sprayed edges. Oh my god, the romance section. *SORRY!*" That last one is to an innocent display she knocks over in her sprint.

Ava grabs all of my books—*two* of each. When I raise a brow, she shrugs. "One for reading. One for collecting. Duh."

By the end of her spree, she's red-faced, grinning, and wobbling under a tower of books that defies basic laws of physics. She dumps another stack on the counter, and I brace myself for the bill.

The total?

Astronomically high.

The cashier reads it aloud, and Ava chokes on her laugh. "Would you look at that," she says sweetly, elbowing me. "Dating is expensive."

"I regret nothing," I pull out my card.

Watching her glow like this is worth the thousands I just spent.

At the car, I grin and open the door for her. She slides in, her eyes scanning the dashboard, the heated seats already warming.

Once I put several heavy bags of books into the trunk, I hop in and put the car in reverse, pulling away from the curb, merging back into the pulse of the city. Streetlights blur past in ribbons of gold. The silence is charged with high energy from two very successful agenda items.

Ava leans back against the headrest, watching me from the corner of her eye. "So... what's next, Pembry?"

My pulse jumps. "Dinner. Somewhere that I hope surprises you."

"Is it a dungeon?"

"Only if you count hanging plants and overpriced farm-to-table menus as bondage."

Her lips curl. "Color me intrigued."

The GPS chimes softly. I take the next turn that swallows us deeper into the night, onto a quiet road winding through a grove of pine and maple, their bare branches dusted in icy lace. At the end of the lane, a structure appears—glassed walls glowing from within.

The greenhouse.

She stiffens as I put the car in park. "What is this?"

"You'll see."

I get out and walk around to her side. Chivalry may be outdated, but I'm leaning into every romance trope tonight. I offer her my hand, and to my surprise, she takes it. Her palm is small and cool, and my stomach somersaults at her touch.

Inside, the greenhouse is warm, scented with earth and citrus. String lights hang in lazy loops overhead, and candles flicker from stone planters and hanging lanterns.

At the center of the space, beneath an arch of ferns and ivy, is a small picnic setup: thick blankets, two chairs, and a table covered with dishes.

"Another favor." I shrug, watching her eyes scan the scene. "The owner of the botanical center's a fan. I promised a signed edition and a quote for their Valentine's brochure."

"Romantic bribery."

I chuckle. "I'm not ashamed."

She walks ahead, fingers brushing a vine of jasmine. "This is..."

"Too much?"

Her eyes meet mine across the candlelight. "No. It's perfect."

My chest expands. I don't let myself grin. Yet.

We sit. Eat. Talk. She teases me for my soup-slurping. I tease her for the way she smells everything before tasting it.

"You remind me of a suspicious woodland creature," I say. She laughs. I light up.

The meal is delicious, and filled with laughter that comes more easily than I expected.

As I retrieve the deck of "Conversation Cards" from my coat pocket, a curiosity crosses Ava's features.

"I have questions," I clarify. "And I thought we could play a game."

"Prepared, are you?"

"Ambitious," I smirk. "Your turn first."

She picks a card. "Favorite book growing up?"

"*The Last Unicorn.* It made me cry, but don't spread that around."

A soft smile. "Your secret's safe."

"My turn." I shuffle, pull a card. "First kiss?"

She snorts. "Middle school. Halloween dance. He was dressed as a cowboy. I was Juliet."

"A cross-genre masterpiece."

She huffs a laugh, then looks away, hair falling over her shoulder.

We fall into rhythm. The cards alternate between silly and soul-baring.

"What's your biggest fear?" I ask.

Not being enough for someone to stay.

Ava doesn't say that aloud, but I see it in her pause. I heard her tonight. I listened.

She finally exhales. "Geese."

Taken by surprise, and very fucking confused, I repeat. "Geese?"

"They have teeth on their tongues, Soren. Teeth. On their tongues. That's not a bird. That's a demon in a down coat."

I laugh, hysterically. "Fair. I was expecting commitment or spiders. But geese?"

"They hiss. They *chase*. I got attacked on a second-grade field trip, and honestly? I still flinch when I see a pond."

Her eyes meet mine. The humor fades, but the openness lingers. It's not the *whole* truth. But it's enough for now.

Geese?

Who knew?

She takes another card. "What's one thing no one knows about you?"

"I learned how to bake during lockdown," I answer. "Got weirdly good at scones and cinnamon rolls."

"You could star in my next book."

"Would love to." I pick the next card up. "What's something you want but won't admit?"

She hesitates. Takes a long pull of her wine, then says, "You."

My pulse is a drumline in my throat, rhythmic and insistent, but my hands stay where they are. I'm afraid any movement will scare her off.

"Ava," I murmur, her name the softest thing I've ever said.

She looks away. Her fingers twist in her lap. "I shouldn't have said that."

"Yes, you definitely should have said that."

Ava lifts her gaze. Her eyes are glassy, bottomless, guarded. But the door's been cracked open.

One more inch.

"You make it almost impossible to keep my walls in place," she whispers.

I push my chair back and stand, the legs scraping softly against the cobblestone floor. Leaning over the table, Sixteen Candles–style, I close the distance until our breaths tangle in the space between us while clutching the edges of he table to brace myself. "Tear them down, Bells. Let me in."

Her breath shivers out, fragile and unsteady.

"I'm not going anywhere. You want me? You've got me. No games. No gutting."

"I don't know how to do this without breaking something."

"Then break me," my voice is just for her. "Just don't lie to yourself about what this is between us."

Ava's answer is in her silence. She tilts her chin up, glassy eyes shining as though she might finally let herself fall.

I lean down. Her breath trembles against my mouth. My hand hovers near her cheek, aching to touch.

And then—

The temperature plummets. A sudden gust rips over the glass structure, rattling it like a warning. Candles flicker, and the moment shatters, leaving us suspended, our lips a breath apart, the world intruding before we collide.

"Come on," I say, rising to stand. "We have one more stop."

She protests, but I wrap the blanket from the picnic around Ava's shoulders, and as I lead her back out into the cold, she yanks a pair of gloves onto her tiny hands.

The greenhouse lights flicker behind us as I guide her to the car, her gloved fingers brushing mine occasionally. Even her subconscious can't make up its mind.

Her cheeks pink from the cold, she watches the frost sparkle on the windows, her lashes dewy and dark.

When we slide into the warmth of the SUV, she sighs and flexes her fingers over the heater vents.

"Okay," she murmurs. "That was disgustingly romantic."

"I know." I grin, pushing the car into drive. "And I'm not done yet."

Her expression is laced with suspicion and reluctant amusement.

We drive up a steep overlook, one of those hidden local spots you only know about if you've lived here or—like me—done an unhealthy amount of research.

At the top, the view opens up. City lights sparkle below, casting reflections on the lake in the distance.

"Okay," she says, squinting out at the skyline. "This might actually be impressive."

"Might?"

"Still debating."

"The silence here is different," I say. "It holds secrets."

Her arm brushes mine. I don't move.

"You did all this for *one* night?" she asks, voice shaky.

"I did all this because I want *more* than one night."

Her pouty lips press together. They're made for kissing. She catches the bottom one between her teeth, trying to hold something in—words, want. Both.

"I know the deal," I say. "But I also know what I want. I want the whole sarcastic, emotionally guarded, wildly brilliant you. And now that I know you want me too...well, prepare for my level up."

"How in the world could you possibly–"

"Wait and see." I reach across her legs and open the glove box to retrieve a tiny Bluetooth speaker.

Her eyes watch curiously as I cue up the premade playlist on my phone.

A few taps later, the unmistakable opening of "I Can't Fight This Feeling" by REO Speedwagon fills the car.

"Oh my God," she says, staring at me in horror. "No. Absolutely not."

"Yes," I say, deadly serious. "Get out of the car, Bells."

"You did not cue up a power ballad."

"I did. And I'm asking you to dance with me."

"It's twenty-eight degrees."

"Exactly. Good excuse to get close."

She eyes me like I've grown antlers. "You are such a sap."

"Guilty."

Opening my door, I rush around to hers and hold out my hand. I'm standing there with breath fogging the air and a stupidly hopeful expression on my face, waiting.

Finally, she groans, then caves.

Ava steps into me as I wrap an arm around her back and pull her in, slow and careful.

The music is ridiculous, and she's fighting a smirk even now, but when her cheek rests near my shoulder, one more crack in her armor splinters.

We move in lazy circles beside the car, headlights casting a soft halo around us. Snowflakes drift like feathers through the air, sticking to her hair. The chorus builds, and I lower my voice to speak in her ear.

"You know what I see when I look at you?"

Her head tilts slightly so her eyes can meet mine.

"I see the woman beyond the name stamped on your books. The one who builds worlds out of heartbreak and hope. Who thinks and works too damn hard and gives too little of herself because it's safer. I see someone who's been burned so badly, she'd rather freeze to death than risk it again. And that's brave as hell, Ava. You are both fire and starlight."

Her arms tense slightly. She's pulling away, not physically, but emotionally, and the moment is threatening to crumble.

"I'm not trying to fix you," I add. "Or push you into anything you're not ready for. I promise I've only been honest with you. And for tonight—*one* night—let yourself give in to the pull between us. Make this *one* moment beautiful. Something to hold onto when those demons creep back in."

Tears well in Ava's eyes. We gaze at each other for a long moment. Then, her head settles on my shoulder, and we sway, surrounded by snow, by music, by emotions.

And we stay there.

Dancing.

Quiet.

Together.

Feast & Fiction

Snowflake Gala

Bookmas Bash

Midnight Kisses &
Paper Wishes

Twenty-One

AVA

I'm not cold.

I'm confused.

Which on some level is worse than freezing, because at least freezing is straightforward. Hypothermia. Shivers. Possible death.

Confusion is layered. Slippery. *Dangerous territory*.

And standing here on my porch, still swaddled in the blanket Soren wrapped around me like I was a burrito.

I'm utterly baffled.

Soren Pembry—Fantasy Heartthrob, Viral Flamebait, Human Sin Against Sweaters—gave me the most romantic *one night* of my entire life.

A surprise art exhibit. A book buying spree. A botanical candlelit dinner. Power ballads. Dancing in the snow.

I'm toast.

Now I'm at my front door, key in hand, heart somewhere between my esophagus and the North Pole, trying to figure out what happens next.

He put the bags on the porch, and now he's standing close enough to kiss me. Close enough to press me into the door and undo all the restraint I've watched him choke back for hours.

I want him to too.

I think?

No. I *definitely* do.

But I also don't.

If I let him in, it's no longer a bit, or a fling, or a PR stunt. It's a shit-just-got-real kind of thing. And real means risk. Real means giving someone the power to hurt you—and trusting, hoping, that *maybe* they won't.

I've been burned. Charred down to the bone by a man who smiled sweetly and left ash in his wake.

I spent years patching the cracks, constructing walls, and pretending my fortress made me strong instead of lonely.

But Soren...

Soren isn't *him.*

He's cocky and *Blade*-level dramatic. But he's also the guy who planned an entire night to make me feel safe. And special.

I've been too damn focused on punishing him for sins he didn't commit, holding him responsible for demons that don't belong to him, that I haven't fully recognized that the version of him the world sees—the glint and grit and swagger one—is the armor he wears to keep from getting gutted too.

What if letting Soren in means breaking the pattern? What if —terrifying thought—I deserve someone good? And honest? Who adores me? One who takes the time to show me that?

I'm tired of being careful.

Right now, as I look at him, I want to know...

What is it like to let someone in and not come undone entirely?

What I'm about to do could ruin me or save me. Fuck it.

I turn to face him. "You want to come in?"

As I wait for his answer, my pulse is erratic. Air to breathe? Forgotten.

Soren's gaze flits down to my mouth. It's quick. Intense.

"Yeah, I do," he replies, voice sultry. Temptation disguised as politeness. "But I'm not going to."

Don't look disappointed. Do not let your shoulders drop. Or your face fall. Appear unaffected.

The words flood out. "I've got wine. And fruit. And at least three different varieties of cheese. We could make a charcuterie board. Roll the salami into little roses if we're feeling fancy." I sound less like a rational human being and more like the host of a midnight infomercial for the lonely and emotionally insane.

A laugh rumbles out of him. "The most Ava Bell offer of all time."

"Well, I'm very on brand."

Soren steps forward. His cologne drives up my nostrils. Without ceremony, build-up, or a dramatic music cue, he kisses my forehead. Thoughtful. Kind. Friendly?

What just happened?

One hand cups my jaw as though I'm made of paper and poetry. His lips brush over my skin with devastating restraint, outlining the shape of the moment.

He pulls back, and my knees are asking my ankles for support. They're not getting it, though.

"That's it?" The shock in my voice is painfully apparent. I almost slap myself for not filtering the question.

Soren's eyes sparkle with humor and control, as well as desire. His stormy grays are all mixed up and cocky as hell.

"Ava Bell, I had an amazing night with you. I'd love to see you again," he says. "Maybe over breakfast tomorrow?"

"Breakfast?" I repeat, still confused.

He nods. "How about I come back tomorrow morning with pastries?"

"Okaaay." The disappointment I've tried to keep at bay takes over. It's thick in my tone.

Taking a step back, a faint smirk tugs at his mouth. "Goodnight, Bells. Dream about a handsome, fantasy-obsessed warlock with half-decent sword skills and an inconvenient weakness for one woman in particular. In case you're wondering...it's you." He winks.

My arms cross, but I'm smiling. "I'll try not to let it ruin my eight hours."

Soren chuckles, turns to head back toward his car. And I just... stand there, arms still folded, body still buzzing, mouth still twisted in a smile I don't mean to wear.

Because hell.

I *am* definitely going to dream about that handsome warlock tonight... might even masturbate to him. And I don't mean the publicist-pleasing version. Or the internet's fantasy prince. The one who took me to dinner. Danced with me. And is now walking away from me to prove he's in it for the long haul, and not just *one* night.

Yeah. *That* version is hard to resist.

Lingering in the doorway, I watch the taillights of that ridiculously expensive SUV fade down the drive. With every inch that disappears, my heart sinks deeper in my chest.

The silence that follows isn't peaceful. It's cavernous. All the laughter and heat and banter that filled our night got sucked out the moment he hopped into the car and shut the door.

I press my palm to the banister on my porch as though it might hold me up, as though I can physically secure myself to something before the ache in my chest tips me over.

Fuuuuck.

Grabbing a few of the bags of books, I make my way inside and set them onto the kitchen counter, then retrieve the rest. I wander through my empty, quiet house, set in the middle of nowhere. I chose this solitude for myself—on purpose, with intention, as a means of control. And silence from the world. Protection, also, if I'm being honest.

But right now, I've never felt more alone in my own house. I'm not sure how to go back to my typical kind of quiet, which doesn't include Soren's voice in it.

My coat is still on, cheeks flushed, fingers shaking. I look out the window at the empty driveway, and my heart plummets. I wish he'd turn back.

I don't want the night to end. Which means, I'm in trouble. And I now very much *want* to be in trouble.

But two seconds ago, I put myself out there, offered Soren more time with Ava Bell up on a silver platter, and... nothing.

He's being respectful. It's fine. I get it.

To distract myself, I toe off my boots. Hang my coat. Wander back into the kitchen where I'm going to do something normal and adult, maybe clean a dish or organize a cabinet.

That doesn't happen. Instead, I open the fridge, stare at a wedge of brie, and close it again.

Why didn't he push?

Why didn't he kiss me?

He said he wanted to come in, Ava. Don't overthink it.

Tonight, Soren gave me safety. Respect. And then he kissed my forehead and promised a tomorrow. A future.

Fucking hell. I'm so goddamn confused.

A few seconds later, I'm standing in my living room. I pick up the blanket from our picnic and wrap it around my shoulders like a dramatic widow in a BBC period drama. I consider calling him back for a second. To... rewrite the moment. Take control. Level the field.

But I don't want control. I want to *lose* control. With him. *Tonight.* For *one* night.

Pushing pride aside, I grab my phone and pull up his contact. He answers on the first ring.

"Okay, so maybe pancakes are better as a post-date snack." My voice wobbled at the end, and I hope he didn't notice.

There's a pause that's full of breath and heartbeat.

I cradle my phone against my ear, staring at the half-finished puzzle on the table. "Soren, I know I do a *phenomenal* job of keeping you out. Award-winning. Tall walls. Strategic misdirection. Chains around my chest."

Silence.

My eyes close, but I push forward before I lose my nerve. "I really need you to storm through one of those walls right now before I chicken out and go back to pushing you away." I laugh awkwardly. "For tonight anyway. And I don't want to pretend I don't care when I do." My voice drops, shaky and small. I'm now entering rambling territory. "I don't know where this goes, and I'm scared. But I know I want to spend more time with you. I don't want the night to end yet." I chew on my lip, nerves kicking up again. "So. Um. You want to come back? We could watch a movie. Keep the night going. No expectations, just time... together."

Silence continues to fill the space.

Starting to panic, I add, "I have popcorn. And wine. And a decent couch-to-lap ratio. And I'm... *really* putting myself out there right now, so if you're about to tell me no, can you at least pretend to think about it first?"

More silence. I hold my breath. He's thinking, which is torture.

"Only if I get to pick the snacks. And you don't judge me for my pajama pants. I'm already halfway to my hotel and halfway into them."

Exhaling, I grin. "Deal. But I'm picking the movie."

"You got it, Bells."

About an hour later, Soren's at my door in fire-breathing dragon PJ pants, a black long-sleeve thermal, holding a paper bag from the bodega in town that smells like buttered popcorn, and several other bags I'm assuming are filled with candy and snacks.

"You came back."

"Of course I did, you tempted me with cinema."

"Well then." I make a grand sweeping gesture toward the couch. "Prepare to be disappointed."

"Bells, you could play the director's cut of *Paint Drying: The Trilogy* and I'd still call it the best night of my week."

Forget butterflies. A tornado touched down in my gut, and debris is flying everywhere.

Breathe, Ava.

"Did I wander into a snow globe on acid?" In the living room, Soren has slowed to a stop. His gaze sweeps over the twinkle lights strung along every surface, the five holiday-themed candles I typically burn simultaneously, and the cluster of nutcrackers on the bookshelf that look as though they're plotting a violent undertaking until finally landing on the disco-ball reindeer above the fireplace.

Soren laughs and spins around slowly, taking it all in again. "This is... a lot of Christmas."

"Don't judge me. I've been avoiding deadlines and nesting like a feral raccoon with a Michaels gift card." I fluff a throw blanket that says *Sleigh All Day* in an aggressive glitter font. "This is a totally normal level of holly jolly."

"Remind me to bring sunglasses next time. It's blinding in here." His eyes narrow in on my couch and look at it like it's the most confusing thing he's ever seen. And then—oh God—he spots the throw pillows.

Those throw pillows.

Cartoon candy canes in, um... compromising positions. One is clearly being spanked. The other is tied up with tinsel. I'm not emotionally stable enough to unpack their origin–which I'm pretty certain happened the night I was two bottles deep in Cabernet–let alone their current placement on my couch.

Soren tilts his head, assessing.

"Yes, they're doing what you think they're doing." Lunging across the room, I suddenly become a defensive lineman and snatch them both up. "You weren't supposed to *see* those. Nobody visits me. They're for fun."

"Fun, huh? Looks more like a metaphor for how Ava Bell likes it—decorative on the outside, filthy on the inside."

I toss one of the naughty pillows at him. He catches it, then I head into the kitchen to pop some popcorn.

While I'm milling about, Soren turns the pillow over like it holds ancient secrets, studying it thoroughly.

"'Naughty but nice,'" he reads aloud, amused. "Is this a seasonal threat or a year-round lifestyle?"

"Depends on the wine," I shoot back.

"Then go ahead and pour yourself a glass, Bells."

The microwave beeps. I pour the popcorn into a ridiculously festive bowl covered in holiday cheer, because I've surrendered to the aesthetic.

When I turn around, he's pointing at a bottle of red on the counter.

"This one okay?" The corner of his mouth lifts. "Does it do the trick?"

Biting my lower lip, I nod and hand him the corkscrew.

Soren uncorks it with surprising grace. Two generous pours. A man who knows exactly what kind of night he wants this to be. Except—what if I'm the only one wanting it to go that way?

We return to the couch. I sit while he sets the glasses onto the coffee table, then Soren drops next to me like a man who's found salvation. He exhales, melting deeper into the plush.

"Okay, this couch is suspiciously comfortable." His legs stretch out. "Is it enchanted? Do I live here now?"

I cue up the movie. "Only if you behave."

"Then, I'm definitely getting evicted."

Soren squints at the screen. "Is this *Twilight*?"

"Absolutely, and if we're up to it, *New Moon*."

"I—" He covers his mouth. He might be having a moment. "You *chose* this?"

"Oh, I did. And we're doing commentary."

His eyes are wide with pure, unfiltered delight. "I get to roast this with you?"

"Obviously. But only after proper reverence is shown for the riotous cinematic masterpiece that is Taylor Lautner's wig progression."

"Ava Bell, you're a genius. You know, they filmed it near my stomping ground."

I take a handful of popcorn. "I thought you lived in Seattle?"

A smirk pulls at his mouth, and it's deeply attractive. "Doing research on me, Bells?"

"I'm thorough."

Soren chuckles. "Every year, I rent a cabin close to the coast. Peaceful. Inspiring. Near some of my favorite bookstores."

Opening a bag of Skittles, I try not to show how much that image undoes me. A rented cabin on the coast. The salt-stung air, waves crashing against weathered rocks, a fireplace spitting sparks while the world outside falls away. No panels, promos, or people pulling at the edges of me. The thought fills me so completely it feels like it's pressing my palm to something warm and endearing.

"I will never confirm nor deny that I've stayed in Bella's House."

My head snaps toward him. "*Bella's House*? The one that's booked through 2050?"

His voice drops, and it makes everything inside me go still. "Have you not figured me out by now? I don't accept defeat. I can find my way around any obstacle."

I know he's not talking about vacation rentals, so I do the mature thing and whip a pillow at him.

Soren catches it with one hand. Effortless. Annoyingly smooth. He doesn't throw it back. Instead, he sets it aside, then shifts closer on the couch.

Touch-close.

His body heat seeps into me. Cedar and the faintest trace of eucalyptus hovers in the air between us. His thigh brushes mine. The contact is barely there, but my whole body reacts to it.

We don't speak, but the urge to touch him is loud. While he sits next to me, undemanding, not pressing—just *there*, I decide that in this quiet little pocket of borrowed time, to let it in, and let it stay.

Maybe it's the firelight. Or the wine. Or perhaps it's him. The man who doesn't run. The one who listens.

Sitting back, I press play and breathe.

We watch. We laugh. I forgot how this could all end in heartbreak and hate. For now, it's happening for one night.

Problem is, I'm already craving the next.

We're twenty minutes into *Twilight* when *it* happens.

I don't mean the sparkling or the light stalking or the confusing biology class stare-down.

No, I'm talking about the *incident*.

It begins innocently enough—me quietly judging Bella's complete inability to operate a backpack, and Soren making some sarcastic comment about how Edward's hair has more volume than the earth's atmosphere.

I respond in the only reasonable way: by flinging a skittle that hits him square in the chest.

He gasps like I've wounded him. "You *assaulted* me with a candy pellet!"

"It was yellow. Calm down. No one likes the yellow ones."

"You monster." Soren clutches his chest dramatically. "Lemon is my weakness."

"You're thinking of vampires, Pembry."

"Them too," he replies, digging a hand into the popcorn bowl for retaliation.

Before I can duck, I'm pelted with several rapid-fire kernels. One bounces off my cheek. One disappears into the couch cushions. The third rolls down my shirt on a journey of self-discovery.

"Uncalled for," I say, batting at my sweater.

"You fired the first shot."

"That was flirtation. You escalated it."

Cocky, and unrepentant, Soren grins. "Well, you should've known I'd retaliate. I'm the fantasy villain, remember?"

Reaching into the popcorn bowl, I grab a handful and rain them down over his head. Most fall into his lap, but one stays in his hair. We both burst into laughter.

After a minute or so in the trenches of our popcorn battle, we declare a truce and collapse back onto the couch, limbs slightly tangled, the space between us smaller now. Popcorn crunches beneath me, but I don't care. It's scotchguarded.

On screen, Edward is giving Bella a speech about monsterhood while brooding from a tree branch as a tragic gargoyle.

"You know..." I half-smile. "For all its cringiness, there's something kind of sweet about Twilight."

Soren raises an eyebrow. "Sweet? Please elaborate on what part of this paranormal stalking saga you find sweet."

"Charlie."

That gives him pause.

"He's awkward and a little emotionally unavailable, but he shows up. Makes her dinner. Checks her truck, cares, without needing credit."

Soren's watching me now, the movie forgotten. "Sounds like someone else's dad I know."

I'm caught off guard by the tenderness in his voice. "Yeah. Mine's like that. He doesn't get the whole ShelfSpace thing, but he understands books. He prints out my covers and keeps them framed in his garage next to his tools."

Soren smiles. "That's so fucking cute."

Pride tightens in my throat. "Growing up, he bought me a new book every birthday growing up. Still does. And every year, he writes a message on the inside cover like he's my personal dedicator."

"Dedicators are underrated," Soren says quietly. "They're the people who believe in you even before the acknowledgments."

That stupid, fluttery ache in my chest kicks up again.

This man. This night. This slow burn unfurling.

"I'm going to need a restraining order against how sweet you're being."

"Nah," he murmurs. "But if I go out, I'm going out with popcorn in my hair and my self-respect intact."

"You had self-respect?"

"It was very brief. I lost it somewhere around the sparkle reveal."

I laugh harder than I have in years. Soren laughs too—deep and rumbling—and then reaches over and tucks a piece of popcorn from behind my ear like he's unveiling a magic trick.

My breath catches—mercifully, brilliantly—then, as the scene changes. Bella's confronting Edward in the forest. He tells her to *say it.*

Soren leans in, whispers, "Vampire," at the exact same time Bella does.

We both snort. The mood lifts again. The tension folds itself back into laughter and sugar and the mess of who we are tonight —two people flirting through their defenses, popcorn in their hair, movie glow on their skin.

I don't know what will happen next. But for now, we press play.

And keep watching.

Twenty-Two

SOREN

Somewhere between *Eclipse* and *Breaking Dawn*, Ava gave up the fight. The fire's burned down to glowing embers, soft orange light filtering across the room. Her TV screen has dimmed to that blue screensaver with the bouncing logo, the movie long since over.

One second, she was curled up with her knees tucked beneath her, making snarky comments about Edward's tragic cheekbones, and the next, she was out cold.

Ava's draped across me, her cheek pressed to my chest, her body slack and warm across mine, one of her hands resting over my stomach. I haven't moved for hours. I should shift. Stretch. At least cover us with a blanket. But I can't seem to do anything but hold her close and watch the firelight dance across her face.

She's beautiful, peaceful, she belongs here, curled into me. God, I never want this *one* night to end.

Every so often, I trace her features with my gaze—those full lips, the faint crease between her brows even in sleep, like she's still a little suspicious of rest. Of comfort. Of me.

I don't want to move. If I do, she'll wake, and the moment will break.

Carefully sliding my hand from her waist, my fingers brush over bare skin where the hem of her shirt has ridden up, exposing soft, creamy skin. My thumb grazes the warmth there, soft, tender, memorizing her by touch alone.

Ava stirs. A soft noise escapes her lips, then her lashes flutter open. With one hand braced against my chest, she pushes herself up. Autumn-colored eyes dart toward the fireplace, the bouncing blue screen, and finally, to me.

For a few beats, Ava only stares down at me. The light in her eyes regards me in the most tender way, as if she's letting me glimpse the part of her she guards from the world, like everything could collapse around us and she'd still keep looking at me.

"You fell asleep," I say, hoping she won't retreat, but stay, *right here*, tucked into me.

When I think she's about to peel herself off me, that light in her eyes sparks into a blaze, and before I'm able to form a single word—

Ava kisses me.

Fierce.

Without caution. Without brakes.

Gentle hands cup either side of my face, holding me in place like she's scared I'll disappear.

My heart flips at that thought. This trusting, uninhibited rendition of Ava has always been the inevitable conclusion for me.

Always.

I don't pretend to play it cool. I kiss her back. I've been starving for those lips since we left Salem. And now, drenched in firelight, interwoven together on a couch with *Twilight* long forgotten and Ava Bell pressed against me, I'm never letting her go.

Ava's lips are soft, sweet, curious, and hesitant all at once. They move like she's testing the shape of surrender, like she's afraid of wanting too much and doing it anyway. When her mouth parts beneath mine, I realize it's not restraint—she wants to drown. To get drunk on this kiss. On me. On *us*.

Ava lifts herself to straddle me, knees bracketing my thighs. My hands instinctively settle on her hips as her body sinks down onto me. At the same time, my hips rise a little too eagerly. There's no mistaking it, she feels my rock fucking hard, fully aroused cock, absolutely aching beneath her.

She halts for half a second. Shit, there it is—the change. Her mental demons scramble to catch up with her body, the logic crashing in, that old Ava defense system blinking red.

No Bells, stay with me.

Taking control, I draw her back down and kiss her with long, deep, drawn-out strokes of my mouth that taste like possession but melt into devotion. I could spend forever here, sustained by her lips alone.

And then—

Ava does the weirdest thing. She pulls back so that she's gazing down at me again, then grabs my hand and puts it on her boob. Over her shirt. Right on top. Palm-to-fabric contact. Suddenly, we're back in middle school, and I upgraded to second base with her parents in the next room.

To say I'm confused—not to mention delighted—would be an understatement. My face must show it because she avoids my gaze completely.

Cheeks flushed, chest rising and falling in tiny, embarrassed breaths, Ava's most definitely nervous and very much unsure of herself. I get it. She's out of practice. Out of her depth. But damn, if it isn't the cutest damn thing I've ever seen.

The number of men she's been with could fit on one hand—actually, a few fingers. That inexperience? This trust? I have to be careful. I'm not just touching her right now—I'm rewiring her, etching myself into places no one's earned the right to go in a very long time. She's let so few in, and somehow, I'm one of them. The fact that she's giving me this drives me fucking feral.

Ava affects me in ways I can't explain. She possesses a fragile magic I don't want to break. And I want to murder the men who helped her build these carefully constructed walls. The one who made her feel like she now has to stay in complete control, carry the risk, read every signal before it explodes in her face, treating intimacy as a field of fire ants she has to tiptoe through barefoot.

My free hand slides around her waist to cup the back of her thigh, and I hitch it higher, opening her to me. The moment my dick presses deeper, her breath breaks.

"Tell me this feels right?"

Ava arches, her body answering me before her voice ever could. That gasp, those tiny shivers, each desperate roll of her hips is all mine. But she's still hesitating, unsure if she should give in completely. And damn, if she isn't stupidly hot and adorably flustered, with pink chinks, her breath shallow. She's standing at the edge of a cliffside, the bottom holding everything she craves... and fears.

"Yes," she exhales, a word that sounds more like surrender than permission.

I let my hand stay. Press gently, show her I'm here, that I get it before I rise off the pillows to meet her where she is. Our gazes connect for the briefest second, then I kiss her temple, her cheekbone, the corner of her mouth.

She sighs. The tension in her shoulders gives.

One more inch.

My hands find the hem of her sweatshirt, and wait. She nods. I lift it over her head in a slow sweep.

Well. That's one way to end my blood circulation.

Pink bra. Perfect tits. Curved, full, flawless. And they are begging to be touched, tasted, and devoured.

Did I mention they're fucking *magnificent?*

A primal noise juts out of me, and I don't even try to hide it because *fuck*, my mouth is watering.

"Ava..." Her breathing quickens as I run my fingers over the soft tops of her breasts. Reaching the straps of her bra, I slip them off her shoulders. "You're gorgeous," I whisper, unhooking the back with practiced ease.

The fabric falls away, baring her to me, and every ounce of clever confidence I thought I had evaporates.

Tight little nipples. Glowing skin. Fuck, she's stunning. And right now...she's all mine.

I stare, awestruck, useless, my throat working around words that won't come. My hands hover as though I've forgotten how to touch.

Huffing out a breath, I laugh a little. "Now I'm the awkward one."

She chuckles, moving her hands to my shoulders just as I duck my head to take her nipple into my mouth gently, giving her every chance to stop me.

Thank fuck, she doesn't.

I suck on one, then the other, swirling my tongue, teasing, giving each equal playing time while Ava grinds over my raging hard cock. Her fingers knot in my hair as she makes a sound that might be a gasp, or might be my name. Might be both.

"Breathe for me." If this is all we do tonight, if this is as far as it goes, I'll still count it as the best night of my life because this is her *letting me in.*

But I'm far from being done. Not if she wants more.

Slowly kissing up the slope of her breast, to the curve of her neck where her pulse flutters against my lips, one hand holds us together while the other trails down her side. Over her ribs. Her waist. Hips. When I reach the edge of her leggings, I pause, letting my fingers rest there, testing the waters.

Ava lifts her hips. Barely. The motion tells me everything.

My fingers tease the skin at her waistband—*so slowly*—until the heat of her seeps into my skin.

She shifts again, grinding harder this time. My fingers dip inside her leggings and move down to her entrance. She's *soaking* wet.

Ava whimpers. "Oh God."

Pressing my lips against her throat, I murmur, "Tell me if you want me to stop."

"I don't," she answers immediately.

Obeying her wishes, I press gently against her clit, coaxing more of those helpless, breathtaking sounds from her throat.

Jesus, I want to fuck her. Of course I do. That's not happening tonight, though. This isn't about me. Tonight, I'm going to peel Ava open with my hands. My mouth. My patience. Layer by layer. I'll give her everything she doesn't ask for—security, and bright fucking stars behind her eyelids when she breaks apart on my fingers. Or my tongue. We'll see how far she lets me go.

Ava moans, "Soren, please."

I give in to the only urge that matters. My fingers pinch the tiny nub. Her entire body arches on top of me. She's gasping now, needy and gripping me tight. I've never wanted to make someone come this badly in my life.

I work her clit easily. It's swollen and begging for attention. The tip of my finger circles it lightly, pressing a little harder as her legs tremble.

"There?" I whisper, kissing her jaw.

She nods frantically, a red flush creeping all the way down to her neck to her chest as I toy with her entrance, coating my fingers in everything she's giving me before pushing one finger in, then two, and she squeezes so tight around me it's like her body's trying to keep me.

Jesus, she's wet.

Ava's fucking strangling my fingers, and all I can think about is how it's going to feel splitting her open on my cock.

"Soren, that feels–" Ava moans into my mouth.

I don't let her finish. My lips crash to hers, blocking the rest of that sentence with one deep and all-consuming kiss.

She's so hot, so fucking *perfect*. Curling my fingers, I learn the rhythm of her hips, the way her breath hitches when I get it right. Ava's close. Her body speaks to me. It's in the way her thighs shake, the desperate little gasps she lets out with every stroke. I drive into her, two fingers buried to the hilt, stretching her until she's whimpering.

"You're doing so good for me, baby." Pressing my forehead to hers, I pump my fingers in and out while my thumb works her clit. "Let go, Ava. I've got you."

Her body goes taut, shudders, her thighs clamp around my hand as she cries out my name. Unhurried, I keep moving her through it, sweet and idle, until she's soft and trembling beneath me.

Once her breathing returns to normal, my fingers slip free, slick and shining, and I bring them to my mouth to lick every last drop off.

"Fucking delicious," I growl. "Next time, I'm going to have your legs over my shoulders while I lap up every moan you make with my tongue."

Ava lets out a shaky sound that lands somewhere between scandalized and *please do that immediately.*

I kiss her again—filthy and affectionate altogether—because *damn*, I'm becoming addicted to this, to her.

And as my lips devour hers, I'm sealing a promise I haven't dared to say out loud yet—one I'll spend forever keeping if she lets me.

Ava peels back and hits me with a surprise blow. "Why wait for next time? Why not now?"

Everything comes to a screeching halt, and my pulse punches the inside of my throat as it does. This woman managed to flip the power dynamic in one sentence. And those two questions *vaporized* whatever thread of control I was clinging to.

Not quite believing I heard her right, I pull back to see her face, her eyes dark and steady on mine, and *fuck me*—I've never wanted someone, or something, as much as I want Ava Bell's pussy dripping on my tongue.

"What?" I ask, clarifying because I'm not walking away from that.

"Why not now?" she repeats.

A wicked smile spreads across my face. I'm not going just to lick Ava. I'm going to shatter her...slowly. Break her into a million fragments, that only I'll know how to hold together.

Twenty-Three

AVA

Why not now?

The words echo in my head the second they leave my mouth, floating in the space between us.

Soren goes stock fucking still. His eyes lock on mine. Everything *shifts*. The air. The tension. The gravity in the room. Whatever leash he's been holding himself back with?

Gone. As if it never existed in the first place.

Cautiously, he slides off the couch, settling on his knees in front of me. *Knees.* In front of *me.* As though I'm something holy. Like he's about to pray.

I'm outside my body watching it happen. This is someone else's night. Someone else's pleasure. I don't *do* this. I no longer let men in. I don't get to have this sort of thing.

His hands come to my knees, thumbs pressing softly into the sides, warm and resolute. I should stop this. I should say something, laugh it off, run into my bedroom and lock the door, do literally anything else—but I don't. I *can't.*

That gleam in Soren's eyes? I'm pretty sure it means he's about to revise everything I thought I knew about my own body.

Fuck it.

I want to forget the walls.

I want to be the woman Soren Pembry gets on his knees for. Even if it's just for *one* night.

Calloused hands trail down the outside of my thighs, so achingly slow, my breath catches, and my toes curl.

Soren isn't rushing. His hands slide to the waistband of my leggings, fingers hooking gently. There's a silent question written in his eyes.

I nod.

Taking his time, he peels them down inch by inch, along with my panties. For him, this isn't about speed, it's about intention. About me.

Cool air kisses the skin Soren reveals, and I shiver from the way he watches every movement. He eases the fabric down my legs, knuckles grazing my calves. My entire nervous system lights up, and by the time he takes them off completely, I'm breathless. He hasn't even touched me where I need him most.

Soren nudges my legs open, and I tense on instinct. I want this—Lord, I *do*—but it's *happening*. This isn't a fantasy anymore. This is Soren between my thighs, peering up at me. And he's about to remake me from the inside out.

I'm not sure I'm breathing. I'm not sure I remember how.

He presses a kiss to the inside of my knee, eyes locked on mine. My brain wants me to bolt. But my heart is doing cartwheels, screaming about every wall I've ever built and how this man kicked them down with a single glance.

His gaze never leaves mine. He squeezes my thighs—gentle, grounding. "You okay?" he asks, voice quiet. He knows I'm halfway to losing my mind.

I nod, too fast. "Yeah. Just... outside my body a little."

His smile is soft. Unbearably tender. "Let me bring you back." Soren leans in, presses a kiss to the inside of my thigh this time, and I nearly come apart from that alone. "You're safe, Bells. And tonight, you're mine. And you matter."

No one's ever touched me like I mattered. Soren wants to *learn* me. The others wanted to conquer. Perform. Take.

Sore rises, and his lips crush to mine as one hand palms the back of my head to hold me in place. He doesn't kiss me like I'm a battle to be fought. He kisses me like I'm the victory already in his hands.

He peels back, and his eyes drink me in. I'm stripped bare in front of him, my legs parted, my breath ragged, my entire lower body trembling—and he's still on his knees, staring at me. To him, I'm something to behold.

I should be embarrassed. But I'm not. I'm *bold*. Confident. He makes me that way.

By the adoration in his eyes. By the fact that he hasn't even touched me down there yet, and I'm already coming undone.

Soren dips down, kisses me higher this time on the inside of my thigh. The scrape of his stubble drags a gasp from my throat.

Another kiss. And another. He trails them closer to my sex, his breath a whisper against my skin. One hand hooks my leg over his shoulder while the other splays over my hip to steady me. Smart. I might fly away if he doesn't hold me down.

His tongue licks straight up my center, deep, slow, *purposeful*, as though he's waited a thousand lifetimes for this and plans to take his time tasting every second.

A moan rips from my chest, and his hand tightens on my hip in response. He likes that. He wants more. And sweet *hell*, I want more too.

His lips are not tentative. Or shy. My fingers clutch the couch cushions beside me while his tongue traces circles that electrify my brain. I'm not outside my body anymore. I'm *buried* inside it, every nerve ending awake. Every thought is a blur. Every inch of me is open and trembling under the weight of this man's mouth.

I can't think.

I can barely breathe.

My body is one long, trembling wire pulled taut, and Soren's mouth is the spark teasing closer and closer to the break.

He doesn't change rhythm. He keeps me on the edge, circling

it again and again until my legs are shaking, my lungs no longer know how to function.

Soren's hands stay firm on my thighs, securing me to him, and the noises leaving me aren't pretty. They're ragged. Desperate. Choked.

His tongue moves with maddening precision, with deep strokes that split me open and devour in the same breath. His nose brushes where I need friction most, and I see stars. *Actual fucking stars.*

"Oh my *god*, Soren—" I gasp, voice raspy and useless.

"Yes, baby," he hums against me–a man proud of his work, and that vibration *detonates* heat low in my belly.

I'm close. So close it terrifies me. So close, I want to run.

I don't.

I stay.

I *allow* it to happen.

Because I fucking want it.

And when my orgasm tears through me, it's not quiet or soft or clean.

It's thunder.

It's lightning.

It's a scream ripped from somewhere deep in my soul.

I *chase* it.

My fingers claw into his hair, holding onto the back of his head so I can grind against his face, feral and gloriously focused. Every fractured part of me is fighting to be made whole through the heat of his mouth.

And Soren doesn't let up. He *groans*. Like he's *living* for this, wants every roll of my hips, each broken sound that spills out of me.

Unashamed, I ride it out on his face until I'm shaking so hard he has to grip my thighs tighter to keep me from sliding off the goddamn couch.

My back bows, a cry tears from my throat. My body shatters and spills over his mouth, wave after wave crashing. He holds me through every single pulse, twitch, and goddamn quake, staying with me, tongue still moving, mouth still claiming until I'm boneless and buzzing and barely human.

I finally breathe, collapse backward, and melt into the cushions as the world tilts and spins around me. I'm panting, flushed, drenched in sweat and sensation, and I don't even care. I came so hard I forgot where I was.

"Fuck, Bells...I could live between your thighs and never need another thing." Soren presses one last kiss to the center of me, sweet and respectful, a full stop on a sentence I'll never forget.

I haven't even caught my breath when I reach for him. I don't think—I *move*. Still floating, still shaky, but I want to touch him. Taste him. Give something back after he obliterated me like that.

But when my hand grazes the waistband of those ridiculous pajama pants, Soren seizes my wrist and shakes his head. "Not tonight."

My face scrunches with confusion. "But—"

"Tonight is about *you*, Bells."

There's a fresh sting behind my eyes. I don't know what to do with that kind of care. That kind of *refusal*.

He kisses the inside of my wrist. "Let me hold you, yeah?"

I nod, too overwhelmed to speak.

Soren reaches for the leggings I'd completely forgotten existed and helps guide them back over my legs and hips with more tenderness than should exist. Once he's done, he settles onto the couch and pulls me into him, tucking me against his chest, protectively.

And here, curled into the warm strength of his arms, legs entwined, heart pounding in the afterglow—I let my eyes fall shut.

I wake up in my bed.

Not the couch.

I was wrapped in limbs and tangled in the man who kissed me into oblivion, fingered me into an orgasm so good it briefly rebooted my nervous system, then licked me as though I was his final meal and savored every morsel.

Now, I'm in my bed. Alone. Which, to be clear, is *not* where I remember falling asleep.

The last thing I recall is that drugging kiss Soren gave me right after he made me see a whole other universe with two of his fingers.

And...

His words.

His tongue.

My body ached for something I've worked very hard at blocking out. Basically, Soren said, *Hey, I'm going to annihilate your pussy. Hope that's okay. And I'm not even going to take my clothes off to do it.*

Apparently, I passed out after that. And "The Blade" tucked me in.

I sit up, the blanket slides down my naked chest, over my fluttering heart. I'm wearing my leggings—which he helped me back into—but nothing else.

Bacon sizzles in the kitchen. Pans clank together.

He didn't leave?

What do I look like right now?

Bolting upright, I snatch a shirt from the laundry basket and power-walk to the bathroom, boobs bouncing with every step.

The mirror does not offer comfort. My hair is a disaster. My mascara is smudged completely, suggesting to the naked eye that my night was either full of sex or sobbing, and my lips are still swollen. From *him*.

Holy Lord in heaven.

After frantically brushing my teeth, I splash my face, tame my hair, swipe on concealer, lip balm, deodorant.

Am I prepping for battle? Or brunch?

I take a breath and head toward the kitchen, but don't make it far.

There he is. Leaning against the doorframe.

Pajama pants.

Bare chested.

Barefoot.

Holding a steaming mug of coffee and wearing a smirk that makes me want to ride his face again, and then expire right there on the tile.

"Awe," Soren's voice is warm with swaggering delight, "were you trying to primp yourself before facing me, Bells?"

I say nothing.

"If so...you missed a spot."

I peek down at my shirt. It's inside out.

I want to die.

Instead of handing the mug to me, he sets it on the counter. Then, to my utter horror and surprise, he steps closer, tugs at the hem of my inside-out shirt, and begins to lift it off me, like he's helping a toddler who got dressed in the dark.

"You look better without the shirt." Before I can process what's happening, he dips his head, pressing a kiss to my bare sternum. His lips trail lower, and when he kisses my nipple with hot, wet lips, I *fucking freak.*

I jump back like I've been tased, and nearly knock over the coffee in the process.

His hands rise immediately in innocent surrender. There's laughter in his eyes. "I was correcting a wardrobe malfunction. *Very* respectfully."

This is the morning *after* our *one* night. And he's still here. Smiling. Which is a problem.

Isn't it?

Last night was obviously a lapse in judgment on my part. And I know one thing for sure—I don't trust morning afters. That's when reality crashes in. When the spell breaks. When the soft looks and slow hands fade into polite nods and awkward silence.

It's when people start editing through what happened. Downplaying it. Folding it into something smaller, something casual. Something that didn't matter. Even though I felt everything crack open inside me.

Morning afters are when one party's gotten what they wanted. And she's left wondering if any of it meant anything at all.

I swore never to be her again.

My gaze slides toward the door, seeking an escape. I'm bracing for the catch. But instead of backing off, Soren steps even closer.

"If you're waiting for the part where I disappear, you're going to be waiting a long time, Bells."

Folding my arms, I try to appear like I'm not hiding behind them. I'm failing miserably. "We agreed it was one night."

"I remember," he's not even phased. "I also remember you crying out my name and falling asleep on top of me half naked, so let's not pretend the agreement didn't get a little...blurred."

My chin drops. Soren lifts it with unfamiliar tenderness, but I don't look at him.

"Ava Bell, you are one tough egg to crack." His thumb brushes my jaw.

My attention then shifts to his handsome face and the thick shadow of facial hair that should *not* be this hot, but absolutely is. The scruff curves over his jawline, his top lip. It's rakish, and I'm remembering the scrape of it brushing against my thighs.

"Mark my words." His eyes lock on mine. "I will break you."

Heart pounding against my ribs, I exhale.

Soren steps back. "Besides, I can't go anywhere—we're snowed in. Must've started somewhere between *Twilight* and your pussy swallowing my fingers."

My mouth tumbles open. He did not just say that.

His lips twitch. "Whatever shall we do?"

A moment later, Soren's setting the table as if he's done it a hundred times before. Plates in one hand, thumb smoothing a wrinkle from the napkin. He moves with this unhurried, quiet confidence.

Forks aligned. Glasses filled. A small dish of butter next to the bread he warmed in the oven because "cold carbs are a crime."

I sit there watching him, unsure what to do with the knot forming in my chest.

Does he do this for every woman he spends the night with?

Is this another trick up his well-stocked arsenal of charm?

Or is this something else?

He's humming under his breath. He's barefoot and comfortable. He's still not wearing a shirt, and I don't know if he even realizes it.

It's messing with my head because I've had men light me on fire. But I've never had one set a table for me.

The thought is either terrifying or attractive. I haven't decided yet.

When he finishes, the table is ridiculous. Scrambled eggs topped with herbs, thick-cut bacon, crispy hash browns, and actual homemade cinnamon rolls—*from scratch*—glazed and steaming. They smell amazing.

"You baked?" I eye the golden spirals like they're going to vanish if I blink.

"I told you, I learned during lockdown. I'm a man of many talents." Soren cuts out a cinnamon roll and winks. "You've only scratched the surface, Bells."

"You mean kind of like how I—"

His brows rise, daring me.

"—scratched your surface last night?"

Soren laughs, head tipped back with the grin that threatens to undo me. "Technically, I scratched yours. But yeah."

We eat in companionable silence for a few minutes, the only sound the crackle of the fire in the living room and the muffled hush of snow falling in thick, lazy sheets outside the window. Everything is soft. Delicate. A world suspended in white.

Sipping my coffee, I stare at him across the table over the rim of my mug. "So, are you this good at breakfast for all your fake dating stunts?"

Soren's forearms rest on the table. "Only for the *one* I want to wake up next to."

The tension electrifies instantly. He doesn't give me time to dodge it.

"I know you're still stuck on that 'one-night' thing," he says carefully, but there's steel behind the words. "You've been spinning all those thoughts in your head about what this means, what it could destroy, where it leads."

I take a bite of bacon.

Soren shakes his head. "Nope. Not today, Spiral Goblin. I'm done tussling with your overthinking brain."

My head tilts.

"The rules have changed." He pushes his plate to the side and sets his eyes on me. "We won't post anything. Not a single photo. No ShelfSpace clues, no cryptic quotes, *nothing*. We'll disappear off the face of the earth. It'll be just us in this cabin, no hovering voices telling us to stay relevant. As long as we're snowed in, our *one* night becomes however many days winter decides."

"And after that?" My voice is barely above a whisper.

Soren smiles crookedly. "We make some decisions."

I stare at him. Soren is so calm. So certain. Grounded in a way I never am. I'm envious. And in this moment, with the snow barreling down, staring back at him, I decide to stop preparing for disappointment and stop scanning for the exit.

I decide to stay.

"All right." Exhaling, I let my shoulders drop. "No posts. No pressure."

His eyes dance with warm mirth.

I pick up a cinnamon roll and take a slow bite, letting it melt on my tongue. "But if you're going to keep baking, you'll need to shovel your way out alone when the storm's over. Because I'm not leaving."

"Good," he replies. "Because I'm not letting you go."

I take another bite. The gooey center is warm and sticky on my fingers. It's pure heaven.

Soren watches me with an intensity that makes it very clear he's no longer interested in breakfast.

"How is it?" His voice deepens, rough around the edges.

"Mmm." I lick icing from the tip of my finger. "It's obscene. I've never had a cinnamon roll *this* good."

"I will never be normal again after watching you lick your finger like that."

With a chuckle, I shake my head, pretending to be scandalized when a wild hair sprouts in my chest—sweet and sharp and totally unlike me.

Reach out, I dip *his* finger into the leftover icing, and bring it to my mouth. Intentionally. Seductively. Keeping my eyes on his, I drag my tongue along the pad of his finger, then take it between my lips and suck—hopefully making him forget what day it is.

Soren's chest rises and falls with heavy breaths. And suddenly I feel *powerful*. Drunk on sugar and whatever the hell this thing between us is.

"What's gotten into you?" he asks, voice wickedly wrecked.

I release his finger with a soft pop and smile, more confident than I have any right to be. "Wanted to see what all the fuss was about."

Shoving his chair back, Soren moves behind me. His hands trail down my arms before settling on my hips. He bends down, lips brushing the shell of my ear.

"You've got icing on your mouth."

"Do I?"

"Mmhm."

I grab my napkin to wipe it off, but Soren beats me to it and slides one hand up, thumb grazing the corner of my lips.

Except, instead of wiping it off, he dips that thumb into the remaining icing on my plate and drags it down the center of my throat.

My heart stops.

"We should put those cinnamon rolls to better use." His mouth brushes under my ear, voice molten, before it finds the spot on my throat, licking the icing away.

"What do you mean by 'better use.'"

Soren peels back, tugs my chair away from the table.

My pulse spikes.

"Stand," he orders, voice deep and commanding.

Without hesitation, I obey, a mixture of curiosity and heat pooling in my core.

Hands slide over my waist. "That's it."

Offering zero warning, Soren grips under my thighs, and hoists me onto the edge of the table.

"You're not serious."

Stormy eyes gleam. "*Dead* serious."

My palms land behind me, bracing against the wood. Soren steps between my legs, spreading them gently with his hips, then leans in until our faces are inches apart.

The fire blazes and spits. Snow falls thick outside the window. His gaze lands on mine, and those eyes tell me that he's about to fuck me sweetly and thoroughly. *Properly.*

Soren picks up the cinnamon roll from the plate beside me and tears off a piece—sticky, hot, glistening with icing.

His lips press to mine, then he says, "Open."

My mouth parts. He places the bite into my mouth. I moan around his fingers. It's that fucking good. *He's* that fucking good.

Soren's lips brush over the icing smeared at the corner of my mouth. "Yeah, we're definitely putting these to better use." His hand slides under my shirt, but pauses. His eyes search mine. "Can I?"

I nod, breath caught somewhere in my throat.

Soren lifts the shirt, his fingers grazing my skin as the fabric rises, and when he finally pulls it over my head and tosses it aside, that gaze darkens.

"I've thought about this, Bells." His hands skim over my bare waist. "You. Laid out for me. My fucking feast. Remove those leggings."

I hesitate for half a second before doing exactly what he asks, dragging my leggings and underwear down my legs.

Soren helps me stretch out along the table—his strong hands adjusting, and coaxing me, treating me as though I'm fragile and precious.

The wooden surface is cool beneath my back, but Soren's hands are hot. He tears the cinnamon roll apart lazily. Icing sticks to his fingers. He drags a piece across my collarbone and brings it to his mouth, licking it off without breaking eye contact.

My thighs clench. He trails another piece over the swell of my breast. His mouth follows, tongue hot and worshipful.

"You taste better than anything I've ever made," he says against my skin.

My hands fist the edge of the table.

Soren continues lower, one knee on the floor, his mouth devouring every sticky, sweet path he lays. And when he places a melting bite of cinnamon roll below my navel, he peers up at me. "I said I'd break you, Bells. Shall I start?"

I cry out. "Fuck, yes, please."

And then—

Soren's tongue.

Hot. Wicked. Sweeping over the icing. Over me. And that's when I fucking lose myself.

Twenty-Four

SOREN

She's stretched across the table, gorgeous as fuck. And that ever-present hunger I've been tucking between every sleepless night and aching pause that has lived in me for a year, whispering: *keep your distance, but don't let her get away.*

Well, that hunger ain't got shit to say today.

Ava's skin is honey-warmed and haloed in firelight.

Defenses? Fallen.

Deflection? Stripped away.

Distance? Obliterated.

Just Ava.

Me.

Nothing left in our way.

I drag my palms over her bare thighs, gaze traveling up the soft slope of her stomach to where her breasts rise and fall with every breath. They're full and begging for my mouth.

Ava's lips are parted, hair a wild halo across the table. She doesn't look scared. No, she's temptation laid bare, ready to be devoured.

Tearing apart another piece of cinnamon roll, I let it melt slightly between my fingers before trailing it between her breasts, letting icing drip down the centerline of her body like I'm glazing a dessert I've waited so fucking long to taste.

My mouth follows, licking every drop from her skin as penance and praise.

"You don't know how beautiful you are," I whisper against her belly, tracing her skin with my mouth. "You're mine right now because you let yourself want me. You stopped running. You let go. *That's* the sexiest fucking thing, Bells."

A ragged breath escapes Ava's lips. Her hands slide into my hair, tugging enough to make my cock jump. My control is fraying, but I'm not rushing.

I kiss her. Hard. Deep. Consuming. She tastes like cinnamon and surrender, and when I pull back, her lips are slick, her pupils blown wide, chest rising fast.

"You ready to serve me breakfast, baby?" My fingers trail between her legs, taunting her. "I'm fucking starving."

Dragging a piece of the roll down lower, I rest it above the place I'm about to claim.

Ava hasn't said anything. Her throat works, presumably swallowing around words that won't come out. One hand lifts, falters halfway, her fingers curl against her palm. Her breathing's quick but uneven, and her eyes—those soft, searching autumn-colored eyes—keep flitting between mine and the space somewhere past my shoulder, like she's not sure which version of herself she's supposed to be right now.

It's not rejection. It's hesitation. She's still learning how to stand still in the light.

"Stay in this moment with me." I kneel. "Don't let the ghosts pull you back."

One hand grips her thigh, the other spreads her open. And then—

My tongue licks straight up her center.

Her back bows instantly, a heavy gasp tearing out of her throat, my name swimming around it like a prayer she didn't mean to speak. The sound spears straight through me, settling brutally and relentlessly.

I take my time, learning her, teasing the edges, pressing deeper, flicking where I know she can't resist.

Ava tastes like sugary icing and something all her own, sweet and addictive, and I know I'll never get enough.

With a growl, my tongue strokes her pussy once, slowly, making her shake, then circles where she's trembling. My rhythm builds—flick, press, swirl—until her hips twitch and chase me, greedy for more.

Pulling back to make her whimper, Ava begs me to come back. "No, Soren, please don't stop."

Lifting my gaze, chin slick, I drag my thumb in maddening circles just shy of where she's throbbing. "You beg so sweet."

I flatten my tongue and lap at her needy cunt. Ava's dripping, and every stroke tastes like a sin I'd die to keep committing. I dip, torturing her entrance, fuck her shallow with my tongue before pulling back up to suck her clit into my mouth. Her cry rips through the air, desperate, and my cock throbs so hard it hurts.

"Yes, baby, sing for me," I moan against her, the vibration setting her off again, her thighs clamping around my head as though she'll never let me go. A deep and guttural groan slips out of me as I lick relentless strokes over her soaking wet heat.

"Oh my, God, Soren." Ava's writhing on the table, muttering curse words and pleading in the same breath.

My gaze holds her stare as I wrap my lips around the little bundle of nerves that's making her fall apart. Her thighs try to close. Not fucking happening. I pin her open and feast.

"You're mine right now," I thunder against her skin. "This body. Those sounds. This flavor. Fucking *mine*, Bells."

Ava cries out again, hips jerking, thighs trembling, breath shattering, and—

She comes on my mouth.

On the table.

Covered in icing.

Snowed the fuck in.

And I'm not done.

Not even close.

Ava's breath stutters in and out as I rise, licking her from my lips like I cleaned the plate—I mean, really, I fucking did, and it was the most delicious meal.

Her thighs are still parted for me, slick and quivering. She's watching me, unsure whether to beg for mercy or more.

Both are welcome.

I run my hands up the insides of her thighs, relishing in how her body twitches beneath my touch—hypersensitive and raw.

"I could keep you here, on this table, all day." My cock strains against my waistband. "Laid out. Dripping. Shaking. You'd let me, wouldn't you?"

Ava's only answer is a whimper.

I lean over her, bracing my forearms on either side of her head, my voice a rasp now. "I'd bury myself inside you right now, Bells —let that needy pussy swallow my cock until nothing else exists. But I didn't plan for this, and I don't have protection."

Ava's eyes widen, and she shifts beneath me, her gaze darting anywhere but mine. One hand lifts. She's about to tuck her hair behind her ear, but then drops it uselessly to her side.

"I don't have any either," she says, the words barely above a whisper. "I... don't have sex. I mean, I haven't had sex."

"You've never had sex," I blurt out before I can process what she said.

"No, I *have*," she quickly recovers. "But it's been... awhile."

My heart splinters. For all her confidence and quips, these innocent moments, in her cabin, are the truest thing she's ever given me. Honesty draped in insecurity. And she's trusting me to hold it gently.

My hands frame her flushed face. "We don't have to, Ava." My voice changes to a warm, husky tone. "I could spend the entire snowstorm between your thighs and making you come over and over, and be totally fine."

Those honey-gold eyes dive into mine, swimming with emotion.

I smile. "Don't need anything else. Just *you*."

Ava laughs, but it catches in her throat. Her expression turns serious. "I want you. *All* of you. I'm here, doing this, and I want it all."

That stills me.

Completely.

"You sure?" My cock is pulsing like this is my first time, because in a way, it is.

She hesitates, then nods. "Yes."

My thumbs brush across her cheeks. "I'm clean. It's been over a year since I've had a partner." My eyes lock with hers. "Despite the reputation you've got swirling in that pretty head of yours, I wouldn't lie to you."

Ava exhales. I can see the walls drop *all* the way down.

This is happening.

We are happening.

She's not running.

She's *choosing* me.

And fuck if I won't make every second of it count.

Reaching down into my pajama pants, I free my cock, and the rush of cool air against overheated skin makes me hiss through my teeth. I'm heavy and pulsing in my hand. My body's been waiting for this release all damn night. When my palm closes around the length, the jolt that tears through me nearly buckles my knees. Every stroke drags a tight ache up my spine. I squeeze hard as a reminder of just how badly I want her.

Ava's gaze drops. She gasps. "That's not going to fit."

The laugh I let out is dark and rough as my thumb smears precum over the head. "Oh, it'll fit, Bells," I say confidently. "Your pussy was made to take me. She's just been waiting for the chance to prove it."

Ava's head tilts as I continue stroking—measured and slick, catching her eyes as I do it. *Yeah, baby. Watch me.*

Her lips part right before she licks them.

"Look at you." My grip tightens as I pump from base to tip. "So fucking hungry for it. You haven't even had me inside you yet, and you're soaking wet again, aren't you?"

She doesn't deny it.

My fist works one last stroke before I release myself and clamp down on her hips. With one quick tug, I drag her ass to the very edge of the table, her thighs opening wider for me like instinct. "So fucking ready for me." My fingers dig into soft flesh as I hold her in place.

I position myself, thick and throbbing, and drag the head slowly through her slick heat. Ava's body jolts, a broken curse tumbling from her mouth as I slide against her clit and down again, taunting her with the promise of everything she's silently begging for right now.

"You want it?"

"Quit teasing me." Her hips lift to meet me.

"Never." The crown of my dick slides through her opening, earning a moan from her. "Every inch of this is yours, Bells. Let yourself *want* it. And now—" My words halt when I push in.

Slow.

Deep.

Endless.

Holy *shit.*

My brain flatlines. Every muscle in my body tenses as her warmth envelopes me—wet, tight, *really fucking* tight—and for a split second, I forget how to breathe.

Jesus. *Mary.* All the damn apostles.

She's so *goddamn* tight I feel baptized. I'm gripping the edge of the table to keep from collapsing on top of her as a man who's just seen God and blacked out from the holiness.

Shit, I've barely moved an inch.

"Fucking hell," I hiss through my teeth. "You're—" I break off with a groan. I'm desperately trying to keep my shit together. But with how tight she is and me feeling her bare, it's damn near impossible. "Your pussy is going to murder me, Bells."

Ava moans beneath me, arching her hips, trying to take more of me, and *nope*, this is officially the hardest thing I've ever done— holding back.

"Fuck, you're taking me so good, baby." I brace a hand beside her head while the other grips her hip. "You feel that stretch?"

She nods, whimpering.

"That's me, Bells. All of me. Just like you wanted, but if I don't start moving soon, I'm gonna come like a goddamn virgin."

"Then fucking move," she breathes.

Deep. Possessive. Thrusts meant to mark a woman from the inside out.

The table creaks beneath us, the fire crackles in the corner, and the snow keeps falling, blanketing the world outside.

I hope to God it never stops. Let the roads shut down. Let the power go out. Let the whole damn world freeze over, because I want to spend the rest of my life buried inside this woman.

Ava moves against me, crying out my name, and the sound creeps down deep into my bones.

This is more than sex.

It's deeper. Wilder.

Beautiful.

This is forever. It's already written into the stars, and fuck, I'm *gone.* Lost in the woman who undid me with a look, dismantled me with a kiss, and is now holding every part of me without even realizing it.

Out there, the world is buried in snow.

But in here, it's her. Me. And every filthy, worshipful thing I've been dying to give her.

"Harder," she pleads. "Fuck me deep."

All reserve inside me *breaks.* My pace goes brutal—months of tension, lust, and unsaid words, exploding into every thrust. Ava arches, clutches at me like I'm her tether to this earth, and I give her everything. Faster. Punishing.

GOING VIRAL FOR CHRISTMAS

The table beneath us groans, legs squealing against the floor, and then—crack. Splinters. We crash down in a heap of limbs and breathless curses, still moving, still chasing it, until the world shatters right along with us.

Ava screams out, her climax ripping through her in waves, and I follow, guttural and crude, pouring everything I've been holding back into the feral ruin of us. Neither of us stops, not until the aftershocks leave us trembling and trapped among broken wood and scattered plates.

Her hair's a wild halo across the destruction, her chest heaving, her lips swollen.

I kiss her messy, still buried inside her, and laugh hoarsely against her mouth. "Oops. Guess that table couldn't handle what I've been holding back for a year. If this is what happens when I finally get to touch you, imagine what's coming next."

Ava giggles, covering her face with her hand. "I'm not sure my house will survive you."

Feast & Fiction

Snowflake Gala

Bookmas Bash

Midnight Kisses &
Paper Wishes

Twenty-Five

AVA

Soren and I are spread out on the thick rug in front of the fire as a pair of satiated heathens in a cabin sex montage.

I'm sticky. Sore in places I didn't know could *be* sore. My thighs tremble every time I shift. I am positively glowing—and not from the heat of the flames licking across the hearth.

Nope.

I'm glowing because I've spent the entire day getting my insides rearranged by Soren Pembry's *massive fucking flesh sword*.

Yes, the rumors are true.

All of them.

Every outrageous comment, thirst post, and five-star review.

His alleged third leg deserves to be carved into Mount Rushmore.

That's how accurate. And he *knows* how to use it.

Soren's currently stretched out beside me, one arm tucked behind his head, the other resting casually across my stomach. I should be overthinking things. Planning my escape. Cataloging all the reasons this is a terrible idea.

But instead, I'm melting into the floor like butter on hot toast, staring up at the wood-beamed ceiling with a blissed-out smile.

"How's your current book coming along?" Soren traces lazy circles on my shoulder.

Eyes half-lidded, I hum. "Mmm. Yeah. It's due in a few weeks. And I'm so not close to being done with it."

"What's it about?"

"The usual—banter, spice, emotional trauma, a man who knows what to do with his hands."

Soren squeezes my shoulder. "Did I inspire it?"

I roll my head toward him, smiling. "Cocky, you are."

"That I am," he says, utterly unrepentant. "What's a book you've always wanted to write but haven't?"

I'm quiet for a few seconds, thinking.

"There's one I've carried around for years," I confess. "A story about grief. And how sometimes people show up in your life like a wildfire, burning through everything you thought was solid. But maybe that's the only way to make space for something new to grow."

Soren watches me, reading between the lines. "You should write that. It matters to you."

I shrug, eyes fixed on the ceiling then roll my head toward him, smiling. "Okay, your turn. What's a story you've always wanted to write but haven't?"

He stretches, arm flexing behind his head. "An dystopian sci-fi where the morally gray hero goes to therapy, stops trauma-dumping on his enemies, and gets the girl *before* the galaxy explodes in the final act."

I laugh. "Groundbreaking."

Soren bumps my leg with his. "There's one problem."

"Oh yeah, what's that?"

"I can't figure out how to keep my hands off of you long enough to type."

I snort, smacking his chest. "Try harder, warlord."

Soren shifts closer, hooking his leg around mine, his hand skimming up my ribs with infuriating ease. "Not a chance, romance queen."

Soren rolls over so he's hovering above me. His lips brush mine, soft, unhurried. I kiss him back, still smiling when he pulls away.

"You know..." His eyes dance with amusement. "...all this snow reminds me of your deeply held belief that snowball fights are a time-honored metaphor for intimacy."

"It's true."

He gives me a quick peck on the lips. "Prove it."

"You want to go outside? Right now?"

Soren's halfway to his feet, bare chest glowing in the firelight, resembling a cocky winter god, *completely naked*, big dick swinging, leading the charge into battle.

I'm torn between hysterical laughter and mild arousal. "You are not going out there like *that*."

A single brow raises, he's utterly unfazed. "What? Afraid the snow's gonna get jealous?"

"You're ridiculous."

"Get dressed, Steam Queen. You're about to catch snow in the face from these metaphorical hands."

"And you're about to get absolutely transformed by snow affection."

Half an hour later, we're bundled up—sort of.

Soren doesn't have clothes here, apart from the outfit he wore last night. Considering how thoroughly we spent the day making sure every layer of it was removed and discarded, it's... less than ideal for a snowball fight.

He emerges from my bedroom, wearing a pair of my oversized joggers that are hilariously snug in the thighs, a too-tight hoodie with a pastel book quote across the chest that reads: *My book boyfriends are better than real men—I regret nothing*, and one of my puffer jackets that *almost* fits... if he doesn't try to zip it.

Soren's also wearing thick pink fuzzy socks stuffed into his boots, which he insists are "gender-neutral" despite the glitter trim and dangling pompoms.

He looks so silly. And doesn't give two fucks while I'm

doubled over as best I can in my snow suit, which mostly means I tilt forward like a bloated marshmallow with joint pain.

"You look like a homeless lady who somehow stumbled into a J. Crew catalog and mugged a toddler for accessories."

Soren does a turn, modeling. "And yet, I *own* it."

"Can't argue there."

"My balls might freeze but my confidence shall remain intact," he announces, slapping on a knit beanie with a sequined unicorn horn. "Let's do this."

Outside, the cold punches us in the face like a scorned ex. The snow is piled thick and powdery, the sky still flaking down in lazy spirals. The woods are wrapped in white silence.

Soren pauses long enough to peek at the driveway where his rented Bentley, now nothing more than a bougie snow mound with luxury tires peeking out from the bottom as a sad, expensive tombstone.

"Well," he mutters, hands planted on his hips, "Guess I'm staying forever."

Not sure I'd object to that.

Soren runs into the snow-covered yard and yells, "YOUR METAPHORIC INTIMACY IS ABOUT TO GET FUCKING PELTED, BELL!"

And then—he sinks.

Immediately.

The snow's deeper than either of us probably realized, and his overly confident charge turns into a slow-motion collapse. He disappears thigh-deep with a strangled grunt.

"Help," Soren calls out, arms flailing slightly. "I've been metaphorically and literally swallowed by intimacy."

"Oh my God, are you *stuck*?"

"Emotionally, yes."

I scoop snow into a perfect sphere, my aim locked in.

Soren's too busy trying to extract himself from the snowdrift to notice. Arms flailing, jacket riding up, talking shit like he's still winning.

Launching the snowball straight at Soren, it nails him in the face with a satisfying *smack*, and explodes in a spray of white across his features.

Soren freezes, snow dripping from his lashes, lips parted in outrage.

"*First blood!*" I shriek and cackle.

His eyes gleam with unholy delight. "You want war, Bells? You got it."

He dives out of the snowbank as a man possessed and one with absolutely zero plan, scooping snow with both hands.

It flies everywhere.

Shrieking, I take cover behind the porch column as a poorly packed snowball sails past my head and hits the door behind me with a sad *plop*.

"You throw like a man who writes poetry in his underwear," I call out.

"I do, and I make women weep," he shouts back, lobbing another one with improved aim.

We're both snow-fueled idiots, laughing, ducking and dodging and slipping on ice patches, shouting insults and declarations of love.

The world has gone white. The cold is brutal. And somehow, I've never felt warmer.

After launching another snowball, I bolt for cover behind the shed, legs wobbling in my puffy suit like I'm running in a weighted blanket. My lungs are burning, my cheeks are numb, but I can't stop laughing.

I hear him coming before I see him—thunderous footfalls in boots, the slap of frozen fuzzy pompoms, and the dramatic war cry of a man with nothing to lose.

"*AVA BELL, PREPARE YOURSELF.*"

Heart hammering with pure energetic joy, I sprint toward the woods, snow spraying at my shins.

I'm fast.

He's faster.

A second later, big arms wrap around my waist and I'm tackled into a snowbank with a shriek, landing in a flurry of white and wild laughter.

Breathing hard, we collapse into the drift, limbs entwined, the unmistakable weight of him over me. Soren braces his hands on either side of my head, breathing hard, his nose red, his lashes dusted in snow.

Chest heaving, I look up at him, my scarf halfway down my face. His beanie is crooked. He's absolutely ridiculous. And completely beautiful.

Soren's eyes search mine, and all that playfulness subtly morphs into softness. "I win," he declares.

"Debatable," I breathe.

A smile. "You're not running...physically, or metaphorically."

"I know."

"Why not?"

Because you're warm, even out here.

Because I can't remember the last time I felt this alive.

Because this might be the dumbest, most romantic day of my entire existence, and I don't want it to end.

But I just say, "Because you tackled me into a snowbank and I'm pinned under two hundred plus pounds of smug."

Leaning down, Soren's nose grazes mine. "Nah, Bells. That's physics in my favor." His lips claim mine, fierce and certain, heat sparking against the cold until every thought of self-preservation is gone. "This? This is me winning. And you're my prize."

There it goes, my heart plummeting straight into his hands, no parachute, no way back.

Feast & Fiction

Snowflake Gala

Bookanas Bash

Midnight Kisses &
Paper Wishes

Twenty-Six

SOREN

Ava and I are sunk into the steaming water of her massive soaking tub. She's between my legs, leaning back against my chest, her head on my shoulder. Relaxing. At least, she would be if my cock weren't making itself very known.

Her elbow shifts, then stills. She tilts her head back to look at me, one brow arched.

"You planning on harpooning me from behind?"

I choke out a laugh. "Not my fault your perfect ass is parked on a very sensitive launchpad."

"Can't even take a bath without you turning into a weapon of mass seduction."

"Correction," I say against her ear. "Weapon of mass distraction."

"Facts."

Ice is still melting in my sock, which is currently slumped on top of the sad little heap of clothes we peeled off like frozen armor.

Correction—*her* sock.

Pink. Fuzzy. Glitter-trimmed. A war crime against footwear I'm now strangely attached to.

Ava's fingers trace patterns on my thigh, doodling her name—

and words she doesn't want to say out loud–in the margins of my skin.

We've been here a while. Talking. Not talking. Letting the steam thaw whatever's left of the walls between us.

Her head tilts back again. "So? Was I right?"

"About what?"

"That snowball fights are a time-honored metaphor for intimacy."

I huff a laugh, reaching for the wineglass perched on the ledge beside me. We popped it open after declaring a truce and deciding day drinking was the only appropriate way to celebrate a well-fought snowball war.

"Well, if you ask me, the metaphor doesn't come from the fight."

"No?" she asks, tone curious.

"No." A wet finger trails down her bare arm. Goosebumps rise in my wake. "It comes from the *after*."

Ava goes quiet, waiting.

I press a kiss to her temple before continuing. "Sitting here. Naked. Warm. Talking about books, writing, dreams, fears... you." My voice lowers. "*Us*. That's the intimate part."

She doesn't respond right away. But something's cracked open in her without force.

"God," she whispers eventually. "You are soooo dangerous like this."

"Like what?"

"All soft-spoken and insightful. Vulnerable. Wet."

I smirk into her skin. "You forgot *hung*."

A small splash follows. "Get out of my tub."

"Too late. You invited intimacy. I'm never leaving."

Ava's back arches, and the movement makes me feel *all* of her. Slippery and slick against my chest, thighs pressed tight against mine.

One shift.

That's all it takes.

The lazy affection between us catches fire, sparking into a darker, heavier thirst that coils low in my belly and dares me to act on every wicked thought currently brewing in my brain. I go from a semi-situation to painfully hard in the space of a breath.

My cock presses into her. She stills, then presses back *deliberately*. And I lose my mind.

Ava exposes her neck, offering me her skin. "You're staring," she says softly.

"Can you blame me?" I set the wineglass back on the ledge without taking my eyes off her. "You're naked. Drunk on snow victory. Dripping wet. You basically summoned this moment."

Her lips twitch. "Careful, Pembry. You're giving me Edward Cullen energy."

My mouth hovers over the pulse at her throat. "Difference is, Bells, I wouldn't stop at just staring."

Ava's lashes flutter. "Well, when you put it that way..."

One of my hands skims over her stomach to the underside of her breast. "Say the word, Bells."

"What word?"

"Literally any of them." My lips skim her jaw. "Pick one. I'll fuck you sweet. Or rough. Or both."

Ava's fingers dig into my thigh. And when she finally speaks, it's not a word at all—it's my name, broken and breathy.

I take that as permission.

My hand slides up to cup her breast, thumb teasing over her nipple until she lets out the softest sound—half sigh, half moan, all mine.

"Still want me out of your tub?" I ask, voice thick with heat.

Sitting up fully, Ava turns in the water, straddles me, her slick heat settling right over my cock—teasing, tormenting—her pussy sliding against me with each tiny shift. It's killing me. I'm so close to being inside her, I can feel her flutter and pulse. Her body's begging me in its own secret language.

Ava stares at me for a delicious few seconds, letting the

tension strangle the air between us before she kisses me, answering my question with her entire body.

"Guess that's a no," I say against her lips.

We stay like this for a while—kissing, tasting, touching—until she relaxes against me again, her breath hot on my throat, one hand idly trailing over my chest.

I hold her against me, my cock standing at full attention—aching, and ready—but I stay still, waiting on her next move. Letting the weight of wanting fall on her.

Then I spot it.

A small black drawstring bag, barely visible behind a cheap little fake plant on the tub's edge. Camouflaged between shampoo and conditioner.

Almost pulled it off, too.

Almost.

I wouldn't have noticed it at all if it weren't for the hot pink lettering printed across the fabric: **Buzz Buddies**.

"Well, well, well." I cock a brow. "What do we have over there?"

Ava stiffens, then immediately glances behind her.

Before she can react, I lunge forward, one arm around her waist to hold her steady while water sloshes around us. Reaching past her, I pluck the bag off the ledge and hold it up between two fingers with a devil's grin as if I've uncovered her deepest secret. Most likely I have.

"Tell me this is what I *think* it is." My eyes gleam.

She scrambles with a splash, cheeks flushing, snatching for it. "It's nothing! That's—it's from a bachelorette party. Years ago."

"Mmhmm," I say, keeping it out of her reach.

"I forgot it was even back there."

"You forgot you were harboring contraband?" I tease, loosening the drawstrings.

"Soren."

I peek inside the bag, fully expecting a cute, modest little vibrator.

What I find?

...Is not that.

High-end. Pink, curved at the tip. It's specifically designed to *beg* her body to respond. There's a defined bulb angled upward for maximum G-spot destruction, and a thick, ridged base that flares out in a way I *know* isn't for grip. It's for grinding.

"This thing's got *architecture*." I hold it up as if I'm examining a futuristic weapon. "This isn't a vibe, Bells—it's an archetype for your undoing."

Ava groans and moves to the other side of the tub. She sinks low into the water, only her eyes and forehead visible above the bubbles now. "Please stop talking."

"I will *not*." Fascinated, I rotate it, searching for instructions. "It has a *curling tip*. *Ten* vibrating modes. Is there an earthquake setting? Oh, this clit base is top-tier. This thing has better engineering than my car."

Her hand smacks over her face.

I can't help the grin pulling at my mouth. "Do you—do you ride this thing?"

"Stop."

"Bells..." My voice drops. "Do you grind on it?"

A strangled sound escapes her throat.

My head tilts.

"You do, don't you?"

Ava doesn't answer, but her entire body is pink and hiding and trembling.

"Oh my god." My mouth falls open. "You *do*. You grind like a needy little slut on this pink rollercoaster, don't you?"

She peeks out from behind her hands, glaring. "*Soren.*"

"My cock just waved the white flag and said, 'Sir, this is above my pay grade.'"

Despite her embarrassment, a laugh escapes her.

"So that's what you like, huh?" My voice turns dark and heady, eager to get this inside her. "Grinding. Pressure. *Full* control."

The way Ava's body shifts is answer enough.

I press the power button on the toy and place it below my navel. The hum kicks through me, subtle but powerful, and I beckon her with my free hand, guiding her to straddle me once again.

She stares down at the setup.

"Trust me," I say. "It's a win-win."

Her expression is still hesitant, but she moves on top of me. I help ease her onto it. The curved tip of the toy slides between her pussy lips while the thick base presses right into her clit, both angled to catch her in all the right ways.

And *my cock*—fuck—it slides between her ass cheeks, snug and hot and perfectly cradled in the slick heat of her body.

She lets out a broken moan the second her hips settle.

I groan beneath her, hands sliding up to cup her breasts. "Jesus, Bells."

Ava grinds forward, testing the movement, and my dick pulses with every pass. Her body trembles with the pressure from the toy, tightening from the buzz of it.

From this angle, I get *everything*—full frontal, flushed skin, her nipples pebbled under my palms, every little reaction in her face as she rides the curve of her own craving.

"You're fucking gorgeous," I rasp, thumbing her nipples.

Ava whimpers, rolling her hips again. My restraint is *snapping*.

"Ride it for me," I growl. "Grind on it like you would when I'm not here. Fall apart for me."

She obeys and grinds harder. My hands palm her breasts with a mix of reverence and filth, fingers pinching her nipples until they're tight peaks begging for more. She's panting now, her rhythm faltering as her body starts to shake.

"You gonna come for me, Bells?" I'm desperate to hear her scream. "Fuck it, baby. Show me how you like it—loud and messy. Soak that toy, make it so wet, it begs for mercy."

Ava nods, helpless. Lost. Her fingers dig into my skin as if I'm the only thing tying her down to this plane of existence.

"Let me see what you look like when you break, baby."

And then she does—loud and raw and blindingly beautiful. A scream tears from her throat as her whole body goes rigid. She shakes through it, hips jerking, riding the storm out.

Before Ava finishes coming, I lift her, remove the toy, and lower her onto my aching cock while she's still convulsing, sinking into her pussy in one desperate, claiming thrust. There's no way I'm not feeling that for myself. But the moment I slide in, I'm instantly sucked into the center of a supernova. Hot. Tight. Drenched in her.

Breathless, she gasps, leans forward and presses her forehead to mine as her lips tremble. "You're my downfall," she whispers, voice cracked, vulnerable.

"You fucking love it." I grip her hips, pulse throbbing, breath ragged as I bury myself deeper.

"I do," she breathes.

"Good," I growl, barely holding on. "Because I'm not stopping until I come so hard you taste it tomorrow."

Ava hits another peak, writhing and gasping, her climax crashing over her. I hold her through the aftershocks as her walls pulse around me, fluttering from her orgasm.

"Fuck, Ava," I grit out, voice shredded, gripping her ass as I guide her rhythm.

She continues to ride me, still trembling, still twitching, her nails digging into my shoulders.

"You feel so goddamn good, baby."

Ava moans incoherent words, collapses forward, her forehead hitting my chest. Our breaths tangling in the steam. I thrust up once, twice, water splashes—and then I fucking lose it, roaring her name as I come, hips jerking, burying myself deep and emptying every last ounce of need into her.

Ava and I shatter together, wet and messy. And in the silence that follows, the only thing I can hear is the sound of our hearts, still racing. Still secured.

"You know," I say, running a hand over the curve of her ass. "That was a pretty strong argument for metaphorical intimacy."

Twenty-Seven

AVA

Two days later, we're not tearing through each other. We're just... being. Normal people, not horny disasters.

The fire pops in the hearth, casting an amber glow over the dining room. It's silent except for the occasional clink of puzzle pieces and the rustle of Soren flipping through the edge pile with extreme dramatic concentration.

I watch him, thinking how right now we're... safe. Real. And I don't know what to think about that.

Normal isn't usually mine to keep. Safe has always felt like a temporary state, something that collapses the second you breathe too hard.

But here I am, sitting across from Soren Pembry—my rival, my fake boyfriend, the man who should be the opposite of safe or normal—but I feel both.

Soren glances up and smiles. I get back to work on the puzzle. We've been working on this thing for over an hour—a thousand tiny pieces forming an old bookshop storefront—and somehow we're still not sick of each other. That's another fact that should terrify me.

Yet, it doesn't.

Outside, the snow has mostly melted. A slushy mess now lines the edges of the road, the mid-afternoon sun having done its job before dipping low again. The charm of our wintry bubble is fading. And tomorrow, they'll start clearing the roads.

Tomorrow means real life.

Tomorrow means this ends.

Soren places a piece into the top left corner and grins. "Boom. That, my Bells, is the corner of a bookshelf."

"You're practically a national treasure," I deadpan, sipping my hot tea.

There's a shift in his gaze. The smirk lingers, but it's quieter now. I'm a little scared.

"Penny for your thoughts?" I ask.

"Have I done a good job?"

The mug hovers halfway to my lips. "On the puzzle? Honestly, I'm impressed. You're a corner-piece king."

Soren huffs a laugh, but it's hollow. "No, Ava. Not that." His gaze drops to the table, and his thumb runs along the rim of his mug. "I mean... have I done a good job showing you that this could be something... More?"

The question sinks between us like a stone in water. I set my tea down carefully, but my hands are shaking. My fingers curl around the ceramic again, searching for warmth that's suddenly harder to find.

"I haven't been subtle about my feelings," he says, voice tender. "I want more than one snowed-in weekend of fucking and flirting. I want *you*, Bells. For *real*. Out there in the *real* world. Not the fake one we manufactured for fans."

Soren looks at me, and it wrecks me. It's open, terrified, and dead serious. He's laid his entire heart out on the dining table between puzzle pieces and steaming hot mugs.

I don't know what to say.

"Soren..."

"You don't have to give me an answer *right* now," he adds quickly. "But I've never felt like this...with anyone. And I've spent the last two days trying to memorize the way your smile curves when you're trying not to laugh. Or how you hum while concentrating. Or how you still smell like sugar cookies even when you've been buried in snow."

I let out a breath. "You've been busy."

Soren chuckles, running a hand through his hair. "I know. It's a lot. But I mean it. And I'll show you that I mean it every single day, forever, if that's what it takes."

A pause. Silence. The hope in his eyes makes mine sting.

"I need to think it over, okay?" I say softly. "It's not a no."

Soren's eyes flash with a mixture of that same hope and now certainty...but also disappointment. He exhales. "Then that's enough for me. For now."

We go back to the puzzle, but the air has changed. It's laced with words we're not saying, a web with a thousand emotions we're both navigating through—but not always the same ones. Some of them collide. Some miss each other entirely. But they're all crashing together in the silence between us.

"Why?" I ask.

Soren eyes shoot up.

"We've been rivals for a year. And then all of a sudden, you decide I'm the girl for you? What changed? What made you *know*, like you said."

Soren sets down a puzzle piece and leans back in his chair, arms crossed, eyes locked on mine.

"As I've stated, I developed a thing for you after I read your book. Your voice was in every line. Every page. And your hero— he got to me. I related to him on levels I didn't even know existed. Not because he was perfect. But because he wasn't." Soren leans forward, elbows on the table, gaze unwavering. "You wrote this man who was angry and messy and trying so damn hard to be better. And the woman who saw through all of it—who loved him anyway. And I thought... shit. That's how I want to be."

Blushing, I bite my bottom lip.

"I didn't know how to be with you," he continues. "You were smart. Funny. You could cut me without flinching. So, I kept throwing jabs online. Made it a game. Kept it fun. But the first time I saw you in person... the real Ava Bell and not the online version, I was done."

"Done with what?"

"Everything that didn't have you in it."

I stare at him, wondering how and why the universe gave me this man.

"You're special." He doesn't smile. Neither do I. And finally, the walls guarding my chest finally crumble to dust. "You came into my life for a reason."

I break eye contact first. It's not that I don't believe him. I do. For some crazy reason. And that's what makes it so terrifying.

My thumb runs along the rim of my mug, mirroring the gesture he made earlier. I stare down into the cooling tea, watching the steam rise and fade like a breath I'm too scared to let go.

"Look..." My voice cracks. I clear it. "Soren, you have to promise to take it slow."

He doesn't argue. He listens. Gives me space.

"You can get swept up in the 'show." And that's the kind of thing that'll make me run away. Fast."

Recognition flickers in his expression, accompanied by a hint of understanding.

"I don't need all the fireworks," I whisper. "I just need you to walk, instead of sprint."

Soren's hand covers mine, grounding, warm.

"Then I'll walk, Bells," he says. "Even crawl if I have to."

My heart shudders at that. It isn't fear. It's relief—over the weight of being heard without being rushed.

A beat passes. My pulse kicks, but I try to smile anyway, because I want this too. I like him too much to let him go.

"Okay," I whisper. "I'll try."

His grin doesn't explode across his face. It blooms—slow and stunned. He wasn't expecting me to say yes.

"You will?" he asks softly, like it's the most important question he's ever posed.

I nod, swiping stray strands of hair from my face. "I'm still scared."

Soren's hand finds mine. His strong touch doesn't demand anything—but promises everything. "You don't have to be fearless," he says. "Just honest."

I exhale through a laugh, a real one this time. "That's not my specialty."

"Good," he says. "I've got enough delusional optimism for the both of us." Soren's mouth curves into that lopsided grin that undoes me.

We don't go back to the puzzle. We channel our inner eight-year-olds and build a fort instead.

What starts as a joke turns into a production. We stack couch cushions against the walls. Drape quilts between furniture. Clip fairy lights along the edge of my bookshelf using hairpins and sheer dumb luck. He even folds my favorite velvet bathrobe into a "throne," because apparently, even make-believe queens need proper lumbar support.

Soren tosses a throw blanket over two dining chairs and declares, in a truly awful British accent, "Behold, the romantic lair of Bellatrix the Bold and her morally conflicted warlock boyfriend."

I laugh and kiss him silly.

Outside, the sky is bruised with dusk but clearing, one star shimmering through the retreating clouds. Inside, it's warm. Dim. The scent of pine trees drifts through the air.

We lie back on the living room rug, wrapped in blankets and entangled limbs. My cheek presses against the soft cotton of his tee, his heartbeat a grounding thrum beneath it. My whole world is syncing to his rhythm.

Above us, the ceiling glows faintly. Soren propped his phone flashlight beneath an overturned whiskey tumbler, the glass scattering light like a prism. It's not much—just a constellation of crooked shapes on plaster—but he swears it's the stars. And somehow, with his arm curled tight around me, I almost believe him.

Soren speaks so quietly, it sounds like a wish. "Okay. Favorite firsts?"

I shift a little, eyes trained on the twinkling pattern above us. "You mean...first kiss?"

Soren nods. "That. And other things. First concert. First lie. First heartbreak. First book that ruined you. Whatever comes to mind."

"Treacherous waters."

His arm moves behind my shoulders, slow and sure. "It's not a game. It's a trust fall in verbal form."

The way he says it, like he's inviting me to lean in and catch fire at the same time, makes my skin feel too tight.

Still, I play.

"My first concert was Alanis Morissette. My mom snuck me in when I was eleven and we sang every word as gospel."

"Jagged Little Pill. Iconic. You peaked early."

"Debatable." I chuckle. "What was the first book that made you stay up all night reading?"

No hesitation. "*Sabriel*. I was obsessed with necromancers for the next three years."

"That explains your fixation with morally gray magic users."

He nudges me with his elbow. "Shut up. Your turn."

I think for a moment. "First book I lost sleep over was *The Name of the Wind*."

He nods, accepting the answer.

"What was your first lie?" I ask.

"First lie I ever told..." Soren breathes in, deep and uneven. "Was telling my teacher I didn't care that my dad missed my eighth grade poetry reading."

My chest pulls tight. My fingers drift across his knuckles.

"That night," his voice lowers, "I came home, went out back, and read the whole damn poem to the trees. I knew it by heart. Still do."

The images come so easily—a gangly boy with too-long limbs and a heart too big for his ribcage, whispering truth to the dark because no one else would listen.

I don't have words for what that does to me.

I crane my neck to peer up at him. "Recite it for me."

Soren's smile tilts, half-awkward, half-boyish, and he rubs the back of his neck. "You really want to hear the tragic eighth-grade emo ramblings of a kid with bad hair and worse posture?"

"Yes," I whisper, my heart already tripping over itself.

For a beat, he stares at me—long, quiet, searching. He's tracking tiny circles on my arm, but then the teasing fades, every trace of humor replaced with something weightier that pins me in place. And with a breath that trembles at the edges, he begins. His gaze never wavers from me, not once, as though every word has waited sixteen years to land exactly here, with me.

"Someday, I'll find her.

The one who sees past the shadows I drag behind,

who doesn't flinch at the storm within me,

but walks straight into it.

Someday, she'll look at me

like I was always worth the wait.

Like the world didn't break me wrong,

just bent me toward her.

Her laughter will be firelight.

Her stubbornness, a shield.

Her heart will burn so fiercely

that mine—ruined, restless, half-afraid—

will finally believe it can be whole.

Someday, she'll make me brave enough

to stop running from my own reflection.

Someday, she'll be my reflection—

and I'll know I was always hers."

My throat closes around air that won't come. The fort, the lights, the faint hiss of the fire—all of it fades until there's only him and the words he's laying bare between us.

No one's ever looked at me like Soren does. No one's ever *spoken* to me like he has—like my existence is not only seen, but *prophesied.*

I want to laugh, cry, and bury myself in him. My eyes sting, and I squeeze his hand. And when he squeezes back, my insides go soft in a way I don't know how to protect.

His voice cracks when he finally manages to whisper, "It was always you, Bells?"

Before I can breathe a response, he twists, capturing my mouth with his, stealing air, and giving it back. This kiss feels like all the years he carried those words alone are finally spilling into me. My chest splinters and mends in the same heartbeat, and the taste of him is salt and heat and forever.

When he finally pulls back, he doesn't let me go. I fold into him, his arms locking around me, my head nestled in the crook of his arm. The fire pops in the hearth, but it's nothing compared to the warmth of his chest beneath my cheek, the rhythm of his heart beating just for me, under my palm.

I exhale into the quiet, knowing for the first time in my life I don't have to run. I don't have to hide.

This man feels like home.

We keep going.

Soren tells me about his first tattoo—badly drawn runes. I confess I once shoplifted a glitter pen from Claire's in middle school and felt so guilty I mailed it back with an apology note.

We laugh. We go quiet. We confess. We listen.

Eventually, Soren twists onto his side, one arm curled beneath his head, the other resting near my hip. The starlight from the glass still glows above us.

"Wanna know my favorite first?" he asks.

My heart picks up. "Do I?"

His fingers find the edge of the quilt and toy with it absently. "You. I've never fake-dated anyone before."

I gaze up at the stars. "That's not fair."

"Why not?"

"Because I don't have anything equally romantic to say back."

Soren lets out a breath that fans warm across my neck. "You don't have to. I didn't say it to get something from you. I said it because it's true."

There's a beat. Maybe two.

"I'm not used to this."

"Which part?"

"The safety. The stillness. Someone wanting more than a version of me that benefits them somehow."

Soren doesn't move. Doesn't speak right away. But when he does, it lands in the marrow of me.

"The only version I want of you is the messy, tired, snarky, post-convention gremlin version. I want the girl who builds pillow forts and gets lost in her own plot twists. The one who wears glitter socks into battle and then hoards all the cinnamon rolls."

I close my eyes. On the outside, it might appear as though I'm hiding. Or running from the moment. I'm not. I'm *feeling*.

There's a soft pulse of heat in my chest. The ache of wanting to believe him. The terrifying, bone-deep comfort of being held like I matter.

A second passes. Maybe more. He shifts. Blankets rustle. A quiet breath escapes his lips. His hand brushes a piece of hair from my cheek. Why does it feel like the most natural thing in the world?

His mouth finds mine. A tender press of lips that says I understand you. I'm here. I'm not going anywhere.

My chest tightens in that sweet, unbearable way that reminds me of falling. And I'm *choosing* to fall.

Aren't I?

Eyes still closed, I tilt toward him, chasing more.

His palm cradles my jaw. And in that tiny, perfect world we've built out of couch cushions and whispered confessions, I kiss him back, hoping he feels what I can't quite say yet.

He does. He's told me as much.

When we finally pull apart, barely breathing, his forehead rests against mine, and he murmurs so quietly I almost miss it—

"I dreamt about you... before I ever met you."

My heart forgets how to beat. This is the beginning of something I haven't allowed myself to want in years.

I don't know how long we stay beneath the stars, under the quiet hush of the pillow fort we built like two overgrown kids avoiding adulthood. But eventually, the night fades.

Soren's hand brushes mine again, but this time he doesn't pull away.

Neither do I.

The blanket above us shakes a little when I roll onto my side to face him. The shadows don't hide the way he's gazing at me with tenderness. I could drown it.

"I'm not sleepy," I whisper, voice barely audible over the gentle crackle of the fire still glowing in the hearth.

Soren's hand lifts. His knuckles skim down the line of my jaw. "Me either."

There's a moment where we just breathe. My body sings, not from desire alone, but from how deeply Soren sees me right now, and how he wants more than my snark or my stats or the way I fill out a dress.

He wants *me*. Only me.

I reach up and trace the edge of his mouth with a featherlight touch. "Are you always this patient?"

"Only when it counts," he says. And then, more quietly, "Only with you."

He kisses me.

Soft.

Searching.

His mouth moves over mine, tasting a secret he doesn't want to lose. His hand cradles my cheek while the other slips to my waist, holding me as if I might disappear if he lets go.

I don't know who moves first. Maybe we both do. But we're shifting together, moving from the fort to the rug in front of the fire. Pillows tumble as we go, but we don't care, too lost in this heart-bonding moment.

No words escape us.

Soren's hands slide under the hem of my shirt and lift, his eyes darkening when he sees my bare skin. He kisses a path down my throat, across my collarbone, the swell of my breast. Every press of his mouth makes my body arch closer, but he doesn't rush.

He undresses, it's somehow more intimate than anything else we've done. There's no performance here. No bit. Only us.

"Still scared?" He hovers above me, gaze drinking me in.

"Yes," I whisper. "But I want this. I want *you*."

His mouth captures mine again, and this time, it deepens, tongues brushing, breaths mingling. He's heat and promise, and when his hard length lines up against me, my hips lift instinctively. Soren groans, a sound full of restraint. I wrap my legs around his waist and pull him closer.

Closer.

When Soren finally enters me, it's a communion. He's tracing devotion into every inch from the inside out.

There's no frantic pace. No rough urgency. Only a rhythm that's made entirely of sweet tension and unbearable closeness–a brewing storm that builds with every stroke, and whispered name, and kiss pressed to sweat-damp skin.

As I fall apart this time, it's quiet. But it's the loudest I've ever felt.

Bells,

You don't even see it, do you? How the icy walls you've built—brick by careful brick—are starting to melt? How your armor is slipping in little places and letting me in?

Don't mistake it for weakness. It's the bravest damn thing I've ever seen.

You've spent years being strong because you had to. You've carried so much expectation, doubt, and criticism on your back until it bent you into someone who thought she had to stand alone.

And yet here you are—choosing to trust me, even just in fragments. Letting me close enough to hold your fear, your fire, your beautiful, chaotic mess.

Do you know what that does to me?

It destroys me. And remakes me.

I told you, I don't take that lightly, Bells.

Each shaky exhale, every stolen glance, and all the kisses you let me steal—it's not just affection alone. It's proof you're letting me see who you really are. The Ava beneath the perfect smile, the viral clips, and the curated confidence. The woman who trembles when the room gets too loud, who makes jokes to hide her panic, who still shows up and shines anyway.

I'm proud of you. God, I'm so proud of you.

You'll never hear me say that enough, because you deserve to know it in your bones. You don't need me to fight your battles—you've already won more than most. But if you ever need someone to stand beside you when your knees want to give out, I'll be there. Not as armor. Or even as a shield. Just as the man who is grateful down to his soul that you'd even let me close to you.

So when tonight's event gets overwhelming, remember this: you don't have to carry it all. You don't have to smile if it hurts.

No longer will you carry yourself all alone anymore. I've got you, Bells.

Love,

S

Feast & Fiction

Snowflake Gala

Bookmas Bash

Midnight Kisses &
Paper Wishes

Twenty-Eight

SOREN

My phone buzzes with a notification, and the name flashing across the screen makes my stomach knot.

Lena.

> This is your last chance to respond, Soren. One day you're kissing me, the next you're parading around with Ava Bell?
>
> With Ava fucking Bell?
>
> Do you have any idea how insane this looks?

I rub a hand over my scruff, biting back the immediate curse snaking up my throat.

My thumbs fly before I can second-guess:

> You kissed me. Not the other way around.
>
> You're unhinged. Not to mention, delusional, if you think otherwise. The fantasy you've built up in your head doesn't exist.

Three dots appear. Vanish. Reappear.

Unhinged, huh? I'll show you unhinged.

Just know, you brought this on yourself. You have only yourself to blame.

I don't even bother drafting a response this time. Instead, I forward the whole thread to Matthew. He needs a heads-up before this blows up into something bigger.

It takes less than a minute for his reply to come through:

Fucking great.

That's it. No lecture. No strategy. Only two words that feel like both a warning and a promise of the headache to come later.

Of all the people you had to piss off after sticking your dick in them, it had to be the one with nearly two million followers?

Spoke too soon.

You're not wrong, but I don't appreciate the tone you're using. I don't need a lecture.

And I need you to stop handing me grenades with the pins already pulled.

Please tell me how to prevent this one from blowing up.

I'm working on that. Keep this between us.

You hear me?

Do not tell anyone, especially not Ava.

I stare at the screen, my stomach tightening. Keep it from Ava? Turn this into a secret? A lie?

After everything we've been through, she's finally started to trust me, and now this?

It's like pulling a thread that could unravel everything.

This won't stay buried forever.

Let me handle it. You've done enough.

Focus on keeping the chemistry alive and your mouth shut.

Chest tight, I pocket the phone. Matthew's trying to protect me. Possibly even Ava. But all I can think is, if she finds out I kept this from her, it won't be a scandal I'm managing, it'll be the end of us before we ever really began.

My insides are burning with rage as I walk into the ballroom of the *Snowflake Gala.*

The place pulses with elegance. Ice-blue uplighting washes the walls in a winter glow, cascading snowflakes project shadows on the walls, while crystal chandeliers drip from the ceiling like frozen icicles. The tables are shimmering with mirrored runners, silver place cards, and candles flickering beside fluted champagne glasses. A string quartet is playing a dramatic orchestral rendition of Taylor Swift's *"Cruel Summer,"* and somehow it works even though it's winter.

Everyone is dressed in tuxes, sequined gowns, and custom accessories that scream, "I read dark academia and I have opinions."

Earlier, before my text exchange from hell, I was stopped twice by execs in bowties who "love the sword content" and want to "talk TV rights," which is code for "let's change your book completely with a streaming deal."

Camille and Renata scurry around like caffeinated elves trying to keep the itinerary on track, but their stressed energy is no match for the anxiety brewing behind Ava Bell's eyes.

The one bright spot is that Ava's book hit the bestseller list this week. Thanks to this PR circus and a couple of well-timed thirst traps—by yours truly, reading her book—the hype train's still rolling.

Her publisher—bless their opportunistic hearts—is sponsoring this event, which means the moment she steps off this parquet floor, someone will corner her about her work in progress.

Her editor has sent three *"Circling back!"* texts to her today. She's currently hovering near the bar like a hawk in heels, wearing a floor-length black gown that fits like it was cut directly from her ambition. Diamond studs wink at her ears every time she swivels her head, scanning the room for her author with laser precision. Even in sequins and silk, she radiates deadlines—poised, polished, and ready to shred a manuscript with one raised brow.

And to add fuel to Ava's fire, Fisher is filming every damn moment, prepping a holiday documentary, apparently.

Ava's talking with Victoria. I can tell she's about to freak the fuck out. If she does, at least she'll look amazing while doing it, wearing a fitted red, floor-length, off-the-shoulder, sultry gown.

Her curls are pinned back with delicate silver clips that sparkle every time she turns her head, and her lips match the dress. Bold. Daring. Hot as fuck. I love it.

She doesn't know she's a fire hazard, but every pair of eyes is staring at her. My caveman instincts kick in, and I cross the floor without thinking. There's zero hesitation in my steps. No pause, only sheer instinct and need.

Ava's face lights up when she sees me. I don't let her speak. I lean in and kiss her, ravenous.

"I need to be inside you right now." The words tumble out before I can cage them. A smirk follows—masking the truth behind why I said them and the weight of what they actually mean.

Her eyes go wide, her lips parting, caught between outrage and desire. I don't let myself linger on it because it isn't about sex. Not really. Yeah, my body's wound tight, my blood's been pounding since the second I closed those text messages. But what

I want—what I can't say—is more dangerous than that, which is, *I love you, and I don't want anything to fuck this up.*

I don't just want to be inside her body. I want to be everywhere. Her laugh. Her walls. Her heart.

Keeping the smirk plastered on, I hide behind it, like I have for so long as The Blade. Because if I let her see the raw need underneath, she might bolt. Even though she told me she would try. It's too early for those three words, and I can't risk her running.

After that, we schmooze. We pose. We mingle with industry types and flirt with several bookstore owners. Ava plays her part, but I recognize the tightness in her shoulders, the same as my own.

Her fingers twitch at her sides, and there's a false brightness in her laugh. She's about five seconds away from melting down in formalwear.

Fisher—saint that he is—keeps her hands full with cocktails, one or two clearly laced with enough Alani to jumpstart a generator. Her smile is glossy. Her voice is fine-tuned. But I know Ava now. I know the signs. And beneath the lipstick and jokes, she's hanging on by a thread.

"If you don't slow those down, your heart's going to explode—or I'm going to have to carry you out of here."

She sighs. "I'm just... so tense."

Understatement of the year.

Ava's breaths quicken, her chest rising and falling in rapid gasps. She's two fake smiles away from either vomiting or sobbing.

Turning to face her, my hands brace either side of her waist. "You need to breathe, Bells."

She tries.

Fails.

An idea strikes.

"Come with me." I don't wait for permission. I grab her hand and guide her out of the ballroom. Down a side hallway. Past the champagne tower and a tray of chocolate mousse.

Around a corner and through a narrow door. It's the wine cellar.

Inside is cool, air thick with oak and earth, dim light pooling across racks of bottles stacked like soldiers. We barely make it past the door before my hand is on her back, guiding Ava forward until her hips hit the rounded edge of a wine barrel.

"Right here, baby," I murmur, voice husky, like a secret slipping out. I lift the hem of her gloriously sexy red dress.

Her hand clutches my wrist. "Soren—"

"Ava, you need to trust me," I assure her, voice even. "I'm going to take the edge off. Let me. Okay?"

She doesn't stop me again. I drop to my knees. Ava gasps when my hands skim up the outside of her thighs. I tug her underwear down her legs. Silk. Cherry red. Fucking hell.

Ava's palms flatten against the wood, breath hitching when her body presses flush to mine. The barrels creak beneath us, aged oak and metal groaning as though they know exactly what's about to happen.

I bend her over the barrel and lean forward, my chest pressing to her back, my lips skating across her ear. "Look at you. Spread out like some rare vintage to be savored. You have no idea what you do to me, Bells."

Then my hands are everywhere—gripping, stroking, worshipping, filthy with need, tender with the way I pepper kisses on every inch I touch.

"Spread your legs wider, baby," I command, nudging my cock into her backside.

She obeys like the good girl she is. Her breath shudders, her stance opens, instinct guiding her somewhere her mind hasn't caught up to yet.

Ava looks back over her shoulder. Her eyes meet mine, wide and wet and wild. Bent over the curve of the wine barrel, she braces herself, knuckles white against the oak.

I sink to my knees behind her, grip her thighs, and drag her open for me. My mouth finds her clit, hot and greedy, and my tongue carves circles, flicks, slows, speeds up—every stroke a torment of precision.

Ava gasps, arches, presses harder into the wood, and I tighten my hold to keep her right where I want her.

Her taste floods me, intoxicating and sweeter than any bottle in this cellar. Reverence drives me as much as lust—I lap her up, coaxing every shiver and desperate moan, until she's trembling over oak and iron and begging me not to stop.

She moans my name once—half-formed and breathless—and I groan into her, letting the sound vibrate against her wet heat. Ava's thighs tense, then she opens them wider for me. She's giving in. Giving up. Giving *me* everything.

And I take it.

The whole world outside this room fades. My mouth and tongue are confident in unison as I lick, suck. And savor. The swirl of my tongue is undoing her. Each breath she takes is a countdown.

Ava nearly screams as she comes, but I don't stop until she melts, utterly boneless and completely unwound.

When I finally rise, I wipe my mouth with the back of my hand and lean close. Her eyes are still half-lidded, cheeks flushed, lips parted.

"You taste like Christmas, Bells."

Her chest heaves. She's trembling, catching her breath. When I stand behind her and drag a hand down her spine, the other frees my cock, hard and heavy, pulsing with tension and need.

"Hold on tight, baby," I say, letting the thick head of me slide against her soaked heat.

Ava's fingers claw at the oak. I grip her hips, yank her back, and slam into her sex in one brutal, glorious thrust.

Her cry splinters through the cellar, ricocheting off stone and wood, and I've never heard anything more perfect.

The barrel groans beneath us, but I don't care if it splits. My hips snap forward again, and again, until all I know is the tight, hot clutch of her body and the way her walls cling to me.

"Fuck, Ava," I grit, leaning over her, lips at her neck. "You were built to break me."

The barrel rattles now, metal bands creaking like they're seconds away from giving out. I drive into her harder, deeper, the wet slap of skin-on-skin echoing in the cellar with every brutal thrust.

Ava's palms skid against the oak, searching for grip. "Soren— God—" she chokes out, voice pitched high and ragged.

"Louder," I snarl against her neck, teeth grazing her flushed skin.

Her answering cry rips through me as I pound into her like a man starved, hips crashing into her ass in a rhythm that borders on savage. Every thrust rips a sound from her—whimpers, moans, gasps—that mix with the slap of my body claiming hers, my groans echoing off the stone walls.

"Christ, Bells," I growl, rutting into her as her pussy clenches around me. "You take me like a fucking goddess."

Her cries mix with mine until the room is nothing but noise —wet, filthy, desperate noise. When she shatters around me, screaming my name, I lose it completely, slamming in one final time and spilling inside her with a hoarse, guttural groan.

We're both panting, ruined, surrounded by glass bottles and the smell of wine. I kiss the back of her neck, laughing hoarsely against her damp skin.

"You okay?" I brush her hair back.

Ava nods. "Yeah. Um... definitely good. More than good."

I grin. "Excellent. Now let's get back out there and show the world who Bell and The Blade really are."

Ava exhales as though she's trying to remember how lungs work. "Right. Absolutely."

I help my girl stand, smoothing her dress back down over those toned, silky legs. She's flushed, glowing. I want nothing more than to throw her over my shoulder, take her upstairs, and sink my cock right back into the tight little pussy again.

But alas, after I use a cloth napkin to clean myself up, we slip out of the cellar and head back down the hallway. Her fingers interlace with mine, and it makes my chest thud with an ache of guilt for what I'm keeping from her.

We turn the corner, only to come face-to-face with Fisher, standing in the corridor like a Bond villain waiting to deliver the final blow. Phone in hand. Eyebrow raised. Lips pursed.

His hazel eyes volley between Ava's flushed face and my smug one, then trail downward as though he's mentally cataloging every fabric wrinkle, hair shift, and indication of—well—exactly what happened behind that closed door.

His voice is low. Ominous. British. "I heard screaming."

Ava freezes. "Fisher—"

"*Everyone* heard screaming. Including the champagne guy, who dropped an entire tray outside that door."

I clear my throat. "Technically, she didn't scream that loud—"

"*Technically*," Fisher cuts in, "you two were *doing* sexual things in the wine cellar during a black-tie event—and I wasn't even *notified*!"

Ava sputters. "We weren't *doing*—"

"Oh, don't you dare lie to me, Ava Bell. I know post-orgasm hair when I see it." He points to her face. "I know suspiciously flushed cheeks. I know the limp of a woman whose knees went on strike."

I hold back a laugh. "You don't know *what* we were doing."

"I don't need a play-by-play," he snaps. "But someone screamed. Loudly. And then another sound shook the catering staff. That waiter will probably need therapy, Ava."

She groans into her hands. "Please stop."

Fisher presses a hand to his heart. "I'm not mad that it happened. I'm mad you didn't tell me this was even happening. You two leveled up and didn't inform me? I had a whole thing planned. I had *pre-drafted pep talks*, Ava. Scented candles. Emergency snacks. A Spotify playlist called "In Case *of First Penetration*.""

I cough. "We didn't—"

"Again, I don't want details!" Fisher throws up his hands. "I want emotional access!"

Ava groans. "This is my nightmare."

Fisher steps closer, hard expression dissolving, like he's not still mentally assigning us trauma homework. "All I'm saying is— if the two of you are gonna slide from fake-ass dating into what-ever-the-hell-*that*-was territory, I deserve a heads-up. A whisper. A flash of Morse code. *Something. I am your person, Ava.* And I cannot be expected to face the party alone while your orgasm echoes through the vents."

Ava's brows furrow. "Wait. You're mad because I didn't *tell* you?"

"Oh, I'm *livid*, love. You didn't even give me a courtesy call! You two have been fake dating, slow burning, sexual tensioning your way through this entire tour, and now it's *finally* escalated— except apparently the only person who didn't get the memo was me!" He crosses his arms defiantly.

I stare, still stuck on what he said earlier. "You made emergency snacks?"

Fisher scoffs. "Don't give me that look. You're the one who ruined the evening with the simple flick of your tongue. Or hell, maybe your cock. I don't know. Nobody told me. And *of course* I made snacks. What kind of friend do you think I am? People get weak after sex, Soren. Blood sugar drops. Knees buckle. Emotions flare. Do you want her passing out mid-thrust? *No.* That's why I pack protein bars and chocolate-covered almonds in my *clutch*. I'm a responsible assistant who's been waiting for this moment to happen since day one."

Ava makes a slight, mortified sound and buries her face in her hands. "Oh my God."

"Jesus Christ," he mutters. "Those noises, Ava. I thought you were being murdered—not climaxing into the afterlife. Honestly, I was halfway to calling security."

Ava drops her hands, her face crimson. "It was a moment. A *panic attack prevention* moment."

"A preventative orgasm?" Fisher sneers. "Brilliant. I support it. Next time, maybe don't hold your crisis intervention in the wine cellar, acoustically adjacent to the event being hosted by your *publisher*. Not to mention agent and editor."

There's a long pause. Then Ava giggles.

She tries to smother it behind her hand, but fails, full-body, shoulder-shaking laughter spilling out as the last of her tension finally breaks.

I laugh too. I can't help it.

Fisher sighs. "You're both disgusting. But I'm happy for you."

"Thanks?" I say, unsure whether I should feel grateful or threatened.

"Now." Fisher smooths his jacket. "Let's go. Your next appearance is in six minutes. If we're late, Renata will sacrifice me to the influencer gods."

He spins on his heel and marches down the hall, muttering about being "scarred for life."

Ava reaches for my hand as we follow behind him. She squeezes once, and the pressure says enough.

Twenty-Nine

AVA

The glitter has settled from the *Snowflake Gala*. The suite is quiet. Lights dimmed. Champagne flutes still half-full on the marble bar. My heels are somewhere near the sofa. And I'm standing at the floor-to-ceiling windows in this costly hotel, staring out at the glittering sprawl of the Chicago skyline, trying to breathe through the gnawing ache in my chest.

The entire night was a *smashing* success. Our photos are circulating online. There's a shot of me laughing in Soren's arms that is a new favorite of mine. A filtered video of us clinking glasses. A clip of him whispering in my ear and my entire body turning toward him as a sunflower in heat.

The world believes we're together.

Our plan is working.

My notifications are exploding. My sales have doubled overnight. *The Boyfriend Deadline* is officially on the bestseller list, climbing, proving a point. ShelfSpace is frothing. There are fancams. Fancams, plural.

It's everything I wanted. But beneath all the glitter and dopamine and breathless headlines, that familiar scratch is back.

The one that whispers *don't get too comfortable.*

The one that hisses *this is all too good to be true.*

354

Because it is. Right?

Soren Pembry is too good to be true. He's every fantasy rolled into six feet of danger *and* unexpected softness, and tonight—he was mine. Truthfully, mine.

He kissed me. He meant it. He *touched* me. He meant it. And then he made me scream in a break room as though I was precious and sweet and deserving.

But what if it doesn't last?

What if I fall, and he lets go?

My fingers brush the cold glass. Soren comes up behind me without a word, his warmth folding over my skin like dusk. His hands settle on my hips, firm and grounding, and then his mouth finds my neck.

One kiss. Soft. Adoring. Laced with fire.

He trails another beneath my ear, and my breath shudders. "Are you ever going to come down from the clouds?"

"I'm...watching it all from a distance," I whisper, voice thick with longing, but also fear. "Waiting for it to vanish."

"It's not going anywhere." The conviction in his voice knocks the breath from my lungs.

His hands rise, sweeping the hair from my back. The tug of my zipper is a whisper against my spine. Then he exposes me inch by excruciating inch, savoring every second and breath.

Fabric slips away, warm air kissing bare skin, until the gown falls in a soft sigh around my feet into a puddle of crimson silk on the floor.

I'm bare except for my bra and panties. My heart pounds. And then he spins me.

I suck in a breath.

He's naked. Completely. No warning. Definitely no apology.

Soren stands before me, gloriously bare, eyes brimming with heat, chest rising.

"Jesus."

His mouth seizes mine in a kiss that's full of hunger and promise and something unspoken thrumming beneath the surface. Fingers find my bra clasp. It falls away. My panties follow, his touch determined, confident.

Soren lifts me, effortlessly, then presses me gently against the cool glass. The contrast of heat and cold is blissful on so many levels.

My arms wind around his shoulders. And then he's inside me. No pretense. Only a perfect thrust which knocks every thought out of my head.

His lips never leave mine. My legs wrap tighter around his waist, and Soren fucks me like he's writing a scene he wants to read over and over again. Deep, achingly controlled.

Stormy eyes lock with mine as the skyline burns behind us. My name falls from his lips, along with a vow that I mean so much to him.

And I believe him.

For once, I let myself believe that I deserve this. That it's not too good to be true.

Soren's hips thrust, each inch of him burrowing into my soul. The glass is cold at my back, but Soren is pure heat. His mouth trails along my jawline, my collarbone, the curve of my shoulder as though he's rediscovering geography he already owns. Every movement is deliberate. Every breath synced to mine.

My nails dig into his back, anchoring myself to him. I'm unraveling—beautifully, blissfully—and he knows it. He feels me.

"Let go," he breathes against my throat. "Tell me what you feel."

"I can't—"

"Yes, you can. I've got you. Let me hear you."

In one fluid motion, Soren spins us around and carries me across the suite. I'm weightless in his arms, legs still wrapped around his waist, heart pounding against his chest, every step powered by need.

When we hit the bed, he lowers me onto the mattress, climbs over me, and thrusts in deep—*so much deeper*—the new angle stealing the breath from my lungs.

"Oh my *God*—" I gasp, arching up into him, every nerve ending lit on fire.

"That's it, Bells," he rumbles. "Don't hold back."

Soren's movements grow harder, more desperate as our bodies chase the end together. My hands clutch the sheets. My voice breaks on a moan.

And when I fall, I cry out his name, raw and unfiltered, and he follows me seconds later with a sound that's torn from his chest. He presses his forehead to mine as we tremble together, wrapped around each other, breathless and spent.

The city glows before us. We glow too.

A few hours and several orgasms later, we're wrapped in white sheets, the city hums beyond the windows. My limbs are heavy and warm, my skin tingling with aftershocks.

Soren lies beside me, one arm draped across my stomach, his other hand gently tracing lazy shapes along my thigh, soothing emotions buried deep within my body. He looks over, and that smile claims me.

"I'm still waiting for the moment the universe rips this all away," I confess.

He gently kisses my forehead. "I know what you've been through, Bells. You've been bruised into thinking that you have to brace for impact every time something feels right, so please...know this." His hand finds mine beneath the covers. "I'm not here to hurt you. I'm here to hold on."

My throat tightens. "Soren..."

He grins, lazy and devastating. "And maybe fuck you against a few more windows, if that helps drive the point home."

I laugh. And then I curl into him, allowing my body to rest against his, allowing the truth of his words to settle deep into my bones.

And I know...I don't have to run.

Not from this. Or from him.

The morning after the Snowflake Gala, the hotel restaurant is buzzing with espresso steam, hushed conversations laced with a hint of hungover glamour, and overpriced granola.

I'm seated at a white-linen table near the window in sunglasses and yesterday's emotional whiplash—the place reeking of truffle oil and clean money.

Behind me, a woman is loudly explaining her Substack. Two tables over, someone's ordering their Bloody Mary with "extra vibe."

Across from me sits Fisher, sipping his brown sugar cortado as though he's channeling the ghost of Miss Marple. He hasn't spoken since we sat down. But he's *looking*. Over the rim of his mug. Through the lenses of his aggressively judgmental tortoise-shell sunglasses. Past the silver cloche the waiter set in front of him. And directly into my damn soul.

Adjusting in my seat, my thighs ache in a very *pointed* way. My dress is new, and my heartstrings are still braided into Soren from last night's pillow talk.

Fisher sets his cup down with the elegance of someone who has seen the abyss and is now ready to conduct the inquisition.

"So," he says, voice calm, casual, and *full of judgment,* "when exactly were you going to tell me that your fake boyfriend turned your cervix into a fogged-up window display?"

I freeze with a forkful of eggs halfway to my mouth. "Fisher."

"Don't *Fisher* me."

I groan.

He sighs. "Just tell me—are you okay? Are you in love? Or was that a very well-earned, PR climax?"

"I—" My eyes skim his. My voice drops. "I don't know. I think it's more. It *feels* like more."

"Okay. Good. Terrifying, obviously—but good." His eyes

dance with curiosity. "So are we talking *exclusive boyfriend energy* here, or did he rail you so thoroughly you blacked out on your publishing deadlines for a full two weeks?"

I roll my eyes.

A nearby guest glances over.

Fisher flags a passing waiter. "We're going to need pancakes. Stat. She just had an emotional breakthrough, and her blood sugar's dangerously low."

Despite myself, I laugh, trying my best to ignore the panic still fluttering in my chest—a bird waiting for the storm.

But maybe the storm isn't coming.

Could this be the time I finally get to stay in the sun? Even if it's only for a little while.

Fisher lets the silence breathe for exactly three seconds while casually stirring his cortado. He's about to decimate me with a smile.

"I mean, I *filmed* you two kissing at the axe-throwing place," he says lightly. "Sure, I played it off like it was all fake dating sparkle for the fans, but let's not pretend I missed the tongue."

My jaw drops.

"And I know," he continues, swirling his spoon, "your ice started melting the second we walked into your parents' house. You were nearly thawed during the one bed situation—don't argue—I saw your face every morning when you came out of that room resembling a woman emotionally rearranged." He lifts his cup again, sips. "Which brings me to now."

I brace.

"When did you actually start...fucking?"

"Jesus, Fisher."

"Don't 'Jesus' me, either, Ava. I'm asking a very valid, very best-guy-approved question. When did the vibes turn into vertical cardio?"

I stab a piece of cantaloupe. "It wasn't some grand moment. It just... happened." Well, actually, there was kind of a grand moment.

Fisher cocks his head, skeptical. "Things don't *just happen*. This wasn't a spontaneous fucking. There's been enough tension between you two to power a small city. I want a date. A timestamp. A *location*. Preferably one I don't need to spiritually cleanse."

"Okay," I sigh. "Soren convinced me to go on a date with him."

Fisher freezes mid-sip, lowers his cup. "A *real* date?"

Nodding, my eyes stay on my plate. "Yeah. No cameras. No Renata. No Camille. *Or you*. Only... us."

"Okay. And?"

"There was a bookish art exhibit. Possibly a bookstore challenge that might've maxed out his credit card. And a picnic. He brought fancy little finger foods. And one of those cozy blankets that somehow smelled like cedar and plot development."

Fisher's mouth falls open. "You slept with him after *that?!* Love, *never* sleep with anyone after an emotionally well-paced outing."

I glare.

"Did he feed you himself? Read you a poem? Quote Austen with a smirk and devastating eye contact?"

"There was... dancing...in the snow."

He chokes on air. "*In the snow?* Ava Bell, you're already married in seven states."

I press my lips together, trying not to smile.

"Oh my God," he whispers, hand to his chest as if I told him I eloped. "He *Nicholas-Sparksed* you."

Shaking my head, I laugh. "Yeah, I guess he did."

"And after that?"

My smile spreads. "We binged the *Twilight* saga."

Fisher goes completely still. "You what?"

I shrug, sheepish. "Started with *Twilight*, then *New Moon*, and... may have made it halfway through *Eclipse* before—well, things took a turn."

He throws both hands in the air. "Oh my God, you're in love.

That man sat through *Bella Swan's* entire decision tree and still wanted to sleep with you? That's a soulmate, Ava. Oh my God, you've imprinted."

"Stop romanticizing it!"

"Too late. I'm already planning your engagement photo aesthetic."

Groaning, I cover my face with both hands. "We agreed it wasn't going to be a thing. Then it *became a thing*. We spent an entire weekend snowed in. And now...I'm scared, but happy. And also scared."

Fisher reaches across the table, resting his perfectly manicured hand over mine. "Here's the deal. You're scared because this isn't about numbers or PR or bestselling lists anymore. This is about him. And you. And how he makes you feel like you *matter*, even when you're clearly spiraling."

My throat threatens to close up.

He squeezes my hand. "So yeah. I joke. But I see it. You trust him. And the way he looks at you? That man would buy every one of your books from every store in America if you asked him to. He probably already has."

I'm laughing, shoulders shaking, when a shadow falls across our table.

"Wow," a syrupy voice says. "So it is true."

Our attention shifts.

Tall. Blonde. A Bond girl type in kitten heels and head-to-toe monochrome beige. She's holding a latte and haughtiness in equal measure.

"Sorry—do I know you?" I ask her.

"Oh, no, you don't *me*," she says, fake-laughing that's too high-pitched for this early hour. "But your so-called boyfriend, Soren, does."

The sound of his name on her collagen-injected lips snaps my anxiety up to a roaring level.

She presses a manicured hand to her chest. "It's so funny.

Right before the Great Booksgiving kickoff party, Soren was waking me up with his tongue in my—well. You get it."

My stomach squeezes around the knife she just inserted.

And twists.

Because *I do* get it. Vividly. Horribly.

I get it so well that my brain helpfully fills in the blanks with flashes I never saw—but now can't unsee.

But worse than the visual, is the math.

The timeline.

Booksgiving.

Her.

Us.

The cabin.

I hear his voice in my head, clear as that first snowfall: *"It's been over a year since I've had a partner."*

My chest goes tight. My breath comes shallow.

If what this woman is saying is true, then he lied. And not just a little white lie—an *emotional landmine*.

And just like that, my demons—so carefully silenced, so neatly tucked away—come drifting back in.

You're so naive.

Nothing but a conquest.

A joke.

Men say what they need to say to get what they want.

You gave it up so freely.

This was never real.

I'm trying not to crumble while this woman beams like she just won something.

And maybe... she did.

She tilts her head, "bitch" dripping from her tone as she continues twisting that knife, "And then—what? Twenty-four hours later, he's dating you? I mean... My God, he moves fast."

I don't give her the satisfaction of a visible reaction.

I *can't.*

Technically—*technically*—I have no right to one. *The Great*

GOING VIRAL FOR CHRISTMAS

Booksgiving happened over a month ago. That's when the contract was born, long before anything real started with Soren. We weren't *together* together then. And I can't hold his past against him like I own it.

What I *can* do is be pissed that he lied. *Really* pissed.

Fisher's foot nudges mine under the table, trying to remind me that we're in public and I shouldn't stab her with my mimosa straw. He should take his own advice because he's holding in a breath like he's about to commit a felony with that butter knife in his hand.

I steady my voice. "So sorry you mistook your hookup for a personality."

Fisher coughs to cover his laugh.

Clearly not used to pushback, she blinks.

"Something in your eye?" I ask.

"Enjoy it while it lasts. I'm sure he'll get bored soon enough. He *always* does. Ask his contact list."

Soren appears behind her, hands tucked casually in his pockets, wearing an easy smile that doesn't quite reach his eyes. He's pretending not to notice the tension, like he hasn't just stepped straight into a flaming emotional dumpster. But I see the slight feather in his jaw.

He's trying to play it cool.

He's not fooling me.

Soren moves around her, leans down, and kisses me on the lips, soft and quick. "I missed you. You were gone when I woke up."

I don't kiss him back. My whole body has gone stiff under the weight of this woman's pretentious grin and the echo of her words still buzzing in my ears.

And now... the images start.

Uninvited. Unrelenting.

I don't *want* them, didn't *ask* for them, but they're here anyway—crashing through my mind like a montage I never wanted.

Soren pushing her up against a wall.

Her head thrown back, screaming his name like it belongs to her.

Her nails digging into his shoulders.

The cocky smirk he gives *me*—aimed at *her*.

Breathe through it, Ava. Try to focus on now—on us.

But her laugh lingers in the air like cheap perfume. And I hate how much it's messing with my head.

I blink hard, willing it all away, but the sting behind my eyes is real.

Soren straightens. His gaze cuts from me... to her. "Lena," he says, coolly, like her name tastes wrong in his mouth, even if it once didn't.

Thirty

SOREN

Lena.

Fuck.

That bitch's mouth is curved into that smug little simper she saves for men who ghost her and women she wants to psychologically decapitate.

"Lena," I say, voice flat.

"Soren," she replies sweetly, batting her lashes. "Long time no tongue. I've been missing you since our little romp at the Great Booksgiving."

Fisher makes a noise that sounds as if he's swallowed a wasp. But I don't look at him. I'm watching Ava. She's gone completely still. To anyone else, she might look unaffected. But I know better.

It's in the rigid set of her shoulders. The way her fingers tighten around her glass. The barely-there flare of her nostrils as she forces herself to keep breathing.

Booksgiving. Fucking Lena.

I know *exactly* what she's doing. She's planting doubt, twisting the timeline just to make it sound recent. And intentional. Like I left her bed and fell into Ava's the next morning.

I didn't sleep with her this year. Hell, was she even there?

But last year?

Yeah. We did.

Biggest goddamn regret of my life. It was meaningless and ended when Lena tried to pitch me her novella idea mid-blowjob and asked if my agent reps reverse harem.

Haven't touched her since.

But Lena didn't say *that*, did she? She let it hang. Vague enough to hurt. Sharp enough to cut.

I inhale slowly, forcing down the heat slithering up my neck. "Funny, don't remember seeing your face there."

Lena's smile turns wicked, her teeth practically glinting. "Well, maybe that's because your head was between my legs at the time." She laughs—a cruel, sugar-drenched sound that lands like broken glass in my gut.

Ava moves, excusing herself, polite and breezy, like she's going to powder her nose, not go completely feral in a stairwell.

I know better for that too.

The moment Ava's out of sight, I round on Lena. "What the *hell* are you doing?"

Lena lifts a shoulder. "Making conversation."

Fisher's on his phone, typing erratically. I catch a glimpse of the screen—Group text: *Mayday. Shitstorm level ten. Suite 811. Bring a mop.*

"Leave," I command Lena.

She leans in. "I warned you. If you wanted to see unhinged, I'd show you. And I'm just getting started. ShelfSpace is going to hate you once I'm done."

"Not more than I hate you." I storm off.

By the time I catch up to Ava, she's barreling into the suite. Camille and Renata rush in behind me, panting. Fisher slams the door and presses his back against it, acting like we're barricading ourselves in a war zone.

"Ava—" I start.

"Don't," she snaps, spinning on me. "Do *not* try to kiss me or calm me or explain *that* away."

My stomach sinks. She's not pissed—she's *hurt*.

"Nothing she said was true," I quickly say. "I haven't touched her—"

"Don't you *dare* lie to me." Her voice breaks a hair. "Don't insult me."

Fisher winces from the doorway. Camille swaps a glare with Renata. They both might want to fry me where I stand. I can tell Renata's halfway between sympathy and strategy mode.

I can't deal with any of them. Not when the only person I care about hearing the truth doesn't even want to be in the same room as me.

"I think it's best if all of you leave," I tell the three of them. They all nod and, without a word, exit the suite.

As soon as the door clicks shut, Ava starts in, "Soren, I've been *trying* to believe this is more than PR and timing and viral clips. I've been giving you the benefit of the doubt, even when I knew your reputation. Because I wanted it. I wanted *you.*"

My chest twists. "Ava—"

"Then that woman walks up to me as though I'm just a pit stop. Or another hashtag in your trail of conquests. And you didn't even deny it. You just stood there."

"I was caught off guard."

Ava laughs—bitter and hollow. "Yeah. So was I."

"I didn't sleep with her at *this* Booksgiving." It sounds like a loophole. A technicality. A soft lie blanketed in omission. And now she thinks I'm another man who sweet-talks his way into her life and leaves her feeling small. Stupid. Used.

"But you *have.*"

Silence.

If I confirm that the woman aiming poison arrows at her once had her hands on my dick and my mouth between her thighs, I know exactly how it'll land.

Betrayal.

A confirmation of every fear Ava's ever had about me.

Proof I'm still the man she's scared I might be.

But I'm not anymore. Not with her. Ava Bell isn't the exception—she's the *goddamn rewrite*. And she doesn't need Lena's name in the footnotes.

My answer is quiet. "Yes."

I pray her mind isn't feeding her images of what my *one* night with Lena might've looked like.

"It meant nothing. I buried it. Shoved it down into the grave-yard of old selves I never plan on resurrecting."

Ava shakes her head, eyes glassy but burning. She turns toward the bedroom, jaw set. I don't know what to say to make her stay, because right now, she's finished with me.

But I'm *nowhere* near finished with this conversation. Ava needs space, though. So, I stand in the middle of our hotel room, watching the woman I care about–the one I've been trying so hard to give me a chance–disappear behind a closing bedroom door, and I feel nothing but helpless.

This is *precisely* the kind of shit Ava's been guarding her heart against. And she's been waiting on it like clockwork, knowing it would end soon enough.

The reason she doesn't let people in. The reason she doesn't believe in soft landings or safe hands or someone staying long enough to mean it.

And I *handed* it to her. On a silver platter. With Lena's perfectly glossed venom on top.

I'm going to be sick.

Ava's been fighting against herself to believe in me. And in *us*. Now, I've given her Exhibit A for why she should've kept her walls up.

My heart aches. Ava's in the other room, wondering if I'm *exactly* what she feared I was from the start.

I want to go to her. Crush every wall. Every defense. Tell her what happened, when it happened, why it never meant anything. Tell her about the texts from Lena. What Marcus said to do. And that I'm sorry. For all of it. For not telling her in the first place. That *she's* the person who makes me a better man.

However, nothing is going to make it better right now. No

amount of clever comebacks or toe-curling kisses or dreamy-boyfriend optics is going to fix it. Ava Bell finally let herself believe in someone. That someone was supposed to be different.

I drag a hand through my hair, chest burning, reviewing the last thirty minutes in my mind.

And you know what? Fuck that.

Ava doesn't get to hold my past sins against me. I've worked too damn hard to prove I'm *not* that man anymore. I've *shown* her who I am now—over and over again.

Fuck her if she thinks I'm going to back down so easily.

I push through the door as though it's on fire. Because *it is*. Ava's pacing near the bed, arms wrapped around her waist. She's trying to hold herself together with sheer force of will.

She spins when I enter, eyes blazing. "Get ou—"

I don't let her finish.

I kiss her.

Hard as fuck.

Desperate.

Furious.

She shoves me back instantly. "Don't *you* dare—"

I throw my hand up when I say, "Yeah, I fucked Lena. *One* time. She left that part out on *purpose*. She planted a seed of doubt in that gorgeous, brilliant, overthinking head of yours. But *you* didn't even let me explain. You didn't *ask*. You decided I was exactly what you were afraid I'd be."

Ava's arms drop, her mouth opening. She wants to argue.

I don't give her the chance. "You want honesty? I've already given it. Time and time again."

She shakes her head, confused, defensive.

"From the moment I found your voice in those pages, I *couldn't* stop reading you. I devoured your entire backlist in a week. I saw the fire and hurt and *hope* in your words and it gutted me. *You* gutted me." I step closer. My voice softens. "I fell in love with you on the page before I ever met you in person. And maybe that's weird. Maybe it's crazy. But it's true. You've held my heart in your hand since the first chapter of *The Lumberjack's Love Letters*. Which is a stupid fucking title, by the way."

She sucks in a breath, lips parting, but I hold up a hand.

"But here's the thing, Bells. You *demand* honesty. Loyalty. Trust. And you *deserve* all of it. But if we're doing this—if we're going to be in an actual relationship—then you have to meet me halfway."

One more inch.

I take another step, gaze unwavering. "You don't get to preach vulnerability and then shut the door the second it gets scary. You don't get to ask me to bare my soul while you hide behind your walls and your sarcasm and that cute little flinch you do every time shit gets real."

She swallows hard. Her eyes glisten—but still, she doesn't speak.

"I love that you're strong, Bells. I love that you've protected yourself. But I am not the enemy. And if you're going to keep treating me like the villain, this will never work."

Her lip trembles.

"I love you," I say, chest open, heart exposed, and with so much emotion, my soul aches. But it's a welcome pain. I've been living with this secret for far too long. "I never imagined this would be the thing that made me tell you those very important words for the first time. But here we are. And I will not spend my life begging for a chance you've already decided I don't deserve."

Silence.

Breathless, aching silence.

"Say it again," she whispers.

Confused, I shake my head. "What?"

Her voice is barely a breath. "Say it again. Say you love me."

"I love you, Ava Bell. And I *am not* going anywhere."

Ava flinches at that, like it physically hurts her to hear. She turns her back. She's going to walk—that's what she does when it's too much.

"I mean it," I say, voice firm, unshakable. "Don't get to shut me out."

Her shoulders tense.

"I know your move, Bells. Pretend it didn't happen. Bury the feelings. Talk yourself into believing I'm nothing but another guy with a pretty face and a decent line. Safer that way, right? Easier to protect yourself if you write me off before I get the chance to do any damage."

Ava still doesn't speak—but her breathing falters.

"You want to be mad at me? Fine. Be mad. But don't twist what we have into something that it's not because it scares you."

She finally turns, eyes wet, voice shaky. *"Of course it scares me!* This whole thing—it felt too good to be true from the start. The fake dating, the cameras, the fans, the chemistry—it's *storybook shit,* and I don't get stories like that, Soren."

I close the distance between us and take her face in both hands before she can retreat again. "You do this time."

Ava tries to look away. I won't let her.

"In our story, you get loved, fully and openly, and without fine print. By *me.*" My forehead presses to hers. "You're not some problem I'm trying to fix. You are the woman I *choose,* Ava. Every single damn time. Choose me back."

Tears spill down her cheeks, but she still fights. "What if I can't do this? What if I'm not enough?"

"Impossible."

"What if *I* mess it up?"

"Then we mess it up together," I say. "But we don't walk away. Unless we've said every truth. Unless we've given it everything."

Ava shakes under my touch. I kiss her tears. I need her to believe it more than I need my next breath, so I repeat, "I love you, Ava Bell," again and again and again.

Thirty-One

AVA

The words detonate, punching through my ribs, seizing my heart in their ruthless grip, and tearing it free. And then, like it belongs to him, Soren cradles it in the open, unflinching.

I love you, Ava Bell.

I want to believe him. But belief has teeth. It chews through you when it's wrong. Right now, his love—his certainty—it's a trapdoor. A story too good to be mine.

The moment I believe it's real, it'll get ripped away, and I'll fall back into the darkness. So I do the only thing I know how to do.

I push away from him and pace.

Turning my back. I try to build the wall again faster than he can tear it down. "I can't do this," I whisper, barely able to get the words out.

"Yes, you can." His voice is firm. "You already are."

"No," I snap, spinning on him. "You don't get it. You don't know. You haven't lived inside my chest, where every time something feels safe, it ends up cutting me open. Where people I've trusted have burned me to ash. Where love isn't a promise—it's a threat."

He doesn't react.

I hate him for that.

I hate him for being so still when I'm coming apart.

But, I think I love him too.

My voice shakes. "Do you know what it's like to be waiting for the good thing to end constantly? The clock ticks on every soft moment. That's what I do, Soren. That's what I've *learned*."

"I know," he says quietly. "I see it. Every time you pull away. Every time you make a joke instead of admitting you're scared. Every time you flinch when things between us are right."

"I'm not flinching," I breathe. "I'm drowning."

It's true. The panic is closing in. My knees buckle before I can stop them, and I collapse to the floor. My body can't carry the fear anymore.

I cover my face as though that'll somehow hide the tears. Hide the fact that I'm breaking.

"I'm sorry," I choke. "I'm sorry I'm like this. But, please, I need you to know that you make me feel things."

"What kinds of things, Bells?"

"You make me feel like a fairytale and a firestorm."

Suddenly, Soren's on the floor too, sliding in behind me and wrapping his arms around my waist, securing us together

One hand slides up my back. He's offering a heartbeat I can borrow, and he's willing to keep rhythm for both of us until I can remember how.

"I'm not leaving," he whispers into my hair.

That's when the final layer—years in the making, brick by trembling brick—*shatters*.

I curl into him, sobbing into his chest like it's the first breath I've had in days. He holds me through it, quiet and constant, as though he knew this was coming all along.

"I don't know how to do this," I whisper.

"You don't have to," he says. "You just have to stay... with me"

My fingers grip his legs. And for the first time in my entire life, I let someone hold me in the middle of the storm—and I don't try to run.

Because he's right. I *do* get this kind of story. And maybe this time, I don't have to write the ending alone.

Soren's arms are still around me when the sobs fade into silence. My cheek rests against his chest, damp with tears. His heart thumps beneath my ear, and for once, I don't need to armor up to match it.

I just breathe.

I'm *safe*.

I shift in his lap, my hand sliding up to cup his jaw. His eyes meet mine. My heart melts at the devotion I see. The patience. The love.

"Soren," I whisper.

His thumb brushes across my cheek. "Yeah, Bells?"

"Take off your clothes."

A brow lifts.

"I mean it," I say. "I want to feel like I haven't lost control."

Soren doesn't ask questions. Or make a joke. He obeys. Piece by piece, he undresses with my help, right there on the floor, until nothing remains but the man who's seen me at my worst—and stayed.

I rise slowly, unhooking myself from the past that's clawed at my ankles for too long. My dress slips off first. Then my bra. Then my panties. Layer by layer, I strip away more than fabric.

I strip away fear. Shame. Doubt.

I move to straddle him, and Soren's hands settle lightly on my thighs, but he doesn't grip. He doesn't guide. He lets *me* control the moment.

Cradling his face in my hands, I gaze down at him, finally seeing him for who he is—which isn't the viral fantasy, or the book boyfriend brand—but the man who braved my family, created a night made special for me, watched the Twilight Saga...

Told me he loved me and meant it.

And got on the floor when I broke.

"I need to do this. My way."

His voice is hoarse. "Anything you want, Bells."

I kiss him. Sure. Deep, pouring everything into it—everything I've held back. The terror. The hope. The way he's unraveled me with every single touch, all of his words, and each time he looked at me.

I sink down onto him, taking him inch by deliciously hard inch. There's no rush. No urgency. I want to feel *every* bit of his eager cock.

Soren groans beneath me, his hands tightening, but he doesn't move. He lets me ride the rhythm, lets me lead us both deeper into this new thing we're building.

My hands slide down his chest. My hips roll. His name leaves my mouth like a song he wrote, and when he answers with mine on lips, it's tender and cherishing.

This man is not a risk.

He's the reward.

I keep moving, grinding, learning the parts of him that tremble when I clench around him. I kiss his throat. I tell him I want all of him—every broken, beautiful piece. His eyes never leave mine. And when the climax hits—when I flutter around him and he pulses inside me—I don't break.

I *become*.

I'm something new. Something more.

We collapse, breathless, sated, and I curl into his chest, no longer afraid.

Soren runs his fingers through my hair, whispering words I can't quite catch.

"What did you just say?" I ask.

Soren presses a kiss to my temple, and the world tilts. The sound of it — so sure, ordinary — punches through my ribcage like sunlight through a shuttered window. "I said... You saved me, Bells. Forever, I am yours."

The words land, and all the places I've kept locked up rattle. My lips part to tell him the truth back, that he saved me too, that he rewired something that had been snapped and rusted inside me, but the sentence dies behind my teeth. Fear crawls up my spine like cold ivy, and the reflex to brace, to fold the fragile parts of myself into a smaller shape where no one can reach them, takes over. I taste salt from a laugh I try to force out and feel ridiculous for wanting to cry and laugh and fling myself at him all at once.

So, I close my mouth and inhale the smell of him, pine and snow, and honesty, and press my hand to the place where his heart would be if I could map it. My fingers tremble. I can feel, in the unbridled ache beneath my ribs, how much he means it. He means so much to me. That should be enough. That should let me say the words, hand him back the gift he's given.

But the memory of promises that turned to paper boats and drowned keeps its hold. Trust is not a light I can switch on. It's a road I'm too fearful to walk down. I want to offer him everything he's handed to me—the safety, the staying, the reckless kindness. But the part of me that learned to survive by leaving a piece of myself at every exit still hesitates at the door.

Therefore, I say nothing. I curl into him in the only way I know how: with my trembling body, with a silence that means yes and maybe-not-yet all at once.

Soren doesn't push. He holds me like I'm the most deadly and most beautiful thing he's ever been trusted with, and that stability almost breaks me open. Because some wounds take longer than one night, one poem, one promise to trust again. I'm terrified of handing him my whole heart and watching him learn how to let go, and proving me right all over again. Proving that love isn't forever, except in stories. That even the best of them leave, no matter how tightly you hold on.

Feast & Fiction

Snowflake Gala

Bookmas Bash

Midnight Kisses &
Paper Wishes

Thirty-Two

SOREN

I've done a lot of humiliating things for the sake of marketing.

Once, I filmed an entire reel in a bathtub full of rose petals reading an enemies-to-lovers novella while making "tortured soul" eye contact with the camera.

I've worn leather pants in summer. I've hosted a panel called *Battle Mage But Make Him Daddy*.

But nothing—and I mean *nothing*—has prepared me for the moment I step onto the floor of the *Bookmas Bash* wearing a matching ugly Christmas sweater with Ava Bell.

Mine has a dragon curled around a snow-dusted castle, breathing fire that conveniently spells *Merry Christmas*.

Hers features Santa's sleigh rocking suspiciously on its runners, mistletoe dangling from the reins. One reindeer peeks back wide-eyed. Caption: *Sleigh My Name, Sleigh My Name*.

We seem to have lost a bet to two overcaffeinated publicists and the ghost of tacky Christmas.

Oh, wait, we did.

Renata's eyes practically glow with glee. "How festive! The fans are going to eat this up. I've uploaded your sweaters to both your sites for merchandise orders."

CEDAR JAMES

"If one more person asks if we coordinated our 'couples look' on purpose—"

"You did," Camille says, casually, but grinning. "For the brand, obviously."

I narrow my eyes. "You love this."

"I do."

Ava snakes an arm around my waist, attempting to calm me. "I think we look cute."

I glance down at her. "Fine. I'll wear it, but only because I'm a man who's about to plunder Santa's workshop and seduce a Jingle Bells heiress." My nose nuzzles into her hair, and she giggles.

Pushing me away playfully, Ava shakes her head, still grinning. "What the hell is wrong with you?"

"Honestly?" My brows waggle. "Very little ever since this morning."

How could I complain? Ava dropped to her knees on the shower floor, lips sliding down my cock until the steam fogged over and I was braced against the tile, bellowing her name while she swallowed every last drop like it was the only thing on the breakfast menu. I barely staggered out of that shower alive.

My girl blushes and shoves a handful of Sharpies at me. "Go sit at your table, Book Daddy."

After hours of signing, the holiday sweater Camille stuffed me into is hot, itchy, and suffocating me like a damn straitjacket. I can't take it anymore.

"Camille," I say, yanking at the offensive wool around my torso. "I'm done with this sweater. You can shove it where the sun don't shine."

Beside me, Ava *snorts* behind her hand.

Camille crosses her arms, arches a brow, then leans in so no one else can hear. "You signed a contract, Pembry. And we pay a *shit ton* of money to make you look good. You will wear the damn sweater."

Ava is grinning, cheeks an adorable shade of pink.

Yeah. Nope.

"I'll take my chances with hypothermia and public nudity," I declare, then I rip the damn thing off.

There's screaming. A woman drops her tote bag. Stickers fly like confetti. I spot a grown-ass man openly weeping near the fantasy map wall.

Without missing a beat, I ball up the sweater and chuck it into the crowd.

"Yesssssss!" someone yells.

"Oh my God!" Another screams.

"Lick his nipple!" a third voice chimes in.

I ignore all of them and turn back to Ava, who is now beet red and mid-eye roll.

I yank her into my bare chest and plant a kiss on her. The cameras go wild and dirty, and she's speechless when I finally pull back.

The crowd loses its mind.

Phones are up. Flashes. Screeches. One woman faints—Fisher fans her with a vendor map while muttering on about OSHA violations.

Ava gapes at me.

"Merry Bookmas, baby." I wink.

"You are *insane*."

"Admit it... you're a little turned on."

One corner of her mouth curls back into the tiniest smirk.

Confirmation received.

My voice drops, for only her to hear. "Bet if I slid my hand between those gorgeous thighs right now, I'd find you wet, and *aching* for my flesh sword."

"You're not wrong."

"Find me a supply closet and five minutes, Bells, and I'll tickle your tinsel."

Ava's eyes darken. She might actually say yes.

"Absolutely not," Fisher snaps, appearing out of thin air as the ghost of Too Much PDA. "No closets. No cellars. No oral situations. No penetration. You two have scarred enough hotel employees to last a lifetime."

Ava coughs into her fist, blushing even brighter.

I pull her up to standing, then step back with my hands raised in mock innocence. "What happened to your magic of Christmas?"

"It's down below," Fisher mutters without missing a beat, "exactly like yours."

Before I can throw back a quip, the air shifts with a familiar presence.

There he is. Matthew. Best friend. Agent Extraordinaire.

His face says: *What in the peppermint-dicked hell did I just walk into?*

Another voice slices through the noise. "I'm confused."

The words. The tone. Both hit like a bucket of ice water down the back.

Ava and I swivel in unison. So does Fisher.

Standing a few feet away, wearing a holly-red lip stain and a face full of arrogance, is Lena. One perfectly manicured brow arched. Arms crossed. Looking bitchy enough to frost the whole damn exhibit.

The crowd hushes, instinctively aware that something is about to shatter the holiday glow.

My gaze cuts to Camilla. One look, one silent question: *How the hell did she get past security?*

Camilla's eyes widen. Her shrug screams *don't look at me*, even as she fumbles for her phone, already barking into it for backup.

Lena's smile is venom and velvet. "Forgive me for being so blunt, but I've been having a hard time wrapping my head around this whole— " She gestures between Ava and me. "—Thing. I mean, Soren Pembry, body collector, fantasy fuckboy, man who practically has a revolving door installed on his tour bus, is suddenly playing committed boyfriend to America's romance sweetheart?"

Ava stiffens beside me. Lena's doing it again. Same sweet

poison, same performative interest. A pinch of empathy to make Ava second-guess everything. Her voice isn't only echoing off the walls, it's reverberating through Ava's cracks, slithering into every dark, doubtful corner I've spent *weeks* trying to silence, dragging Ava's deepest fear into the light, using it for gossip and nothing but entertainment.

I should've known Lena wouldn't let it go after the last encounter when she cornered Ava and dripped those same venom-laced doubts into her ear.

I told Ava I loved her that night.

She didn't say it back.

I've told myself it was just a matter of timing. Nerves. She was overwhelmed. But a part of me wonders if Lena's doubt missiles hit their mark.

And now Lena's back—reloading.

"I mean, your viral feud was fun while it lasted," Lena purrs, voice dripping with rotten sugar. "The insults, the clips, the trends—you two were practically made for ShelfSpace. Was this the plan all along? Fake a rivalry, fake a romance, cash in the numbers?" Her smile cuts wider, cold and satisfied. "Because if that's the case—*bravo*. Really. You've played the whole internet like a fiddle. But guess what?" She leans forward, like she's about to share a secret. "I'm not buying it. And I'll make damn sure nobody else does either."

Tension pours off Ava. This is the type of moment where most people would fold, duck for cover. But she doesn't move.

Lena sees it, and her smirk grinds like a jagged blade. "Let's see what happens when this little charade burns to ash. I'm going to expose the truth to everyone. Soon, they'll see what's *really* going on."

The silence in the room thickens, weighted and ugly, until it's begging to be broken.

So I fucking do.

I step forward, voice calm, eyes locked on Lena. "You know what's funny?"

"Mmmm, what's that?" Lena purrs.

"You strut in here acting like you've cracked some code, when really? You've missed the entire plot."

Lena's lips curl, her heavily lined eyes flashing challenge.

I don't flinch. "If you think I need to fake-date Ava Bell to sell books or stay relevant, you clearly don't know her. Or me."

A ripple of nervous laughter breaks through the crowd, but I don't take my eyes off Lena. I take another step closer, closing the space between us. She peers up at me, smirking.

"And here's the real kicker—you call it fake, but I don't need to pretend to want Ava Bell. Nor do I need a marketing plan to explain why I'm standing next to the most brilliant, infuriating, stunning woman I've ever met."

Phones tilt up, cameras snapping.

I smile, wicked and deliberate. "So no, Lena. This isn't some carefully staged stunt. It's me. Wanting her." I point to Ava. "Choosing her. Every damn day." I back up, arms open wide, until I'm next to Ava. "This is me falling in love with the woman I was supposed to hate. This is her seeing through every bullshit layer I've ever built and kissing me anyway. This, *Lena*, is real."

I let that hang there. Let it *land*.

Lena's painted-on smile doesn't falter, but her eyes harden to tiny shards of glass. She moves toward us, the click of her heels like gunshots in the silence, and once she's close, she leans in and says, "We'll see."

My smirk turns deadly. "That we will. And if that threatens your worldview or your follower count, that sounds like a *you* problem."

The crowd bursts into applause. But all I'm watching is Ava. Her eyes. Her mouth. Her lips parting slightly, as if she's forgetting how to breathe.

I hope to hell she knows—

That wasn't for the audience.

That was for *her*.

Later that evening, the *Bookmas Bash* plunges into its nighttime phase. With *The Great Interrogation* now safely in the rearview, thanks to an open bar, increased security, and Lena mysteriously developing laryngitis shortly after my speech.

Ava has traded the ridiculous sweater for a dress that cheats the room of oxygen—a short silk slip in a red so deep it drinks the light. Thin straps thread over her shoulders, the low back reveals the pale sweep of skin between her shoulder blades. The fabric doesn't sit on her so much as melt into her, clinging to the curve of her hip and the soft swell of her thigh, catching the candlelight and turning it into molten lava.

Moonlight pools along the window and finds her as if it's drawn by a compass, slipping across the silk, picking out the highlights of her hair, and slithering over the slope of her collarbone, making her every move look like liquid. She walks like someone who knows exactly how the light will love her, a slow tide of silk and shadow.

My heart is so damn full at the sight of her, drenched in all that light—vulnerable and impossible and absolutely mine. Later, I think, I'll show her exactly how much I love her, with a thousand kisses and even more licks.

I've salvaged some of Camille's dignity by putting on a shirt after my bare-chested stunt I pulled earlier, when I ripped off Camille's tragic attempt at an ugly Christmas sweater. Crisp, black, fitted—safe. Something that doesn't get me a million views on ShelfSpace, like my torso does. Well, one million four hundred thousand thirty-two to be exact.

We are now at a twinkle-lit mixer in one of the hotel's luxury lounges, complete with mulled wine, book-themed cocktails, and a curated cheese board.

Ava moves across the room to post up near the fireplace, drink in hand, laughing with Fisher and a debut author wearing a cape. Her cheeks are glowing. Her smile is real. She looks so goddamn beautiful happy.

A nudge at my shoulder. Matthew.

He's nursing a glass of a bourbon-based cocktail, eyes tracking Ava, running calculations.

"You two holding up okay after the whole Lena Laceration?" he asks, nonchalantly, as though we didn't get verbally shanked in front of half the industry.

"My definition of okay might differ from yours."

He grins. "She hasn't set you on fire yet. That's a promising start."

My eyes drift back to Ava. She's throwing her head back in laughter now—God, that sound—it's champagne uncorked, bright and effervescent, fizzing straight through my veins until I'm drunk on nothing but her.

"So, you're really in it, huh?" Matthew sips his bourbon and watches me watch her. He's studying me, cataloging everything, posture, breath, expressions. Classic Matthew.

"I'm in something, alright."

Shaking his head, he laughs, takes a sip from his glass. "You're in deep, man. You've got *the* look."

"What look?"

"The one you used to make fun of me for when I saw Christina get out of the car in that 'Good Trouble' shirt. I was a man watching his emotional downfall walk across a parking lot in pink heels."

"I remember that day vividly."

Matthew's gaze shifts. Ava. Back to me. Ava again.

"She's hot," he comments.

"Careful." Arching a brow, I side-eye him, blood sparking.

"I'm married. Not blind." He takes his phone out of his pocket, glances at it, then slips it back in. "But that's not what I meant. She's got spunk."

"Yeah, she definitely does."

"And you like that?"

"I *love* that."

Still assessing me, Matthew hums. "Not gonna lie. I figured you'd write through this little crush of yours. But now that I'm here... and she's here... and I'm watching you, and..." He turns his full attention to me. "...So, is this the one?"

My lips press together. Ava is now crouching to sign a fan's book on the armrest of a velvet chair. She points to her signature. They giggle as if they just got away with something dirty. It melts my heart.

Ava finds me watching, and softens. I refocus my attention on Matthew. "I'm all in for this one."

He studies me for another beat. "Okay."

"Okay?"

"I mean, I've got more questions. For instance, when the hell did you become a panty-melter with principles? But okay."

"You're not going to interrogate her?"

"I might. But not tonight. She's happy. And you look like a man who finally realized the life he once thought was out of reach was waiting for him all along."

I stare into my glass, then huff a breath. "Guess I have."

"Besides," he starts, clamping a hand on my shoulder with a mock-grimace, "have you met *her* agent. Fucking terrifying."

Huffing a laugh, I grin. "Victoria?"

He nods, but his expression is full of some war crime PTSD. "That woman made me rewrite the contract three times, change the font to be 'less aggressive,' and sit through a three-hour Zoom where she compared your brand synergy to a layered trifle. And then—*then*—she made me role play as a toxic fan to test Ava's publicist response time."

"You're kidding."

Matthew's eyes turn haunted. "She gave me a script. It had stage directions. I had to use an alias—*Thornblade69*—and argue that romance is ruining fantasy. I haven't slept right since."

Covering my mouth with a fist, I wheeze out a laugh. "Oh my God."

"Laugh it up," he muses. "That woman could out-strategize a CIA advisor while wearing fuzzy slippers and sipping a turmeric latte. I'd rather be drop-kicked into a live cobra pit than ever work with her again."

Matthew's posture straightens. His features—formerly amused—morph into an eerily unreadable expression, as though he's spotted a mythical creature in the wild. One that he's read *extensively* about in my books, but now has to verify for himself. I don't even have to turn around to know Ava's there.

"Speak of the devil and she arrives in candy cane couture," I say brightly.

"What? This old thing?" Ava teases, the silk catching the light as she steps up beside me, the dress clinging in all the ways it shouldn't be legal to, her bare back a weapon all on its own. She holds out two glasses of red wine, cheeks flushed from her earlier pour. "Here." She hands me a glass. "It's either this or hot cider that smells like a Yankee Candle store exploded."

Matthew steps in smoothly, extends a hand. "Ava Bell."

Ava appears surprised by the confident greeting. "Hi."

"I've heard a lot about you." Matthew shakes her hand.

"All good, I hope."

"Nothing but." His finger taps on the rim of his glass. "But, you do know that I'm here to confirm if my best friend's complete personality shift is warranted, right?"

Her brow lifts. "Personality shift?"

"Oh yeah. The man who used to drink bourbon for breakfast and mock emotional monologues is now quoting your paperbacks and baking muffins."

Ava side-eyes me. "Cinnamon rolls, actually."

With a chuckle, my head drops.

Matthew's brow quirks. "*Are* we still talking about baked goods or..."

Ava's cheeks flush a suspicious shade of guilty.

"Let's just say that frosting was *everywhere.*" My lips press together while my arm snakes around her waist.

One of Matthew's hands goes up, silently begging me to stop. "Nope. Nope. I'm tapping out. I did not come here to hear about Soren's sticky buns being used in a biblical sense."

Ava grins, eyes sparkling with mischief. "You brought up the muffins."

"Yeah, but I didn't expect it to be a Pillsbury-sponsored foreplay." Matthew clears his throat, the sound resembling a benevolent threat. "Anyway. I'm here for the usual things—support, temperature gauging, and a vibe check."

Ava's arms cross. "So this is an interview?"

"Let's call it... an informal review panel. I'm trying to understand the woman who managed to make *this guy*"—he jerks a thumb toward me—"watch the Twilight saga and do a puzzle."

Ava sips her wine. "He likes the Volturi drama."

"I'm a man of taste." I shrug.

Matthew turns back to her. "So. Serious question."

Ava braces. Uh oh. I'm nervous now."

"Don't be. I promise I won't bite." He grins. "Tell me, what's your stance on dogs in Halloween costumes?"

Ava doesn't hesitate. "Pro. Strongly pro. But only if the dog consents via tail wag."

Matthew nods solemnly. "Correct answer."

Ava smiles, lighting me up on the inside. "Was that the test?"

"No," he says. "That was the warm-up." His eyes glide between Ava and me. "Now tell me, Ava—is this all still a fake dating publicity stunt for you? Enemies with benefits? Your numbers have reached record highs due to this scheme. Is that all it still is?"

Thirty-Three

AVA

The question knocks the air out of me.

Matthew asks it so easily—as if he's tossing out a joke. But this one isn't funny. Not even a little. It's very serious.

Shifting my weight, my attention snaps to Soren, who's watching me with that calm, steady patience that drives me a little insane. He already knows my answer. He's waiting to see if I'll say it out loud.

For a second, I want to lie. Come out with a breezy line. Tease. Deflect. But Matthew isn't *some* friend. He's Soren's *Fisher* —his only family. And Matthew is obviously fiercely protective of Soren.

More than anything, I'm exhausted from the performance. Smiling on cue, bantering for the cameras, selling a relationship that isn't supposed to be real. The idea of dropping the act and telling the truth for once feels less like relief and more like a risk.

Heat rises to my cheeks. I inhale, exhale. Answer him. "It stopped being fake the weekend we got snowed in." My voice is light, but sure. "Between the cinnamon rolls and the way he looked at me like I was the whole damn world."

Matthew listens. Soren's expression softens so fast, I nearly dissolve.

"I kept trying to push him away," I go on, shrugging, playing it cool. But fail. "I didn't want it to be real. Because if it were real, then it could hurt me. Or I could lose it. And I've lost enough in the realm of love."

Soren's fingers caress my hip, a small, tender offering.

"I wanted my cake," I admit. "I wanted to eat it too. Soren, though, didn't want crumbs. He wanted all of me. But I kept trying to offer half. Turns out, he doesn't settle."

Matthew's eyes narrow, despite a smile dancing on the corners of his lips.

"I get it now." My eyes are still on the man who changed everything. "So, to answer your question, Matthew, it stopped being fake the second Soren felt like home."

Soren exhales as though he's been holding it in for months.

"Well, shit." Matthew huffs a breath, swiping at his eyes like something is stuck in them. "Now I gotta go call my wife and tell her I love her or some shit like that. Fucking authors, man. You're all emotional terrorists in cute shoes."

Soren chuckles.

Matthew claps him on the back, sets his empty glass on a passing tray, then turns to me. "It was a pleasure, Ava. If you ever need someone to dramatically read one of your steamy scenes at an open mic night, call literally anyone else."

I grin. "Duly noted."

"She's got me for that." Soren winks.

"No doubt in my mind." With a final head nod, Matthew fishes his phone out of his pocket, strolls off into the crowd.

I turn back. Soren's gaze roams over me like I signed my name on his soul. Stormy eyes glitter with hunger, heat crackling in the space between us. The man before me is a lit fuse.

"Uh-oh," I breathe, taking a step back that's not really away. "I know that look."

Soren keeps staring. Pretty sure he's about to start a holy war in the name of my thighs.

I tilt my head. "Are we about to find another back room?"

That delicious mouth of his curves. "That depends."

"On what?"

His voice becomes a blazing whisper of desire. "On whether or not you want to walk tomorrow."

Soren's hand curls around mine. He's got that gleam that screams *sex and sabotage,* and he's on a hunt to find the nearest coat closet to fuck me in the name of holiday spirit.

But I dig my heels in with a smirk. "Whoa, whoa. Where exactly are we going?"

Turning back to look at me, his brows raised, Soren squeezes my hand, "Trust me, Bells?"

"I do. I'm just trying to get the itinerary. Is this a one-orgasm detour or a multi-course tasting menu?"

"Definitely multi." Soren yanks me into him, laughing wickedly before continuing.

We barely make it halfway down the hall before he veers left, tugging me with him through a closed-off area marked *Holiday Memories Station.*

A red, ornate chair is the center of attention, with two shelves looming behind it, filled with Santa hats, elf ears, reindeer antlers, and numerous other props, including candy cane glasses and various festive trinkets. A camera sitting on a tripod faces it.

"You've got to be kidding me." I peek back toward the hallway we came from.

"Nope." Soren grins like the Devil in December, making his way toward the props. "Nothing says holiday cheer better than fucking in a corporate-sponsored photo station."

I'm a little breathless over the suggestion. My eyes roam over the candy cane glasses, and suddenly, the reindeer ears are oddly erotic.

A flutter ignites low in my belly, tightens my thighs, and makes my breath heavier. I hesitate. No one's here. But still, this isn't exactly soundproof. Or locked.

Soren sees it in my eyes and leans close, voice low. "No one's coming in. And even if they did... You'd be too far gone to care.

It's a holiday-themed role play, Bells. You, me, a tight little space–other than, well, you know–and a countdown camera? Feels like Christmas to me."

Heat pulses through me. I swallow as his hand falls from my back. He peruses the props, plucks a reindeer headband, and a pair of wire glasses from the basket. He dangles them in front of me. "You want Mrs. Claus or a naughty reindeer?"

Sleigh bells thud in my chest. I eye him for a beat. "Mrs. Claus. *Duh.*"

His grin turns absolutely filthy. "I've always thought Mrs. C was hot."

Secretly snatching a prop and hiding it behind my back, I eye him. "You have an age gap kink?"

"Don't we all?" Soren grabs a Santa hat, plants it on his head, and sits. The world narrows to the two of us. My heart slams in my chest as I gaze down at his beautiful face.

"Sit, on Santa's lap, Bells." A dark demand that curls under my skin.

Soren draws me toward his lap, those strong hands waste no time burrowing under my dress. But I don't budge. I meet his eyes, let the corner of my mouth curve into a saccharine smile, and slowly shake my head no.

His brow furrows, confused. I sink to my knees, and his body stiffens. Kneeling before him, I short-circuit his central nervous system.

"What are you doing, Mrs. Claus?" he asks, voice a little croaky.

"Being festive." I fashion a pair of elf ears on with deliberate care. Tilt my head. Let him take me in.

"Fucking hell," he growls. "You have no idea what you just did to me."

"I have a pretty solid one, actually."

"You wearing those—" His eyes blaze. "—on your knees...like that?"

I cock a brow. "Something wrong, Pembry?"

391

Soren leans back against the ornate chair, as if to give himself a better view—or to avoid prematurely climaxing on the spot.

"Wrong?" he echoes, laughing darkly. "No, Bells. I've just had this exact fantasy since I was sixteen and downloaded my first elf-ridden smut fic off a fan forum. And now you're down there—looking exactly like a pervy holiday wet dream—and I swear to the stars, if you start speaking Elvish, I will marry you on the spot."

I peer up at him, flushed and sultry, then tug on one of the elf ears as though I'm adjusting a crown. "And here I was thinking all your teenage fantasies involved swords and sorceresses."

"Oh, they did," he breathes, heavy with desire. "But none of them knelt."

My grin is wide, wicked, and full of menace. "Well then," I purr, my palms clutching his thighs. "Guess I'm about to make your fantasy canon."

His hands grip the rounded ends of the chair. The groan that slips from that delicious mouth of his could sanctify this whole damn room.

I spread his legs wider. As I reach for his belt, he's so hard and thick beneath the fabric of his pants, my pussy tingles from the feel of him.

Soren drags his bottom lip between his teeth as I undo the button. One slow pull. Then another. The zipper gives way with a soft *shhht*.

His breathing shortens. The pulse in his neck is wild. My fingers slip under the waistband of his briefs, grazing the length of him, teasing the tip, making his whole body tense.

Soren mutters a curse as his head tips back briefly before locking eyes with me again, as if looking away will cause him to miss the whole show. "You're going to kill me."

"At least you'll die happy."

One hand threads into my hair, needing contact to stay grounded. "Bells..." He's eager, ready, lifting his hips to help me as I pull down the waistband past his cock. Once it springs free, I dip my head and slowly lick up his shaft, pressing my tongue flat all the way to the tip, treating him as my own personal candy cane.

A groan rumbles from his chest. "Shit, Bells, Fuck, I love that."

"Mmmm...but why nibble when I can devour?" My tongue traces circles around the head of his cock, savoring every twitch, before easing him down into my mouth until he's pressed against the back of my throat.

Soren hisses, ragged and sharp, his fingers tightening in my hair as storm cloud eyes darken with small flashes of lightning. "Oh, baby, yes."

My mouth works his cock in an unrelenting rhythm until Soren trembles beneath the weight of my tongue while my hand curls around the base, stroking him, each movement a promise, each pull meant to undo him,

"Fuck, Bells," he growls.

I take my time, exploring him, lifting him with my hand and dragging my tongue along the thick veins standing out beneath his skin, teasing every inch with wicked care.

"You're so good at that."

Dipping lower, I flatten my tongue once again on the underside of his cock and lick all the way up to the tip. Wrapping around his crown, I take him deep.

His other hand clutches the armrest. "Deeper," he demands. "You can take more. You want to, I know you do."

The husky, desperate sounds spilling from him only make me crave the stretch of my lips, not because he's demanding it, but because I want to give him everything.

His cock is obscenely rigid. It's becoming impossible to take him all the way down my throat. I build a slow, unyielding pace, quickening as I swallow him with every pass. He's tense beneath my touch, every muscle drawn tight. The rhythm building between us is faster, deeper, and the air itself feels heavy with hunger.

Soren's hips buck, trying to stay in control, but his grip in my hair says otherwise. "Just like that, fuck yes—" His head tips back, groans pour out of him, rough and guttural. "You keep doing that, and I'm gonna come so hard you'll taste me for days."

That's all the encouragement I need. I force myself down, farther, until he nearly steals my breath, the pressure burning and exquisite, my body caught between gagging and wanting more.

His breath saws out in ragged bursts, hips twitching beneath me, the grip in my hair tightens, then suddenly he tugs me back. He's close.

"Fuck—no. Stop." Soren's voice is a rasp. "I need to be inside you, Bells."

Lips wet and swollen, I pull back and look up at him. The expression on his face nearly undoes me. That raw, aching hunger. His restraint is barely hanging on by a thread.

Soren reaches for me, voice urgent. "Ride me."

For a second, the words hang heavy and daring in the air. My breath quickens, heat sparking low in my belly. Slowly, I shift and rise, Soren's hands skimming up my thighs as I do, the power of his gaze scorching every inch of skin.

As I straddle him, the hem of my dress rides up obscenely fast. His hands are under it within seconds, gripping my hips and securing me in place. And when I settle on top of his lap, Soren's mouth meets mine in a kiss that's all tongue and teeth and power.

"Your heart is racing." His lips move to my neck.

"Maybe I'm excited for the photo op."

"Oh, you'll get your photo op."

Soren growls into my mouth, squeezing my hips so hard that bruises are inevitable. I welcome his mark.

"That pretty pussy better be ready for this cock, Bells—because the second you slide down on me, I'm not stopping until you've come—twice."

The flash on the camera goes off. We both freeze.

"...Did it just—?"

"Yep. Pretty sure that was frame one."

"Make it stop," I half laugh, half pant.

394

"Can't. Booth's analog. These are getting developed." He bucks up, his eyes glittering with wicked promise. "Better make the rest worth it."

My panties are gone in seconds. Ripped off and tossed away. So is my ability to form a rational thought. His cock is hard and perfect, and when I sink onto each inch by perfect fucking inch, we both break.

"Fuck, Ava."

Soren's hands seize my ass, guiding me, clamping me to him while I ride his cock fast, and so filthy deep it feels like my soul might explode.

I'm biting down on a moan when another flash goes off. I freeze, breath snagging in my throat, and glance over my shoulder.

Soren grips me tighter, thrusting up so hard the chair groans. "Good. I want it all. Every picture." The bastard doesn't stop moving. His cock spears me deeper until my eyes roll back.

I fist his shirt, gasping. "Stop—stop moving," I say through gritted teeth, though my body betrays me, walls clenching around him, never wanting to let go. "You're going to break the cha—oh, God—Soren—"

His Santa hat falls from its perch on his head. "I don't care if we break the space-time continuum. You feel too good." Soren doesn't let up, hips driving into me until I'm trembling.

Another flash. I halt.

"Stop worrying about the fucking camera, Bells. Let it see. Let the whole world know who makes you come like this."

Another flash bursts, catching my parted lips and the choked sound clawing its way out of my throat.

"We're absolutely going to jail," I pant, riding him faster.

"Maybe–maybe not." His grip tightens. "But we're definitely going viral."

Thirty-Four

SOREN

There are good nights. Great ones, even. And then there are the nights where your fantasy-hating, mayhem-bringing, mind-melting girlfriend puts on a pair of elf ears and ruins you for all other women—past, present, or theoretical.

Last night? Top. Fucking. Tier.

I'm not even entirely sure what happened after the photo booth. I remember grabbing the photos from the dispenser, the two of us nearly fucking again and again every five steps on the way to our suite, the click of the lock on our hotel room door, and the sultry way Ava bent over the minibar in stolen reindeer antlers and asked if I wanted to unwrap my Christmas gift early.

Reader, I did.

And even better, I plundered the entire prop station, treating it as my own personal treasure hoard. I'm not proud. Actually, that's a lie—I'm incredibly proud. Somewhere in my suitcase is a sparkly candy cane tie, two Santa hats, the aforementioned antlers, a suspiciously phallic snow globe, and one single velvet glove I've decided to keep for reasons I will not be explaining.

Now, here Ava and I are, on the bed—after some of the most intense sex I, for one, have ever had.

We're curled in sheets and each other. Ava's pressed against my side, one leg slung over mine, her fingertips drawing lazy circles on my chest, etching her name into my soul.

We're existing. Breathing the same air. Skin to skin. Glowing.

I'm dangerously close to asking her if we can live here now. Right here, in this bed, in this moment. Forever.

Then she says it—softly, but not accidentally. "So... what are we going to do about that Lena chick?"

Fuck.

I keep my breathing steady, but inside, every one of my organs winces in unison. I was hoping this wouldn't come up, but of course it did. Of course, Ava would ask.

Shifting to gaze down at her. "She's noise. She'll fade. You and me—we're what matters."

Ava lifts her head, eyes searching mine. "Is there more to you and her than what you've told me? It seems strange that she would be so extra with her scorch-earth shit if the two of you were only together once."

The question's fair. Reasonable, even. But it lands disgustingly hard in my gut—a punch thrown by someone who knows precisely where the bruise is hiding.

I take Ava's face into my hands. "Lena and I have zero history. One night. One mistake." *One too many times in a single goddamn evening.* "I told you. It wasn't romantic. Or meaningful. Or anything close to what I have with you. But it happened. She tried to come back for seconds this past summer, and I told her no. Now she's making it everyone's problem. I wish more than anything I could erase *that* mistake."

Ava studies me a second longer than I'd like.

I move one hand to her back, trace a line down her spine. "She likes attention. And drama. She can't stand being told no, apparently. And she hates that you stole a spotlight she never even had."

Ava doesn't press. She settles back into the crook of my arm and hums a soft, thoughtful sound, resting her cheek on my chest again.

"I love you."

She still doesn't say it back.

I kiss the top of her head, eyes fixed on the ceiling. And I promise myself—it will resolve itself. Lena will disappear. I'll keep doing what I've been doing from the start. Whittling away at every last wall, Ava Bell thinks she needs to survive.

An hour later, room service arrives. Breakfast should not feel like aftercare. Yet here we are, basking in the glow of culinary comfort and recent sexual relations as two vainglorious criminals sipping overpriced lattes and pretending we didn't defile an entire holiday photo booth sponsored by a romance imprint and their corporate partners.

I look at Ava—eyes still sleepy, lips still kiss-swollen, hair a beautiful mess—and all I can think is: *I'm fucking gone.*

Honestly, I don't even want to be saved.

Ava takes a sip of her peppermint mocha, still flushed and warm from the night before, and I catch myself.

I said Girlfriend earlier.

Fantasy-hating, mayhem-bringing, mind-melting... girlfriend.

I freeze.

Girlfriend?

Shit. I said that without thinking. Not out loud—but still. That's a word—a *loaded* one.

I mean... we travel together. Sleep together. Text like lunatics when we're apart. Which is practically never. I've met everyone from her terrifying agent to her aggressively endearing grandmother. I've worn her shirt. I've watched her cry. We binged Twilight together. I've told her I love her. We do all the things couples do. We just haven't... labeled it as anything else.

My thumb taps the side of my mug. I should let it go. Let it stay easy. Let the definition remain vague so no one gets spooked.

Ava peers at me over her cup with those sleep-heavy eyes and that wild, no-one-else-gets-this smile and—

Yeah. No. I want the word.

"Hey," I say, casually. *Too* casually, maybe. I sound suspicious. "Random question."

She narrows her eyes. "That never ends well."

"Would you say," I begin, drawing the syllables out as though I'm prepping for a dramatic reading, "that we are...label toeing?"

Ava's face scrunches in confusion. "Label toeing?"

I nod solemnly. "Yeah. You know—like camel toeing, except with relationships. A little too tight, a little too obvious, but we're all pretending not to see it."

Ava's cheeks flush, but her glare could slice me in half. "Oh my God. You did not just compare me to a wedged-in yoga pant situation."

"Metaphorically speaking," I say, smirking. "It's the part where we toe the line without crossing it. Except in my head, I may or may not have just called you my girlfriend."

"Just now?" she asks.

"Literally two sips ago," I admit. "I didn't mean to. It was a reflex. Like breathing. Or stealing prop antlers."

Her lips twitch. "So you're telling me I've been demoted to a hypothetical mental girlfriend?"

I grin. "No, I'm trying to find out if you'd consider being officially *upgraded* to something with capital letters. I mean...I told you I love you, soooo..."

Ava's eyes soften. The moment stretches a breath, long enough for me to panic. And then she leans over the table, grabs a sugar packet, and flicks it at my chest.

"Well, if I'm going to be labeled, I expect stickers. Glittery ones. Or maybe edible."

"Done," I say, instantly relieved and also a tad hard. "I'll text Camille. She probably already has branded relationship stationery."

Ava rolls her eyes, but she's smiling. "You're lucky you're cute, Pembry."

"You're lucky I've already mentally monogrammed your initials next to mine."

Ava leans across the tiny café table, her robe slipping and showing those beautiful breasts of hers. I meet her halfway,

399

cupping her cheek and kissing her deeply. I've earned the right to every inch of her. Repeatedly. In holiday-themed headwear.

She tastes sweet, like mocha and mischief, and when I deepen our kiss, her breath catches a little. My hand slips beneath the robe, grazing over soft skin and lower, lower—until I find her slick and waiting.

"Goddamn, Bells," I murmur against her mouth. "You're already *this* wet for me?"

She bites her bottom lip, eyes dancing. "You do things to me, Pembry."

I drag my thumb through her arousal. "I'm going to fuck my *girlfriend's* pussy so hard, they're going to hear it at the North Pole."

"Harder than last night?" she asks, breathy, teasing.

I growl. "Harder than—"

BANG BANG BANG.

We both freeze.

The knocking is *intense.* Someone's trying to break down the fucking door. And I'm about to break their fucking face.

"Soren?" a voice calls. Camille. "Ava? Are you decent?"

Ava yanks her robe shut. I glimpse at the very not-decent state of my lap.

Fisher's voice comes next, too cheerful to be trusted. "There's been a... situation. We need you to open the door. Now."

Ava stares at me. "What kind of situation?"

"Honestly?" I sigh. "I have no idea."

BANG BANG. "NOW, please!"

Groaning, I shove off the chair, adjusting my robe and cursing whoever decided the hotel didn't need deadbolts strong enough to keep our PR team out.

Ava's scrambling to tie her sash tighter while I reach the door and crack it to peek out.

Standing there as the weirdest version of the Four Horsemen I've ever seen are Camille, Renata, Fisher...and Matthew.

400

Matthew raises his brows at my half-dressed state. He can sense what was about to happen.

"I was promised breakfast," Matthew says dryly.

Camille ignores him. "Are you going to let us in, or are we holding this intervention in the hallway?"

"Intervention?" Ava echoes, appearing behind me and peeking out from under my arm. Her cheeks are still flushed, her hair a mess of post-coital curls, and yeah—if four extremely annoyed adults weren't currently staring me down, I'd be dragging her back to bed.

Instead, I step back. "Fine. But know—whatever this is— we've been a *little busy*."

Fisher walks in first, already unlocking his phone. "Oh, we know."

Ava freezes. "Wait. What do you mean, *you know*?"

Renata shuts the door behind her, like she's locking us in for questioning. "Have either of you checked ShelfSpace today?"

"No," Ava says, gnawing on her nails. "We told you. We were... distracted."

Camille gives us both a look that could cancel Christmas. "Well, congratulations. You're trending. Again."

Fisher flips his phone around and hits play on a video.

The sound plays:

"Ava—this whole fake dating publicity stunt has been *gold* for you. Enemies with benefits! You're trending daily. Your numbers are off the charts. But tell me the truth... is that all it still is?"

"It hasn't stopped being fake." Her voice isn't her voice, but it still sounds sure. "Just because we started fucking for real."

The video cuts off.

Ava pales. "That's *not* what I said. That's *not* how either of us said it—"

"Somehow Lena recorded it," Matthew says grimly, arms crossed. "Then she edited it using A.I."

"But she wasn't there with us," Ava counters.

"That we know of," Matthew replies.

The video continues:

"When authors fake date for publicity, what lines are they willing to cross? Bell and The Blade's story isn't romance—it's a scam. I didn't want to believe it, but this audio says it all. Their 'relationship' was nothing more than a launch strategy. For the views, the sales, the algorithm.

And if you needed more proof? I'm about to show a clip of what went down—at a professional venue, mind you—where the 'Queen of Steam' got on her knees for her co-star because, apparently, for Ava Bell, the only thing hotter than fake love is fucking in public.

Guess sex sells, even if you have to crawl for it.

To anyone who ever believed in this pairing—don't worry. So did I. And that's what makes this so disturbing. So manipulative. They have deeply mocked every one of us who thought their story meant something."

Lena's face transitions into a shot of the photo booth, Ava clearly on her knees inside. There's a big enough slice in the curtain to show her between my legs, head bobbing, leaving no doubt what's happening.

My hand is tangled in her hair, head tipped back in pleasure. The fake fireplace backdrop in the room flickers behind us as though it's cheering on the performance.

Then the camera zooms in, freezes on Ava's position, and a red circle highlights the elf ears on her head as Lena's voice returns, cold and cutting:

"Let's break this down, shall we? First, we have Ava Bell—self-proclaimed Queen of Steam—inside a branded photo station, at the Bookmas Bash, *wearing elf ears in some twisted author cosplay. Not even an ounce of discretion. Just straight-up sex on company property. Classy."*

The video cuts to a slow zoom on the curtain gap again, freezing on Soren's hand in Ava's hair.

"Soren Pembry, award-winning fantasy author, clearly enjoying his front-row seat to the Bell & Blade Circus. But don't let the charm fool you. This was never about romance. It was strategy.

Calculated. Cold. Fake dating to drive up engagement, turn readers into shippers, and manipulate sales with heat masquerading as heart."

The following slide flashes screenshots of their hashtag stats—#BellAndTheBlade climbing ShelfSpace charts, preorder numbers, even event footage of Ava and Soren laughing together.

"*They didn't fall in love. They fell into bed. And they let you believe it was more. Now they're out here giving blowjobs behind closed doors for bonus views—mocking the industry, their readers, and every author who actually works for it. Still don't believe me? Well, here's the Queen of Steam explaining it all.*"

It cuts to the faked audio again.

Ava's manipulated voice: "*It hasn't stopped being fake. Just because we started fucking for real.*"

The screen fades to black.

Lena's Voiceover (quiet, controlled): "*Bell and The Blade wasn't love. It was a lie you paid for. If you'd love to see the* entire *video, join my Patreon for a small, nominal fee. Fan art coming* soon.

　#EnemiesWithBenefits
　#FakeLoveRealReceipts
　#QueenOfSteamOrQueenOfSchemes
　#BellAndTheBlade
　#ShelfSpaceScandal
　#PublicityPorn
　#PublishingExposed
　#SexSellsIntegrityDoesnt
　#Fauxmance
　#SexSells
　#PublishingScandal
　#PRPlaybook
　#WhoEvenIsRealAnymore
　#ScriptedShipping
　#LiesAndLikes
　#ScriptedSizzle

#FauxmanceConfirmed

#PromoNotPassion

#BellAndTheBladeWasBusiness

Renata exhales through her nose. "There are over a hundred thousand comments. ShelfSpace is having a meltdown. Half of them believe it's all a scam. The other half are defending you like it's their full-time job."

I run a hand down my face. "Unbelievable. Matthew, get that Patreon taken down. Now!"

Fisher's eyes bounce between us. "We need to respond. Immediately. Preferably before the New York Times gets wind of it."

Ava is staring at the screen as though Lena's voice climbed out of the speakers and slapped her across the face. And despite everything, all I want is to pull her into my lap and whisper that we'll fix this. Together. This isn't only about the photo booth. It's about whether the world believes in *us*. It's her livelihood and her career reputation on the line.

Still, Ava isn't crying. I don't see a hint of rage in her expression. She hasn't even screamed. Like I am on the inside.

She stands there, pale-faced, seemingly in a state of shock. Then she whispers, "I need a minute."

"Ava—"

"No." Her voice cracks—it's not breaking, but it's being held together by force and sheer will. "I need a minute, Soren. Alone."

I watch her as she slowly exits the hotel room. I want to follow. Fuck, every muscle in my body is pushing me to chase her out that door, stand in that hallway with her, and make this right. But I saw the way her fingers trembled as they wrapped around the doorknob, and pushing right now will only make it worse.

So I let her go. And then *I* unravel. Yep, in front of everyone.

Twenty minutes later, I've chewed every nail down to the quick—and I'm not even a nail biter. I'm also two whiskies in. It's not even ten a.m.

The room still smells like her. Peppermint. Vanilla. Sex and sadness. The clothes she wore the night before are draped across the chair like a ghost.

I can't sit still. I can't breathe right. So I go looking.

First, I check the lobby.

Nothing.

Then the café. The bookstore nook. The little lounge across from the elevators, where she sometimes hides when she needs quiet. I even checked the rooftop terrace and that stupid faux igloo setup from the influencer dinner. Nada.

"She's not in the room?" Camille asks, scrolling her phone for clues, oblivious to the fact that Ava left at all.

"She never came back here," Renata confirms.

"Maybe she needed air," Matthew says, though he doesn't sound convinced. "Did you check outside?"

I call the front desk and talk to them again. They tell me a woman wearing a bathrobe walked out the main entrance forty-five minutes ago. Alone. No coat. No bag. No clue where she went.

My blood runs cold. And for the first time since this whole thing started, I feel an emotion I don't know how to write through.

Panic.

Ava Bell didn't walk away. She fucking vanished.

Thirty-Five

SOREN

It's been a week since the world split open.

Seven days.

One hundred sixty-eight hours.

Ten thousand, eighty minutes since Ava Bell disappeared like smoke from the air.

And yes, I've counted every fucking one.

I'm back in Seattle. My house is quiet. Cold. And despite what the thermostat says, I haven't been warm since I lost Ava.

Her phone is with me. Her laptop. Her notes. Everything but the woman herself. She left her life as if it were a book she no longer needed. A complete DNF. And left me holding it outside in the cold.

The first two days, I stayed in New York, where the *Bookmas Bash* was held. Just in case. I retraced every step she took, or could've taken, scoured the hotel's security footage, and bribed every doorman and concierge within a ten-block radius for information.

Nothing.

We texted her friends and family. Nothing. Fisher checked her credit card activity. Zero. No flights. No ride shares. No receipts. *Nothing.* Nothing on socials. Nothing from her agent. Not even a breadcrumb from their group chat.

It's as though she never existed. As if she flicked off her own switch and ghosted the whole fucking planet.

So I did the only thing I could think of. I rented an SUV—nothing flashy, no black Bentley, no tinted windows to draw attention—and parked outside her house. For two days.

Didn't sleep.

Didn't shower.

Just waited.

Every passing car made my pulse pound, thinking maybe it was her.

It never was.

Only rain. Fog. Silence. And the creeping realization that she might not come back.

All I've got are haunted thoughts and a heart full of unanswered questions. *Where the hell are you, Bells?*

I drove to Salem after that. Thought maybe she went home. I knocked on her parents' door with a bottle of whiskey and eyes that hadn't closed in days.

The first night, Mandy made me soup. G-Ma held my hand. And Uncle Marty made me a cocktail so aggressively festive, it came with a candy cane stir stick and a cinnamon stick crossbow.

"Rudolph's Regret." He slid the glass across the counter. "Twelve ounces of bourbon, three of cranberry liqueur, a whisper of nutmeg, and the tears of an emotionally devastated man."

I took a sip. It tasted like Christmas and burned like shame.

"Yeah," Uncle Marty nodded, already shaking up another. "That one's a two-hanky drink."

Later that night, after five too many Rudolph Regrets, I froze my ass off sitting in Ava's treehouse, curled up in the world's most dramatic sad-boy position under a plaid blanket that smelled of pine and sorrow.

Around 2 a.m., Tom came out in flannel pajama pants and said, "I've seen some shit, but this takes the cake," and coaxed me back inside with the promise of leftover pot roast and central heating.

I lasted maybe twelve minutes on the couch in front of the fire before I caved and zombie-walked up to the guest room.

Worst decision of my life.

Sleeping in the same bed we shared, hugging her pillow while trying not to ugly cry into the flannel sheets?

Yeah. That was rock bottom.

I cried. But only a little. Two tears. Three, max.

Okay, I sobbed. Once. I sounded vaguely the same as a dying goat, and I will never recover. But that pillow still smelled heavy with her shampoo. And I couldn't let it go.

So maybe I squeezed it. Maybe I buried my face in it. Maybe I humped it in a fit of heartbreak and self-deprecation.

Sue me.

Judge me.

Hell, write a song about it.

I'm not proud of it. I wasn't in the right headspace. I was still there—pathetic, pining, and very much in love with a girl who'd stopped believing in happily ever after. I missed her so damn much it hurt to breathe. The worry crawled under my skin and settled there, gnawing, all-consuming.

The next morning, her family had officially had enough of my pity party. Tom greeted me with coffee and a look reserved for stray dogs who've overstayed their welcome.

Mandy muttered something about "grown men and their melodrama" while scraping eggs onto a plate. Even G-Ma gave me a side-eye so judgmental that I briefly considered therapy.

I tried to act normal, made small talk about the weather, thanked them for the hospitality, pretended I hadn't wept into their guest linens like a man auditioning for *Les Misérables*. I also, mercifully, left out the part where I may or may not have gotten overly affectionate with a pillow.

Mandy finally said, "Soren, sit down. There's something you need to understand about Ava."

G-Ma began, "Ava tries to outrun heartache. The worst of the worst was after she broke up with *I Hate Your Face*."

"I hate your face?" I parroted, confused.

"Jon Perry," G-Ma clarified with a dramatic sigh. "Look him up."

I reached for my phone. She waved a wrinkled hand. "You'll find him under *walking red flag with a book deal.* He'll pop right up. And if you ever see him in person, I've got a shovel in the trunk, a full tank of gas, and no fear of jail time."

Mandy shot her mother a look, then turned back to me. "Jon put Ava through some shit. For a long time. The whole ordeal left her unable to trust her own instincts, so when things overwhelm that overthinking brain inside her skull, she runs. Hides. It's her armor."

"I'm not that guy," I say, softer than I mean to. "I've shown her, over and over. And that I'm here."

Mandy's face falls. "We know. Look, Ava would kill us if she knew we were telling you any of this, but there's no sense in keeping it a secret after all you've done to try and find her. Hell, to try and love her."

For the next half hour, I sat at the table, hands wrapped around a mug I wasn't drinking from, eyes somewhere beyond the curtains while they told me the whole story. Not every detail —just enough to wreck me, piss me off, make me want to commit murder.

Jon Perry. The mentor who wasn't. The man who slid into Ava's life when she was young and trusting and turned her world into a maze she couldn't escape. He painted the broad strokes: the gaslighting that made her doubt her own mind, the isolation that cut her off from everyone who might've pulled her out, the control disguised as concern. He fed her praise, then used it like a leash.

Hot, uncomplicated anger rose within me as they spoke. I wanted to find Jon Perry and unmake him, and be a wrecking ball for the men who believe ideas and access are fair trade for a girl's trust. But anger wasn't enough. Ava needed steadiness, an unshowy presence, proof—day after day—that a person can be safe.

By the time they were done, I could see how deeply it rewired her. Every instinct she has now is a survival tactic. The constant second-guessing. The need to stay one step ahead, to keep every emotion at arm's length. She doesn't just protect herself from heartbreak, she protects herself from *hope*.

I get it now.

Every time she pushed me away, she wasn't punishing me. She was trying to avoid believing I might be different.

I thought of the times Ava disassociated in the middle of a smile, the way she flinched when a hand moved too fast toward hers. Like when I grabbed her leg under the table. I also thought about the casual cruelty of comment threads that reduce people to clickable fantasies and how easily the wrong person can turn those fantasies into a weapon. Like what happened once Lena ran her story.

In that moment, the promise in my chest changed shape. It became a simple, practical plan. Once I found her, I would close the space between us and hold her tight. Stop promising the stars and begin building scaffolding: patience, proof, time.

More than anything, I needed to tell Ava:

You are not the damage.

You are not the reason anything broke.

You are not the fault line.

They finished sharing Ava's story, and I walked out of that kitchen with the image of her shrinking away still burned into my retinas. Then, I started to shrink myself. Questions tumbled in.

What if I'm not enough to undo a past built on manipulation? What if she just wants to be alone? I would have to respect her boundaries. But isn't what we have the only thing that should matter?

Regardless, I was done being dramatic about it. If she shows up, I'll do the same, quietly, every day, until she stops believing that the worst of what happened to her is the map she must follow forever.

Later that night, I flew home, Ava's story still coursing through my veins as I sat on the plane. I searched online for *I Hate Your Face*. Found where he lives. What he looks like. He definitely has a nose I'd love to break. His DM's were itching for some Pembry charm. But I haven't done anything... Yet.

Ava deserves to return to someone who won't unravel entirely. However, it's a little too late for that, if I'm being honest. Just ask Ava's pillow.

Wherever she is, I need her to know I'm never going anywhere. Even if I have to camp out in a fucking treehouse again to prove it.

It's been a few days since I left Salem.

I drink too much. Barely sleep. I haven't written anything in days except Ava's name in margins. Her initials on my notepads. Her scent still lives in my skin. Her voice in my head. Her smile lurks in every inch of me. And I can't stop replaying that goddamn video Lena posted. I saved it to my phone before Matthew got it taken down. She's posted a bazillion more. I'm told her cease and desist letter is coming.

I keep hoping I'll hear a knock. Ava will show up. Coffee in hand. Eyes apologizing for everything before her mouth even speaks.

But the door doesn't knock. The texts don't ping. The world keeps turning without her. All I can do is watch from a distance and hope—

Hope she's okay.

Hope she knows I'm not mad.

Hope she believes in us enough to come back.

Wherever she is... I miss the hell out of my girlfriend. Even if the whole damn internet thinks she never was.

At 3:14 a.m., I decide to text Emily. She messages back three hours later.

> Hey. I know you told Fisher you hadn't heard from her. Just checking again. Anything?

> Nothing. I'm so sorry. I've called. I've emailed. I've even reached out to people she knows in Boston. In case they've heard anything. But it's total radio silence.

> She doesn't have her cards. No ID. How would she even travel?

> I don't know. But if anyone could disappear like a ninja librarian, it's Ava Bell.

I stare at those words—a ninja librarian. They're so Ava, it makes my chest ache. She left her life mid-sentence. No punctuation. Or goodbye. Just an ellipsis and a vanishing act.

I'm still here—flipping pages, rereading every chapter of us, praying the story's not over. I don't want another book. I don't want another heroine.

I want *her.*

My chaos. My calm. My comet that set my whole sky on fire.

If this story has to wait—if she needs more time before she can come back to me—I'll wait.

Every chapter. Every page.

Until she writes her way home.

> Please let me know if you hear from her.

> I will, Soren.

Soren Pembry

New York Times Best-Selling Fantasy Author

Bells,

Know one thing: I'm not mad. Not even close.
I'm hurting, yeah. The pain inside chews straight
through bone. But anger? No. I couldn't be angry
at you for protecting your heart the only way you
know how.

I get it. I do.

But I miss you.

I miss your laugh and how it bubbles up
when you least expect it. I miss the way your
eyes dart around like you're always ten steps
ahead, even when you're pretending you're not. I
miss the warmth you bring to every cold corner of
my life.

I need YOU, Ava.

I need the woman who snorts a little when she
laughs too hard. The one who builds pillow forts
and hides inside stories when the real world claws
at her too sharply. The one who trusted me—piece
by trembling piece—with her heart.

I know you're hurting. I know you're scared.
But I believe in us. I believe in the way you

kiss me, in how your hand finds mine when no one's looking.

You finally started letting me see the tiny fissures in your walls and didn't bolt the door shut after.

Which means...

We can overcome this, baby. Together. You just have to believe.

I don't care how far you run or how many doors you slam—I'll be here, waiting. I'm not trying to cage you or drag you back like some caveman.

Please understand, I want to hold you. When you're ready.

I want to remind you that you don't have to carry it all alone anymore.

So take your time if you need to. Disappear if you must. But make no mistake, Bells:

There's no world where I stop loving you. No universe where I let go of what we have.

You're my story now. And I'm not letting the last page turn without you.

Love,

S

Thirty-Six

AVA

I'm in Port Townsend. Curled up on Emily's oversized armchair in her cottage-style rental, buried under a throw blanket that smells of sea salt and peppermint tea, trying not to unravel like one of the fraying seams on this damn afghan.

Outside, the Washington wind lashes the windows. Pretty sure it's got some vendetta against me.

Inside, I'm warm in body but not in spirit. I got here with no money. No phone. No ID. No plan.

I borrowed someone's phone and called Emily. Told her everything through sobs and adrenaline.

Emily—who is terrifyingly competent even when she's microwaving soup—made things happen.

Apparently, a friend of hers, Rorie, lives in Port Townsend. Rorie then sent two of her friends—Jeremy and Maya—to drive me *across the entire fucking country* to drop me off.

That's real friendship.

That's also slightly certifiable.

The road trip was unforgettable, and a tad terrifying. Jeremy played only early 2000s boy bands and insisted on narrating all of his love life regrets through dramatic hand gestures and Taco Bell metaphors.

Maya made us stop at nearly every roadside convenience store we passed, and if she saw a magazine with Asher Cross on the cover, she'd snatch all the copies, shred them like confetti, toss a hundred-dollar bill at the stunned cashier, and storm out in a blaze of righteous fury.

I chose not to ask.

Days later, I made it.

I'm here.

Emily's house is quiet, filled with the smell of lemon candles and overachieving academia. She's currently at her desk, toggling between her day job—some medical journal on neurodivergence and maternal inheritance—and a fantastical erotica manuscript with a main character who may or may not be hooking up with a morally ambiguous pirate-fae hybrid.

Soren got her number from Fisher and texted her a couple of nights ago. I made her lie. I hate myself for that. But I'm not ready. I know he probably hates me too—for what I've done, and what I've put him through. And leaving like I did, he'll *never* forgive me.

Everything is my fault. Soren agreed to a stupid PR stunt to help me. *Me.* He didn't need the hype or the numbers. He *was* the numbers. He had the credibility, the career, the loyal fandom. And now, because of *my* desperation, *my* need to make this work, *his* career is caught up in the shit show. What was supposed to be a bump. A push. Became a demolition.

I'm mad at myself for ever signing on to do it. For dragging him down. And for falling for him so fast, and hard, and so *completely* that I forgot to protect either of us from my curse.

Emily keeps reminding me that if I hadn't agreed to the fake dating scheme, I never would've been with Soren. She's right. That doesn't make this pain any less cutting.

A log shifts in the fireplace. I flinch.

Emily glances over from her dual monitors, chewing the end of a pencil. "Uh, Ava? You might want to come see this."

Groaning, I drag myself from my cocoon. "If that's another of your DM's from that dude named **FeralFucker**, I'm not emotionally equipped."

She snorts but stands, motioning me toward her chair. Her screen is split.

On the left: a private chat thread with someone named **BrandDom4U**. And the profile pic is a man, neck down, wearing a black power suit, crisp white dress shirt, black tie, and what is *very clearly* a riding crop in his hand.

I don't ask. I've learned.

On the right monitor is Soren.

My breath catches. He's standing on the cliff where we danced. Bundled in a camel-colored coat, hair whipping in the wind, eyes locked on the screen, staring straight at the camera. Straight at me

A livestream.

ShelfSpace.

Over fifty thousand people are watching. And counting.

Emily nudges the volume up. I sit. Frozen. Heart in my throat.

Soren's there. I'm here.

He's talking.

To them.

To me.

Thirty-Seven

SOREN

After writing Ava's last letter, I stared at that paper until the words blurred, the ache in my chest pulsed, syncing to every sentence.

And then... It hit me.

A terrible, reckless, probably-doomed idea.

I put down that letter. And I started to plan.

Fast-forward a few days and here I am—outside, freezing my nuts off on the same snow-covered cliff where I first slow-danced with the love of my life in the middle of a flurry, with city lights on the horizon, and a sky full of stars and hope.

Matthew is beside me, wearing a down jacket and gloves. His expression screams *I hate this, but I love you, so I'm here*. He's holding my phone with a cautious thumb hovering over the livestream button.

"You sure about this?" He eyes me. "I think you've fully lost it."

"Nope. Not sure at all. And you're right." I rub my hands together for warmth. "But when has that ever stopped me?"

He mutters words under his breath about me being a walking liability and a poetry-reading lunatic, but he hits the button anyway.

418

"And we're live."

I inhale. Exhale. Speak.

"Hey, everyone. Soren Pembry here. And before you ask—no, I'm not about to promote a preorder or tease a new morally gray warlord with dagger kinks. That can wait."

"The feed is flooding with laughing emojis, heart eyes, and gifs of you wielding a sword," Matthew says.

I hold up a hand. "This, friends, is going to be different. This is personal." I pause. Let it sit. "I know you've probably been waiting for a response to Lena Divine's posts about Ava and me. And that's fair. But you also need to understand something—Ava and I? We're human. Real. Flawed. Messy. She's out there somewhere right now, and I don't know where. Before you start making up rumors that she ghosted me, it's not that. It's because this—*all of this*—got to her. And that's on us. On me. On Lena. And yeah, on *you* too."

Matthew stiffens in front of me but doesn't stop the stream.

"What I'm here to do today is tell you the truth. Not the cropped version. Definitely not the AI-generated, maliciously edited clip that Lena posted to get more Patreon subscribers. And if we're *truly* being honest... to get back at *me* for denying *her*. Sorry, Lena, I just wasn't that into you." Widening my stance a tad, I clasp my hands in front of me. "Lena is a liar. That part's easy to say. But even worse—she's a manipulator. Her *theme* might've held water. Yes, our relationship started out as fake. Yes, we were a publicity stunt initially. But Lena twisted that narrative. She exploited private moments, repackaged them for drama, and slandered a woman who's already been through more than any of you know. Lena monetized it all. *She's* the true villain. Not Ava. Not me."

Matthew shakes my head in awe, mouths, *One hundred thousand.*

"Lena's behavior is disgusting," I continue. "And if you still follow her after this, that's on you."

A beat.

"And yeah. Ava and I fucked in a photo booth. God forbid we get a little spicy under a string of twinkle lights and the illusion of privacy. How many of *you* haven't done something questionable in a semi-public space with someone you love? Or even someone you don't. Be honest."

Matthew grins. "The comments are lighting up. Laughing, gasping, heart reacting, many are giving their stories, man. Keep going."

"We started out as fake? Yeah. But I've been in love with Ava Bell for over a year."

"Whoa... dead silence in the comments," Matthew updates. "They want to hear this."

I nod and continue, "Ava didn't know it. Hell, I didn't even realize it fully until she was sitting across from me in the Genre Feud panel at The Great Booksgiving, snarking about her holiday heroes and wearing those glasses that made me want to rip her skirt off and propose at the same time. I've loved her since she sent me that first DM last year, calling my main character an emotionally stunted woodland chump with rage issues. Since she threw a snowball at my head. Since she told me I make her feel like a fairytale and a firestorm." I swallow. "So yeah. When our managers floated the idea of fake dating, I saw an opportunity. Albeit a selfish one. But there was no other way a woman like Ava Bell would look twice at a guy like me."

A gust of wind rips past. I keep going.

"To prove it, I'm going to read you a letter. One of many. I've written dozens to Ava. She's never seen them. She doesn't even know they exist. But this one... this one started it all."

Pulling a crumpled paper from my coat pocket, Matthew steadies the camera, and I read all the letters I've ever written to Ava Bell, starting with the first and ending with the last.

Bells,

I stood on our cliff and told the world the truth—that I've loved you for longer than you'll ever believe. And that none of this, us, was fake. Never for me. Not for one single second.

I hope someday you'll know that I don't care about the fallout. I don't care if people laugh, or sneer, or turn it into a meme that lives on the internet forever. None of it matters if it means you finally understand that I was never playing pretend.

I need you, Ava. YOU. The real you. The messy, brilliant, stubborn, beautiful disaster who makes me want to be better just by standing in the same room.

I feel your pain in my own soul. But I told you that you don't have to carry that weight alone anymore. We've both been broken, Bells. We've both been bruised by people who swore they loved us and then ripped our hearts out for their own reasons.

That will never be me. Ever.

I want to hold you, put my arms around you

until the noise fades, until you believe, really fucking believe, that I'm yours, forever.

Together, we will survive this. We will rewrite the ending. We will reclaim the story Lena tried to steal and make it our own again. That's what you are to me, Ava Bell—my story.

My beginning.

My middle

My every damn word ever written.

So come back to me. Or let me find you. Just... don't close the book yet.

Because I swear to you—I'll never stop reading us.

Love,

S

Feast & Fiction

Snowflake Gala

Bookmas Bash

Midnight Kisses &
Paper Wishes

Thirty-Eight

SOREN

I flew home straight after reading exactly sixty-five letters aloud to ShelfSpace.

Sixty. Five.

One a week. Every damn week. For over a year. Plus a few more over the past few weeks.

They weren't for me. They weren't for publicity.

They were for her.

My Ava.

Every single one.

So even if Ava doesn't see the stream today, tomorrow, or ever—if it gets buried in noise or drowned by the next scandal—it doesn't matter...

It's out there.

Like me.

Still waiting.

Still hers.

Christmas Eve is upon us. My house is still. Lonely. Lit by twinkle lights I've had up since last year. Not because I'm festive. Because I never got around to taking them down. They've dulled over time, flickering, trying to die quietly. They know joy doesn't live here anymore.

The fireplace crackles, the vodka and tonic in my hand is barely touched, and the view out my windows is objectively gorgeous. Snow, evergreens, the Seattle skyline in the distance. It's a goddamn postcard.

And yet?

Also a painting I can't step into. Because none of it means anything. Not without her.

I don't even realize I'm crying until a tear plinks into the glass and makes the saddest little ripple in the universe.

I wipe it away. It didn't happen. (It did.)

Knock. Knock.

The sound startles me. No one knocks on my door. My neighbors text or throw pinecones. My manager FaceTimes before showing up. And Matthew always barges in as if he pays rent.

Knock. Knock.

My glass hits the table with a thud when I set it down. My feet are moving before my brain even catches up. And when I open that door, I nearly black out.

Ava.

A deep crimson coat hugs her body like she's Christmas incarnate. Snowflakes cling to her lashes. Her cheeks are flushed. Her lips are pink and perfect.

She's real.

She's here.

I do the only rational thing I can think of and launch myself at her. The door flies open so hard it bounces off the wall as I grab her the same way a drowning man would grab a life raft.

"Holy shit, Bells," I breathe, clutching her as though someone's going to rip her away again. "You're alive. You're okay. You're here. You're—you smell amazing—"

And then I start sobbing. *Ugly* crying. Full-body, gasping, snot-dripping man-wailing.

"Oh my God." Ava squeezes me tighter, her hand stroking the back of my neck. "Soren, breathe. It's okay. I'm okay. You're crushing my lungs."

"I don't care," I sob. "I'll buy you new ones."

She laughs, and it's the most beautiful fucking sound I've heard in days. "You're going to kill me before I can even apologize."

"You better apologize! I've been—" I hiccup. "I've been hallucinating your voice in my shampoo bottles. I almost slept in your treehouse. I hugged your pillow so hard I dislocated emotional cartilage."

"Emotional cartilage?"

"It's a thing," I say. "Search it up on WebMD. Right after you search: 'can heartbreak cause spontaneous personality collapse?'"

She sniffles. I realize she's crying also now, so I pull back to gaze into her eyes. They're glassy and red-rimmed, but still Ava. Fire and starlight.

"I'm sorry," she whispers. "God, Soren I'm *so so* sorry."

"No, I'm sorry," I whisper back.

"I disappeared on you."

"I faked dated you to try and get you to go out with me."

"I left without a word."

"I might've humped your pillow."

Her head tilts. "What?"

I wave it off. "We'll circle back."

Her hand cups my jaw. "I missed you so much it hurt."

"I missed you so much I lost all my abs," I say. "They're gone. From sadness."

A laugh crawls out of her throat. "They're not gone."

"Okay, they're maybe sulking under holiday bloat."

We both exhale. We stare at each other.

And then the emotional whiplash hits. Because underneath this joy, there's still the bruise that she left.

"Where. The *FUCK*. Were you, Ava?"

Her forehead crinkles.

"You vanished! Houdini'd right out of my life!"

"I broke. I needed space."

"Why, Bells?" My voice cracks. "Why run? I waited outside

your house until my legs went numb. I went to your family's. You had Emily lie for you. Every damn day since we came face to face with each other, I've been proving I'm here—showing you I'm not going anywhere—and you still disappeared on me."

Ava's back stiffens under my hands, but she doesn't pull away. "I wasn't running from you. I was running from everything. Being humiliated. I nearly ruined your career, *and* mine. I failed. I'm sorry I left and didn't tell you. I'm sorry I didn't talk to you. Or trust you enough with that fear. I was so wrong, and I'll carry the weight of that mistake for the rest of my life."

My hands find her hips. I yank her closer. "You think I can't handle your fear? I can. Throw every insecurity you've got at me so I can knock them the hell down. Because I will."

A thousand apologies swim in her eyes. "I've spent so long holding on to these trust issues—they're a part of me, and I didn't realize I was cutting myself on their jagged edges. But... I'm done. I'm handing them over to you now, Soren. Swing away. Shatter them. Please. *I beg you.* Just forgive me."

My face falls. My heart sinks. "Oh, Bells, come here.." I guide her to the sofa, sit down, and ease Ava onto my lap. My arms lock her in. "You left your phone. Your wallet. Do you know how many gas station managers I bribed trying to find you?"

"Why gas stations?"

"I thought maybe you hitchhiked!"

She laughs at that. "Not exactly."

"It's not funny! I thought you were gone forever. Or DEAD!"

"I was...dealing. The only way I knew how."

"Well, I'm sorry, Bells, but I can't help but wonder—if you can leave once, what's stopping you from doing it again?"

The tears on her lashes catch the light. "Soren..."

"No." My voice falters, but I don't let go. "I need you to hear me."

She nods slowly.

"When you walked out," I say, quiet and rough, "it wasn't just a bad day for me. My mother left when I was a kid, Ava. One day

426

she was there, the next day she was gone. Never came back. Do you know what that does to a child?"

Ava shakes her head no.

"It rewired me, made every goodbye feel like the last one. It made every knock at the door feel like hope, only to be severely disappointed."

Her mouth opens, but nothing comes out.

"And my father was a joke as a dad, so I built my whole life around not needing anybody. I never wanted to be the little boy left standing on the porch, watching the taillights disappear, ever again. And then you show up in my life, snowball to the face, fire on your tongue, photo booth sin—everything I didn't know I needed. I let you in. I stayed. I proved myself every damn day. And you left."

Her eyes squeeze shut. *"I'm so sorry."*

"I don't need sorry, Bells." I brush a tear from her cheek with my thumb. "What I need is to know you're not another person who's going to prove I'm easy to walk away from."

"I was scared," she whispers, cheeks soaked with tears.

"I was scared too," I rasp back. "Difference is, I stayed."

Ava flinches at that. She twists to straddle me, her small hands gripping my biceps, anchoring herself to me. "I didn't know how to stay. I thought if I disappeared, I'd save you the trouble. I was drowning in shame, in noise, in every whisper of a world waiting to judge me. My demons kept telling me I'd ruined everything. And the one thing I thought I could control was walking away first. Before you could."

I swallow the stone that's lodged in my throat. "You're not saving me when you leave, Bells. You're *breaking* me."

"I see that now." Her voice trembles.

"You know it's funny," I say, tracing circles on her lower back. "When we first met, on that panel, you said: Sometimes the one who hurt you the most is the only one who can help you heal." I huff a laugh. "You were right. You hurt me. And here you are."

427

"I'm here because I don't want to run anymore. Not from you. Or from what we have."

My hand cups her cheek. "Then don't, Bells. Stay. Let's heal *together.*"

She nods.

"If you ever do that again, I'll follow—I'll find you... In every city, whatever fucking crowd you try to hide in, and every single shadow you try to disappear into, until you finally understand there's nowhere in this world you can go where you're not mine. You are my fire and starlight, Bells, but I'm not built to be left in the dark anymore."

She nods again, something like determination flashing through the tears. "I promise I'll stay in the light with you." For a beat, neither of us moves. Then Ava lifts her palm to my cheek. You, Soren Pembry, are the death of me."

My throat tightens, but Ava keeps going, eyes on mine. "Not the kind that ends something—the kind that begins again. You killed the version of me that only knew how to survive. And what's left..." Her thumb traces my jaw. "What's left is someone who finally knows how to live. *You* are my heart." Her bottom lip wobbles. "I love you."

The words knock the air right out of me. My own heart kicks hard against my chest, wild and erratic, like it's trying to leap straight into her hands. I've imagined hearing those three words from her—hell, I've *agonized* over them—but nothing prepared me for the way my chest feels too full to hold it all, and Ava has no idea how she just leveled me.

After processing all that, I say, "I know," giving the Star Wars reference to her again. Because why not?

"You're the worst." She laughs through her tears.

I brush my lips over hers. "I'll fight through a million wars, curses, and every damn monster in the realm to hear you say that again."

Ava's head drops to my shoulder, nuzzles into my neck. "I love you."

"There's no out with me, Bells. You're it. Endgame. My final battle. Do you get that?"

"Yes," she whispers.

"Fucking finally." I hold the woman I love as the man who's finally found the last page of a story he thought the world had burned. I'm here, with the girl in the red coat who captured me with a look, did unforgettably inappropriate things with a cinnamon roll, and healed me with a knock on the goddamn door.

Pressing a kiss to her temple, I breathe her in, the scent of her shampoo wafting up my nostrils: Jasmine and sandalwood.

"I'm so happy you're in my arms again. Merry Christmas, Bells," I murmur. "I love you."

"Merry Christmas," she whispers back, then pops up to look at me. "By the way, I have a present for you."

Surprise wraps around me. "You—you do?"

Eyes twinkling, she nods. "It's not wrapped. But I think you'll approve."

For a second, I can't answer. Christmas gifts have never really been a thing for me. My childhood sure as hell wasn't filled with anything from Santa. After that, the only ones that came my way were obligatory—publishers sending corporate baskets, fans sending things that belonged behind a paywall.

I go wonderstruck. "Bells, no one's ever really given me a Christmas present before. Not one I actually wanted."

Ava wriggles to stand, a devilish smile curving her lips. "Then you're overdue."

With careful fingers, she unbuttons her coat.

One.

Button.

At.

A.

Time.

My heart flatlines when the coat slips from her shoulders and puddles at her feet.

Holy. Fucking. Shit.

She dressed as my main character—the one inspired by *her*. Only... sexier. And more scandalous than anything my cover designer ever approved.

What's standing before me should absolutely be banned in these United States of America, along with several high-fantasy realms with strict morality codes.

There's leather—deep forest green and scandalously fitted—laced tight through a corseted bodice that pushes her tits *way* up. Silver filigree vines curl along the boning, glinting in the firelight.

Ava's magic, ready to be whispered. Her waist nips in, hips flaring into barely-there high-cut bottoms that leave *nothing* to the imagination. The thigh-high boots are laced up the front with slivers of iridescent ribbon and etched with runes that I'm eighty percent sure translate to "your doom is imminent... and you'll enjoy every second of it."

A sheer panel runs up the center, and every inch of revealed skin scrambles my not-so-polite thoughts, sending a rush of blood due south.

Then—*then*—she reaches down, slips two fingers into the valley of her cleavage, and pulls out a pair of sparkly elf ears.

"Can't forget the ears," she teases, her voice pure sin and jingle bells.

My jaw? On the floor.

My soul? Ascending.

My dick? Leading the way.

I can't speak. Can't *breathe*. Every nerve ending in my body is screaming *Mate*.

One brow arches. "Still breathing over there, Pembry?"

"No," I manage, my voice an octave higher and very much sounding like middle school me. "Absolutely not."

Ava steps backward, toward the fireplace, boots clicking on the hardwood, sounding like a countdown to my total ruin.

So yeah—this is happening. And I'm one elf-ear away from proposing with my *entire body*.

"Your boobs must hurt," is what I croak, still stunned.

"Worth it," she says.

"How—how did you even—between the ShelfSpace chaos and vanishing off the grid—*when* did you make this happen?"

"I have resources."

My eyes narrow. "Do those resources include Emily and a dark underworld of insatiably horny fandom crafters?"

She shrugs innocently. "Maybe."

"I forgive her for lying." Standing, I close the distance between us and wrap an arm around Ava's waist. "And bless every single elf-loving seamstress in her contact list."

Ava bats her lashes. "So... Do you like your present?"

"Bells, I'm about to write a ten-book saga in your honor, complete with the same number of orgasms. Or more. Let's go for more."

Swooping her up in my arms, she yelps, giggling, and I carry her across my loft as the battle-worn fantasy warrior who conquered the final war, claimed the crown, and is about to plunder this elven woman's pussy because it holds the key to the entire goddamn realm.

"Soren!"

"Shhh," I growl, already halfway to the bedroom. "I'm in character."

"What character?"

"The one who's going to spend the next several hours worshipping the elven goddess who saved his soul with a knock on Christmas Eve."

Thirty-Nine

AVA

Never—*never* in a million lifetimes did I think I'd be in Soren Pembry's bedroom wearing a naughty cosplay outfit based on *his* book.

A book he said was inspired by me.

A book that hit number one on the fantasy charts in twelve countries.

A book I originally roasted on a livestream because the main character said, *"Saddle my rage, princess."*

And yet—here I am. Thigh-high boots. Corseted leather. Glittering elf ears that are definitely crooked but still make me a feral woodland sex witch.

Soren's looking at me as though I *invented* orgasms. But what *really* messes with my head isn't the lust in his eyes. It's the reverence. The tenderness. That broken sort of love people write sonnets about and tattoo on their ribs like bleeding heart psychos.

And I'm the one he feels that way about.

Somehow, this infuriating man who once corrected my grammar in a meme caption has become the single most grounding, electric, soul-stretching force in my life.

Never saw that one coming.

Soren didn't just chip away at my walls. Oh no.

He brought dynamite. A sledgehammer. A crowbar. Probably a Dremel.

And when I slathered on another layer of emotional concrete for him to break through, he smiled, rolled up his sleeves, and said, "Challenge accepted, Bells."

Sometimes I wonder if I kept stacking bricks in front of him on purpose. To see if he'd leave. If he'd finally sigh and say, *"You're too much, Bells. This is too hard. I only wanted one thing, but you're not worth the trouble to get it."*

Soren Pembry proved me wrong. Again. And again. And again.

I'm not completely fixed. Who the hell is? But I'm more balanced. More grounded. More *me*. Thanks to him. And his tenacity.

And his heart.

He strips out of that cozy green sweater, muscles rippling beneath golden skin, jeans hitting the floor as an offering, and that long, thick cock swinging like it's a prophecy written in the stars—

Yeah. I'm one *very* lucky elf.

"You're staring." His lips twitch.

"You're *naked*." My voice isn't nearly as stable.

"Is that a complaint?"

I shake my head. "It's a blessing."

Soren steps toward me, eyes dark, muscles tight. "Ava Bell, you came home."

Warm breath brushes the curve of my jaw. His hands—those large, greedy, loving hands—trace the edge of my leather panties with a look like he's unsealing something sacred. Or sinful.

Really, it's both.

With maddening precision, he drags them down my thighs—inch by reverent inch—until the cool air hits my slick heat and I *shudder*.

Soren doesn't break eye contact, and with the way his jaw tightens, I know he's barely holding himself back from devouring me right where I stand. But he doesn't rush. After he slides the panties off completely, he twirls them once on his finger before tossing them behind him.

"They're mine now." He smirks, voice feral. "For inspiration."

"Planning to write a sequel?"

He grins, villainous. "*Sequel* to your orgasm."

My laugh stutters out on a breath I don't remember taking. He notices. As though he's approaching a throne he intends to kneel before for the rest of his life, Soren sinks to the floor in front of me. My boots still on. My corset, untouched. Elf ears sparkling in the firelight.

Apparently, this fantasy warrior has *zero* intention of letting me take off a single piece of this costume–other than the panties– before he fucks me six ways from the solstice.

My tongue sweeps over my bottom lip, wetting it before I catch it between my teeth and bite, hard enough to feel.

"Jesus, Ava," Soren groans as though I granted him a dying wish. "I want your pussy on my tongue so bad it hurts."

Lightning bolts down my spine, ripping a gasp from my chest, when in one deft movement he hoists me up onto the bed. Calloused fingertips skate over my inner thighs, scratching lightly, leaving trails of sparks in their wake. My nipples pebble beneath the corset, the contrast of cold air and burning need lifting me higher.

Soren's hands settle on my thighs, spreading me open as a sacred text he's been desperate to study, chapter by dripping chapter. His head lowers, kissing a slow path along my right thigh, teeth grazing, lips branding. When I think he'll give me what I need, he detours, nuzzling across to the other thigh.

"Soren," I groan, writhing, but his grip tightens.

His nose bumps my slit, and he breathes me in. It's obscene and sexy as hell. "Fuck, Bells," his voice is thick and heated. "You smell like mulled cider and second chances."

I whimper. Or maybe I sob. It's a thin line. Soren doesn't wait for permission. He dives in, tongue sliding up from my entrance to my clit in one long, devastating stroke that has me seeing stars behind my eyes. My back bows. The air leaves my lungs. This man knocked it out of me with one flick of his mouth.

He does it again, but slower this time, tasting each syllable of my arousal. A moan rumbles deep in his chest and vibrates against me. Soren pushes my legs wider, his shoulders wedging in between, massive and immovable as those gifted hands slide under my thighs, lifting, securing, making me the offering I clearly am.

Then he *devours*.

His tongue works me in slick, punishing strokes, each pass over my clit more electric than the last. My whimpers melt into moans, my hips rising off the mattress in search of more, more, *God*, more—

The only background noise is the fire crackling in the hearth. Otherwise, it's the slick sound of his mouth on me. The scrape of his scruff. The wet heat of his tongue. The raw desperation in every gasp he pulls from my throat.

When his hands tighten around my thighs, I know what's coming, and he's not letting up. Not until I fall apart on his tongue and repent for leaving him.

The world fades. All I know is the pressure building, cresting, *teasing* the edge. And then—Soren pulls back. Blows a slow, hot breath over the place he just left.

I nearly scream, "Please don't stop."

"That," his voice hoarse, tone punishing, "was for disappearing without a goddamn trace."

"What's for coming back?" I pant.

Soren rises from his knees like a storm gathering strength, he catches my wrist before I can grab at him, snatching my hand and pressing it flat over his chest. His heart pounds frantically beneath my palm. He stares at me like it's the only truth he has left.

"This," he rasps, squeezing my hand tighter, "is for coming back. It's yours, Bells. Every beat. Each broken piece. My heart hasn't belonged to me in a long time—it's been spelling your name with every pulse. You left, and it still beat for you. You're here now, and it always will."

Tears prick my eyes, his words tangling around me while his heartbeat drums beneath my palm. I blink through the wet droplets, a laugh breaking free even as I choke on it.

"You're insane," I whisper, pressing closer, clutching his chest as though I can hold the rhythm myself. "Insane for loving me like that. Insane for waiting, for forgiving me, for still beating my name when I didn't deserve it." His silver eyes shimmer, steady on mine. "But if your heart is mine, then you need to know—" My voice breaks, then steadies again. "—mine's been yours since the moment you looked at me like I wasn't just another storm. But like I was worth being ravaged by it. Keep spelling my name, Soren. And I'll be here—*right here*—to read every letter."

Those silver eyes turn dark. He doesn't give me a chance to breathe before he grips my hips, spins me, and yanks me to the edge, pressing a kiss to my shoulder, then murmuring against my skin:

"I love you," he says with a low voice, ravaged with need and too much restraint.

Calloused palms drag up my sides, over the curve of my corset, and back down again—slow and possessive. Soren kicks my legs a little farther apart to expose and brand me in the best possible way.

"Bend over the bed, Bells." A hand slides down to squeeze my ass. "I'm going to split you open and make you beg for every inch."

Glancing back over my shoulder, a wicked smile tugs at my lips even as my body trembles. "Begging's not really my style. But if you think you can fuck it out of me...try."

A just as wicked grin spreads across his face as his other hand curls around my waist, tugging me back so my ass presses flush to his hard, thick cock, twitching with anticipation. "Challenge accepted, Bells. Now, fist the sheets," Soren commands, hot breath dragging over my ear.

My fingers toy with the fabric instead of gripping it. My voice comes out as a teasing dare. "What if I don't? What if I make you work harder for it? What'll you do then, Soren?"

I know exactly what I'm doing. I'm baiting the wolf—also the man I broke. Every moment I shut him out built this one like kindling. Now I want him to strike the match, punish me in the best way.

"Baby, I'm not stopping until your screams make the walls bleed and the glass shatter. So," Soren grits, sliding the head of his cock into me—infuriatingly slow. "Fist." He pulls out, leaving me clenching on nothing. "The." Another sharp thrust of just the tip. "Damn." Out again, deliberate torture. "Sheets." Back in, deeper this time, holding me there, his transforms into a snarl. *"Now."*

Forty

SOREN

Ava bends for me, hands braced on the mattress, legs spread exactly the way I need, every last inch of her wrapped in that criminally tight costume that I now consider legally mine.

I step in behind her, curling one hand around the back of her neck, while the other grips her hip, securing myself to reality. Because holy fuck. Ava's here. She's real. She's mine.

And I'm about to demolish her.

I will not be gentle.

I will not be sweet.

No—I'm going to fuck every emotion I've swallowed for the last week straight into her.

My cock presses against the seam of her pussy, hot and aching and *ready*. Her heat soaks through the air. It's in my lungs.

God, I've *missed* her.

I've missed her voice. Her laugh. How she blushes when her name dances off my lips. I've missed her *too much* to be calm.

Underneath this lust, I'm still cracked, still scared shitless. She disappeared without a word. Now she's bent over my bed as if nothing happened. Like she didn't take my heart and fucking eviscerate it.

I line myself up, dragging the head of my cock through her folds, slow enough that her legs tremble.

"You scared the hell out of me," I grind out, voice rough.

She whimpers, hips pushing back into me—begging for it.

"I thought I lost you, Bells," I whisper, leaning over her back, pressing my chest to her spine, my mouth to her ear. "I'm gonna remind you what you came back to."

I deliberately drag two fingers over her clit before dipping down to her entrance. She's so wet, so slick, my fingers slide in with no resistance. My eyes nearly roll back in my skull when her pussy clenches around them. *Jesus.*

Ava tips her head back, lips parted, lashes fluttering closed as I curl my fingers inside her, tempting that perfect little spot. My thumb circles her clit in a steady rhythm. The noise she makes— half gasp, half needy whimper—shoots straight through me.

She moans again, hips rocking, chasing it. One of her hands comes up, slipping beneath the tight leather corset to tug at her nipple. The sight alone makes my cock twitch in my palm as I give it a slow stroke. I can't wait any longer.

When my fingers pull free, they glisten with her arousal. I bring them to her lips. "Open," I command. "And suck."

Ava's lips wrap around them. She moans while she sucks my fingers off, tongue licking every drop.

"Filthy little elf. I'm going to keep you locked up here–in this outfit–forever."

Pulling back, I tap the head of my cock against her ass to tease her with the weight of it before grasping her hips and lining myself up.

"I should take your ass right here," my tone comes out dark, "make you beg for it. Would you like that, baby? To know every inch of you belongs to me—front, back, everywhere?"

Her answering whimper could make me come.

I drag my teeth along her earlobe, savoring the way she shudders against me. "One word, Bells. One. I'll have you shaking, soaking wet, forgetting how to breathe, let alone stand."

"Yes," she says.

To tease, I press harder against her. Ava's nails bite into the sheets, desperate, needy. I grin against her neck. "Yeah. I bet you would. But not right now, baby. Right now, I'm about to make your pussy feel so fucking good."

A second later, I *drive* in, balls deep in one thrust. Ava's a velvet vice gripping me hard. I have to grit my teeth so I don't fucking lose it on the spot. I'm barely holding on as I let her adjust, allowing me *not* to explode before she does.

My hand curves around her throat, turning her head to mine. As she melts under my touch, I press forward, chest to her back, closing every inch between us.

"Soren," she breathes.

"You can take more, baby." One hand on her hips, my other working her clit rhythmically between my fingers, I pull out halfway only to sink back in—slow and deep—over and over until she pushes back, meeting my thrusts,

And then, I give it to her.

Every. Fucking. Inch.

The sound of skin meeting skin fills the room. Sharp. Wet. Relentless. Each thrust lands with a slap, echoing through the loft like applause.

Our show.

Her breath stutters every time I bottom out, and she tightens around me with every stroke. Her body's trying to drag me deeper, keep me buried. It *knows* I belong there.

"Yes, Soren, fuck me," Ava cries out, and I swear I see fairy sprites dancing overhead in that moment. Or maybe just Ava Bell in thigh-highs and elf ears, which is honestly better.

Gripping her hips, I drive in at a brutal rhythm, chasing the obscene sounds our bodies are making, never letting up, never stopping.

"Hear that, Bells?" I rasp, slowing down. "That's the sound of your pretty pussy getting fucking obliterated."

"You feel so good," Ava moans, high and broken. She presses back against me, greedy for more. "Please don't stop."

Shifting my weight backward, I pull out of her. Immediately moving between her legs, my entire palm rubs against her slick heat. She whimpers at the loss of my cock but grinds against my hand, surrendering to the friction.

"Fucking say it," I growl, fingers working over her dripping cunt with punishing precision. "Tell me who you belong to."

"*You*, Soren," she gasps, voice catching. "Always you."

That word undoes me. *You.*

"Now, please fuck me," Ava cries out again.

I slam my dick back into her, once, twice, deep, and final. Wrapping my arms around her waist, I pump hard until we both shatter. My body shudders against hers, she gasps beneath me, trembling, unraveling, her pussy pulsing and clenching around my cock.

For a long moment, we don't move. Our bodies remain locked. Breaths mingled. Hearts syncing. I press a kiss to the back of her neck, one to her shoulder, another above the corset's edge. Tender. Loving.

"I missed you so fucking much," I whisper against her skin.

She reaches back, threading her fingers into my hair, pulling me closer. "I missed you, too," she whispers. "Even when I was trying not to."

The words land right where the hurt's been festering all week. My forehead presses against her shoulder blades. I breathe her in, trying to decide if I want to fuck her again or finally demand the answer that's been clawing me apart.

I settle for both.

But for now, my cheek rests against the top of her head. We stay there, stitched together, sweaty, breathless, elf ears forgotten, the fire popping in the background. There's nothing else in the world right now.

Just her.

Just me.

Just us.

Forty-One

AVA

The day after Christmas, Ava and I released a joint statement on ShelfSpace.

There weren't any flashy graphics. Nor was there dramatic music or over-edited videos. Just the two of us. Me, in one of Soren's sweaters. Him, in pajama pants, holding a mug that read *World's Most Dramatic Love Interest*. Our hair was mussed. Our cheeks were pink from the heat of the fire.

And our hearts? Well, they were worn all the way on our sleeves.

We told the truth. Yes, the way we started was built on fiction. A publicity stunt. A spicy marketing scheme with the shelf-life of a sugar cookie. But if it hadn't happened that way... we never would've found each other, away from the screen.

We apologized for the deceit. For making it messy. We acknowledged the hurt it might have caused.

Then we said this:

"We're in love. Time will show you the truth of it. That's fine. We're not rushing it. But you won't see Bell and The Blade *battling it out online anymore. The sarcasm will be less. The insults will die. The genre wars will look a little different. Less war. More healthy debate. From here on out, our feeds are spaces of support. Of light.*

Of bookish love. We're dedicating ourselves to helping aspiring authors—and championing readers—no matter what they choose to read. Books are for everyone. No matter the tropes. Period."

The reaction was overwhelming. Some rolled their eyes. Some called it a PR pivot. But most cheered.

Now, it's New Year's Eve. We're walking into *Midnight Kisses and Paper Wishes,* hand in hand, deliriously in love.

We don't know what to expect. We don't care. We're together. That's all that matters.

The past week has been a blur. Soren rented us a cottage in Port Townsend for a little writer's retreat, filled with manuscript edits and coffee-fueled plotting. We mostly wore pajamas, or nothing at all, and argued about who got to eat the last cinnamon roll. I'll let you infer how that argument ended.

I saw Emily. She took us to a charming bookstore called *North & Anchor.* The owners are a couple named Rorie and Nolan. They're disgustingly in love. Even worse than us.

They bickered over shelving. Flirted over coffee cups. He tried to smuggle her romance novels into the fantasy display. She made heart eyes at him while threatening to burn his limited editions. I adored them instantly. And apparently, Rorie's a massive fan of mine, carries every book I've ever written in the store.

All of this made a new small-town romance series percolate in my brain. I've already started the outline. It opens in a coastal bookshop with a secret second floor. But that's a next year project. Right now, I'm too busy being *disgustingly* in love myself.

A weird warmth blooms in my chest as we make our way inside the ballroom, where Camille and Renata swirl around us as nervous little hummingbirds. Renata keeps fake-laughing. Camille might throw up on her own clipboard.

I don't blame them. This whole event is press-heavy. Fans. Media. Authors. ShelfSpacers.

It's *a lot.*

Soren squeezes my hand, tugs me toward the dessert bar, not a care in the world. We pass Matthew on the way. He's standing in the corner, nursing a bottle of wine that I'm pretty sure was meant to be decorative.

"Why does Matthew look like someone kicked his puppy?" I whisper. "Also, he's downed that whole bottle himself."

Soren presses his lips to my ear. "Don't say anything. Pretend you don't know whenever he finally says something."

"Know what?"

He hesitates at a beat before finally saying, "His wife left him. *On* Christmas."

My heart lurches. *"Oh my God."*

"Yeah. He's not well."

My eyes shift back to Matthew, who lifts his bottle in a sad salute.

"We'll talk to him later," Soren whispers. "Just leave him to his feelings for now."

I nod, then, as if summoned by magic, readers start to approach. Authors, too. Some teary. Some giddy. Some with a gleam in their eye that says, *I've been there. I understand.*

They tell us our story gave them hope. It reminded them that even if two people start as fiction, it doesn't mean their love can't be real.

After hours of mingling, my cheeks ache from smiling while my feet beg for mercy. I'm mid-sip of my water when Soren leans in.

"Come with me," he says, tugging my hand. "I have a surprise for you."

"Is it another photo station?"

He laughs. "No, this is better. Sort of. Actually, I don't think anything can top that."

We slip out a side door, down a path lit by fairy lights and silver lanterns. At the end of it, there's a gazebo. A very familiar gazebo.

Twilight fans, brace yourselves.

The white wooden trim. The dangling icicles. The warm glow

445

of light strung through every beam. It's a scene from a fanfiction dream.

"You did *not*." My jaw drops.

"I did." Soren pulls me in, hands on my waist, spinning me in slow circles.

Somewhere behind us, the speakers shift. The first haunting notes of *Flightless Bird, American Mouth* float around us. My breath catches. It feels too perfect, too fated, as if the universe just pressed play on our love story.

"Care to dance, Miss Bell?"

"In a gazebo that's a replica of the *Twilight* prom scene?"

"Only the best for my vampire lover."

Laughing, we sway under the stars, the sounds of the countdown distant but rising.

As it nears midnight, I peer up at him. "You gonna turn me?"

Soren's smile softens. "Already have, my love." He dips me—a full swoon-worthy, leg-lifting dip—and presses a soft kiss to my neck. Just like Edward.

"Happy New Year," he whispers. "Here's to every chapter we haven't written yet."

When our lips meet at the stroke of twelve, it tastes like stardust and forever. I never expected this. Soren Pembry started as the enemy. A fantasy-reading, romance trope-hating, livestream-trolling nemesis with a body that belonged in a graphic novel.

I hated him.

Until I didn't.

Until he chipped away at my walls with so much patience and fire that I had no choice but to let them burn. *This* man proved me wrong. He made me stronger. Softer. Whole in ways I didn't believe I could be.

I let him in.

I let myself love him.

When he rights me from the dip, I smile and brush snowflakes off his collar. "I have a surprise for you too, Mr. Pembry."

"Oh yeah?"

Rolling up on my tiptoes, I whisper my secret in his ear. Soren's eyes go wide. His hands fly to his head. He spins in a frantic little circle. His body can't contain the excitement.

"Are you serious?" he yells.

I grin, nod.

"Holy shit. *Holy shit.*" Soren clutches my head, kisses me again, passionately, as though we have a thousand New Year's ahead of us.

Because we do.

Forty-Two

SOREN

Eight Months Later...

"Move, move, move!" I barrel through the hospital hallway like I'm leading a last-stand cavalry charge, minus the sword but definitely with the same panic level.

Matthew trails behind me, huffing, puffing, wrangling an overstuffed bear the size of a Fiat.

"I told you not to stop for coffee," I hiss over my shoulder.

"I didn't think she'd go into active labor during a red light!" he snaps. "Besides, she loves the new hazelnut roast."

We round a corner, nearly plowing through a gurney. The nurse gives me a look. She might tase me. Honestly, fair.

The sign reads MATERNITY WARD in soft pastel letters that do nothing to match my heart rate.

"Pembry? Soren Pembry?" A voice calls out.

I whip around so fast I almost dislocate something.

A nurse in lavender scrubs waves me over. "Come with me. We've got to prep you now."

Matthew clutches the bear as a shield. "I'll be out here. Rooting for you both. And, uh, this thing has a built-in lullaby button, so... bonus?"

I nod, clapping his shoulder. "Thanks, man." Then I'm through the doors.

Everything becomes a blur. Hair nets. Booties. Scrubs. Sanitizer. More sanitizer. Another nurse practically swoons when she sees me.

"Oh my God, my sister *loves* your books. That scene in *Blades and Bone* when Calla rides the wyvern? Masterpiece."

I nod. I grin. I consider eating a latex glove to pass out and escape the moment.

"Can we talk about this later?" I whisper. Maybe scream-whisper.

They lead me through the final set of doors. Relief washes over me. There she is. My Ava. Hair piled on her head in the messiest bun ever. Face flushed, eyes half-lidded. She's ethereal. Serene. A goddess in a delivery gown.

She turns her head, sees me. Tilts her head. Smiles.

And then the contraction hits.

"You!"

"Me?"

"You did this to me, you fantasy-loving, elf-eared, orgasm wizard!"

A nurse glides in with sprinter speed. "She's fully dilated. We're ready to go."

"READY TO GO? I AM NOT READY. NOTHING ABOUT ME IS READY!" Ava panics.

Rushing to her side, I take her hand, immediately regretting everything.

"When did your grip get so strong?"

"When your penis broke my cervix!"

Another contraction.

Another scream.

Another threat to my life.

"We are *never* having sex again. Do you hear me? I don't care if your abs sparkle or your tongue is poetry."

"Okay," I wheeze. "I deserve this. I deserve all of this."

The doctor appears like a war general. "Let's push, Ava. Deep breath. One... two... three..."

What follows is a symphony of primal screams, encouragement, a monologue that might've been excerpted from a horror film.

"I hate you! I love you! If you ever try to touch me again, I will hex your balls off!"

"Fair!" I agree. "So fair!"

A high, perfect, wailing cry shatters the air and stitches it back together with wonder.

A nurse lifts the tiniest little bundle I've ever seen. Wraps her in pink. Our tiny banshee's screams are the sweetest sound I've ever heard.

Ava collapses back against the pillows. Glowing. Radiant. Tears sliding down her cheeks. She smiles. "She's here."

I kiss Ava's forehead. "She's perfect. You're perfect."

Ava gazes at me for a beat, sweat trailing down her temples. "I know."

Laughing at our little Star Wars reference, I crush my lips to hers. "I love you."

"I love you too."

"I love you more."

"I love you most."

All the pain. The panic. The profanity.

Gone.

Just a mother. A father. A little girl who already owns our hearts. And a bear outside the door, playing lullabies.

Epilogue

AVA

If someone had told me a year ago that I'd be spending the following Halloween dressed as Morticia Addams while *breast-feeding* a one-month-old at my parents' annual "Monster Bash and Margarita Crawl," I would've laughed.

Or cried.

Actually, probably both.

"Okay, but hear me out." Fisher holds up his phone, angling it for the millionth picture. "What if the baby had *fangs*? Tiny ones. For aesthetics."

Fisher is Lestat by way of a Paris runway. The man is wearing a bespoke velvet cape lined in crimson silk, tailored so sharply it could cut glass. His lace cravat is pinned with a brooch shaped like dripping blood, and his black boots sparkle with tiny Swarovski bats. Those fake bite marks on his neck? Diamond-studded.

I chuckle. "She's only a few weeks old, Fisher."

"She's committed to the bit," he argues, gently adjusting the bat-winged baby bonnet over my daughter's ridiculously round head.

My daughter. *Our* daughter.

"Besides," Fisher continues, "the vampire bat onesie was my gift. You're welcome for her entire future TikTok following."

451

"Her name is Aisling," I remind him, "not Count Chompula."

"Aisling Elara Pembry," Soren adds from across the room, his voice smooth, intoxicating. "The dream and the spark."

Devastating in a perfectly tailored pinstripe suit with a red carnation tucked into his lapel, Soren's dressed as Gomez Addams, with his hair slicked back. The way he's seductively holding a glass of blood-red wine is illegal. Just fucking illegal.

Stormy eyes find mine. Soren's smirk deepens—private, knowing. It says *I love you, Bells,* without saying a single word. Even dressed like a fictional gothic cartoon husband, he somehow makes my entire world feel real.

Because it very much is.

"She's an angel," my mom croons, snapping at least fifty blurry iPad photos from two inches away. "Look at her little mouth! Like a rosebud! A milk-slicked, dribbly rosebud!"

"Mom," I mutter, "boundaries."

"Wait until you see the outfit I got her for Christmas!" She continues, unbothered, possibly a little tipsy. "It says *I sleighed Santa's heart.* Isn't that cute? With glitter!"

With a glittery witch hat jammed over the top of her head and a feather boa draped around her petite neck, G-Ma cackles from her perch on the leather recliner. She's holding a skeleton glass full of spiked apple punch. "I like this baby. This one doesn't cry when I talk. Unlike your cousin's kid—what's her name? Tractor?"

"Trinity."

"Right. Little demon."

My dad dressed up as Ghostface for reasons that remain unclear. He tries to hand me a mimosa, pauses when he realizes I'm still nursing, then panics, averts his eyes like my boob is a solar eclipse, stammering, "Oh—uh—okay. I'll just, uh..." His eyes bounce to the ceiling, the floor, looking anywhere but my chest. Then he flees. Ghostface indeed.

Mom has since moved into the kitchen, where she's now

whipping up something pumpkin-spiced and questionably alcoholic, sporting devil horns and her vintage "Hot Mamas Club" apron.

"Baby's first Halloween." Soren crosses the room, kneels in front of me. He adjusts the blanket over Aisling. "She's going to be a legend."

"Please," I say. "She slept through two costume contests, one fake séance, and an argument about the moon landing. She's thriving."

"She gets it from you."

"The ability to nap through drama?"

"No." He presses a kiss to the top of my head. "The ability to make everything around her better. Just by existing."

I roll my eyes, but it's mostly for show. Aisling shifts against my chest with a sleepy grunt, melting me into a caramel apple of emotion.

Right then, G-Ma shuffles up behind Soren. She gently pats his head like he's a golden retriever who fetched the paper. "Well, Morticia's boy toy," she drawls with a wink. "You really put the *bone* in *bona fide daddy material?*"

"I—uh—" Soren stammers.

G-Ma beams, entirely unbothered. "You planted a phenomenal seed, Pembry. I knew those strong hips of yours would make good."

"G-Ma!" I cough, mortified. "Oh my God—stop talking."

Soren's shoulders shake with silent laughter as he drifts closer to me, eyes sparkling with mischief and that devastating tenderness. "I love your family."

"Good, cause you're stuck with us."

"I'm counting on it."

Across the room, Emily sips from a wine glass. She tries very hard not to make eye contact with Fisher. He, in turn, is *definitely* adjusting his vampire cape in a way that implies something happened upstairs that required... redressing.

"For science," he tells me later when I corner him by the candy cauldron. "Also? Emily's thighs? *Spooky strong.*"

"You're going to hell."

"Only if she lets me."

Meanwhile, G-Ma has convinced Soren to judge a costume contest featuring the family dogs. Brinley's chihuahua is dressed as a sexy nurse. Uncle Marty is trying to glue googly eyes to his cat. Soren has our baby strapped to his chest, a clipboard in hand.

And me? I haven't slept in forty-eight hours. My boobs are sore. My stretch marks are visible. I feel like a cracked pumpkin—yet, I've never felt more full. I'm not talking about being full of stress, hormones, or even panic.

But of joy.

Of love.

Of *Aisling Elara Pembry*, the softest, most ridiculous thing I've ever created.

Of Soren, the man I love, forever and ever.

That gorgeous man leans in later, when the baby's asleep and June's reading tarot cards for the dog. "Think she'll be a writer?" he asks.

"I think she'll be whatever she wants to be."

He grins. "Rebel."

"Pembry."

Soren takes my hand, his thumb tracing slow circles against my skin—a quiet promise in the middle of the noise.

Around us, laughter collides with clinking glasses. The fading light blurs into gold, my family's chaos swells like a song I've always known by heart.

For once, I don't fight it. I let myself feel *everything*—the warmth, the ache, the dizzy, terrifying beauty of being seen and wanted all at once.

It's glorious.

Messy. Miraculous.

A moment you don't dare breathe too loudly in, afraid it might vanish if you do.

So with that I say,
Happy Halloween.
And happily ever after.

Bells,

A year ago, we signed on for a lie. A scheme. A viral stunt with manufactured captions and staged smiles.

Now, here we are. Cameras, gone. Contract, ripped up.

I still think about that first panel sometimes. You glared at me like you wanted to set me on fire. Your voice shook with fury when you called me tolerable.

My entire chest burned because I knew I was done for.

Since then, we've fought. We've broken. We've lost things we thought we couldn't survive losing. You vanished. I begged the universe for a miracle. Somehow, impossibly, it gave me one. Christmas has a way of weaving miracles where logic fails.

You, Ava Bell, are mine.

I never believed in destiny until you.

I never believed in family until now.

You and our daughter are asleep upstairs as I write this. Her tiny fingers curled like commas, her breathing a steady rhythm that stitches my entire life together. I watch her, and I realize that this is what it means to be whole. Bestselling lists, packed auditoriums, or critical acclaim will never compare.

It's you. It's her. It's us.

You've given me more than love, Bells. You've given me a home. A place to belong. A family I thought I'd never deserve. There were so many broken, scarred-up pieces of me I used to think were unfixable, and you've held them, softened them, made them into something new.

When I look at you, I see every chapter of our story: the sparks, the fight, dancing on snowy cliffs, stolen kisses, naughty time in wine cellars.

There's the tough stuff, too, with so many moments when we could've let go, but didn't. We chose each other. Over and over. Even when it was hard. Especially when it felt impossible.

So tonight, with an early blessing of snow falling outside our window, and our newest miracle sleeping peacefully, I take comfort in knowing that this is the only story I've ever wanted to write.

My love, my partner, my fire and starlight. This is our fairytale and our firestorm.

Thank you for believing. For choosing me. Thank you for letting me choose you.

Forever yours,

S

Acknowledgments

It takes a village. I'm honored that you are all a part of mine.

To my husband, Ben—thank you for letting me chase this dream, for enduring every creative outburst, and for somehow keeping your patience as I hop from one project to the next. Your constant support make this possible. I love you.

To my kids—your laughter, craziness, and unconditional love reminded me daily why stories matter. This book wouldn't exist without you being my biggest cheerleaders.

To my sister—thank you for being my sounding board, another one of my cheerleaders, and the one who always reminds me that I can do hard things.

To my incredible alpha and proofreaders—Renata, KaiDee, Kristen, Felicia, and Marisela—thank you for generously giving your time, insight, and encouragement. Your feedback elevated this story, and your belief in me means more than I can ever put into words. This book is stronger because of you.

To Jasmine, my editor—thank you for seeing the heart of this story and helping me bring it to life in the best way possible. Your editorial eye and thoughtful guidance pushed me to dig deeper, polish harder, and believe in the words when I couldn't see them clearly myself. This book is better in every way because of you, and I'm endlessly grateful to have you in my corner.

To Autumn, my PA—my career would be in shambles without you. Thank you for keeping me organized, sane (mostly), and moving forward when I'd happily drown in the chaos. From being the Queen of Engagements to working your social media sorcery, you're the glue that holds this all together, and I wouldn't have the success I do without you.

To Kristan—Thank you for rooting for me. I look up to you in so many ways. Watching you gives me hope and endless inspiration. You're an absolute Goddess, and I can't thank you enough for always being there, for answering my questions, for shooting me straight when I need it, and for offering your kindness so freely. You'll never truly know the drive you've given me—without even meaning to—just by standing in your brilliance and showing the rest of us what's possible. You pour so much love and light into the world, and I'm endlessly grateful for you.

To Rachel—one side of the triangle. Your positivity and your light have carried me through the dark days and made the bright ones shine even brighter. You've been more than a friend—you've been a safe place, a constant reminder that love and laughter can exist even in the mess. Someday you will bring Ava to life in a way only you can, and when that happens, it will be magic. I love you endlessly, and I'm so grateful for the piece of my heart that will always belong to you.

To Nicole—the other side. My gorgeous best friend, my person. You get me in a way no one else ever could. This journey wouldn't mean half as much without you walking beside me, celebrating the highs, surviving the lows, and reminding me I'm never alone in this. You are my manifest, the proof that the universe sometimes drops the right people into each other's orbit at precisely the right time. I cannot wait for what *our* future holds—for the books we'll write, the dreams we'll chase, and all the laughter still ahead of us. Thank you for being a lifetime friend, my sister in everything but blood, and the constant I never knew I needed. I love you more than these pages could ever hold.

And finally, to you, the readers. This book doesn't just belong to me—it belongs to you. You're the reason I sat down at the keyboard on the days I'd rather have binged Netflix or read someone else's book. You're the reason these characters get to breathe beyond my head and onto the page. Thank you for laughing at the banter, swooning at the kisses, gasping at the drama, and supporting me no matter what.

Every review, every post, every friend you've said, "You *have* to read this," to—it all matters more than you'll ever know. You've turned my little dream into something bigger, brighter, and so much funnier than I ever imagined.

You are the HEA I didn't know I'd get. And I'm endlessly, ridiculously grateful for every single one of you.

Also by Cedar James

Text Me, Never

Amazon

Signed Copies

Book Stores

Let's Get Social

Website: authorcedarjames.com

Social Media: @authorcedarjames

Facebook Group: CJ's Swoon Room

About the Author

CEDAR JAMES writes swoony romance for readers who love witty banter and their slow burns deliciously drawn out. An Oklahoma native now living in Houston, Texas, she juggles life with four kids and a brain full of fictional stories. When she's not writing, Cedar's spending time with family, falling in love with her next set of characters, or plotting spicy comebacks she'll never say out loud. She believes every love story needs a little heat, a little heart, and a whole lot of trouble.

www.ingramcontent.com/pod-product-compliance
Lightning Source LLC
Chambersburg PA
CBHW010650100726
47901CB00012B/2499